BOOK TWO
SURVIVAL

RISE OF
ASUR

Printed in Australia

Cover and internal design by New Found Books Australia Pty Ltd
Images in this book are copyright approved for New Found Books Australia Pty Ltd
Illustrations within this book are copyright approved for New Found Books Australia Pty Ltd

First printing: SEPTEMBER 2024

New Found Books Australia Pty Ltd
www.newfoundbooks.au

Paperback ISBN 978 1 9231 7232 6
eBook ISBN 978 1 9231 7244 9
Hardback ISBN 978 1 9231 7256 2

Distributed by New Found Books Australia Distribution and Lightning Source Global

 A catalogue record for this work is available from the National Library of Australia

More great New Found Books Australia titles can be found at: www.newfoundbooks.au/our-titles/

*We acknowledge the traditional owners of the land
and pay respects to the Elders, past, present and future.*

BOOK TWO
SURVIVAL

RISE OF
ASUR

JULIE FINN

To my family and close friends for always inspiring,
supporting and encouraging me. Thank you.

For all the dreamers who are
busy creating their own reality.

CHAPTER ONE

Misplaced

Fear, a primal echo from forgotten wars,
spurred them onward, an ancient enemy
had arisen ready to claim their world.

Ogda

The sun beat down on the group of people as they made their way to the craggy peaks of rock that rose on the distant horizon. They were tired, close to exhaustion, but an unsuppressed terror drove them forward. Dust swirled around the crowd before rising and disappearing into the thick foliage of trees that lined the road.

Tallot scanned the path they had just crossed, concern written on his face. They were like sitting ducks walking on the road. He swept his gaze back towards the throng of people; he would have to make the decision to send them into the forest, and soon. When the group had heard their former leader and chief of the village had been killed by the Asur, it had almost driven them into a panic. Merek, the former chief's son, had barely managed to contain them. It had taken all his patience and strength to convince them they had to keep on their journey to Dorhall Pass.

The trees seemed to sense Tallot's dilemma and began to whisper a mystery that only the forest understood. Tallot looked towards the trunks of foliage that rose, stretching and reaching for the sky. The leaves rustled, vibrating against each other, calling to Tallot, urging him to come into their realm. Tallot frowned. The forest had always been a haven, a place that offered sanctuary to troubled people. It provided a space for important rituals and ceremonies to take place. But a large part of the forest had been burned to the ground by an evil entity intent on destroying and removing humanity forever. The forest now beckoned Tallot, inviting him to seek shelter and hide from a common enemy. Tallot knew that this was the only choice he had and that the forest would help protect them. He wheeled his horse and raced to catch up to the group.

As Tallot approached he noticed the slight tremble in Merek's hands as he tightly clasped the reins. Dark circles sat under his eyes; his shoulders drooped as if the weight of the world were upon them. Tallot could only imagine the strain his friend was under not to mention the loss of his father. He knew despite Merek's exhaustion a quiet fury remained driving him to outmanoeuvre an ancient enemy and seek vengeance for what he had lost.

'We need to hide in the forest; we are too exposed on this road,' Tallot swept his gaze from the road to the forest. Merek glanced over at the people he now led: a group of six hundred. They were one of the four groups Merek's father Eijanbrook had decided to split to allow a better chance of survival. Merek had tried to conjure an army to fight the Asur while his father had been forced to flee when the forest had started to burn. Eijanbrook had been left with little choice but to take his people to the Pass. He had only recently returned from the ancient Seer Ogda who had foretold the rise of the Asur. Merek did not answer immediately he rubbed his chin a slight frown on his face. Tallot wondered if his leader was thinking about what Eijanbrook would have done. Eijanbrook had been a wise and strong leader, he would have known what to do. Tallot sat waiting for Merek's response. Time was not on their side; they had to get to the Pass as quickly as they could.

'Get them into the forest and tell the scouts to focus on the rear. I will lead. You and Flamma are to protect the flanks,' Merek said at last. He turned his horse, making his way to the front of the group.

Tallot gave a brief nod and set off to find the scouts. The burnt forest still smouldered, and a smell of smoke hung heavily in the air along with a deep sense of loss. It was difficult to comprehend the death of their beloved forest the enormity of it was slowly sinking in.

Krea tore her gaze from the charred remains, willing herself to focus on the road ahead. She could hear the whispers of the Seer, her mother and niece inside her head; they were able to mind travel, something she was still getting used to. Her world had changed so much in the last month, starting from when her brother and his family had arrived at their village and warned of an old enemy that had come to seek and destroy them. Now, along with Kacha and Ulric, she was searching for the secret underground tunnels that the Asur were rumoured to use.

Krea whistled for her wolf, Romulus, who had bounded after a hare. She wanted him to stay close, as she could not shake the feeling of being watched. The hairs on the back of her neck rose. She whistled again, but the large wolf did not show. It was not unlike him not to come to her first call. She shaded her eyes, scanning the charred skyline, feeling her heart beating a little faster.

'Romulus chasing a hare?' Ulric asked his aunt. Krea turned in her saddle to face Ulric and noticed his own dog standing by his master's horse, tongue lolling. She frowned. Kanji had joined Romulus in the chase, yet here he was, which was unusual as they ordinarily would have come back together. Panic was beginning to rise within her as she once again swept her gaze over the blackened forest. '*You need to call him again Krea, you have to leave. The Asur are searching for you,*' she heard her mother Anja's voice whisper inside her mind. Again, Krea let out a loud whistle, her concern building for her beloved wolf.

'I see him!' shouted Kacha. He had moved some distance away from the trio, eager to be on the move. Kacha was a warrior from a tribe that lived on the other side of Dorhall Pass and become friends with Merek who had been separated from his family after injuring his back in a fall during a violent blizzard. Kacha had fallen in love with Merek's daughter Ada after he had seen Merek's family living with a different tribe a few days' ride from his own village. Together, they had set off to be reunited with a family that Merek had never given up hope of finding.

The large black wolf came bounding from where he had been chasing the hare. He found it hard to give up the chase when his mistress called him. Krea jumped from her horse when she saw him. The wolf dropped and then rolled on to his back when he sensed her displeasure. She scratched his belly, her anger instantly disappearing.

'You had me worried, Romy,' she said. The wolf licked her hand, begging for her forgiveness. Krea smiled at his goofy look. 'Who would think that you are a big, bad, scary wolf?' She stood, turning towards her horse and grabbing a piece of dried meat from the saddle bag to give to him.

'*Krea, it's time to go!*' This time, her mother was shouting at her. Krea jumped at the sound of her mother's voice and hastily mounted her horse. She swept her gaze around her, noting that Kacha and Ulric had started to move towards the blackened forest. '*You must follow them. Hurry, they are coming!*' Krea kicked her horse into a fast trot as fear crawled within her.

Within the blackened copse of trees, she felt a vibration. It seemed to pulsate from the ground under her. A sickening sense of dread festered as she swallowed down the nausea that had risen; it was time to get far from this desolate place and as quickly as possible.

The sun was slowly dipping in the afternoon sky and Merek had stopped his group to rest for the night. His body ached, and he was growing tired of the constant struggle of not only keeping his people alive but managing their daily life. He knew that until they had gotten to the Pass and even then, there would be no guarantee of safety. His only goal had been to get to the Pass. After that … he shook his head and sighed, trying not to think too much on the future that lay ahead.

'Merek, you need to rest.' He looked at his wife who had stopped beside him. She had an uncanny sense of knowing that something was troubling him.

He forced a smile, clearing his throat. 'I am fine, Norrie,' he told her. He started to unsaddle his stallion, his mind reaching back to the last couple of days seeking the memories that lay there. Merek tried in vain to stop it, but it was to no avail. The image of his father came to mind, the cruel death of a man he revered and loved. Eijanbrook had sacrificed his life for his people and his family, brave to the end.

He felt a hand on his arm as Elenore turned him to face her. 'Merek, we need to organise food and a fire, or should we eat the dried food again so as not to attract attention by lighting fires?'

Merek frowned. He had to focus on the people he now led. Pushing

4

the memory of his father's death away, he turned his attention to the question his wife had just asked.

'We will make a fire. We can't eat dried food forever. Besides, there would not be enough. We have the cover of the forest I will send out a group of hunters to get fresh meat.' He handed the reins to Elenore to finish tending to the horses while he went and organised a hunting party.

Elenore watched him go. He had not been the same since Eijanbrook's death and she could not blame him. *We have lost so much and still stand more to lose. Will we ever be safe and live a normal life?'* The question begged to be answered. Only the death of the Asur would ensure their safety and future. Another fear pressed upon her, one that had started to grow only a few weeks ago. With each passing day it seemed to manifest and confirm her suspicion. The tiredness and nausea had increased. She had not had a chance to meet with the healer like she had planned, fate had intervened with different plans. She did not want to confess this new fear with Merek – the Gods only knew he had enough on his plate. She would have to wait. Nothing was confirmed, it could just be something she caught. The thought made her feel a little better and she set to work on grooming the horses.

People gathered around the fire. It had been over a week since they had had fresh meat, and the smell of cooking made their mouths water. A line had formed as people held their plates while Elenore spooned the meat and gravy mixture onto them. She smiled and noted the shift in their demeanour, the smell of a fresh meal had revived them. However, after some time she suddenly felt a pang of sorrow. They had left their homes, taking only the barest of things, and now were facing an uncertain future.

She scanned the back of the line and noticed a familiar face. Sabin's black curly hair was sticking out from the cap he wore. A small woman with dark hair stood beside him, a child balanced on her hip. It was Edyth. Elenore had barely spoken to her since the day she had met her with Eijanbrook when they had come back from the Seer. It seemed so long ago now.

She smiled as the memory danced in front of her. Eijanbrook had insisted she come with him and meet Edyth, but the woman had not been welcoming and barely concealed her contempt for her. Now it appeared she had fallen for her best friend, Sabin. Elenore was curious to find out more about her. She was Merek's best friend's wife, who had lost her husband and one son to the Asur. Her twins had arrived four months early, dying soon after birth, only seven of the ten children she had birthed survived. Huxley, her eldest son stood in line behind her. He had not been the same since the Asur had taken him years earlier, preferring to stay hidden in a small bungalow behind his mother's small farmhouse.

Huxley towered above his mother. His hair was long and unkept, and matched the beard that covered his face. Elenore thought he resembled a lost bear that roamed the forest, forever seeking answers to the questions that would not stay quiet. He never smiled, and a vacant, distant look was permanently settled on his face. She felt a stab of sadness for the young man; the Gods only knew what he had endured. A thought struck her: maybe he held some clues to the Asur's weaknesses. The Seer Ogda had told them they had to look for any flaws, it would be the only way to penetrate and infiltrate their enemy. If Merek could speak with Huxley, it may help, but Huxley hated Merek. He blamed him for the loss of his father and brother. Elenore's mind whirled. She still did not know all the details of her husband's former life, and now it was even more important for her to learn what had happened.

CHAPTER TWO

The Tree

*The air that day held a tremor, not of wind, but of something
older, something sinister. In the depths of my mind fragments
of a memory linger. Echoes of a demon's touch, a chilling
reminder of the day innocence fled.*

Merek

The smell of burnt timber hung in the air; Ulric could not only
smell it, but taste it. He cleared his throat, hawked, and spat,
trying to rid the soot that seemed to be lodged there. Blackened
ash fell from the sky with bits of timber still smouldering. The once
majestic forest of large oaks that seem to reach to the Gods, now lay in
dark ruins. A heavy sense of sadness hung in the air as the trio carefully
made their way alongside the silent woods.

'It will take years for the forest to come back, if ever,' Ulric
announced. The others barely nodded, so taken aback by the
destruction. Ulric could hear Ada; she too could see and sense
the destruction, using her mind to weave its way into her brother's.
'Ulric, you have to look for a labyrinth of tunnels,' she whispered. Ulric
frowned, not sure if he had heard right. *'I know how it sounds, but
please trust me, it's important.'*

'Okay,' Ulric replied. He turned in his saddle looking at Kacha and
Krea, who also it seemed had received the same message.

'The trees will let us know,' Kacha said.

As Ulric gazed towards the blackened forest, doubt pulled at him.
Only darkened stumps were left, charred limbs remanent of the trees
that represented life. Confusion clouded his mind. From afar, he could

see movement. He stiffened as he squinted, focusing on where he had seen it. There! Something was moving!

Once again, he turned in his saddle, this time to alert his aunt and friend. They too had seen the movement, concentrating on the same spot Ulric had been looking at. One tree stood among the darkened ruins, seemingly untouched by the fire and its destructive flames. Standing tall and lush, branches like tentacles that flared reaching up and out. A splash of green, like a light in a dark night beckoning them to safety.

The trio looked up in awe at the giant tree. How it had managed to escape the ravaging fire was a mystery.

'The Gods have spared this tree for a reason,' Krea said, marvelling at its beauty. The tree seemed to lean into them as if it was acknowledging their observation.

'I can feel its energy. It's a warrior, a fighter, a soldier of the forest,' Kacha said in return. The leaves rustled as a wind swept through the now dead forest. *'Come closer,'* a voice whispered, beckoning them.

'You must listen, Ulric, it's important. The tree will help us,' Ada said quietly inside her brother's mind. The three of them stepped closer to the tree, feeling its energy become even stronger.

'We fight the same enemy, one that will destroy us all if we leave it too late. Look for what you seek, a place that holds the secrets of the evil that lurks,' the tree said. They waited, as they all frowned, thinking about what the tree had just told them. Silence. The wind started up again, blowing the fine ash into the air and lightly covering the people that stood under the branches of the ancient tree. Ulric fidgeted as he waited, unsure what the next move should be.

'Be patient,' Ada told him.

'We don't have time,' Ulric's mind replied. Ada did not answer him.

More silence. It seemed to stretch for an eternity, agonising and slow. Ulric closed his eyes, taking a calming breath. He felt tired as he waited for a tree to speak to him. Images of the past weeks dashed across his mind. It had been so long since life had been normal, now he felt he wasn't even sure what that meant anymore.

As he focused, an image flew up in front of him. A dark, damp tunnel stretching as far as the eye could see lay before him. He frowned.

Not only could he see the tunnel, he felt like he was in it! It was cold and dark, and a strong earthy smell penetrated his nostrils. Surely, he was dreaming.

'*Look closer,*' a voice commanded. Ulric examined the tunnel as he felt himself take a step, entering the shaft. '*It will be closer than you think. Look for something that doesn't seem to fit. This will lead you to them, but you don't have much time, you need to hurry!*'

'But—' Ulric began.

'*You know the why, you will figure out the how,*' the voice told him. The image instantly vanished, and Ulric blinked against the sun that beat down from a cloudless sky.

'*Ulric, you need to hurry,*' this time it was Ada who was talking to him. He shook his head, trying to clear his thoughts. He felt motionless, locked within his own confusion.

'Ulric,' he heard his name being called as if from a great distance away. 'Ulric!' he heard it again, but he could not move rooted to the spot under the tree that had offered them hope.

'*Move!*' this time it was Ada who screamed at him. Ulric felt his senses return as his sister's voice reverberated inside his head. He opened his eyes and for the first time since making their way through the burnt forest Ulric felt he like he finally knew what he had to do. A sense of urgency pulled at him as he cast a quick glance at Krea and Kacha, they were waiting, seemingly understanding that he would lead them to the place they had to find.

'We have to look for something that will stand out and be in a place where it's not meant to be.' Ulric made his way to where they had tethered the horses not far from where they had stood under the huge tree.

Kacha frowned and hesitated before following his friend.

Krea also seemed a little confused. 'Wait, Ulric, what exactly are we looking for?' She grabbed her nephew's arm.

Ulric turned to face her. She was a formidable looking woman, strong and powerful. He could feel her grip on his arm. 'The Gods will show us Krea, that is all I know.'

She continued to hold his stare for a moment longer before releasing her grip on his arm. Ulric mounted his horse, not waiting for the others as he set off through the ash-laden forest.

They combed the woods, stirring the blackened dust, seeking the key to finding the Asur's underground tunnel system. Minutes turned into an hour, and an hour turned to two. They searched, looking for something, anything that would be a sign, but their search was starting to appear futile.

'Ulric, are you sure there is an underground tunnel system here? How long will this take?' Krea demanded. Ulric ignored Krea's questions. Doubt pulled at him, but he pushed it away. He scanned the tree line before sweeping his gaze over the ground. Nothing, there was nothing except dead trees and blackened ash. Ulric felt an overwhelming desire to give up.

The sun had reached its halfway point as the trio reined in their horses. It was hot and the sun beat furiously down upon them. Ulric wiped the sweat from his face. He longed for a cool bath and a soft bed, but he knew it would be a long time before he would be able to experience any sort of luxury, let alone some sense of normal.

He let out a loud sigh before he dismounted. Krea and Kacha had already unpacked some dried fruit cakes to eat, and they watched him silently. Ulric didn't feel like eating; the heat had snatched his appetite. He spread out a small deer hide to sit on. If only he could find where their tunnels were hidden it would be a way into their world.

The group had stopped for a quick break, snacking on the meat they had dried the night before. It was a hot day, and the forest offered a welcome reprieve. Elenore struggled to hold back the wave of nausea that threatened to overwhelm her. She coughed, choking back the bile that had risen in her throat. Merek turned to his wife, a frown on his face.

'Are you sick?' He was direct.

Elenore forced a weak smile and shook her head. 'I am just tired, Merek. I will be fine.'

His gaze lingered. 'You better have something to eat. We have a long journey ahead.'

She nodded. Her brow puckered into a frown. *I have never seen this side of him. Will we ever find peace again?* The thoughts churned through her mind.

Merek was a large man, tall and powerfully built, his long dark hair pulled tightly back into a bun his beard also tied with a thong. Tattoos of blue swirling symbols decorated his arms, making him appear more menacing. As Elenore ran her eyes over her husband, she realised that perhaps she really didn't know him at all.

She had learned more about him the last few months than she had in their whole married life, and it was a sobering thought. She sighed inwardly; her life had changed so much and now it was beyond her control. The man she called her husband was leading them back to Dorhall Pass where they had crossed not that long ago, fleeing from an ancient enemy she had only thought was something of myths and legends. Regardless of her gnawing curiosity, or the fear that had started to take seed about her future, she willed herself to only focus on the present.

A cloud passed over the sun, darkening the sky for a moment before the light reappeared. Ulric rolled the hide into a small bundle. He paused as a thought came to him: only the tree knew where the tunnel was. Ada, his sister, Anja, his grandmother, and the ancient Seer Ogda, who were mind travelling watching their progress had no idea of where the tunnel system lay. His brain crawled and squirmed, trying to wring out the idea that was forming. If the tree was the only thing that knew where the tunnel lay, why did it not tell him directly? Could it be that the Asur could mind travel too and would be able to detect the tree? If that was the case, the tree could not reveal their secret to him for fear it would alert the enemy.

Ulric looked back over to where they had come from, back to where the ancient tree stood. It was almost unbelievable that this enormous tree was the only one that survived. It had to be more than a coincidence. The Gods had protected the tree for a reason. The more Ulric thought about it, the more sense it made to go back to the tree. There had to be some clue to where the tunnels lay, and Ulric had a hunch that the tree was keeping something from them.

Merek rode at the front of the group of people he led, his best friend Sabin beside him. He estimated they were still another three days' ride away from the Pass. The army he had tried to gather before his father had been slain still had not reached them, and he had doubts they ever would. It was quite possible they had been overcome and murdered by the Asur. He sighed when he thought of this. *If we make it to the Pass, then what?* He took a deep breath. On the other side of the Pass lay open forests, and more villages. He had thought going to his parent's village would protect him, keep him safe at least for a while, but that had been short-lived. The Asur had followed them and now were chasing them back to where they had just come from.

Merek was starting to question why they were now fleeing again. Where would they run to? Where could they hide from an enemy that would always be able to track them down? Was it all just hopeless and had his father's act of sacrificing himself been all for nothing?

Merek had first come across the Asur after he had begged his father to join him on raids. The legends and stories of a mysterious enemy had always intrigued him and when he had heard of talk that they were real, he was determined to see for himself. His mind drifted back to a memory from his childhood. He had been around thirteen years of age, far too young to join a band of warriors that hunted monsters, but he was stubborn and argued with his father until he'd given in to his demands.

Merek wished he had listened to his parents. What he'd seen on that first raid had haunted him for years, and he felt a shiver run down his spine as the memory surfaced.

Eijanbrook was not only a good leader, but a strong and powerful warrior who led a band of equally powerful men, known as the 'Protectors' scattered throughout the world. Merek did not know how many of these were left; he had lost contact a long time ago and his father had not revealed any further knowledge.

There were so many things he needed to ask his father, if only he was here. Merek closed his eyes. His father was not here. It was up to him to lead and make decisions that would determine the fate of the people that followed. It was an enormous responsibility, but the Gods had chosen him. His father had never lost faith in Merek, even when he'd left his family home all those years ago. The memory of his first raid pulled at him, the young, headstrong boy who was to face the biggest enemy of mankind.

It had been a clear blue day when a young Merek followed his father and his men from his village. It was not long before Kwan Eijanbrook's best and most trusted friend turned his stallion and shouted out to the boy that was tailing them. Merek, surprised at how quickly he had been spotted, sheepishly walked his pony from the cover of trees. His father had a dark look on his face; it was a formidable sight.

'You need to go home,' his father had told him sternly. Merek shook his head defiantly.

'Let him come, Eijanbrook. He wants to see, and it might make a man of him. Although it will be early, it might be a lesson for the others. Axel has been begging to join us as well, and being that they are best friends, it may act as a deterrent if Merek sees what we are fighting. My son may listen to yours after this day has passed.' Kwan shook his head.

Eijanbrook stared at Merek, his lips pursed into a tight line. 'Join the back of the group and don't stray or get behind!'

'Yes, Father!' Merek could hardly believe it. Finally, he had gotten his own way to join the Protectors.

The band of warriors followed the river that snaked through the land providing a valuable water source for all that used it. Eijanbrook had heard that the Asur had been seen camping close to where the river split into two, south of where their own village lay. He had been surprised at how close they had come to his home, and he was thankful for the lone horseman who had rode in the previous day to tell them. As the group neared where he suspected they were hiding, he heard a horn, low and forlorn, that sent a shiver down his spine. He instantly remembered his son and fear clutched him; this was no ordinary hunting trip, the prey they sought were monsters. He looked at Kwan, motioning that they split into two and circle the enemy's camp.

Merek was ordered to stay with Jabari, a young warrior not much older than Merek himself, and to hide in the field that lay behind the tree line that followed the course of the river. Jabari was not amused that he had to 'babysit' their leader's son or that if they had not heard from the rest of the group when the sun had reached its midday point, they were to head for home and alert the village. Merek stole a quick look at the young man beside him. He was short. Merek already towered over him and since he was only thirteen, he had not yet stopped growing.

Jabari was powerfully built, his muscles rippling as he clutched his shield and sword. He wore a permanent scowl on his face making him a menacing figure. Tattoos covered his body; two cobras were carved into his arms, snaking down the length of them. The tattoo of an eagle graced his back while the face of a sabre-tooth tiger in a silent roar was plastered on his right thigh. An image of a God was imprinted on his right cheek while a pattern of swirls adorned the other. His head had been completely shaved and his green eyes flashed as he scanned the surrounding landscape. A scantly clothed female warrior, carrying a bow and arrow, embellished his stomach. Jabari had been with the Protectors since he was fifteen and had proved himself many times with his unwavering courage and his talented use of the sword.

Merek attempted to make conversation, however was cut off with a threatening look. He shrugged to himself and looked towards where his father had left just moments before. The horn sounded again, causing the young teen to jump. This time it sounded closer. Merek's heart began to race, and he turned to see what Jabari's reaction was. The warrior had showed no fear and continued to scan the tree line that lay closer to the river's edge. Suddenly the cries of dog's howls and shrieks began to sound, echoing across the field. Jabari tightened his grip on his sword and his expression hardened. His horse, sensing its master's tension, began to paw the ground and fidget, snorting and throwing his head. Merek waited for Jabari to say something or give a command on what they should do, but the young man only waited and watched.

The silence was deafening as the pair waited. No further howls or shrieks were heard, it was as though the dogs had vanished. Merek could see Jabari debating whether to stay or follow his peers into the dense forest that lay in the near distance. He fidgeted, re-adjusting his grip on his sword in between rubbing his horse's neck to calm the animal. They continued to wait and slowly a trembling could be felt. The ground started to vibrate, shaking slightly. A loud shout pierced the silence as movement could be seen among the undergrowth of trees. Jabari gestured to Merek to move further among the grasses so as he would not be seen. Merek begrudgingly obliged.

He turned his pony, manoeuvring him among the tall stalks until Jabari nodded his approval. Suddenly a riderless horse burst from the tree line. Merek squinted, trying to find out whether it was one of theirs. It was a dark bay and Merek remembered one of the Protectors riding one very similar. As he continued to watch the horse make its mad dash from the trees, a larger beast also burst from the foliage. It was enormous! It was a much bigger horse, and a hideous beast sat astride it. Large and powerful, wielding a club, the monster urged its mount faster.

They were gaining on the horse as it fled from its attacker. Closer and closer it got to the now tiring animal as Merek watched in horror as the creature lifted the club and hurtled it effortlessly at the horse. It found its mark, crushing the skull of its victim and bringing it down with one fatal blow. The creature let out a loud whoop and pulled its mount to an abrupt halt. Merek felt an icy chill run down his spine, he could not tear his gaze away from the thing that stood not far from where he was hidden. It sat there for a moment before it began to sniff the air like a dog tracking its prey.

Jabari, who had silently ridden alongside Merek, startled him by whispering,

'They have an extreme sense of smell. We have to be careful as the wind seems to be blowing in his direction.'

Merek continued to stare transfixed as the beast inhaled the air, slowly it turned its head towards where Merek and Jabari were hiding.

'It knows we are here. You need to run, Merek, as fast as your pony can carry you. Go home and alert the rest of the Protectors we will be needing reinforcements today.'

Merek did not move.

Instead, he watched in horror as the thing sniffed and searched, trying to find the source of the smell. Suddenly, it kicked its mount into action letting out a loud blood curdling cry.

'You need to move!' Jabari growled at the young teen. Merek kicked his pony, panic now grasping him as the creature hurtled towards them. As he looked over his shoulder Merek saw the ever-brave Jabari ride towards the beast, his sword drawn.

Merek urged his pony to run faster as he lay flat against his mane, his legs gripping the saddle as they flew across the meadow. He could hear cries of anger and pain, but he dared not look, instead he forced himself to focus on getting home. A moment later, he heard the sickening howl of dogs followed by shrieks of pain. Guilt came over him like a wave crashing on a beach and he pulled the reins of his small horse, forcing him to slow and come to a halt. Merek whirled the pony around and he took in the scene he had just fled.

There were many more of the hideous beasts. They rose, standing tall among the grasses of the field, wielding their clubs and whistling to the dogs that Merek now saw were huge, ferocious wolf-like creatures. The Protectors had caught up with their enemy and were locked in a vicious battle. Merek's breath came out in ragged gasps as he watched the battle unfold. It was not long before he remembered Jabari's order to go home and gather more men. Digging his heels into his pony's flanks, he headed for home.

'Krea, Kacha!' shouted Ulric as he hastily mounted his horse, turning back to where they had come from. 'Follow me!' he ordered them.

Krea watched her nephew with a puzzled look on her face. Kacha came to stand beside her. He too was bewildered.

'Guess we better follow him. Seems like he has seen something of interest,' Kacha murmured. Krea nodded in agreement and went to mount her stallion. She shivered involuntarily and rubbed her arms.

'Trust and follow him, my daughter,' her mother's voice whispered inside her mind. Krea needed no more urging and raced after Ulric, Kacha not far behind.

Ulric came to an abrupt halt in front of the tree, his horse panting. Ulric rubbed his gelding's neck soothingly, looking up at the ancient tree. It stood tall and majestic, its branches stretching towards the bright sky. It was beautiful, a stunning work of nature, a creation of the Gods themselves.

Ulric took a breath, trying to calm his racing heart. He searched the ashen ground around them looking, seeking, and willing himself to find a clue. Something, there had to be something. But there was nothing! He could find nothing, but he refused to give into the doubt that was beginning to tug at the corners of his mind. Wiping the sweat from his face, he took another breath and another.

He heard his aunt and friend arrive, their horses giving out a soft wicker. Ulric dismounted, throwing the reins at Kacha and placing a finger to his lips, letting them know he did not want to hear questions. He had to concentrate, and he would explain later. Walking around the base of the tree, he once again looked up, searching for a clue. As his gaze took in the marvel of the giant tree, he noticed something: a branch devoid of leaves stuck out away from the cluster of others.

Ulric frowned as he wiped the sweat from his eyes and stared. The branch was thick at the base but started to taper down to a point that jutted out to the side of the massive trunk. As Ulric stared, he realised it looked as if it was pointing. He peered harder and it began to dawn on him that maybe, just maybe, it *was* pointing. As if the tree was reading his mind, it swayed, its leaves rustling fervently. Ulric knew this was a sign and that he was right; the tree was trying to tell him where to look! He turned in the direction the branch pointed and began to walk, once again his eyes sweeping the area before him.

It was not long before Ulric noticed that the land seemed to dip undulating into furrows. He hadn't noticed it when they had ridden there before. As he observed the lay of the land, he saw it taper down to a ravine. Ulric hurried over to it.

Carefully, he scanned the landscape. It had escaped some of the fire's destructive flames with bits of burnt vegetation that blended against a sea of green. The gully had not been badly burned as it lay on the outer ridge of the forest. Maybe it was being protected for some reason, Ulric thought. He rubbed his chin, trying to make sense of the ideas that were crowding his mind. If it had been protected, it meant that the Asur were trying to hide something.

Ulric looked behind him and noticed Kacha and Krea watching him, dumbfounded. 'Quick, you have to help me look. It's here, the tunnel, they are hiding it. It's here!' he said. They rushed over to Ulric as he quickly explained his theory about the ravine. They combed the gully, looking for a clue or some indication of something out of the ordinary.

An hour went by before Ulric heard Kacha call out, 'Over here, hurry, I've found something.'

Krea and Ulric raced to Kacha who had disappeared into thick grass. Pushing away the green stalks, Ulric caught a glimpse Kacha, not that far ahead, kneeling beside a pile of rocks partially hidden by dense foliage. Kacha had pulled out his small axe to begin to hack at the thick vegetation before Ulric cried out for him to stop.

'Stop Kacha!' he yelled. Kacha turned to him, frowning. 'We can't let them know we have found it. I don't know when they are coming back or even if this is the thing we are looking for.' Ulric explained. Kacha nodded. Both men kneeled to study the strange rock formation, Krea burst through the undergrowth only moments later and joined in their examination.

'We have to move the rocks,' Kacha said as he began to lift the heavy stones carefully placing them to one side.

Slowly, they removed the rocks and stacked them in a pile. It was heavy work, and it was not long before the three of them collapsed, sweat running down their faces and soaking their tunics. A large pile of rocks lay to one side and Ulric could make out a gap under the last rock that blocked the hole underneath. Relief swept over him. His hunch had paid off; this had to be the tunnel system.

They waited until they had caught their breath and some energy had been restored before removing the last few large rocks. A gaping hole stared back at them as they peered over the rim staring into the depths of darkness that extended in front of them.

'This must be it,' Kacha said. Ulric smiled in return.

'Good work,' Krea added.

Ulric, although elated at finding the entrance to the tunnel, was now not sure on what to do next. He also had a niggling doubt if this was the actual tunnel system, or perhaps some burrow that was home to some poor creature. He waited for some whisper of reassurance in his mind from his sister or grandmother, but it seemed they both had grown quiet. He was puzzled. Why had they not tried to connect with him? Especially since they had now discovered or thought they had discovered the Asur's tunnel system.

As Ulric contemplated this, he heard Kanji, his beloved canine friend, let out a low growl. Romulus, Krea's pet wolf, also let out a growl, and his hackles raised. The three quickly turned in the direction where the two canines were facing. A heavy stomping could be heard in the distance it sounded like the heavy footfalls of people marching. Kacha laid his hand and ear to the ground; he could feel the ground tremble.

Not taking any chances, Krea signalled Ulric to grab the horses and lead them further down the ravine while she and Kacha would do a reconnaissance to find out who was marching through the now dead forest not far away.

CHAPTER THREE

Mohsin

In the rasp of their guttural tongue, a single word escaped his lips, a parched whisper, of a truth waiting to be revealed.

Mohsin

The small army of men made their way through the burnt timber. There were less than a hundred of them. Following the procession were a few women and children who had chosen to go with their husbands and leave their homes behind. They were terrified of the Asur having heard the myths and legends which had compelled them to flee. Now, as they looked upon the dead landscape, they realised their nightmares were true. A small herd of well-bred horses followed the women and children, driven by young boys whose fathers had made them go, not only to tend to the horses, but to give the women and children a chance of survival.

When Eijanbrook had sent his sons Merek and Flamma to ask if the nearby villages could help with the fight against the Asur, most had come to the forefront offering their best horses and warriors. However, Flamma and Merek had not made it to Borak, the village renowned for their reputation of owning and breeding the fastest and toughest horses in the land before they were summoned back early by Eijanbrook. The Asur had been swift in their attack on mankind and the brothers were needed to help their loved ones flee from a common enemy. The villagers who had put their hand up to help when Merek and his younger brother had ridden into town managed to alert other villages of the enemy that they now faced. The leader of the town that prided itself with its beautiful horses had fought alongside Eijanbrook in times past and did not hesitate to help a former ally and friend.

Kacha and Krea watched the group of people file past. They peered out from the edges of vegetation that had been spared by the merciless Asur after they had set fire to a once majestic forest. They were relieved that reinforcements had come but there were not enough.

'Should we meet them and let them know where Merek is seeking shelter?' Kacha asked Krea.

She frowned at the young man beside her. 'We do not know for sure where Merek is, Kacha, and I do not want to be questioned or to alert people to what we are doing.'

As the last of the procession faded into the distance, the pair made their way back to Ulric. They could see him perched at the edge of the tunnel that led towards the bowels of the earth. He smiled briefly when he saw they were back from their recon.

'It's the reinforcements that father ordered before he left,' Krea explained to her nephew. 'That's good.' Ulric paused briefly before continuing, 'I think these tunnels will help infiltrate the Asur as the Seer said.' Ulric could barely hide his excitement as he continued to look down the tunnel.

'What do we do now?' Kacha asked. Ulric rubbed his chin. He had just been intent on finding the tunnel system. As for to do with them when he found them ... well, he had not thought that far ahead.

An unfamiliar voice whispered the answer to him. *'Hide the horses but take the wolf and dog. Seek and you will find.'* He was not sure of the identity of who had spoken to him. He thought it may be his grandmother, Anja, but he could not say for sure. He repeated what he had just heard to Krea and Kacha, and it was not long before they had watered the horses and tethered them to graze not far from the tunnel. Satisfied they would be safe until the trio returned, they made their way into the darkness and onto an unknown path.

Merek walked his stallion alongside Sabin's smaller horse. As they continued Merek ran his gaze over his remaining warriors. They looked tired, dishevelled but a grim determination were etched on their faces. He felt a sense of pride before the memory of Jabari came to surface again.

Merek's pony had been close to exhaustion as he'd neared his home. Merek called out to the village Councillors as he jumped from the saddle. The Councillors, hearing Merek's panicked cries for help, rushed from a large stone hut that sat in the middle of the village.

'What is it, son of Eijanbrook?' Ranco asked, barely masking his irritation at being disturbed. Merek looked at the young Councillor who had just had his twentieth birthday and had already managed to climb the village political ladder.

Merek did not like the ambitious young man, sensing a lack of integrity.

Merek blurted, 'They need help you need to get more men they are—'

Ranco interrupted the young teen, 'Take a breath, Merek, you are not making sense.'

Merek narrowed his gaze, feeling his irritation mount.

'Father said I could go with them.' Merek decided not to tell the Councillor that he had followed the Protectors that morning, he had a feeling that information would only prolong organising a rescue group. 'We were following the river where the last sighting of the Asur had been when they were alerted to our presence.' Merek brushed over this part of the story as he had been waiting with Jabari. 'They attacked us. I was told to get help. We need to hurry.' he said, watching the Councillor's reaction.

The Councillor looked sceptically at Merek. 'I am surprised your father let you go, Merek. You are ... thirteen?' The Councillor inclined his head a smirk on his face. Before the youngster could reply he continued, 'I was sure Eijanbrook is quite strict with his policy of no boys under fifteen running with the Protectors. In fact, I am sure he would not even contemplate his son going until he was at least fifteen since he may be the next village's leader.' Ranco's voice had risen as he said the last part of his sentence.

Villagers had gathered around, by now noticing the Councillors surrounding their leader's son. They were listening transfixed to what the Councillor was saying.

Merek could feel anger beginning to bubble, steaming, gathering momentum, waiting to explode. He swallowed, forcing the anger down. He had to remain calm. Ranco was waiting for him to lose his temper, and if that were to happen, there would be no reinforcements and men would lose their lives.

Merek cleared his throat. The crowd had continued to grow.

He replied, 'the Protectors are in danger. I was with them this morning, following the river where it splits into two where the Asur had last been sighted and we were attacked. They are, at this present moment, fighting for not only their life, but for the sake of this village. We must hurry if we are to save them and the village!' Merek had completely ignored Ranco's question and had gone straight to the point again.

The other Councillors began to murmur, looking at Ranco.

'Ranco, you need to gather the rest of the men that can fight, what are you waiting for?' Pancome glared at the young Councillor.

Ranco nodded at Pancome, choosing not to argue. He was aware of the growing audience.

'Hurry, we must summon our best warriors that are still here and anyone else that can and is willing to fight!' he yelled.

It was not long before a group of men were gathered, ready to follow Merek back to where he had left Jabari earlier that day. Ranco threw Pancome a scathing look as the group left. Merek watched the exchange between the two men; he knew that the older man would pay for undermining his plan to make the prodigy of Eijanbrook look like a foolish and disobedient youngster.

When the group reached the place where Merek had last left Jabari, it was a completely different scene. Men, now unrecognisable, were covered in blood and bits of flesh. Some still sat on their horse's others sat slumped where they had killed the Asur they had battled with. A strong smell of death hung in the air, pungent and overwhelming.

Merek gagged as he took in the scene before him. The men that had followed the son of Eijanbrook began to look for survivors and to hunt down any remaining Asur that were alive. Merek caught sight of a familiar face: Jabari! He dismounted, running towards the warrior slouched over a fallen tree. As he approached, he noticed a large gash. At first Merek thought the man had passed out from all the fighting and the wound that he had sustained.

Maybe he is tired from all the fighting, his young mind mused. As he inched closer, cautiously kneeling beside the man who had protected him only hours earlier, he could make out the long extension of sausage-like intestines protruding from an even larger wound.

Merek's stomach heaved, the smell of death overwhelming him. He retched, spilling the breakfast he had had that morning. Wiping his mouth, he turned to take a better look at the lifeless body. It was obvious Jabari had put up a strong fight, his body was riddled with bruises, scratches and deep wounds. His tunic had been ripped to shreds, his dagger lay beside him covered in blood and chunks of flesh. His face was frozen in a look of hate and fury. Blood was smeared across the tattoos that covered his arms.

Merek searched for Jabari's sword and noticed it lying not far from its owner, beside a hideous creature. Merek made his way to the Asur that lay twisted, its back broken when it had been brought down from the beast that it once rode.

It was grotesque.

Merek's wildest imagination could never have conjured up a beast like this. Not even when he had listened to the tales of beasts that would take children if they went out after dark. A cold shiver ran down Merek's spine as he continued to stare at the thing that lay with its mouth open in the silent scream of death. A mixture of human and monster blended into one was all Merek's young mind could interpret as he peered closer.

A strong, foul odour permeated the air. It too had put up a good fight before Jabari had brought it to its death.

The memory of Jabari brought a feeling of sadness and a fresh wave of determination washed over Merek as he encouraged his people to travel faster.

A gloomy grey morning greeted the six hundred villagers who had fled their home from an enemy that threatened their existence. The mood was sombre as they gathered their belongings, finished off a light breakfast and prepared for another day of walking through the forest that offered them protection. Merek stroked his long beard that hung in a plait he estimated that they had another day's hike before they would reach the Pass. He was unsure on what to do once they got there, he assumed that they would have to cross it and then what? The question screamed at him, then what? He closed his eyes, exhaustion always threatened to claim him, but he pushed it away this was not the time to give into sleep. A familiar voice could faintly be heard, he concentrated harder, was it his mother? Daughter? The Seer? It was there, he was sure of it trying to communicate, to break through whatever it was that it needed to break through, to speak to him. Merek forced himself to relax he needed to hear what it was trying to say it must be important and it could very well help save their life.

Tallot could see Merek in some form of meditation as he approached the village leader. He hated having to interrupt him, but it was important and could not wait, Tallot cleared his throat. Merek barely masking his annoyance stared at the warrior in front of him. 'It had better be important' he growled at Tallot. 'The scouts have notified me of a large group of horsemen heading our way' Tallot said. Merek nodded, he would have to try again later to listen to the voice that seem to be whispering in the back of his mind, there were more urgent matters to tend to. Merek got up from where he had been seated, grabbing his sword he ordered Tallot to ride with him and meet the mysterious group who was following them.

Merek urged his stallion into a gallop, he had left his younger brother Flamma to start the daily procession, they would be slow, and Merek had no doubts that he could catch them up after he had dealt with whoever it was that was trailing them. As they came over the rise one of the scout's came to meet him. 'They're about a kilometre away Merek, they seem like they are from the neighbouring village of Borak, the horses they ride are exquisite', a slight smile played on the scout's mouth. Merek too felt the beginnings of a smile as relief swept over him. It would make sense how this group of horsemen had been able to catch them so fast when they rode the best and fastest horses in the land, not to mention that he and Flamma had asked for them to come to their aid before they had been summoned back by their father. It was not long before Merek and the scout were proven right, a large procession of men followed by some of their families, a collection of farm animals and a few possessions they had managed to bring tagged along. The leader of the group rode a huge buckskin coloured stallion the horse was a sight to behold in itself, it pranced snorting and half rearing as Merek approached. The man who sat astride the horse was also a rare sight, his hair was the same colour as the first falls of winter snow it fanned out behind him as the breeze caressed the morning air. Merek could not wipe the grin from his face Amzi was leader of the village of Borak he was a strong and fair leader taking on the legacy from his fathers before him in breeding the best horses in the land. Not only were their horses prized but the men who rode them were said to be the best with the bow and arrow and could outdo any man or woman in their endurance. To have such a force unite Merek knew that maybe just maybe they may have a chance in their conquest against the Asur.

The tunnel smelled of earth, a powerful aroma mixed with leaves, soil, and dampness. Ulric had hurriedly lit a torch as they made their way in. The labyrinth of different paths was convoluted, intriguing yet eerie, they spiralled out in each direction.

'Which way?' Kacha asked as they came to a stop. Ulric frowned and waited to see if he would be given a sign of where to go from here. Kacha and Krea waited patiently. They too heard the whispers inside their minds as they were guided by Ogda, Ada, Ulric's sister, and Anja, Ulric's grandmother.

Follow the path to the left, Ulric, his sister's light voice told him. Ulric nodded and gestured to the others to follow. The path extended before them, tree roots that were buried deep in the ground searching for water and nutrients protruded from the edges of the dark corridor. Ulric swept the torch along the tunnel, alert for any sudden movement or sounds. An eerie silence deafened them.

They continued to follow the tunnel as it wound and twisted, looping back before stretching out again. Ulric felt like it could go on forever, like he was not getting anywhere. He cast a brief look at Krea and Kacha. They too seemed to be dubious about where this path would lead. Their canine companions had come with them and were hesitantly following behind.

'You will come to a bend soon, Ulric, be careful. They are not in this part of the tunnel, so please do not be afraid. They do not know you are here that is why we are guiding you. Up ahead there is their arsenal of weapons, so do not be alarmed when you come across it. We need to see

it, and the only way is through you,' Ada whispered in Ulric's mind helping to calm the anxious young man.

As the trio of humans rounded the next bend a door was wedged between the top and bottom of the earth walls of the tunnel effectively blocking off their way. For a moment they looked dumbfounded at the grey wooden door not sure on what their next move should be. Ulric waited patiently for instructions, but his sister remained silent. Krea moved forward; her patience had begun to run out. She hated not being in control of what they were doing. She gently pushed past her nephew, grabbing the doorknob. Her wolf let out a low growl as he watched his mistress. The door was not locked, which seemed a little ridiculous. The reason for its existence now begged to be answered. Krea frowned as she twisted the knob slowly edging the door open a crack. The wolf whined and the three of them held their breath as she pushed the door open further.

The room was stacked to the roof with a vast array of swords, shields, bow, and arrows and torture implements. A large cage stood in the corner next to a pile of shackles and chains. Krea made her way over to the cage, curious to find out if anything or anyone was being held captive within it. Ulric watched her make her way over to the iron barred device as Kacha studied the stockpile of bows and arrows. As she came closer, she could see a pile of clothes seemingly left behind by the person who owned them. She held her breath as she took yet another step curious to what else was there.

Be careful! warned the voice inside her mind. Krea took a step back, her heart in her mouth as the pile of clothes began to move. Ulric and Kacha had heard her sharp intake of breath and rushed over to where she stood transfixed. The pile of clothes rose. Krea drew her sword, preparing to attack whatever it was that was making it move.

A small, stick thin man peered out at them from hollowed eyes. It was evident he had been beaten and had not eaten for some time. The pathetic creature held onto the bars of its cage, leaning against them as he tried to speak but nothing came out of his mouth.

'He is close to death. Ulric, you must give him water and find out what he knows,' Ada instructed her brother.

'We need to give him water, Krea' Ulric whispered. Krea pulled out her skin of water along with the wooden cup that she had tied to her pack. The man eyed her suspiciously as she passed the liquid between the bars, he took it and greedily drank from the cup. He handed it back indicating he would like more. Krea obliged, handing him another.

The man's clothes hung off him like he was a clothesline, and he thirstily drank four more cups of the liquid. He smacked his lips as he finished the fourth cup, eyeing the strangers fully for the first time since they had stumbled into the room that held him captive.

'You must want to know what I am doing here?' He cocked his head slightly, his voice raspy like dry crackly paper.

Krea nodded. 'Yes, why are you here? Who are you? Where are you from?' She could not contain the questions that poured out. Ulric lightly touched her arm as they waited for his response. Kacha held his hand at his sword, ready for anything. Ulric and Krea were not only friends but had become family. The Gods had led him to them when his village had rescued Merek from a blizzard on the Pass.

The small man noticed Kacha but was not alarmed; he had already been to hell and back, a young man with a sword was nothing compared to that.

'What is it you seek?' the man asked. The question caught Ulric by surprise. He had no intention in telling him feeling that it best kept a secret for the time being. 'Where are you from? What are you doing here?'

Ulric stared back at the man who seemed to be assessing him. The small wretched human that clung to the iron bars closed his eyes. Taking a deep breath, he slowly shook his head. When he did not answer immediately Ulric cast a quick glance at the two people beside him, they too were waiting for the man's response.

'Do you have some food for me?'

Ulric startled for a moment, blinked. He leaned forward, peering in at the man who had let go of the bars that kept him prison. Ulric knew he would be starving, ravenously hungry, the need for nourishment overwhelming. Ulric gestured to Krea to give him one of their dried fruit cakes they carried while travelling. It would give him instant energy and some sustenance, allowing him to be able to tell his story.

Krea passed the food through the iron bars. The man snatched the cake, tearing into it and gulping it down in hungry mouthfuls. The three of them waited until he had licked every crumb off each of his fingers, relishing in the delight of having food once again.

Ulric felt his patience beginning to fade. 'Now that you have been fed you have to tell us what happened to you,' he demanded.

The man again closed his eyes. He had slumped to the floor, leaning back on the metal rods that held him prison. 'I will tell you,' he replied, not opening his eyes. 'I feel like I have been here forever, in a prison in which I will never escape. Maybe that is for the best.' He paused, taking a breath. 'The evil that wants to take this world is all around. I doubt you will conqueror it, though I admire your courage.' He opened his eyes, an intense sea of green, staring at Ulric. Ulric nodded, not wanting him to stop. The man continued. 'You never asked my name.' He cocked his head to one side, waiting for Ulric to reply.

Ulric felt annoyance brush over him, but he knew the man had been through a lot. The least he could do was introduce themselves. 'My apologies. I am Ulric, son of Merek. This is Krea, daughter of Eijanbrook, and this is Kacha, to be married to Ada, daughter of Merek.' Ulric was unsure how to introduce Kacha but thought that the title he had given would please him, since his love for Ada was so profound.

The small man shifted his gaze from Ulric to Kacha as he took in the other young man in the group. Kacha had a huge smile on his face. The man looked back to Ulric. 'I know of Ada. She is in my dreams; she helps me through the dark times; she told me you would come.'

Ulric took a step closer to the man's cell, his curiosity spiked. 'She comes to you? What does she say? I mean, what did she say about us?' Ulric asked.

The man chuckled. 'She did not tell you that she knew me? I can understand. They travel through the mind too, you know. I guess she was worried they would find out, pick up on her since they have me here.' He gestured to the cage he was in. Ulric waited for him to continue. 'Sit down Krea, Ulric and Kacha I have a long story to tell you, don't worry they won't be back until the moon is full again and by that time, I would have died so we are safe for the moment,' he chuckled again as he waited for the trio to take a seat on the damp earth floor.

'My name is Mohsin, which means courage.' Mohsin smiled weakly. His gaze took on a faraway look as he continued. 'I was born in a village many days ride from here, possibly weeks if not months, where the sea meets the land, and you can watch the ships come in. My father would sail on those ships, helping bring fish to feed the community. Sometimes he would go trade with other villages in faraway places. I heard about the Asur as you all probably did when we were only but very young. They were the boogey man, the dark creatures that would steal you away if you were out after dark.'

Ulric had been listening to Mohsin, but another question tugged at him: what had Ada told him and how come she never said anything? Mohsin looked at Ulric expectantly as the young man turned the question over in his mind.

'She will tell you, Ulric. In time, she will tell you, but first you need to listen to my story.'

Ulric nodded, temporarily at a loss for words. 'Of course, please go on.'

Mohsin cleared his throat and asked for some more water. Krea once again obliged. When the elderly man had drained another cup of the liquid of life, he once again took up his narrative. 'I never truly believed those stories I just thought they were something adults told youngsters to help keep them in line.' He shifted uncomfortably. 'If only I had known better. The Asur came to our village two summers ago. I was a grown man, but by the Gods above me they were exactly like they were described: the epitome of the boogey man. I had a family, four sons and two daughters, a beautiful wife, we were happy. My sons had grown up and left their family home to have their own families, my daughters were still young, not yet ready to marry.' Mohsin paused again. Tears welled in his eyes and trickled slowly down his sunken face. 'I had married late, waiting for the woman I had fallen in love with when I was only a young teen. She had married another, and I knew she was not happy and would never be happy, so I waited for her. We were so in love, a match made in heaven as some may say, our lives were complete, content.' He chuckled softly, brushing the tears from his face with wrinkled hands. 'Then they came, and our lives changed forever.

They were the devil, killing, raping, and pillaging everything in sight and torching our homes with fire. They kept some poor souls captive, mostly the young girls and men.

I don't know why they kept me, maybe to use as a tool for their cruel games. I could not save my family. Only one of my daughters survived they threw her in a cage on wheels with the other young people, I was taken bound and gagged in the back of a wagon.'

Mohsin covered his face, trying to control the rush of emotion that swept over him like a huge wave. Slowly he uncovered his tear-stained face and went on with the nightmare that had changed his life forever. 'They beat me, set fire to me, dragged me, spat on me, starved me, used me as a form of pleasure. Their queen is pure evil, the devil's wife.'

'The devil's wife, a queen, a female?' Krea blurted.

Mohsin nodded. 'Yes, the devil's wife, she is leader of the Asur.' he smiled sardonically. 'Believe me, you will never want to meet her. She is the essence of Satan himself. So cruel, so unbelievably cruel.' He paused. They could see he was struggling with the memories. The things he had endured made them cringe. The Asur, it seemed, would be a bigger threat than they had first thought.

The man seemed to have aged more since he had started retelling his past. Welts, leftover scars and horrific burn marks crisscrossed the taut skin, signs of the torture he had endured. An immense sadness swelled and filled the room.

The threat that loomed and teetered mankind on the edge of existence, hovered within the tunnel that had been dug and burrowed within the bowels of the earth.

'Can you give me more to eat? It's been so long since I had a decent meal,' Mohsin whispered. Ulric reached into his pack, pulling out a chunk of dried meat and offering it to the starving man. Mohsin reached for the meat, devouring it within seconds. Once again, they waited for him to finish as he licked his fingers savouring the leftover flavour of the food. Mohsin asked for another cup of water. This time he drank slowly, enjoying it. He settled himself against the bars of his prison. Closing his eyes, he let his mind open to the memories he had buried, the nightmare would be replayed.

CHAPTER FOUR

The Dream

The veil between worlds thins with sleep, a whispered vision
beckons, a haven where evil cannot lurk.
Merek

Tall craggy peaks loomed like immense rocky towers reaching high in the sky. The procession of humans paused to take in the stunning scenery. Merek had pushed his group a little harder, and faster, the threat of their enemy constantly on his mind. Amzi had advised Merek he had spotted the army of the Asur not far behind them as they took a large berth from the evil that was intent on ruling the world. The Councillors who had been instructed by Eijanbrook to split into groups before he turned back to fight the Asur, had not been found. They had, it seemed, disappeared.

Merek was at the foothills of Dorhall Pass, from here he was unsure what was expected of the Asur. The Pass would not stop their enemy from chasing them. It would put them in a perilous position.

'Merek, we have to rest before we go into the Pass, you have been pushing them too hard.' Elenore pleaded with her husband, glancing back at the community of people behind them.

Merek knew she was right, but he had had no choice. He nodded. 'We will rest once the scouts have come back. I need to know how far ahead we are.'

Elenore studied her husband for a minute before turning to look up at the enormous stone formations. She remembered the last time they had crossed the Pass and the blizzard that had separated their family, she shivered involuntarily. She'd thought Merek had perished. Thank the Gods, they had returned him safe to her. A wave of nausea swept over her. She waited for it to pass, vowing she would see the medicine woman that night after the evening meal. She could not put it off any longer. Her thoughts were interrupted when Amzi rode up to the couple.

'We have good news, Merek,' the young man announced, a smile lit his face.

Merek returned his smile. It had been a long time since he had heard those words. 'Tell me, Amzi, what is this news?'

'An enormous army has been seen travelling from the north, and it is not the Asur.' The young man chuckled. 'It is a coming together of different villages. I think your word got out and they have come to help.'

Merek closed his eyes, sending a quick thank you to the Gods. 'How far are they?' he asked.

'Two days ride if the weather favours them.'

'Have the scouts returned?' Merek silently hoped he could let his people rest for a couple of days so as they could wait for the coming army to arrive.

'Not yet, but I expect their return within the hour. Why don't we share some tea?'

Merek nodded. It would do him good to stretch his body and have a brief reprieve.

Elenore left the men to share tea. She didn't trust her stomach, and she did not want to alarm Merek until she knew what was causing her illness. She decided to find Sabin, her curly haired dark-skinned friend. She had been avoiding him of late due to her mixed feelings with his new relationship with Edyth. The woman had been less than welcoming when she had gone to her home with Eijanbrook. It seemed so long ago now when she had accompanied Merek's father to offer support to the families that needed help due to tragic or unforeseen circumstances. She felt a pang of sadness as the memory played out in her mind. Dear sweet Eijanbrook, a leader that everyone would follow, who had given his life to save his people. Tears began to well and run down her cheeks. She hastily wiped them away. This was not the time to weep, she had to be strong, they all had to be or Eijanbrook's death would be for nothing.

Elenore weaved her way through the throng of people who had taken advantage of Merek's short reprieve as they waited for the scouts to come in. They had seated themselves under the old oak trees to cool down from the sunny day. Children chased each other around while the adults chatted. Some snacked on the corn cakes that had become part of the staple diet since they had fled their village a few weeks ago.

It seemed they had been travelling for so long and the normality of village life was a long distant memory. Elenore searched for Sabin, and it was not long before she saw him, his dark curls jostling as her ebullient friend engaged in conversation with some young teens. He noticed her before she had time to say hello, his enthusiasm evident as he greeted her.

'Norrie! What a pleasant surprise! It has been so long since I have seen me favourite lady.'

Elenore blushed and was secretly thrilled at being called his favourite. 'Hello, Sabin. Where have you been and what have you been up to?'

Sabin grinned lopsidedly as he wagged his finger at her. 'Tisk, tisk Norrie, ye have been checking up on me, I know ye have but, please let me introduce you to these young men that are dying to meet the wife of our leader, Merek.'

Sabin imitated a bow as if he was in front of a queen. Elenore laughed. Sabin never failed to make her laugh it was part of his personality she had fallen in love with and the part she had missed so much.

'This is Levi, Chad, and Monte' Sabin said. The three young men said hello, slightly blushing as they shook Elenore's hand. Elenore was quietly amused at their sudden shyness. The three young men explained that they had always wanted to be part of the Protectors and hoped that one day they too would be a brave strong warrior as their leader Merek was. Elenore assured them that Merek would be proud just to hear them say that, which caused them to blush again.

'Well look at this, Norrie, ye are making grown men blush.' Sabin threw his head back letting out his infamous infectious laugh. They all joined in. After they had quietened, the three young men excused themselves leaving Sabin and Elenore alone.

Elenore watched them leave, suddenly feeling at a loss for words as she stood beside Sabin. 'So, Norrie, what have ye been up to? Ye never talk to me anymore,' Sabin asked as he turned to her.

She smiled. 'Sabin, you know it's hard now and …' her voice trailed off. She had wanted to ask and tell him so much, but now she was at a loss for words. She looked down at her feet.

Sabin gently took her hands. 'How about we go find somewhere quiet to talk?'

She nodded. Tears sprang to her eyes, and she quickly brushed them away. She was so angry with herself. Why am I so emotional? she thought.

Sabin led her towards a large patch of bushes that grew on the edge of where the camp had decided to pause and wait for further instructions. It was a quiet corner, giving space for a private conversation.

'Okay, please be honest with me. Ye must tell me, what is going on? I don't see ye these days ye never come and chat with me nor offer a cuppa. I can understand Merek, but yeself?' His voice was gentle, but Elenore could detect a slight hint of irritation.

She could not blame him. Sabin was making the most of current circumstances, moving on and making a relationship with probably a lovely woman. She certainly had made an impact on his life.

Elenore sighed. 'I don't know what is wrong with me. I am going to see the medicine woman, I haven't been myself of late.'

Sabin looked at her with concern in his eyes. Frowning, he asked, 'How long have ye been not feeling yeself like?' Elenore looked away. She didn't want to go into detail, and she suddenly felt she couldn't ask anything about his relationship with Edyth. 'Ah, I know what it may be,' he said as if he had just had a revelation. Elenore looked at him taken aback. 'Is it because I have been spending time with Edyth?'

His face had taken a serious look, something Elenore was not used to. She shook her head fervently, feeling ridiculous that she had even wanted to talk to him about it.

'No! Sabin, of course not! No, I, um, I am happy that you have Edyth.' She swallowed. It was hard to say those words. 'I have just been feeling unwell and I was going to see the medicine woman, that's all.' She forced herself to smile.

Sabin stared at Elenore for a moment before giving his characteristic lopsided smile. 'Well okay then, we will go to the medicine woman. She will know what it is, I'm sure.'

As if the Gods themselves had heard Sabin's words shouts of 'break for camp!' were heard across the small sea of humanity. 'Break for camp' meant they could roll out their tents, make a fire, cook some food, and tend to the things that needed tending to.

'Ah the Gods themselves agree, Norrie, looks like they have given their permission for us to go and see the woman who heals.' Sabin took Elenore's elbow as he steered her in the direction towards the back of the camp. Elenore felt dread clutch at her, but there was little she could do as they made their way to the medicine woman.

Thoughts raced through Elenore's mind. She had come to talk to Sabin about Edyth with the possibility of getting to know her more, and uncovering what attracted him so much to her. Now he was taking her to the medicine woman to find out what was wrong with her!

She felt herself cringe, she wanted this to be kept a secret and she wasn't even sure she wanted to know anymore.

'Sabin' she stopped.

He turned, frowning. 'Aye, Norrie? Ye have me worried, why don't ye want to see the doc?' Concern was etched all over Sabin's face as he studied Elenore.

She forced a smile. 'Guess I am nervous, that's all.'

Sabin immediately put his arm around her waist, pulling her close to him. 'Now, now, missus, it's me and we are friends, aren't we?' He continued, not waiting for her to answer. 'We have been through so much, Norrie, and I am ye friend, right? And I will take ye to the lady who heals and get this sorted ye have my solemn support.' He chuckled as he said the last few words.

Elenore smiled weakly, knowing she could not argue any further.

The medicine woman had chosen a spot away from the main camp, preferring to keep to herself when she was not tending to patients. It was rare for her to have some time to herself as there was always someone who needed tending to and she was the only medicine woman available. She saw the dark-skinned, curly-haired man with the woman with the long flowing hair that was the colour of a sinking sun making their way towards her small fire.

She sighed and added more water to her cast iron kettle, she would now be making tea for three not just one. Her old horse gave a soft nicker as Sabin and Elenore approached, the medicine woman looked up and smiled at the man and woman in front of her.

'Aye hello, woman who heals, how is ye today?' Sabin's kind brown eyes twinkled as he greeted the medicine woman. Serenity returned his smile. She recognised Sabin; he had been helping take care of Edyth and she was most grateful for it, as it had helped lessen her burden. Serenity was not just a physical healer, but also helped people with their personal problems, this at times was an arduous task.

Elenore stood beside him, a stunning woman with her fire-coloured hair and green eyes, Merek's wife, Serenity was sure. The healer pushed a strand of hair away from her face that had come away from the bun perched high on her head. She swept her gaze over Elenore, giving her a reassuring smile. She immediately knew what her condition was.

'Come sit. Tell me what ails you, girl.' She motioned to the fireplace and a long timber log that stretched itself in front of it.

Elenore was not sure what to do. Part of her wanted to run back to where she had tethered her horse and now, she fervently wished she had never said anything to Sabin.

'Come on,' Sabin encouraged her as he went to take a seat on the log. Elenore hesitantly made her way to the log and carefully took a seat.

There was an awkward silence before the medicine woman offered tea and took out a pouch of herbs. 'Are you comfortable letting this lovely friend of yours know what it is that you seek clarification on?'

Elenore was taken aback and at a loss for words. This woman, it seemed, already knew what was wrong with her.

Serenity saw the reaction on Elenore's face and smiled at her. 'It is okay, Elenore, wife of Merek, you will grow to love the life you will give.'

Elenore felt the blood drain from her face. She took a breath and felt her stomach clench. Sabin looked from woman to woman. 'Aye, what's goin' on?'

Serenity could barely keep the laughter inside her. Sabin was such a funny, adorable man seeing his puzzled dilemma was almost more than she could bear. She continued to wait for Elenore's response patiently as she watched her digest the comment she had just made.

At last, Elenore nodded. 'Yes, you can tell him what is wrong with me.'

Sabin was more confused than ever. 'What is goin' on with ye?' He shook his head his curls jostling around his face. 'Norrie, do ye know what is wrong? Ren has not even checked ye properly,' he said, frowning.

Elenore swallowed, turning to look imploringly at Serenity. She could not put into words what she had been pushing away, refusing to acknowledge what was the cause of her mystery illness.

Serenity smiled at Elenore, trying to put her at ease. 'Elenore, please do not be afraid. It is probably your fear that is getting in the way of accepting what is a miracle and what, my dear, may mark the start of a brighter future for us all.'

Anger built inside Elenore. 'I disagree with you, Serenity! How can I bring a life into a world such as ours? We may not even have a future!'

Serenity shuffled closer Elenore. 'You have to be strong. The Gods have blessed you with a new life. Cherish it, they would not let this happen if they knew we had no future.'

Elenore was still not convinced but she did not want to argue further.

Sabin, bursting with curiosity let his frustration be known. 'Can you please tell me what is going on?'

Both women turned to look at Sabin. 'I am with child, Sabin,' Elenore blurted.

Silence descended as the news settled like flurries of snow falling to the earth below.

Serenity was the first to break the silence. 'Sabin, your friend will need you more than ever.'

Sabin nodded, shock still etched on his face. Elenore felt an enormous weight lift off her. What she had already known had been confirmed, but she wondered how this woman knew, when she had not even asked her the usual questions. Serenity, as if hearing Elenore's thoughts asked Elenore to join her in her tent, a makeshift room that was used to see her patients.

The two women left Sabin to drink his tea, promising they would not be long and would come and join him once the physical check was over.

Serenity pushed the opening flap up and ushered Elenore inside. A curtain hung in the middle of the small space, strange patterns and swirls covered it. Elenore frowned. She was sure she had seen something similar before, but couldn't remember where or when.

Brushing the thought away, she lay down on the stretcher that the medicine woman used to examine her patients. Serenity washed her hands in a bowl that was set on a small timber stool before grabbing a bottle from a leather bag. Pouring oil made from tea tree leaves, she rubbed her hands together, warming them as she made her way to Elenore's exposed belly. Gently, she massaged Elenore's stomach, carefully feeling the size of her uterus, checking, and probing the life growing inside.

Elenore watched her and began to feel a familiar maternal instinct rise within her. She had denied the truth for so long she had almost convinced herself that it was all in her head yet here she was her fears and intuition being proven.

'Is everything okay?' she asked timidly.

Serenity was quiet for a moment before she answered her, 'You need to eat a little more. This one is small, but a fighter,' she said reassuringly. 'How long has it been since you menstruated?' she asked Elenore.

Elenore thought for a moment; it had been quite a while, she'd thought she was going through the change as her cycle had become unpredictable.

'I think around three months,' she told the medicine woman.

Serenity tutted shaking her head. 'Your baby is very small, Elenore.' She stopped herself from saying more as she did not want to alarm her. Stress for a pregnant woman was never good, and the Gods knew they had more than enough stress now.

Elenore studied Serenity, wanting to ask her more. But fear held her back, she bit her lip. Though she had been unsure, she now wanted this baby more than ever. The medicine woman was right, it represented hope, the start of a new beginning, a future to look forward to.

'Eat plenty of leafy vegetables. I know it is hard at the present time, so I will keep some aside for you when I am out foraging. I do it for the other pregnant women and you will all need as much help as you can for your babies to grow. I will give you some herbs for the nausea to help settle your stomach so that you can keep food down. The other pouch of herbs you make into a tea they are for you and the baby's health.' She turned away from Elenore to collect the herbs to put into small leather pouches for her.

Merek pulled on his beard, taking another sip of his wine. He closed his eyes, letting the relaxing effects of alcohol wash over him. It had been so long since he had wine and let himself relax. Once, in a former life not that long ago, it had been one of his favourite habits to pour a cup of his favourite wine after an evening meal. He had dared not do that in the last few weeks for fear of letting his guard down and let an enemy crawl and worm its way inside his small community. He felt a responsibility, an obligation to the people his father once led, he knew he must protect them and keep them safe; they were an extension of his own family.

He took another long sip of the red drink. Amzi had brought wagons of the delicious drink, it had been too good to leave behind. Merek was grateful that the blonde leader of the Borak tribe had had the insight to bring alcohol.

Merek smiled; it was good to unwind. They still had such a long journey ahead of them, but the good news that an army to help fight the Asur was on their way was a reason to celebrate. Resistance to the red drink was futile and as the sun moved past its midway point Merek had asked Amzi to open one of the crates. Amzi was only more than happy to oblige; he too had longed for the sweet fruity taste of the wine. Now the sun was slowly descending, clouds stretched grey, streaky finger-like projections across the blue sky. People happy to finally have a reprieve from the exhaustion of travel, lit fires, talked a little louder and even let laughter fill the camp. It was a more joyous atmosphere than there had been in many days and nights. Merek had told them of the army that was to join in their fight against the Asur. It was vital to keep up the morale of the people that followed him.

Elenore searched for Merek, she had gathered up the courage to tell him the news. He deserved to know he was going to be a father again. She saw their small tent strung between the trees, a fire burning. Sabin had begged to walk her back, but she had refused him. Just because she was pregnant did not make her incapable and she had told him so.

She felt a slight quiver of remorse at speaking a little harshly at him, but she knew he would not have listened otherwise. She sighed as she made her way to where the bed rolls were spread out, no Merek.

Where could he be? she asked herself as she turned and headed back out towards the small fire. She stood indecisively, looking in both directions, a slight breeze blew ruffling her long hair and caressing her face. Elenore closed her eyes, soaking in the moment of time, letting her intuition come and guide her in the direction of her husband.

She had a feeling he was probably with Amzi. He held a great respect for the leader of the Borak tribe and his camp lay west of where Merek had set up his own tent. She turned and began making her way to the Borak camp, smiling and nodding to the people she saw on her way. As she came closer to the camp, she could make out a group of men standing to one side. They were laughing and joking. Under normal circumstances this would have been ordinary, if not welcoming, however these were not normal circumstances – an enemy was hunting them, intent on destroying them all.

Elenore stopped, a sense of unease settling over her. She wondered about the security of the camp. She could see Amzi, his long blonde hair hung loosely down his back. He was engaged in a deep conversation with Merek. A beautiful young woman stood beside him. She too had the same pure white hair that hung loosely down her back. It made Elenore think of her own daughter, Ada, she had the same coloured hair. Elenore felt a pang of sadness; it seemed so long since she had seen her.

Ada was such a gifted, talented girl, and her mother missed her terribly. Ada had been chosen along with her grandmother Anja to help the ancient Seer Ogda guide Elenore's son Ulric, her sister-in-law Krea and future son-in-law Kacha to infiltrate the Asur and learn their weaknesses. Elenore wondered where and what they were doing at this very moment. She sent a silent prayer to the Gods to keep them safe.

Her sadness deepened and she felt tears begin to well. As she quickly wiped them away, she heard a man call out to her.

'Hey Elenore, is that you?' he stepped out of the shadows a cup of wine in his hand. Elenore felt herself blush. It was Tallot, Merek's second-in-command. She felt embarrassed that he'd caught her spying on her husband and crying.

'Yes, Tallot, it's me,' she said in a small voice.

The tall, muscular man smiled when he heard Elenore's voice, seeming oblivious to her embarrassment. 'Are you looking for Merek?' he asked. Elenore nodded, not quite trusting herself to speak. 'Ah, Elenore, we have all had a bit too much wine.' Tallot chuckled.

Elenore was surprised by Tallot's laid back attitude. He was usually so focused and serious; it was nice to see this side of him.

'Yes, I was wondering where my husband had got to, guess he came here.' She waved a hand towards the Borak camp.

Tallot chuckled again. 'We have been here since we decided to break for camp, where have you been, Elenore?' Tallot teased.

Elenore once again felt herself blush. The last thing she wanted to tell him was where she had been. She quickly searched for an answer.

'I was um, with Sabin, just catching up,' she finished lamely. She wiped her face, suddenly feeling self-conscious. She had seen Sabin, now, he was making her blush and tell a small white lie. It was all she could do to keep herself from running back to her own tent.

Tallot smiled. 'You are an amazing woman, Elenore. Merek is lucky to have you.'

Before she had time to react, Tallot gestured for her to follow him as he turned and made his way to Merek.

The group of men and one woman stood near a large fire. The sun had finished setting, giving its way to the dark of night. A moon had risen full and bright, beaming a soft glow on the Earth below. The forest had come to life with the fires of the camp and the humans that lit them. The Asur, it seemed, had been forgotten, for the moment. Wine had filtered down to other families and they all took turns in enjoying the effects it brought them.

As Merek saw his wife and second-in-command approach, he suddenly realised he had not even thought about Elenore that afternoon and he felt a sudden pang of guilt.

'Norrie, my love, where have you been?' He smiled broadly at his wife.

Elenore returned his smile, trying to hide her discomfort at being the centre of attention. All eyes were on her. She swallowed as she cast her eyes on the faces that now were turned to her waiting it seemed for a response.

'I, um, was with Sabin, we were talking about old times.' She forced a smile. Merek let out a loud laugh, it was clear he had too much of the red drink.

'Ah, that curly haired maniac, where is he? We need to catch up. My wife can't have all the pleasure at seeing him!' The rest of the group joined in his laughter.

Elenore did not like seeing Merek like this. He had become a different man. She wished she had just gone to bed and not bothered looking for him. The beautiful girl beside Amzi grabbed Tallot's hand.

'I don't believe we have met?' she said as she batted her eyes. Tallot blushed, at a loss for words. She was exquisite, possibly the most beautiful woman Tallot had ever met. Her eyes were the darkest of blue surrounded by her long, dark eyelashes. Pure white hair framed a heart shaped face, and skin the colour of honey. Her tunic was white too, patterns graced the front and back of it.

She had completely ignored Elenore, acting as if she did not exist, her focus on Tallot. Tallot melted as he stepped forward, letting the woman lead him away.

Elenore felt a wave of jealousy wash over her as she watched them go and she chided herself. *I need to go to bed, this is a waste of time. I don't belong here.*

She turned away from Merek, not bothering to answer his drunken question. She felt a hand on her shoulder and turned back to see who it was.

'Norrie, I asked you: where is Sabin?' Merek asked. His eyes had narrowed, the former joviality had disappeared. Elenore frowned. This was so unlike her husband, but she reasoned he had been under enormous stress in the last few weeks.

'He went back to his camp, Merek. He is probably asleep, don't worry about it.' Now, more than ever, she wanted to get away from him as she felt his grip tighten.

Merek considered her answer for a moment. 'Ah you are probably right. That fool has probably gone to bed.' He waved his hand at

Elenore. 'Go home, Norrie, it's not right for a wife to see her husband being a drunken fool.'

Elenore wasted no time in exiting the group of drunken men as she quickly made her way back to her own bed.

In the early hours of the morning, Merek stumbled into the small space he shared with his wife. He clumsily pulled off his boots, his coordination slurred in his drunken stupor. He reached for the skin of water they kept near the furs they slept in and greedily drank the cool water. After he finished, he wiped away the droplets that had dribbled down into his long beard and rubbed his face. He knew he would have a splitting headache come the time when he would wake, he groaned inwardly at the thought.

His tunic smelled of dried vomit; he had thrown up earlier as his body tried to rid itself of the excess alcohol. He forced himself to take it off but had no desire to find a fresh one. Leaving his undergarments on, he laid down on the spread of furs. It was not as comfortable as a bed made of straw, but it served the purpose, and he was glad to be back in his own tent.

He felt the warmth of Elenore's body beside him. She snored lightly, and he was thankful he had not woken her. He had neglected her lately and he made a promise he would take more care of her. It was just that he had had so much to do and think about. He sighed. The last few months had taken a toll and he wished fervently that it was all just a bad dream he would wake from.

He lay there for some time thinking of all the things that life had thrown him and the sacrifices that had been made. He knew he should not question the Gods, but he could not help himself; it just didn't seem fair. He took a deep breath. The alcohol was still running in his veins, it made him feel lightheaded and weary. Slowly, Merek closed his eyes and drifted off into a deep sleep.

The path led up the mountain, a dense growth of trees overarched the rocky trail creating a green canopy of flora. Merek held up his hand as he surveyed the trail ahead, unsure if it was wise to continue. The scouts could not go round as it was a single file track and he was hesitant to send them ahead. He continued to observe the path, stuck in a moment of indecision. It seemed to worm itself into an even thicker tunnel of foliage, creating a mystery immersed in the unknown. He felt his stallion grow restless under him and he rubbed his neck trying to soothe and calm him. Merek grew uneasy with how indecisive he felt. It was something he worked hard against, a leader needed to make decisions whether they were right or not they needed to be made and sometimes quickly, the very lives of his people depended on it.

The people behind him fidgeted as they waited for his decision. Panic began to nip as he waited, his mind refusing to give a verdict. He looked up at the craggy peaks intimidating in their appearance as they reached high into the sky.

'I bet they can touch the Gods' he mused to himself. People began to call out, asking what was taking so long. The sun seemed to have reached its midday point and was quickly descending, ushering in the darkness. The panic that had nipped was beginning to bite.

Merek still could not decide, and he felt at a complete loss, totally helpless. He sent a quick prayer to the Gods, calling on them for their guidance. The sun suddenly left, leaving behind an eerie gloom. Merek looked all around, frowning. The panic was now almost too much to contain and his heart beat furiously in his chest. He closed his eyes, taking a deep breath to slow down his breathing that now seemed to come in gasps.

After a moment, he could hear his daughter's voice, it was faint, and he was unsure of what she was trying to say. He concentrated, willing himself to make sense of her words. 'Papa, take the path.' He frowned. Had he heard correctly? 'Take the path.' There it was again. He leaned forward in his saddle peering into the black night, the path had gone, and he could not see a thing. 'You must take the path, Papa. Don't delay! Take the path!'

Merek sat up, the remnants of the dream still in his head. He blinked, trying to focus on what he had just dreamed and where he was. Elenore lay beside him. He could hear her breathing, rhythmic and peaceful. He closed his eyes, trying to collect his thoughts. Wisps of what he had dreamed still lingered. He rubbed his temple trying to remember what his daughter had tried to tell him.

She had told him of a path, yes! A path that would lead them to safety when they crossed Dorhall Pass. He shook his head as doubt crowded his thoughts, making him feel uncertain if it really was his daughter telling him of a path that would help hide them from the Asur, or just the effects of a day of drinking wine. He got up, leaving the warmth of his furs as the sudden urge to urinate took precedence over anything else. He made his way to the back of the tent and unfastened it, letting himself out into the night air. He drew in a deep breath before stumbling towards a huge oak tree, where he relieved himself. When he was finished, Merek made his way back to the entrance of the tent. Pausing before he entered, he looked up at the moon that graced the dark sky above. He sent a prayer to the Gods, trusting that they knew what they were doing. Not only did his life depend on it, but the lives of the people he led.

CHAPTER FIVE

Exposed

Their putrid breath is just a moment behind, but I run
toward the light, where a monster's grip will be withdrawn.
Pancome

Mohsin let his mind slip into the murky depths of a past that he had done his best to bury and forget. He had known he would be asked to dig up the hurt and torment he had experienced; Ada had advised that it would prove valuable when the time came. That time was now.

He took a long cleansing breath as the images of the horrors he had endured came to play and he began a dance with terror itself. The one thing that stayed within in his mind and filled his senses was the smell; he had found it impossible to get rid of. The rancid smell of rotting flesh, putrid and overwhelming, floated back to him as he began to speak about the first night when his life was forever changed.

'They put us in the back of a wagon. I was the oldest male, all the others were just boys. As I said before, the women and girls were put in another, including my daughter. I knew I had to stay alive so I could save her.' Mohsin paused and cleared his throat. A low scornful chuckle followed. 'How naïve I was to think that. I never saw my child again.'

Silence followed as Mohsin wrestled with the demons that lurked in his thoughts. He loathed to think of what had become of his beloved daughter.

'Take your time, Mohsin, you are doing well. This is very important,' a soft voice told him. Ada had been his companion, his motivation to live. When he had first heard her, he thought he was going mad. She had helped him through the darkest of times when his thoughts had threatened his existence. He had come to rely on her soft, soothing

voice and let it guide him as he clung to the fabric of life. Now, as she had predicted, it was time to tell his story. It was vital that he describe every detail; it would provide clues about a way to bring down the Asur.

Ulric looked doubtful as he glanced over at Krea and Kacha before returning his attention back to Mohsin. They waited for him to continue as a sicking sense of gloom manifested.

'I don't know where they took us, we were locked in that wagon for days. They never fed us, just gave us barely enough water to survive, and threw a blanket to cover the roof of the wagon that way we couldn't see where we were going. We stopped a couple of times, and all I could hear were the sounds of death and destruction. We could never see what happened, they made sure the wagon stayed covered. The last stop we made, an older man, even older than me, was thrown in the wagon. I must say I had forgotten about him until now. He was a very clever fellow said he had tried to outrun the Asur for several days after they burned the forest down.'

Ulric threw Mohsin a questioning look. Was he talking about the Majestic Forest? Ulric stepped closer to the iron bars. A slow smile played across his Mohsin's mouth. 'Ulric, the Majestic Forest covers more land that you think.'

Ulric frowned.

'*Let him tell his story dear brother,*' his sister breathed inside his mind. Ulric shook his head. Nothing seemed to make sense and he was starting to realise that this was how it would be from now on.

'Ada tells me that you know this man, his name is Pancome.'

Once again Ulric felt perplexed. He ran his fingers through his brown hair before nodding.

Mohsin continued, 'Pancome became my friend over the next few months. He was a wise, kind man. I don't know how many villages they conquered and captured; it all becomes a blur after a while. All I could think of was having something to eat.

When we finally stopped for more than a few hours longer than our usual routine of listening to people being killed and tortured, I knew something was going to happen. They took the blanket off the wagon. It was the first time I had seen the light of day for some time, and I soaked up the sun as she beat down on us. We were put in a hole underground – I think they like that, the underground – I reckon that is where they come from. The devil themselves, that is what they are!' Mohsin face was distorted by anger as he spoke.

'Keep going, Mohsin. Please, we are learning so much, don't stop,' Krea encouraged.

Mohsin closed his eyes and nodded. He had to finish his story; he did not have much time left, soon it would be his time to go and meet the Gods. 'They kept us in underground prisons and would randomly pick one of us to inflict torment and torture. We were at their whim.

I shared the same cell with Pancome. He was so intent on escaping, it was all he could talk about. I just wanted to see my daughter, but that never happened. When they would pick us for their sport, we were taken up to the outside world and paraded around to those hideous beings.' Mohsin shivered. 'They whipped us, chased us around in a big arena, and used us as a form of entertainment. That was when I first met their leader, the queen of the Asur. She was the vilest thing I had ever seen; her hair was like tentacles that grew and extended like the roots of a tree. She would unleash these tentacles of evil when she was displeased with her captives. They would reach out and grab some poor soul and she would devour them. If you pleased her, you would live.' Mohsin shifted his posture. It was clear he felt uncomfortable, but continued anyway. He stood and paced his small prison cell, the water and food had given him energy. He looked up at the roof of the tunnel and sent a silent prayer. He wanted to be reunited with his family, he was ready to severe the tie with life on Earth. Mohsin wanted more than ever to finish his story, for it would mean peace at long last, an end to the suffering that had been his existence for so long.

'The place where they had taken us was dark, there were tall mountains that rose trying to reach the Gods themselves. We were only taken out for short periods of times, and I can't remember how many times I was taken, but I remember the mountains of craggy peaks. They were so big. Stony monuments, giants of rock that seemed to have been Gods themselves once, they were so daunting.'

Krea and Kacha both looked at Ulric, Mohsin must have come through Dorhall Pass, the very place that Merek was now heading.

Ulric returned their puzzled gazes, he grabbed another chunk of meat from his pack, it was imperative that Mohsin save his strength.

As the prisoner reached for the food Ulric said, 'I have a few questions I need to ask, I can't wait they need to be answered and Ada I have one for you too.' Mohsin merely nodded. Ada remained quiet. 'Firstly, how big is the Majestic Forest? I mean how far did you travel? I am trying to get a timeline in my head, it just doesn't make sense. Also, the mountains of rock you mentioned, I—' Ulric shook his head things were starting to become confusing. 'I think you must be referring to Dorhall Pass. I know of no other mountainous ranges. And if it is, it must be where the queen lives!' Ulric took a breath to steady himself. 'You also mentioned Pancome, he was a Councillor of our village. I am unsure whether he left with my grandfather or stayed behind.'

Instead of Mohsin answering, Ada began to whisper, '*This is the reason why we need his story so much. No one has survived the Asur like Mohsin, that is, as far as we know. And I know you are going to ask me why I didn't just read his thoughts…*' Ada paused before she continued, '*I could not penetrate Mohsin's thoughts, so traumatised was he from his experiences, he had buried them too deep they were impossible to infiltrate.*'

Ulric nodded. It made sense.

Mohsin finished eating the meat. His stomach was starting to hurt; it had been a long time since he had eaten this much. He sat back down on the dirt floor and the comfort of sleep began to tug at him. Reluctantly, he pushed it away. He wiped his face on the rag of material that had once been his shirt. Taking a breath, he continued to tell them the last chapter of his life, though he knew the effort would cost him. 'I lost track of time not long after they had captured us. It all became a blur and I struggled to cling to life. It was only the hope of seeing my daughter again that kept me going. As for your question of Dorhall Pass, I had heard of it way before the Asur came and I do believe that it could well be it. The queen was not always at the arena, sometimes it was just the generals. The Majestic Forest stops where the land greets the sea, where I am from you can see it from our lookout as far as the eye can see. Pancome stayed for a bit and then he escaped.'

'He escaped!' Krea interrupted. It shocked her that someone could escape; the only other person she knew was Huxley, and he had not been the same since.

Mohsin nodded. 'Yes, as I said, he was a very clever man. I do not know completely how he did it but, the Gods must favour him. He did not have to endure the torture for as long as I did.'

'So, we know the queen may live in Dorhall Pass, the Majestic Forest is larger and extends further east than we ever thought, and our Councillor managed to get captured and then escape from the Asur,' Krea said. 'But what we don't know is the timeline of events. We left the Seer almost a week ago, which means if Pancome stayed behind he was taken not long after they raided and set fire to the village. This means they must have several groups. This is the part I am trying to work out. If they took you to Dorhall Pass, that would mean they are ahead of Papa, and it would make sense if they lived there that is where they would take you. But how come they brought you back here? And how did they get to the Pass so quickly?'

The three young adults looked at Mohsin, waiting for an explanation.

'Ah yes, well, this tunnel here leads all the way to the mountains. It's their quick route to get there. Thinking back now, I recall we had to wait for some time for them to dig something. As I said, I could not see my surroundings, but it is coming back to me. I am pretty sure they had to widen a tunnel because I remember the smell of the earth.'

'That would make sense,' Krea said. 'It would explain how they got ahead of Merek and left some other group to hunt them down. They could not fight a big battle with wagons full of people they must have been on a raid, conquer and capture mission.'

'Yes, I think you are right.' A brief smile crossed Ulric's face. It was coming together.

Mohsin closed his eyes. Exhaustion was descending like the darkness of night. He felt Ada inside his mind, and he slowly opened his eyes. He had to finish his story; the long sleep of death would have to wait just a little longer. He cleared his throat once more.

'Pancome kept telling me they were not as clever as they thought they were. He said they did not guard all the passages that lay underground, and all you had to do was work out how to get away without them noticing. As I said, the Gods favoured him. One evening, the queen wanted to have a celebration. She wanted as many as the captives up in the arena to fight with the hounds. They are vile creatures and certainly not man's best friend,' Mohsin said disdainfully. 'They dragged us all up, but just before we left the tunnel there was some sort of commotion. I don't know what it was, but it got them going, that's for sure. They left one guard for all of us. Some saw the opportunity that it presented. A few started to try and escape, the guard of course could not go after all of them, they scattered in all directions.' Mohsin let out a low chuckle. 'That was a sight to behold, I can tell you. Anyway, Pancome managed to slip away, probably back where we were held captive and then down one of the tunnels that led from the prison cells. All the others were killed or caught. Pancome was clever. He must have doubled back; they would never have thought to look for an escapee who went back towards the cells. I only hope he managed to find a place to hide once he got out of the tunnels.'

Silence descended on the group when Mohsin finished talking.

Mohsin finally let his eyes close. This time, Ada did not try and stop him from falling into the deep dreamless sleep that would last an eternity. Instead, she said a prayer to the Gods and asked that they let him have peace and reunite with his family. She had the answers they had been seeking and it was time they all left. The Asur would come looking and they were all in a vulnerable position.

She tapped Ulric's mind, bringing his attention to her presence. *'It is time to leave now, dear brother. Mohsin is finding his way back to his family. You still have so much to do, and I must take my leave as well. Hurry and go back to the horses, find camp and rest for tonight. You will need to leave early tomorrow, there is much to be done.'*

'We need to leave,' Ulric said.

Krea and Kacha did not need any more encouragement. The trio took one last look at the man asleep in his prison. He seemed finally at peace, and they vowed to take revenge on the beings that had taken so much from him.

Flamma had kept a quiet solitude since witnessing his father's murder and had started to grow a quiet respect for the older brother he had met not that long ago. The jealousy he had felt when he had first met him still simmered but had cooled somewhat. Now as he watched the man who was destined to fill his father's shoes, he became intrigued and the desire to know him more began to take seed and grow.

As Merek woke the camp and set about organising the group to make their way to Dorhall Pass, his brother walked his horse over to his white stallion.

'So, brother, where is it that you lead us now?' Flamma asked.

Merek was surprised to see Flamma beside him. Since their father's death he had made himself scarce, preferring his own company and staying at the back of the camp. Merek had left him alone, feeling that he needed some time by himself. He was a lot younger, and he had just witnessed the murder of his father.

He regarded the young man before him and could see that the last few weeks had aged him. Flamma would make a good leader himself one day, once he had sorted out his anger issues, but that was a long way off. Merek knew his temper still simmered and would be tested in the days to come.

It was time for his younger brother to be given more responsibilities. If he was ever to become a leader himself, he needed someone to show and challenge him on things that would matter.

'Dorhall Pass,' he replied.

Flamma frowned, slowly shaking his head. 'Why?' he asked.

A brief smile played across Merek's face. 'The Gods have told us this is where we need to go.'

Flamma cocked his head. 'And what after that, brother, do we just wait in the Pass? Or do we cross it to some magical land that will hide us from the Asur?'

Merek detected a hint of sarcasm but chose to ignore it. 'No, we wait and hide until we are told what to do next after that you will help me put together a reconnaissance team.'

Flamma shook his head his temper suddenly flared. 'So let me get this right, we ride into the Pass and just sit there and wait? That's it?! That is your plan?!' Flamma's voice had risen, and he struggled to hold himself back from shouting. This was the most ridiculous plan he had heard.

'In time, little brother, you will learn that not every plan has to be complex. Sometimes the simplest things are the best.' Merek clicked his tongue, urging his stallion to jump to attention and leave a puzzled Flamma behind.

Merek led the procession of humans from the Majestic Forest out into a landscape that unfolded before the tall, craggy monuments of rock that had formed thousands of years before. The view was breathtaking as summer was at its full height, enjoying its turn on the stage of seasons. Merek paused, halting the parade of people who followed him and turned his face up to the brilliant sky of blue above.

He wanted his people to have a positive state of mind before they ventured into the Pass, he knew it had been hard for them, but they had yet to meet the full wraith of the Asur. So far it had not been a too difficult journey, but this could change at any time and having a positive, determined attitude would help them overcome the difficulties they had yet to face.

He sent a message to the people behind him, telling them to enjoy the view and take the time to thank the Gods and be grateful for all they had and the present moment that was offered to them. A murmur rippled through the crowd as they looked toward their leader. It was not long before a silent hush descended upon them as they realised what he was telling them, and they gave thanks to the Gods, not only that they had been spared and were still alive, but they had a leader like Merek. The other groups who had split and made their differing ways to Dorhall Pass had not been found and no evidence had been discovered that they still existed. The probability that they had perished was now becoming a reality.

The land gave way to a steep gradient as it creeped its way up the rocky trail that led to the mountains in front and above them. Elenore halted her horse next to her husband's as she breathed in the fresh air.

'Norrie,' Merek said quietly, but she did not hear him, lost in a prayer to the skies above. He called her name again. After a moment she turned to meet his gaze. 'We need to make it to the end of the first trail by end of day, the Gods have a place for us to hide.'

Elenore slowly nodded, and a faint look of surprise crossed her face.

She was silent for a moment as she digested what he had just told her. She had felt better than she had in weeks, and she put it down to the herbs that the medicine woman had given her. Elenore sent a silent prayer to the Gods, giving thanks to Serenity and her healing powers and that they had helped Merek find a place to take refuge from the devil that trailed them. She placed her hand on her abdomen and closed her eyes. Maybe their baby had a chance, a place in the world that would follow the demise of the Asur.

CHAPTER SIX

Anja

My mind became a battlefield, where thoughts
clashed with unseen horrors.

Anja

The Seer opened his eyes and looked at the two women sitting in front of him. Large dark circles sat under their eyes and their eyelids drooped with exhaustion. Ada stifled a yawn. Ogda knew he would not have been able to learn as much as they had without them, especially Ada. He knew she was more than talented; she was gifted. They still did not know the full extent of her powers, but in time, this would be revealed. He called for Ludwig and asked him to organise a banquet and bring out the best wine they stored for special occasions.

Ada frowned. 'You are going to drink wine?'

The Seer let out a soft chuckle. 'We need to celebrate! We have had our first win.'

Ada was silent for a minute.

'He is right, Ada, we need to have time to celebrate. It has been a big revelation what we have learned from Mohsin.' Anja added. Ada nodded but something, however, seem to tug at her, a wisp of doubt.

'Tell me what concerns you, Ada.' Ogda had lost his former jovialness and had taken on a serious tone. The more he got to know Ada, the more she intrigued him. The Gods had blessed her with gifts for a reason and he was beginning to understand why. They had known the future of mankind and the prophecy that was to unfold, they also knew they needed to have some type of defence to fight back, and Ada was key.

She shook her head, trying to concentrate but the thought danced away keeping out of her mind's reach. 'I am sorry, I can't quite get it, but there is something. It will come to me, I'm just not sure when.' She sighed.

Ogda got to his feet and stretched, releasing the stiffness from his body. He often wondered how long the Gods were to keep him on Earth before letting him join the people he loved in a more peaceful place.

He suggested they get some rest before meeting him back at the kitchen table. It would take Ludwig a while to prepare and cook the food they would be eating.

'I will help Ludwig, it is an awful lot of work he has to do,' Ada announced. Anja nodded. Her granddaughter had so much more energy than she and the Seer had, and she too needed time alone to reflect on the mind travel. She had not quite come to terms with her husband's death, instead she had pushed it away, concentrating on the work that they had to do.

Anja made her way to the room she shared with Ada, it was small, clean, and tidy. A twin-size bed where they slept sat under a window that looked out to the enormous vegetable garden. Fruit trees graced the space behind it while the Majestic Forest created a scenic backdrop. She walked to the window and looked out breathing in the fresh air. Memories that she had kept at bay came to surface and she let out the torrent of grief.

Eijanbrook had been her best friend, her lover, and her soul mate. The Gods had promised her to him from the moment she had been born and she never regretted their choice. Eijanbrook came from a land far to the South, where the winters were bitterly cold, and summers were a season that was barely there. He had left his home, scarcely a teen after having a dream about her. Eijanbrook had travelled months to find her and when he had arrived, her mother had demanded what had taken him so long.

She smiled through her tears when she remembered this. Her mother was gifted too, however she ruled with an iron fist and was the Chief of their village. Eijanbrook had been surprised to learn a female reigned a village. There were not many women leaders, and she was the first he had met.

Anja's mother instructed the couple to marry when her daughter came of age. Anja was only ten when Eijanbrook first met her. Anja had felt no fear of Eijanbrook he was only a few years older than herself, and she had had the same dream as her future husband. Her mother had told her she shared the gift of seeing too, a blessing from the Gods themselves.

The couple stayed with Anja's village for a month before her mother told them to leave. She wanted them to get to know and trust each other, the best way was to fend for themselves. Making the trek back to Eijanbrook's village would present challenges and they would also be racing against the seasons; winter was not too far away.

The young couple had set off the following dawn and Anja never saw her mother in real life again. From that moment on she only saw her in her visions or dreams until she died almost thirty years later.

Anja let out a sigh and turned away from the window. She made her way to the jug and basin that stood on the bedside table and washed her tear-stained face. Changing out of her tunic, she put on a fresh one. Exhaustion settled over her and she laid down on the bed; images of the Asur pushed away her memories of Eijanbrook and she rolled onto one side. Squeezing her eyes, she willed them to leave and tried to think of more pleasant times. Sleep descended and Anja drifted into a deep slumber.

The tunnel wound deep into the earth, creating an underground labyrinth of pathways. Anja floated through the passageways, seemingly pulled onwards. Time sped up as she raced towards the end goal. She could see some of the Asur working inside the tunnels but did not have the time to stop and find out what they were doing. Finally, the tunnel she had been travelling through opened to a space that was filled with light. Anja looked up and the sky greeted her. She felt herself hover briefly, before coming to the surface leaving the tunnel behind.

A vast forest of trees extended itself as far as she could see. They were not like the Majestic Forest, instead they were dark and leafless, creating a grey, drab landscape. She made her way through, intent on finding out where she was going. A gloomy, eerie feeling wrapped itself around her, and she was unable to shake it. She pushed forward until a voice whispered for her to be careful and tread lightly. The sounds of construction could be heard along with the guttural noises made from the Asur. Anja stepped from the forest into a large clearing and looked in fascination at the scene before her.

There were hundreds of Asur gathered around a large stone throne that a female Asur sat upon. Her hair long dark hair flowed behind her like a mass of tentacles that wormed and reached into the dirt at her feet. It was as if they were seeking something, the finger-like tendrils of hair probing the earth.

Anja held her breath. This must be the queen of the Asur that Mohsin had described, she knew they could not see her, but she did not want to let down her guard. The sounds of hammers echoed in the distance behind where the woman sat, but Anja couldn't see what was being built. There were no humans present, and she thanked the Gods she could focus on what was happening around her without the distraction of the misery and torture of her fellow humankind. She listened intently to what the queen of the Asur was saying and the soft voice came back to her.

The queen spoke in an unfamiliar language, but the voice offered a translation: 'She is probing the ground to look to where they can create new tunnels, close to villages, allowing ease of access and surprise. It will be a big help to take over the human world. She says they are always distracted by their own egos and petty problems.'

Anja frowned. 'Our petty problems?'

'Yes,' the voice answered. Anja waited for an explanation, but the voice stayed quiet. When she thought that the voice would not speak again, her thoughts were interrupted. 'The sounds of the work being done is made by the sweat of humans. The tunnels where you saw the Asur is where they are creating new tunnels. You will have to work fast, Anja – time is of the essence. There will be a great battle and your son will need all the help he can get. Now, leave this place before they catch a whiff of your presence.'

A shiver ran down Anja's spine as she took one last look at the evil queen. An impressive line of warriors formed a precise formation on both her sides. As Anja turned, something caught her eye. She paused, taking a step closer.

'I told you to leave. Now, go!' This time, the voice shouted inside her mind. Fear gripped Anja as she recoiled from the words. The queen had paused in her dialect, and she turned to look in Anja's direction. A icy chill descended upon Anja.

The queen sniffed the air, not unlike a dog that had caught a whiff of an intriguing scent. Her eyes gleamed and her mouth opened into a wide grin revealing a set of sharp fangs. She ran her tongue along them and chuckled to herself as she summoned one of the Asur.

Anja's breath came in rasps; she could not move, she was rooted to where she stood. Her mind screamed at her to move but she was paralysed.

The queen continued to stare. The Asur she had called forward sniffed the air before it too smiled exposing a set of needle-like teeth. Suddenly Anja felt her mind being invaded. She struggled to hide her thoughts, but it was like they were held hostage, a dark net cast over them holding them captive. Panic threatened to overcome her, she had never encountered anything quite like this.

She pleaded with the Gods to help her as she forced her memories and her new revelations to a deep corner of her mind.

The queen probed her brain, searching for what she had hidden. She knew they could not see her physical form but that mattered little as they sought her thoughts, her memories, all that made her who she was. Anja realised if the Asur were able to grow stronger with mind travel they would not need to fight physical battles; they could conquer by sabotaging the mind. Anja felt sick as this revelation swept over her.

Suddenly she felt the presence from before entering her mind, 'Enough!' the voice screamed at her but still she could not move. If she did, her body would awaken and alert the Asur to all what she knew. Anja felt a hand on her shoulder as it gently pulled her away. Slowly it dragged her from where the Asur called home. She struggled to keep her mind blank as questions sought her nipping and begging to be asked. The queen loosened her grip on her the further she was pulled away. Finally, she felt like she could release her thoughts, the strange invasive presence had gone.

Anja woke in a sweat, the last of wisps of the dream still clinging to her. She sat up sweat caused her tunic to stick to her and she wiped her forehead. Anja ran her tongue over her lips, a metallic taste was in her mouth and her throat felt dry. She got up from the bed and poured herself a large cup of water and drank. She frowned as she let her mind dive back to where she had just come from. This was not just a dream, but a journey of mind travel. She learned where the Asur called home, had informally met their queen, and learned some of their strategies of how they planned to take down humanity. She had to tell Ogda and Ada.

Anja poured herself another cup of water, 'Eijanbrook, this is a win we will bring them down; our son will bring them to their knees your death will not be in vain!' Tears began to run down Anja's face, she wiped them, but they refused to stop. Anja made her way back to the bed. She thought she had cried out her grief earlier, but she was wrong. Anja would never stop missing, loving, and wanting the man that had been such a big part of her life. 'I miss you so much,' she sniffed.

Silence followed. Anja had to be strong, her family and so much more depended on it. Forcing herself up, she washed her face and grabbed the comb that sat beside the jug and basin. Pulling the comb through her long hair, she tied the strands into a plait. It was time to tell Ogda and Ada, it was time to start the great battle.

The sun graced the sky with the promise of another perfect summer day as Ulric woke from a dreamless sleep. He stretched before fully opening his eyes. Sleep still clung to his mind as it took its time to fully awaken. He shook his head, trying to shake out the memories that began to stir. Frowning, Ulric sat up and tossed back the furs, he paused a moment, as the memory of the last few days came to life. Groaning, he fell back against his bed roll, staring up at the roof of his tent.

Ulric was not born a fighter like his father and grandfather; he was far too sensitive to have become a warrior. He constantly struggled using the sword, preferring the bow and arrow, and to hang out with his dog in the woods that surrounded his home village. Ulric would have easily become a victim to the town's bullies were it not for two things: first, he could outrun any boy his age, and secondly, his father was a force to be reckoned with.

Sighing, Ulric knew it would do no good complaining about it, he had to accept reality and get on with the hand he had been dealt. He stood up from his bed roll. The morning felt cool against his bare skin, he hadn't bothered putting on a fresh tunic before falling into an exhausted sleep the night before.

Krea burst through the tent's small opening. Startled at seeing Ulric naked, she quickly turned her back giving him some privacy as he hastily put on his tunic.

'You could have knocked!' Ulric chastised her, his face blushing.

Stifling the peals of laughter that threatened to overcome her she managed to answer him. 'There is no door to knock upon, dear nephew, or I may have used the opportunity to do so.' As she said the last few words, she could not control herself any longer and broke into a fit of laughter. Ulric soon joined her. It felt good to laugh, it had been such a long time.

Kacha, curious at what they were laughing about, arrived to find both doubled over in fits of hilarity. After learning what had caused their merriment, he shook his head with a grin stretched upon his face.

Anja entered the kitchen where a large oak table stood in the middle of the room. Various dishes of food graced its top and tantalising aromas filled the air. She wrinkled her nose and felt her mouth water. She had not realised how hungry she was. Ada and Ludwig were engrossed in conversation, their heads bowed close together.

Anja quietly seated herself and reached for the bottle of wine that sat in front of her. It had been a while since she had had the red drink and she suddenly felt she needed it. Her newly acknowledged grief was still raw and clawed mercilessly at her. She took a large swallow, savouring the fruity taste as it slid down her throat. Anja took another and then another, enjoying the relaxing feeling it was giving her. As she put down her glass, she saw Ada staring intently, a slight frown on her brow. Anja wiped her mouth with the back of her hand, feeling guilty for relishing the drink. She cleared her throat as if to speak, but remained silent. This was not the right time to tell her about the dream she'd had. She needed more time to reflect and consider all that it represented.

Ada smiled, breaking the tension between the two women. 'You have to eat, grandmother, we have a lot of mind travel ahead of us and as you know it can be exhausting.' Ada continued to look at Anja, her gaze unwavering.

Anja nodded, relieved that Ada had not chastised her. Her hunger suddenly came back with a passion. She reached for the large pot in front of her and began to fill her bowl with the beef and vegetable stew.

Anja was onto her second bowl of stew when the Seer joined them. He appeared rested and a determined look was set on his weathered face. He nodded to the three seated at the table and a smile crossed his face when he saw the banquet in front of him.

'You have outdone yourself again, Ludwig,' he said. Ludwig smiled a lopsided smile, happy to know he had pleased his master. 'I believe you had an assistant?'

Ludwig nodded. 'Yes, she was a great help.'

'I have no doubt that she was. We need to eat and gather our strength, I believe the Gods have a plan for us.' The three turned to look at the ancient man, wondering what he would tell them. Seeing their reaction he chuckled. 'I will reveal all, after our meal. Now, please eat!' They needed no further encouragement and ate until their appetites were satiated.

After the meal they gathered around Ogda, perched on overstuffed cushions sipping a relaxing tea that Ada had made. Ludwig had joined them, his curiosity spiked from what the Seer had told them previously.

'Anja, before I tell of the plan the Gods have made, I think you have something to say to us.' The Seer raised an eyebrow.

Anja nodded. She had wanted to tell them at the kitchen table but had pushed it away preferring to enjoy and savour her meal without thinking about the Asur and how they had nearly caught her. Shaking off her embarrassment of being nearly caught she cleared her throat.

'I had a dream. It was enlightening, to say the least, but something was guiding me. I am not sure whether it was the Gods or...' her voice trailed off as she became unsure of what to say.

'We will focus on that later, it is not as important as the dream itself. Please, tell us,' the Seer encouraged her gently. Anja nodded and recounted the dream she had had earlier. 'What you have told us is extremely important not to mention helpful. We must use it to our advantage. The queen is key, however she will be difficult to get to. For the moment, we must gather as much of an army as possible. The Gods want Krea, Kacha, and Ulric to go to as many villages as they can to tell them about the great battle that lies ahead. We will mind travel to each of the village chiefs and open their minds with dreams of influence. This will help the job of convincing them. We must make haste. As Anja has informed us, the queen is using her powers to feel, or should I say probe, for the villages she plans to raid. Once the Gods have told me it is time for us to leave, we will prepare for our journey too.'

Both women threw each other a questioning look. Neither had been able to foresee this change of events. Ogda looked bemused at their reaction, but did not offer further explanation.

'Master, will I be coming with you?' Ludwig asked.

Ogda shook his head. 'You will be safer here, Ludwig. I trust you will take care of the place as you always do.' A brief smile crossed the Seer's face before it became solemn again. Ludwig did not argue with his master and remained silent accepting that it was his duty to stay behind. They spent the evening discussing each of the villages that they would be telling the trio to visit and ask for their help. It was something that Merek had started before being called back by his father when the Asur came hunting for them. Time was running out, and a sense of urgency filled the room. The Seer however felt a small sense of relief; finally the Gods had given him a plan. It all hinged now on how much humans could come together as one to fight a common enemy, hopefully for the last time.

CHAPTER SEVEN

The Stranger

Beneath the cracked earth, a pulse quickens. The roots awaken, secrets waiting to bloom. A time to return.

Ulric

U lric heard the shrill cry of a hawk as it circled above looking for prey on the land that lay beneath it. He felt his sister's presence as he turned his face to look at the large brown bird flying above. *'Brother, you need to make your way to the villages that lie to the east.'*

Ulric frowned at his sister's words. 'I don't understand. We have to catch up to Papa and find out more about the Asur,' he told her.

'You will in time but first you must gather the army that our father could not, we need as many to fight the evil that lingers in the world. The Gods have a plan.' Ada stopped herself she already had revealed too much she did not mean to tell Ulric of the plan that she had yet to find more about. It was dangerous to reveal vital clues. The Asur were becoming stronger in their mind travel, and it was hard to know who was listening in, regardless of whether she could feel their presence or not.

Ulric took a deep breath and let it out slowly. He wondered when all this would come to an end. Memories of when he would go to the river that ran behind his home village with his dog were becoming distant. He longed for the world to be normal again and for this ancient enemy to be put to rest for an eternity. *'Patience, dear brother, I hear your thoughts. We need to be strong and united, we will conquer and overcome.'*

Ulric smiled, his sister had always been the stronger one, confident in who she was and had the courage to set sail in her own ship trusting the Gods to guide her in the right direction. She will make an excellent Seer when we finally return to a life resembling some type of normalcy, he thought.

'*Don't I make a good Seer now, Ulric?*'

The question caught Ulric off guard, and he chuckled. 'I stand corrected. Yes, dear sister, you make a fine Seer.' He heard her soft laughter inside his mind and was grateful for her presence and strength.

The trio turned east, heading for the villages that lay closest to the sea. This new turn of events both intrigued and surprised them. The sky was a breathtaking blue and a slight breeze blew, cooling the perspiration on Krea's forehead, she looked at the sun that had started to climb and cast its warmth on Earth below her. She had been a little taken back when Ulric had told them they had to head east and gather an army, but she understood the reasoning. Her nephew had come a long way since she first met him, and she knew that this was difficult for him. A kind, sensitive soul that relished his own presence, who had now been thrust into making critical decisions. Ulric, the boy with the tear drop shaped birthmark, now led them on a quest that would help save humanity. Krea understood why she and Kacha had been told to go with Ulric, they were skilled warriors but struggled with making the human connection that came so easily to the son of Merek. Krea understood all that now, and she was both grateful and honoured to have been given the task to protect and serve her young nephew.

Ulric pushed his horse as much as he dared. They had no extra mounts, and he was careful not to make his bay gelding lame. The day was ending when they came across their first village. Charcoaled remains were all that was left, a town blackened by the fire that had devoured it. It was not an unfamiliar sight; they had come across villages before this one that had been torched and destroyed by the Asur. They combed the surrounding area for any survivors, but the landscape revealed none.

As the summer evening descended, Ulric decided to set up camp for the night. Krea made a small fire and roasted the hare she had caught not that long ago. Ulric seemed deep in thought, reflecting on the day that had just passed.

Kacha came to sit beside his newly found best friend. 'Ulric, I have an idea.'

Ulric turned to look at the young warrior beside him.

Kacha held Ulric's gaze as he told him of his idea. 'Mohsin told us of Pancome, your grandfather's Councillor, who had been caught and then managed to escape. I think he may have come this way or be heading back to the east coast; it makes sense.'

Ulric tilted his head, frowning at his friend. 'Go on,' he encouraged.

Kacha nodded. 'It's simple: the Asur have come from there, taken everything they could, burning everything in their path leaving a trail of destruction. There would be no need to go back. They are heading north, towards the Pass. Time is of the essence, so they would not come back this way, it makes no sense.'

Ulric considered this. It made sense that Pancome would not have to encounter the enemy if he went back to where they had just come from. The only thing would be if the Asur had left a recon party to find and slay any survivors. He voiced this concern to Kacha. Kacha shook his head, 'No, they would be long gone. They would not have the time to hang around looking for survivors.'

Ulric nodded. 'I think you are right. But the next few days will tell us.'

The trail began to gradually become steeper as it slowly wound its way up the mountain path. A forest graced the sides of the path, giving off a sweet scent of pine. Elenore let the aroma fill her senses. It had been so long since she had enjoyed the sense of smell without it making her feel sick. Merek had decided to go with the scouts to look for a place where they could rest for the night, leaving Tallot to lead the group. Elenore decided to join him, urging her mare into a trot to catch up to him.

He gave her a broad smile when she came alongside him. 'Ah, Norrie, my favourite person how are you? Feeling better?'

Elenore blushed. She had forgotten that she had not told anyone about her pregnancy. 'Yes, I am feeling better.' She returned his smile. Tallot held Elenore's gaze a moment longer than usual before he looked away. Elenore frowned. *Is there something wrong?* The thought tugged at her.

Tallot was usually straight forward and to the point, he now appeared a little perplexed. She pushed her concerns to the back of her mind. She had always felt comfortable in front of Tallot, but now she felt awkward, almost shy, as she contemplated about what to say to him. Her mind was at a loss, and an uncomfortable silence followed between them. She gazed out over the tree line and took a deep breath of fresh air. If they hadn't been running for their lives, she would have felt giddy with exhilaration.

Suddenly, Merek could be seen up ahead as he made his way back with the scouts. He approached Tallot and Elenore, a smile upon his face as he told them he had found a place to camp for the night.

The place Merek had chosen was a little way from the trail, the tree line had hidden a small patch of grass that offered a place to set up a fire and shelter for his people. The sun was still high enough in the sky for the men to organise a hunt. Merek felt more in control than he had since being told to go find an army to fight the Asur, and it felt good. He summoned any man wanting to go hunting and was surprised at how many were willing. Most wanted to have a break from the monotony of being on the run and having to set up a camp every night not knowing what lay ahead. A hunt offered adventure and time away from the reality they now lived.

'I can't take you all but' – he held up his hand as a murmur of disappointment rippled through the throng of men standing in front of him – 'I promise there will be another hunt. Those of you who don't go now will come on the next one. I will take twenty men, those that stay behind, give your names to Tallot and I promise you will be on the next hunting party.' A quiet cheer rang out when they heard their leader's offer. Most followed Merek not because he was son of Eijanbrook, but because he offered them hope. He was a fair and kind leader who loved his people and truly cared. Many offered a prayer of thanks for being in his group.

Elenore watched the group leave the camp. An excitement had rippled through it as the men quickly bid their families goodbye and mounted their horses. An energy of positivity descended upon them, and soon laughter and conversation filled the air. Elenore smiled the feeling of euphoria that she had felt before had not left and she quickly gave thanks to the Gods that they were still alive and that she now carried the future in her womb.

After the hunting group departed, she decided to look for Sabin. He would not have gone, preferring to stay behind and gossip. A smile crossed her face when she thought of this. She made her way through the camp, looking for the curly haired man and was pleased when she spotted him not far away. As she neared, she noticed that he was talking with Huxley, Edyth's older son. Elenore hesitated for a moment before Sabin caught sight of her and called out. There was no turning back now and she forced a smile as she waved to the two men.

'Ah, here is a sight for one's sore eyes then,' Sabin chuckled. Elenore giggled as she embraced him. Huxley watched the pair, not showing any sign of emotion. His beard was long and matched the length of his hair that hung down to the middle of his back. A vacant stare filled his eyes and when Sabin introduced him, he barely nodded an acknowledgment. Elenore felt unsure of what to say, but as always Sabin broke the awkwardness. 'Ah, Huxley, Elenore is a good one. Ye can trust her,' Sabin said.

'Should we have some tea? I can make us some, if you like?' Elenore asked the young man that stood in front of her. Huxley shook his head but did not speak.

'Aye must confess, dear Norrie, that we are having some lovely beverage. That is, well, let's say is the *relaxing type* that is not tea.' Sabin chuckled as he said this. Huxley offered no response and continued to stare blankly at Elenore.

'Shall we come back to my camp than?' Elenore asked. Sabin nodded, smiling.

The three of them made their way to Elenore's camp. Elenore was unsure of how she would start a conversation with Huxley; he seemed to be quiet and indifferent. She was relieved that Sabin was coming, he would help break the silence. When they reached her small camp, she set about making some tea. She knew Sabin had said they were drinking the red drink, but the tea would help reduce the headache they would have the next day. Sabin sat on the log in front of the fire, throwing on more kindling that Elenore had collected earlier.

'Ye need a bit more of a flame to heat that kettle for ye tea.'

Elenore smiled, 'The tea is for you and Huxley as well, you are both going to need it. You will thank me for it later.'

Sabin chuckled, shaking his head. 'Aye, I guess. I should be thanking the Gods that I have ye, lucky man that I am.'

The three sat in silence, the men drinking their wine and Elenore sipped her tea. She thought about what to say to break the silence.

'So, Huxley, how old are you?' It was the only thing she could think of, and she chastised herself for not being more creative. At first, she did not think he was going to answer her but to her surprise he did.

'I'm twenty-two, but I don't like to have birthdays anymore.' He offered no more information instead going back to his silent self.

'Why is that?' Elenore asked. The young man did not meet her gaze, instead, he kept his head lowered staring at the ground. Huxley sighed and took a long drink from his cup. Sabin had kept quiet. He knew Elenore wanted to get to know Huxley more. Another long pause.

'I have seen the devil. She took my Papa and my brother, it's not right that I have birthdays.' Huxley's words sent shivers down Elenore's spine.

'She?' Sabin asked. Elenore frowned. Most people presumed that the devil was male.

Huxley took another long drink and wiped his mouth with the back of his hand and took a deep breath.

'Yep, she is the devil.' Huxley offered no more information, instead, he stood up from his seat, looking awkwardly at Sabin and Elenore murmured a quick goodbye.

Elenore thought about what Huxley had said. It didn't quite make sense that the leader of the Asur could be female and why was that? She looked at Sabin.

'Aye, Norrie, not sure what to say to ye. Huxley has never said anythin' to me like that. Sort of makes ye think.' He rubbed the stubble on his chin.

'We need to find out more. I mean, he knows things and it would help us find out more about the Asur, don't you think?' Elenore asked her friend.

Sabin nodded. 'Ye have a point, Norrie, but how do we do that? I mean he doesn't talk very much, as you found out.'

Elenore smiled. 'I have a plan, and you have to help me with it.'

Sabin chuckled, 'aye, I would love to.'

As the three travelled east, the scenery began to change. The forest that had graced the landscape with its beauty had been reduced to a blackened mass of ash, now slowly it seemed, some of the trees had been spared. Ulric, who all his life had felt a connection to nature, noticed the change. It was subtle at first, but the green curtain had slowly been descending.

He reined in his gelding, taking a good look at his surroundings. 'Can you notice something?' he asked his aunt and friend. They both stopped beside him, finally taking a good look at the landscape that unfolded in front of them.

'What is it?' Krea asked.

'You can't see it?' Ulric asked again. Krea shifted in her saddle looking front to back, not quite understanding what Ulric was asking. She shook her head. 'Do you see anything Kacha?'

Kacha frowned. 'There seems to be more trees,' he mused.

'Yes!' Ulric almost shouted. 'Don't you see? Nature is on our side, they are fighting back too. The forest is not only coming back to life, but some parts are still alive and thriving. I think it is their way of saying they will not be defeated. They are true warriors, fighting for survival.' Ulric appeared euphoric.

Krea took a closer a look at the forest that flanked their sides. The blackened stumps had given way to a slight green and as the land travelled further the green grew to trees that were standing tall and very much alive! Krea could see why Ulric had become excited; it meant there was hope and that they had a formidable ally.

The group of three seemed to be invigorated by Ulric's discovery and moved at a quicker pace. They passed villages that had been burned to the ground, nothing but a pile of ashes and crumbled stones. It brought a sadness, but Ulric would not give in to the despondency, instead he pushed forward. The forest had offered a taste for a future, and Ulric hungered for more.

Four days passed, bringing the same scene of burned-out villages and no survivors. As they neared yet another village, Ulric asked for them to stop. Something didn't seem right. He couldn't shake the feeling it seemed to smother him in uncertainness.

'What is it?' Kacha asked.

Ulric frowned, peering down at the village. They had been travelling at a fast pace and the weather had been kind so as not to slow them down. This meant they had covered more ground than they thought they would have been able to. It had been a few weeks since the fire and the forest had slowly thickened, parts were still blackened, and yet others appeared untouched. This had puzzled Ulric. Even though he knew that the forest had bounced back he had been amazed at the speed that it had. The village had the familiar blackened ash and pile of stones as all the others they had passed, but this one had some houses still standing. The forest that grew alongside it appeared to be healthier full of green foliage, birds and insects buzzed alike.

Ulric looked back at the village. *'You are full of inner wisdom, Ulric. That is your weapon, your armour, do not ever doubt yourself. This is why the Gods have chosen you,'* the voice gently whispered. Ulric was unsure of who had spoken the words to him. They did not come from his sister, nor his grandmother. He was uncertain if they had come from the Seer, but regardless of the speaker, the words helped.

All his life he had doubted himself and had sought refuge in the forest that lay behind his home village. He preferred the company of his canine companion rather than boys his age and loved to run the trails that zig zagged behind his home. Nature had always beckoned him and he understood that it was all a precursor to the present moment. Ulric who never wanted to be a warrior or a leader now was leading the way and discovering that nature was the best and biggest friend he had at that moment. The difference he had always felt, was becoming the difference in the world. Humanity needed more than hope, it needed a saviour to help them overcome a threat that was intent on destroying their existence. As this came to fruition in Ulric's mind, he began to feel strong, confident, and empowered. Once again, he scanned the village below before giving the signal to move forward.

The three looked for survivors, skimming the surroundings as they entered the village.

'I will look in the remaining houses,' Krea said. Ulric looked over at his aunt, he could feel her energy, she was intent in finding a human alive. But the hunt for survivors brought nothing, it appeared again that no one had been able to survive the destructive grasp of the Asur. 'Nothing!' Krea almost shouted.

Ulric could see she was upset. 'Keep looking.' He did not quite understand why he encouraged her to do this, but something tugged at him. He looked for Kacha and could see the strong, young warrior looking towards the forest. Ulric frowned wondering what had caught his eye. He made his way to his friend's side.

'Kacha, what is it?' Ulric asked.

'I am not sure. I mean, I thought I saw something but … I am not sure.'

Ulric pushed past Kacha, urging his gelding into the dense undergrowth. As he pushed through, he thought he heard someone running. He pulled on the reins, bringing his gelding to a stop as he listened. The forest remained quiet except for the occasional hum of an insect and the call of a bird. He urged his horse forward. Something was pulling, luring him deeper into the forest.

Ulric scanned the tree line, a mixture of blackened trunks and thick trees. He urged his horse forward focusing on his surroundings.

'There! Was it a shadow?' He could not be certain. He stopped. Leaning forward in his saddle, he peered ahead. There. He saw it again, a slight movement. So slight, that if he had not been fixated on the spot ahead, he would have missed it. Ulric waited. Kacha joined him, quietly pulling up alongside. Kacha had been trained to hunt, to stalk and kill his prey and understood the importance of being patient. Ulric placed a finger to his lips and pointed in the direction where he had seen the movement. Kacha nodded and waited beside his friend.

A breeze blew, rustling the leaves of the trees revealing a figure standing to the right of a large oak tree. The person was only half hidden and appeared to be debating whether to remain hidden or show themselves.

Ulric called out to him, 'We do not mean you any harm. Please, we only want to help. I am Ulric, son of Merek, and we are searching for survivors.'

The man stepped fully out from behind the tree, putting his hand up he gave a wave and waited. Kacha went to greet the man with Ulric following behind. As they drew closer, they noticed how unkempt he was. His tunic was in tatters, he had a receding hairline that did not match his long filthy beard. He looked malnourished and strips of rags were wrapped around his feet in a futile attempt to protect them.

'You are a sight for sore eyes, praise the Gods, I have not seen anyone. I thought I was the only one left and the Asur had won their battle of ridding the planet of humans.' Tears ran down the man's face as he kneeled, looking up at Ulric and Kacha.

The men waited patiently until the newcomer stood again. 'I am so relieved it is you, Ulric. I knew Merek would not let them win. Eijanbrook must be so proud. Thank the Gods.' Ulric frowned as the man said this and a thought crossed his mind: could this be Pancome?

CHAPTER EIGHT

The Attraction

As the shadows darken, the memory

of your light guides me.

Anja

Ogda led their minds east of the land, searching for any villages that may have remained. The Gods had wanted him to come this way, certain they would find survivors. As they travelled, he discovered that the once thriving land had been reduced to rubble and blackened earth. Soon Ogda began to wonder why the Gods had showed him this way, they had not indicated for him to go south or west, it had to be east. This was a mystery however the Seer knew better than to question the judgement of the Gods. They combed the area, sweeping the countryside, desperately searching. The forest began to change the closer they got to the east coast; it had begun to become alive again. This both intrigued them and gave hope; the Asur had not destroyed everything.

The vast blue of the sea could be seen, an expanse of water that had offered food, trade, and a means of transport for the villages that had once lived beside it. A mountainous range lay to the north, while the forest lay to the south, creating a natural backdrop of beauty. The minds of the three travellers were awed by the sight. The forest seemed untouched. To their surprise and relief, a small village lay nestled under the fringes of the trees. The village also seemed untouched. A community of people could be seen quietly going about their daily routine, seemingly mindful of how much noise they made. Ogda, Ada, and Anja would have to infiltrate their minds through dreams to enable them to want to fight the Asur when Ulric would come to ask them. This would not be an easy task, the people of the village appeared content with their lives.

Merek rolled to one side; it didn't matter how much he slept under his tent, he never could get used to the cold, hard ground. His body felt stiff and sore, and he longed for a mattress made from feathers or straw. The sun pierced through the lining, reminding him that the day had already started. He closed his eyes, rolling back onto his back. The night's dreams came back to him in wisps and as the fog of the last one lifted, he abruptly sat up.

Frowning Merek tried to recall what it had been about. Slowly, it returned. He knew there was more, but he could not quite grasp it. The trail that had been shown to him in a previous dream had once again been in the latest one he had just had. The trail head wound higher up the Pass turning into a narrow path. As the path turned in his dream, a small, spindly tree grew to the left of it. Merek had been pulled in this direction. He had left the path, pushing past the tree where a rocky trail descended and curved disappearing into a small forest of trees. Merek shook his head, as if to clear and dislodge more of the dream, but he could not remember any more details. He knew it meant something, but he was not quite sure what.

Elenore began to stir beside him. She had been fast asleep when he had come to bed exhausted from the hunt. The party had managed to find some hares and a couple of small deer, just enough for everyone to have some fresh meat. Now the sun had risen, Merek knew it was time for the camp to be on the move again. He hoped that the dream he had had would become clearer as the day wore on.

Merek let his people breakfast on the meat they had got from their kill the previous evening before urging them to gather up their belongings and be on the move again. Most were in good spirits; the morning meal had filled their bellies and given them energy to set off again.

Elenore finished her food and started to pack up their things. She felt tired, and once again wondered when she would finally have a home again. She knew the Asur would have burned down the one that Eijanbrook had made for her and Merek, a gift he had given upon their return. She sighed and willed herself to think of other things, but it was difficult. As she rolled up her fur and strapped it to her saddle, she noticed Tallot coming towards her. He smiled, and her cheeks flushed and her stomach fluttered. Elenore chastised herself; she was a married woman and in love with Merek.

What is wrong with me! It must be the hormones, this is not right. I pray that this feeling leaves. It is not right, she thought.

'Ah here she is, the lovely Elenore. How are you today, Norrie?' Tallot said.

Elenore blushed again and grew even more frustrated with herself. She had hoped that he had not noticed and kept working on fixing the straps on the bundle of fur.

'I am well, Tallot, thank you. How are you?' She glanced briefly at him.

'I am very well. Having fresh meat for breakfast does wonders for a man's appetite. You look like you are almost done?' He paused, waiting for Elenore to answer him.

She knew it would be rude if she did not look at him and give him her full attention. Forcing the butterflies that continued to flutter inside her stomach aside, she looked at the handsome warrior standing in front of her. The summer sun had turned his skin into a deep dark tone and his muscles bulged under the tunic that seemed to have gotten too small for him. Tallot was tall, standing higher than the other warriors, his good looks had attracted many women. A fresh tattoo of a large oak tree could be seen peeking out from the sleeve of his tunic. Elenore saw how the roots of the tree snaked down his arm, replicating a similar looking tree that they had found in the forest of witches.

He smiled as he saw she was looking at his arm. 'Do you like it? I only just had it done.'

Elenore frowned, the image of the tree seem to trigger a memory, something that Huxley had said but she couldn't quite grasp what it was. She had a feeling that it would reveal a clue about the Asur. She made a mental note to reflect upon it later.

'It's nice.' She offered him a smile. He held her gaze for a moment before looking away. Elenore felt herself blush yet again and turned to mount her mare.

Tallot nodded, offering her another charismatic smile. 'I better get saddled too, best we make haste.'

The sun hovered at its midway point, beating down on the group of humans below. The summer was hot and humid, whisking away energy levels and providing a steamy bath. Some of Merek's people began to complain; there had been no rest since they had left earlier that morning and with the sun's melting rays, they were beginning to grow tired and restless. The mountains offered little shade as the trees had thinned, replaced with clumps of gigantic grasses growing alongside the trail. Merek searched desperately for the small thin tree that had been in his dream indicating where he should turn.

He heard someone shout at him to stop, but he ignored it. Sometimes a leader had to be hard they were on a path for survival, and it was up to him to make sure they stayed on it. He heard the soft sound of hooves come up behind him and he reined in his stallion.

'Merek have you not been listening? Your people are begging you to stop!' Elenore's face was livid. Wisps of hair had come loose from the ponytail high on her head. Merek repressed the urge to shout back that it was for their own good and he was trying everything to lead them to safety. He clenched his jaw. Sweat ran down his face; the heat only made his temper shorter.

'Well, they have to wait a bit longer. I am trying my best to find somewhere where they can be safe.'

Elenore brought her horse alongside Merek's stallion. Leaning forward and barely able to control her own anger she retorted, 'You are their leader, you are responsible for their welfare. If you don't tell them to stop and rest, I will.'

Merek felt his temper flare and it took all his strength not to slap her. He clenched and unclenched his hand trying to calm the fury that threatened to overcome him. He could not lose face in front of his people, and he also knew that Elenore had the will of a small country when she set her mind to things. He turned his stallion back around and went to tell Tallot it was time for them to take a small break from the heat. They would have a short reprieve before they set off again.

Merek refused to speak to Elenore for the rest of the afternoon, and the summer heat did little to cool his anger. Elenore longed for them to stop and rest the whole afternoon, but her husband had other ideas. Merek had acted in a similar fashion when they had been on the run from the Asur in the past. They had planned to get through Dorhall Pass and seek refuge at Merek's parents' village. It seemed such a long time ago and it had been winter then. She shuddered at the memory.

Merek had been as determined as he seemed now, leading them to safer lands. She knew he was under enormous pressure and took his place as leader seriously. He prided himself that not one person had been lost since he had taken the place of his father as leader. She debated whether to approach him and talk to him, but he seemed busy with Amzi and Tallot, both men he regarded with deep respect.

Instead, she trailed behind, trying to listen to their conversation and learn where Merek thought he would be taking them. He had not spoken to her much the last few days, preferring to talk to his warriors. She did not begrudge him for this, but she felt a little hurt he had not discussed any of his ideas with her. He had always valued her opinion, or so she had thought.

She looked at the three men in front of her; one, she felt an immense attraction to, which had caught her off guard, and the other, her husband, whom she loved dearly. The third man was a blonde-haired man who rode a magnificent buckskin stallion. She had learned he was leader of the Borak village, the breeders of the finest horses in the land. She knew little else about him, except that his sister had taken a liking to Tallot. This thought stirred up feelings of jealousy. His sister was very attractive and had done little to try to get to know Elenore, preferring to keep her distance. Elenore thought this odd. It was customary to get to know another leader's wife, especially if you were related to a leader yourself.

As they made the steep ascent, the afternoon sun seemed to grow hotter, stifling them. No breeze blew, and the air seemed heavy. Elenore thought about asking Merek to stop again but thought better of it. She continued and rubbed her mare's neck, she knew her horse was also feeling the heat and the arduous climb.

Suddenly Elenore saw Merek hold up his arm, halting the procession. On his left, a tall spindly tree grew. It seemed barely alive, and it was odd that it was the only one that had a sparse number of leaves. Elenore squinted against the sun's glare, trying to see why he had stopped abruptly. Merek directed Tallot back to where she now stood and ordered Amzi and some of the lead scouts to follow him. Merek and Amzi disappeared behind the tree and Elenore caught her breath as she watched her husband.

Moments later, Tallot pulled alongside her. 'Elenore come help me tell the people they are to rest until their leader returns.'

Elenore frowned. 'Where has he gone? He doesn't seem to tell me anything anymore. I think he has been searching for the path all day.' She looked directly at Tallot when she said this. He smiled at her and again she felt her cheeks grow warm. She quickly looked away, hating herself for the way her feelings had grown.

'I think he said something about a dream and Ada your daughter helping guide him. Don't let him know that I told you this.'

Elenore looked up at Tallot. He was still smiling, but the mention of Ada sent her in a spin. How she missed her only daughter, it seemed an eternity since she had seen her, held her, spoke to her. She also felt annoyance brush over her at the thought that Merek had not even told her that Ada had been communicating with him. She swallowed the lump that came to her throat, refusing to give in to her emotions.

'Okay,' was all that she could manage to say. Turning her horse around, Elenore followed Tallot back to the crowd of people who had taken it upon themselves to rest under whatever bits of shade they could find.

Pancome tore off chunks of bread and dipped it into the meat casserole. Food had never tasted so good. He looked over at the three people who had saved him and the two canines that also watched him with curiosity. Ulric shared similar looks to his father and had inherited the same integrity and compassion. He reminded Pancome of when Merek had been a teenager and how much he wanted to know about the Asur. His gaze drifted to Krea, she looked more like her father. Her physique was tall, lean, and muscular. The wolf at her feet watched his every move and seemed to read his mind, letting out a soft growl.

'So tell me, Ulric, where are Eijanbrook and Merek?'

Ulric had been waiting for Pancome to ask this question, but he knew it was best to wait until the man had decent food in his stomach. They had done a quick hunt in the small forest, bringing down a pig that would provide meat for the next few days. Pancome had nearly finished his second bowl of food. In his hunger, he reminded Ulric of Mohsin. Ulric knew his grandfather had been murdered by the Asur but could not think how this knowledge had come about. Sadness crept over him, he had had little time to get to know his grandfather and now there would be no chance for that to happen. Ulric sighed and pushing this thought and his feelings aside, he cleared his throat and answered the man sitting in front of him.

'Eijanbrook has passed, giving his life for the people he loved, slain by the Asur. Merek, my father, and son of Eijanbrook, is now leading a group of people to safety. We have been sent to look for survivors.'

Pancome nodded. 'I guess I am your first?'

Ulric smiled. 'Yes, you are the first.'

Pancome pulled at his beard. 'You do know that Eijanbrook asked me to lead a group to safety.' Ulric frowned. This was news to him, he had always thought that Pancome had stayed behind. He looked at the man, a former Councillor, and shook his head. Pancome placed his bowl on the ground, sighing. 'If I could turn back time, I would. I refused him because I thought I could not lead anymore. I was an adviser to Eijanbrook, but not in the formal sense anymore. I had long since retired, only offering private advice. My concerns had always been for the people and Ranco. He was not a good Councillor. The man had a heart made of stone, he only ever thought about himself. I despised him! I pray that the people he led were able to get to safety.'

Pancome looked at Ulric, seeking an answer. Ulric shook his head. He had heard nothing of the groups that had split, except for the one Merek now led.

Pancome glanced at the ground, dark circles sat under his eyes and his shoulders drooped. It had been such a long time since he had had a good night's rest. Running from the Asur had meant always being on the lookout and keeping one step ahead. He'd kept on the move only having snatches of sleep before moving on. Now, he looked like he could sleep forever. Pancome shifted his position and took a deep breath. The people who had rescued him were waiting for an explanation, a story of how he had escaped the Asur.

He owed it to them to tell them. He sighed, once again, sleep would have to wait. 'I will tell you my story, but please let me sleep when I am done. It has been a long time since this body has slept.' Ulric nodded his approval and waited for the old man to tell them what had happened the day the Asur had come to take his village.

The village chief was a small man by size, but his kindness radiated a warmth that his people fell in love with. His insight had helped them escape the wraith of the Asur when they came searching for humans. He had dreamed of the place they now lived and had thought that it was a sign from the Gods. The forest had helped hide them sheltering them from the fire that was lit to destroy and erase them. For reasons unknown, the fire had not reached the very edges that grew closest to the sea, thus offering the refuge they sought. Dumas thanked the Gods every night for the place they now called home.

It came as a surprise when he began to have dreams of a group of people who would come to ask for them to leave and help fight the Asur. These dreams left him in turmoil. He longed to repay the Gods, but he was unsure of what he could offer. His people were sheep farmers, not warriors, and did not know the first thing about fighting.

The next time he dreamed the same dream, the answer was made clear: strength was in numbers, everyone had something to give, and it all contributed to saving humanity. Dumas had no choice, he had been asked to leave and go north to join Merek, son of Eijanbrook. The hard part would be to convince his people, as they had grown used to the life by the sea.

Surprisingly, the Gods had made his job easier by letting his people dream a similar dream of the ancient man and his two female assistants, letting them know of the plight that all humans now faced. Dumas and his people soon were packed and following the path to Dorhall Pass, leaving their small village behind.

The Seer, Ada and Anja returned home to rest and gather strength for their next mind travel. Although their bodies remained behind, the mental exertion of using their minds to seek had to find left them exhausted. Ludwig was waiting for them, providing a meal fit for a king. Ogda ate little before retiring to his room. Anja noticed that the mind travel was taking a toll on him; he seemed to have aged and was tiring more quickly. She knew that his time was running out and that the Gods would invite him to join them in the not-too-distant future.

Anja sighed. These moments reminded her of how much she missed her husband. As she reflected on the events that had taken shape over the last few days, a thought began to take form: Ogda would not live forever. If humanity was to triumph and move forward, who would take the role of ancient Seer of the world? She did not know of any other Seers that held the same wisdom and respect as the one she now followed. She frowned. There were none and probably less now that the Asur had decimated so many. A new thought came to her, and she tried to push it away, however it would not budge instead pleading to be acknowledged. What if Anja, wife of Eijanbrook, mother to Merek, was to be a Seer!

She silently groaned and closed her eyes. The more she thought about it, the more sense it made. If Eijanbrook had been alive, she would have welcomed the revelation, basked in it perhaps, but this was like a life sentence. All she wanted to do was to reunite with Eijanbrook, her only true love.

Tears rolled down her cheeks and sadness enveloped her in its cloak of misery. She could not stop the stream of tears and welcomed them as she pushed her face into her pillow. As she cried, she slowly became aware of a presence quietly trying to make itself known. Pushing herself up on one elbow, she frowned. Who was trying to intrude into her thoughts?

'Hush now, Anja. I understand how you are feeling, I was like you so many years ago. Please remember, Eijanbrook will always be by your side in spirit. He is a favoured child by the Gods, and you will need his guidance and advice in times ahead. You will live a long life, be prepared for that, but you will have great influence on the people you will meet. Anja, be honoured that the new world will welcome a new Seer, the first female in the line of ancient Seers, it will be a change that the world will embrace.' Anja sat up as she heard these words. Instead of feeling overjoyed, the feeling of despondency descended upon her once more and she fell back on the bed, falling into a restless sleep.

CHAPTER NINE

An Announcement

Within the labyrinth of memory, a key lies slumbering.
Once awakened it will be the doom of the Devourer, a
forgotten clue buried deep within the past.

Elenore

Pancome leaned back on the base of the tree and stretched his legs out before him. The sun felt strong, and he was glad to be resting under the shade of a tree in the oppressive heat. He had started to feel a growing despondency with each passing day that he had not found a single soul since escaping from the Asur.

Ulric had explained how they had found Mohsin and learned about Pancome's escape, perhaps the only human who had ever accomplished such a feat. He took a sip of water, and wiped his brow. Sweat trickled down his face, however he was more comfortable than he had been in a long time. Taking a slow breath, Pancome began his story:

'The Asur are merciless, evil, and cruel. Everything they encounter is left broken or dying, or both, even the forest was not spared. I knew I had to escape and thank the Gods they heard my prayers.'

'What do you mean?' Krea asked.

Pancome took a long drink from the water skin. It was warm from the summer heat, but it quenched his thirst and gave him the energy to continue. He handed the skin back to Kacha, giving him a quick smile of gratitude. 'I will tell you in time, Krea, I think I have got a little ahead of myself. I will start from when your father left the village and I along with some other fools stubbornly stayed behind. We thought we would be safe inside our homes just by closing and locking the doors. I went to my neighbours' home and helped him push all their furniture up against the front door to stop any of them from trying to break through. We could hear the forest burning, shrieking in pain as the flames tore and engulfed the trees and everything in them. It was soul wrenching. I have never heard anything like it before.'

Pancome repressed a shiver as he remembered the forest's screams. 'We waited all day and into the next evening. I think it was a false sense of security. We thought perhaps they had gone around us, that maybe they just wanted to burn our precious forest, but we were gravely mistaken. They came during the night, setting fire to the buildings and waited for their occupants to come out. The traditional way an army flushes out their enemy. As we fled from our burning homes, we were met with clubs, whips, and swords. They slaughtered men, women, and children, seemingly undiscriminating in who they killed. I ran and hid, and watched the people I had known and loved all my life be killed in front of me.'

Pancome grew quiet as the memories flooded in. Kanji, Ulric's small brown dog trotted over to Pancome he let out a soft whine before settling himself at the older man's feet, placing his head in his lap. Pancome smiled and his eyes twinkled as he stroked the dog's soft fur. Kanji thumped his tail in response. After a moment he cleared his throat and continued his story.

'I hid while they continued their killing spree. They laughed, relishing every person they brought down. The sun was coming up by the time they had finished setting everything on fire and torturing and butchering their prey. Quite a few of us had stayed behind. It really did surprise me, as everybody in our village loved Eijanbrook. I think there were a few still left alive, these ones they threw in a large cage. I hadn't seen it until the very end. It was like they had kept it hidden. I know I told Mohsin that I was able to hide from them for several days, but in truth it was only several hours. They knew I had been hiding the whole time because as soon as that cage was wheeled out, they came for me. I ran, but I was no match for their dogs. I was pushed into the cage with the other poor souls. They had a cage for each village they passed, keeping a handful of humans as souvenirs and to use as toys for their sick amusement.' Pancome hawked and spat, anger descending upon him.

'We continued for days until we came to a large river. I have no idea where we were, but I do know that here was where they spared the forest from being set on fire. I have a theory for this that I'll share later. Most of the captives had died, either from the wounds inflicted by the Asur or malnourishment. Once a day, they fed us some sort of tasteless soup, served with a cup of water. I knew I had to escape.

'By this time I had become friends with Mohsin. We had stopped to camp by the river, and they had put all the survivors in one of the cages, like I said there were not many of us left. Mohsin told me he was from the village near the sea to the east. After a few days of being camped near the river, they started to sort through the survivors. The ones that were selected, including myself and Mohsin, were led to this tunnel. It turned out it was a labyrinth of an underground travel system. It was huge! The Asur travel through the network and send scouts to look for villages, sometimes surprise raiding them. Other times, they would send a party of warriors to burn, pillage, and take captives. They also are learning to know how to mind travel. I know Anja was quite good at this.'

Ulric frowned. Hadn't he heard about this before? He tried to dislodge the thought as he suddenly remembered his sister Ada who had been mind travelling when she had felt the breath of the Asur. They had tried to intrude in on her thoughts and this had concerned and frightened her. 'How do you know this, Pancome?'.

The older man smiled. It was almost a smirk and he looked up at the vast blue sky above. 'Because it is what the queen wants, and what Dardanos wants, she gets.' Pancome shifted his gaze back to the audience of three sitting in front of him. A vacant look seemed to have transcended upon him. 'Water, please,' he said.

Krea gave him the skin and he drank. Ulric had heard Mohsin mention the queen of the Asur but who was Dardanos? He wanted to know more about this mind travelling. It was unsettling to know that the Asur were increasing their capacity to do this. It meant humanity didn't have an upper hand, and this was a grave concern.

'Who is Dardanos?' Pancome looked hard at Ulric before throwing his head back and giving out a loud sardonic laugh. Ulric was taken aback by how Pancome was acting at that moment but waited patiently for the man to finish laughing and respond.

'Ulric, Dardanos is the queen. Her name means "to devour" and that is exactly what she intends to do: devour us, all of us.'

Ogda, Anja and Ada let their minds glide through the moonlit night seeking for signs of human life, desperately seeking something that would show that the Gods had been right and that there was hope. They scanned the horizon. At least this part of the land the forest had been spared. A green canopy of trees created a breathtaking scenery of how exquisite mother nature was. The backdrop of the sea was a blur of blue and green, the waves crashing gently on the sandy beach. The Seer led his two followers over the thick canopy of green. Doubt had pulled at him when he had first started the night's mind journey but now a sense of excitement began to tingle within him.

He searched and searched, eager to find out what was causing this flood of anticipation. He was certain they would stumble across something soon. He felt Ada's presence within his own mind, she too indicated that she sensed a great discovery. They travelled along the coast, heading south. As they did, Ogda started to remember the stories of a large village possibly the largest in all the lands that was rumoured to be in the far south. It was the stirring of this memory that Ogda realised why the Gods had showed him this way. Their numbers would be great and if they had survived the Asur, there would be a good chance they could come and join their fight. With renewed determination the Seer began to concentrate peering deeper into the huge, magnificent forest that spread out before them.

A billow of smoke made its way through the canopy of green, acting almost like a second chimney. The grey cloud of smoke indicated that people were living below the tree line, hidden within the camouflage of flora. Ogda, Ada and Anja made their way towards the wisps of smoke like moths drawn to a light. Anticipation building, they were soon among a gigantic village that sprawled among the trees, cleverly entwined between the huge trunks of oak and pine. It was a typical scene of an everyday evening routine of cooking and preparing the night's meal. Quiet conversation, children playing, the sounds of fires being stoked all sounded like music to the Seer's ears and he could not help but smile. They had found the reputed village of being the largest in all the lands.

As Ogda searched for the village chief, he felt a presence tap into his own mind. At first, he thought it was either Ada or Anja, but quickly realised it was someone else. His first reaction was to withdraw and flee back to the safety of his own home, but he knew the presence would follow him there. Instead, he demanded to know who it was.

'Ah! Do you think that you are the only one who can travel just using one's mind leaving the physical body behind? That surprises me since you are the oldest and wisest Seer that has ever been.'

'Who are you?' Ogda demanded. Laughter echoed around him, and Ogda felt his temper spike. He forced himself to stay quiet until the laughter had subsided.

'I am not unlike you. I am the Seer of the village of Shakurta ruled by the leader Takeo. I too can mind travel. It seems the Gods have forgotten to inform you of this.' Again, the laughter rang in Ogda's ears. *'Unlike* you, I knew you were coming, and I know what you are going to ask. *You seek our help in ridding the world of the Asur I can't blame you but...'* – the Seer of the village of Shakurta paused – *'We are the people that are directly descended from the ancient ones the last line that exists on earth today. We have been battling the Asur long before you were born, Ogda. They hunted and killed us taking what they wanted. Slaves for work and torture, entertainment anything they could dream up they took to fill that quota. We despised the Asur like you do now. We fled to Dorhall Pass hoping that we would be safe, but they found us. They drove us out like a wolf flushing its prey and we fled to the south near the coast and made ourselves fishermen. They tracked us again, determined to wipe us from existence and that is when we made our deal.'*

Ogda began to feel the beginnings of dread. When the other did not answer, he asked the obvious, 'What was the deal?'

Again, the eerie laughter rang in his ears. *'Oh, you would love to know, I am truly amazed that the Gods have not told you. They have forsaken us for the deal we have made.'*

Ogda scowled as a hundred thoughts raced through his mind. *'You have learned that the Asur possess mind travel. You are curious on how they came to know about this or even how they can do this at all. Believe me, they simply are not equipped to manage the travel that involves leaving the physical body behind. Let me enlighten you, Ogda. I have given them the means of mind travel so my people can live! We are the longest and largest community of people that has and will ever live! Thanks to me, they have a place in this world that cannot be taken from them. We must do what is best for our people Ogda don't you agree?'* Ogda felt his stomach drop and he sucked in his breath. *'Your days on this earth are limited you have taken too long all ready. I am surprised that the Gods have led you here. They have known for some time that we now dance with the devil.'* Ogda shuddered. His energy was ebbing, and he felt exposed. So many questions pulled at him, demanding an answer. He longed to be back in his home so he could meditate, prayer and seek answers.

He could feel the other Seer listening to the turmoil of thoughts going through his mind. 'We will leave now. I wish you well, but be warned there is a reason why I was led here, and you should never trust the devil.' Before waiting for an answer, he retreated, calling Ada and Anja and vanishing to the safety of their home. There, hopefully their thoughts would not be compromised.

Pancome was starting to tire; he was not a young man anymore. He thought about the last few weeks and all that he had endured. It had to mean something. As far as he knew, apart from Huxley, he was the only one who had escaped. Surely that meant the Gods had a plan for him. He looked at the three young people in front of him, waiting for him to finish his story. He gave them a brief smile, took another long gulp from the water skin and began again.

'The queen has hair like tentacles. They grow from her, probing the earth like giant octopus arms searching for movement. That is how she can find where humans live; she is determined to kill every one of us. She loves to watch us become entertainment for her warriors. I knew if I did not escape, I would also become her plaything. I waited and watched, and then I made my move. I must let you know that I had help in getting away from the devil.'

Krea tilted her head. 'What do you mean you had help?'

An ironic smile spread across Pancome's face. 'Our beloved forest saved me.' The three people in front of them leaned in, curiosity had not only lured them, it had them hook, line and sinker. Pancome chuckled. 'The Majestic Forest saved me. The Asur are not the only ones probing, looking for life, but so too is the forest. I have no idea why they chose me but' – Pancome let out his breath slowly – 'they did, thank the Gods.'

Ulric gave the older man a long look. It was hard to believe someone could escape the Asur. If he hadn't found Mohsin and was now talking to Pancome he would never have believed it. 'So how does a forest help you escape?'

Pancome stared over Ulric's shoulder, into the forest. He held a deeper respect and love for the very thing that was responsible for him being alive.

'They probe too, just like the queen Dardanos. I learned about their probing one night when I was put in a cell under the ground. I was separated from the others after I was caught trying to steal some food. I felt something scratching trying to push through the earth behind the steel bars. I waited. I thought it strange that the queen would want to seek me out in a cell! Eventually, a tree root pushed its way through like a giant earth worm tunnelling its way through deep soil.

It seemed to sense I was there, as if it was me it was seeking. Then it withdrew back into the soil. I thought this strange and waited to see if it came back. It did. The following night I had a dream. I am sure that the Gods were working with the forest, advising me to have patience and courage.'

Pancome leaned back against the tree, he had shifted forward when he was telling his story and now his back hurt. 'The dream told of how there would be an altercation with some of the prisoners when it was time for us to become the devil's entertainment; this would be my opportunity to escape. The dream prepared me and when an argument broke out between my fellow hostages, I knew it was time to leave. Instead of trying to escape the ground, I ran back towards the cells. The guards were too busy trying to control all those trying to flee, and they never would have thought that a human would have the courage to go back down the burrow of hell. But as I told Mohsin, they are not as clever as you think. I must say I felt bad leaving others behind especially Mohsin he had been such a strength and a friend.'

Pancome felt emotion well within him and he longed to burst in a river of tears to relieve the guilt of leaving his friend behind. But this was not the time to let his emotions rule, he had to tell his story. It would be wise to let them know that the Gods did care and listen, and they had not been forsaken.

He cleared his throat. 'I took my chance running for my life in the labyrinth of tunnels. The forest helped me as I could hear the backfill of dirt behind me. This way the Asur would be unable to find me. Some of the tunnels the forest showed me had been dug by the Asur, others were created by the gigantic trees above me. I know now why the Asur had been so determined to rid the world of it. The forest is our ally, our friend, it provides so much. We need to do everything we can to protect it.' Pancome grew quiet, reflecting on what he had gone through and how grateful that he was the one they had been chosen to be led from the bowels of hell.

The afternoon was heavy with heat intensifying Merek's people's irritability. The summer had only just begun, and it had the promise of being a hot one. They longed to swim in a cool river and sleep with no fear under the stars at night. Tempers had begun to fray and if it had not been for the deep respect they had had for Eijanbrook and now his son, they would have given up long ago.

Elenore could feel their frustrations as she waited with them, sweat trickling down her spine. She turned to look back at where Merek had disappeared, but he still had not returned. She sighed and wiped her brow before casting her gaze back to the crowd of restless people. She watched Sabin and Edyth talking to the people around them. It seemed they were trying to take their minds off the heat and the current situation they now found themselves in. Elenore dismounted, handing the reins to Tallot before going to talk to her people.

She made her way to a family that had young children, offering to take the baby from her exhausted mother. They seemed grateful for Elenore's presence and complained about the oppressive heat. She stayed with them for a while before moving to a couple who had elderly parents. Elenore could see that the journey and the heat were taking a great toll on the older couple. She knew they'd had no choice but to flee their village but the niggling question that always nipped at her began to tug at her again: *when is all this going to end?* She forced herself to smile, engaging in light conversation. Their son was a blacksmith and Elenore had seen him a few times working on the horse's hooves. He was a short stocky man with a large bushy beard. Flecks of grey ran through his dark brown hair. He touched Elenore's elbow and steered her away from his parents, wanting to talk to her in private.

'I appreciate your kindness, missus, but there is something I need to ask you.' His face was creased in worry and Elenore nodded for him to continue. 'I know you don't know when and where we will be able to stop and make a home again, that I guess is up to the Gods.' He cleared his throat and glanced back towards his wife and parents that were sitting under the shade of a tree. He looked back at Elenore, 'My wife is with child and I—' he took a breath and shook his head.

Elenore reached out and touched his arm. 'I understand I am with child too.' He looked at her in surprise, nodding but remained quiet. Elenore continued, 'I was like you, worried about bringing a child into a world full of chaos, but I think the Gods have a plan for us and our children. They will be the future, the very thing that the Asur do not want. And it is that reason that there is hope. I know we will overcome and beat our enemy, but we need to remain strong and united. It is the only way that will ensure humanity will triumph.'

The man returned her smile and nodded. Tears glistened in his eyes and he wiped his face, embarrassed that she had seen him become emotional. 'It is okay, we are all in this together. Please, go be with your family.'

Once again he nodded, giving her a quick embrace before turning and hastily making his way back to his family. Elenore watched him go and turned looking to find more people that she could help. She was in deep conversation with a young teenage girl when she heard a familiar voice.

'Aye, I knew we would find ye.'

Elenore looked up and saw her curly haired friend. Sabin chuckled softly. She threw her arms around him, giving him a warm embrace. He chuckled again. 'Aye, I think I might have to leave ye alone a bit more if I am going to get this sort of hello.' Tears welled in her eyes, she was so happy to see Sabin.

Sabin gently extract himself from her embrace. His smile was still spread across his face as he turned to the small woman standing next to him. Placing an arm around her, he looked back at Elenore. 'Aye, Norrie, I think you and Edyth may have already met.'

There was an awkward silence as Elenore struggled to put her emotions under control. She felt her cheeks go red as the small woman in front of her gave her a cold, hard look. Elenore felt like fleeing she was so embarrassed at her open display of affection to her friend. 'Aye Edyth, this is Merek's wife, Norrie, I know ye has met but well there is no harm in meeting for a second time.' Sabin chuckled, winking at Elenore.

'I remember when we met before. You came to my home with Eijanbrook. I have seen you around the camp, but I guess...' she shrugged her shoulders before finishing. 'It is only Sabin that has brought me to come and meet you again.'

Elenore's mouth went dry as she racked her brain for an answer, but her mind was blank.

Sabin came to her rescue, as he always did. 'Aye, my love, Norrie is a wonderful lady. If it wasn't for her and Merek, I might not have had the good fortune to have met ye.'

Edyth looked up at Sabin and the hard look on her face softened. 'I don't owe anyone anything. As far as I am concerned, it was the Gods that brought us together. Now come let us go, the children will be wondering where we have gone.' She turned, not giving Elenore another look pulling Sabin along with her. He mouthed an apology before letting himself be pulled in the direction of the back of the camp.

Elenore watched them go. She knew that it would take a long time before Edyth would accept her, if ever. She still held a grudge against Merek and Elenore could feel her jealousy regarding her and Sabin's friendship. Sighing she went to search for Tallot.

The stone cottage provided a sanctuary as they became one with their body again. Ludwig served warm tea and biscuits as the three reflected on the news they had received from the Seer of the Shakurta village. A heavy silence descended upon them as they ate and drank in silence. Exhaustion always followed mind travel, but this time fear and trepidation replaced it.

Darkness filled the sky outside, a black backdrop against the small window. Ogda looked out towards the darkness, he was puzzled as to why he had been shown a path that seemed to be fraught with danger. He thought maybe the Gods had wanted to reveal the other enemy, one that was perhaps just as or more threatening than the ones they already knew. The two women in front of him waited for him to give an explanation to what had happened and what it all meant, but he had none.

Sighing, he took a sip from his cup, savouring the rich sweet taste. He loved a strong, sweet tea and Ludwig never failed to disappoint. 'The village of Shakurta have forsaken us, preferring to make a deal with the devil instead of helping their fellow mankind. I have no idea why the Gods led us there, except to show us another enemy. We are, as you may have already guessed, in grave danger.' He took another sip and went quiet, trying to calm his mind and think of a solution to the current dilemma they found themselves in.

'I may have an answer that could help.' Both Ogda and Anja turned to Ada, giving her a puzzled look. She smiled. 'I need to go and meditate and spend time reflecting before I can disclose what I think it might be.' Both the Seer and Anja nodded, hoping that this special girl could somehow turn the tide of evil.

Elenore scanned the ridge where she had left him. The sun stung her eyes as it's fiery gaze beat furiously back at her. She felt her eyes sting and begin to water as she tore her gaze away. 'Where could Tallot be? And where is my husband?'

It seemed like an eternity since he had followed the path beside the small tree. His people waited under the hot summer sun and had long grown restless. The heat had sapped their energy and they had given up protesting, instead they rested under patches of shade and waited for their master to return. Elenore walked up the stony path her patience had started to wear thin. Not only did she need to talk to Tallot, but he had her mare. She had told him to wait, and he had promised her he would and now there was no sign of him or her horse.

As she neared the top, she could make out riders coming down the sloping path. She shaded her eyes, blocking the sun's rays so as she could getter a better glimpse of who it could be. She drew in a sharp intake of breath when she recognised her husband's long beard tied in a thong riding his large white stallion. Moments later, Tallot was standing next to her an infectious smile stretched from ear to ear. She was caught between being furious at him for not being there and the desire to smile back at him.

'Hey Norrie, I took your mare to graze down the path a little, hope you didn't mind.'

Elenore shook her head. It would be pointless to remain angry at him and Merek would be joining them in a few minutes. She stared at Tallot for a moment and desire swept over her. She felt her cheeks flush. *What am I thinking? My husband is risking his life for them all and I am having feelings towards another man!*

Elenore gave a murmur of thanks before she mounted her mare and made her way to meet her husband.

Merek was happy to see his wife. Tallot come to greet him too. 'Good news,' Merek said, 'I have found a place for us to camp and rest for a while. We should be safe there for the time being. We must tell the others and get everyone moving, it is going to be a little tricky getting there.'

Elenore turned her mare and followed her husband back to where she had just come from. It would be a welcome relief for all to finally take the time to rest and replenish.

Merek had not been exaggerating when he had told them the path was tricky if not dangerous. He organised small groups as the path was narrow and wrapped itself around the stony wall of the mountains. Getting the wagons down into the hidden valley below would prove the most difficult and he left them until last. There were more than thirty wagons, since most families used them to transport what goods they could carry and their children.

'What are you going to do about this, dear brother?' Flamma had watched the procession over the course of the afternoon and even though his jealousy towards his brother had calmed somewhat it still lingered like a soft flame, barely burning.

Merek frowned. 'I am not sure, little brother, do you have any suggestions?' He looked at the young man next to him, he reminded him of himself however he was sure he had not been so arrogant. Flamma shook his head, he had nothing to offer. Merek stroked his beard. There had to be a way, they could not leave the wagons behind. Not only did he not want to leave the goods they carried they also would alert any passer-by of their location and that was too big a risk to take with the Asur.

'Bring me the wagon builders, we will dismantle them and put them back together once we get to the valley, I can't see any other way.' Tallot went to find the wagon builders, leaving Merek and Flamma to unload the goods.

The men worked into the night; it was painstakingly slow. Everything had to be disassembled, and packed onto the horses which were led single file onto the treacherous path. Merek had ordered Tallot to set up the camp and for Amzi and his men to help with the wagons. He felt exhausted, but knew that he would be able to rest after the night's work without having to worry about the Asur finding them.

His dreams had been the Gods way of showing him the path to safety, even if for just a short while. It would allow them to develop a strategy for their next move and he needed time to think. The valley was protected on all sides by the craggy peaks of Dorhall Pass and the narrow path they were on was difficult to find unless you knew where to look. A small river flowed from a spring located at the base of the rocky mountain providing fresh water and fish to eat. The land was fertile and perfect for grazing their horses who also needed a rest. Merek had been delighted by the find, it was more than he had hoped for.

The moon rose high in the sky, lighting the ground below as the men worked furiously to pull the wagons apart. A renewed hope had started to ripple among the people that followed Merek once they entered the valley. At last they had found a sanctuary, if only temporarily.

Elenore instantly fell in love with the valley and immediately set up her tent under some large oak trees that flanked the eastern side. She loved the old trees; they reminded her of the Majestic Forest and all that it had provided them. She had learned never to take them for granted, life could be so fragile and precarious. When she had finished making a makeshift home, she went to help other families settle in. It had been a long time since she had felt this happy.

It took only a few days for the valley to be filled with laughter and the daily routine of life. There was much to be done. Men hunted and fished, women repaired clothes, cooked, and spent time with their children. The energy of the camp was light and full of joy, they all were thankful to the Gods that they had been given the valley to seek shelter and refuge from the evil that hunted them.

Elenore was full of renewed hope and enthusiasm and as Merek busied himself with organising hunting parties and repair work that needed to be done, her thoughts returned to Huxley. She knew he held the key that would enable them to bring down the Asur or at the very least assist with their demise. The only trouble was he was a recluse, and his mother did not like her very much.

Since entering the valley, Huxley had moved to the back of the camp and rarely ventured out. She knew Sabin would help, however, he was always by Edyth's side. Grabbing the water pail, she decided to go to the river to fill it, she was in a dire need of a cup of sweet tea. She had an idea to help Huxley tell them about his experience. That, she thought, was the easy part, the hard bit was getting him out. As she bent down scooping the fresh clean water into her pail another idea occurred to her. What if she brought the medicine woman, Serenity, to him? A smile played across her mouth before a new thought entered her mind: how would she get the medicine woman to him without Merek finding out? She knew he would not approve and would forbid her from doing it. He would not agree that the medicine could help, and she felt that it would be easier without having to explain her plan to her husband. Elenore was not even sure if it would work, and she would only have herself to blame if it didn't. Sighing she headed for home the only option was to ask the medicine woman to keep it a secret and that would be difficult.

The medicine woman lived at the rear of the camp, preferring the far-right corner, nestled under the looming peak of rock that stretched itself up towards the sky. She had made a shelter using her tent and large branches creating something that resembled a cabin. Elenore was impressed with her ingenuity and thought to try to make something similar for herself and Merek.

As she approached, she noticed two cups placed near the fire a plate with some uneaten food was on the ground. Elenore frowned. The medicine woman must have a visitor. She took another step forward and instantly heard a familiar laugh: it was Sabin! A smile crossed her face.

'Hello!' Elenore called.

Sabin's head poked from the tent flap 'Aye, it's Norrie!' Sabin embraced Elenore holding her a moment longer before releasing his hold. 'Is everthin okay, Norrie?'

Elenore nodded. 'Yes I just needed to see the medicine woman about something.'

'I thought I heard right, it is Merek's woman, how are you, dear?' The medicine woman came through the tent opening smiling at Elenore. Her gaze flickered over her, pausing briefly at her abdomen. 'Have you been eating enough, dear?' Elenore nodded reassuring her. 'So, may I ask what it is you seek, wife of Merek?' The medicine woman looked closely at Elenore. Her grey eyes twinkled and there was a kindness in them.

Elenore suddenly felt at a loss for words, the courage she had earlier seemed to have vanished. 'I was looking for, Sabin,' she gestured towards Sabin, smiling back at Serenity.

'Aye ye must have a sixth sense, Norrie, I was looking for Serenity cos I have some exciting news!' Sabin did not wait for a response. 'Edyth and I are gettin married!'

Elenore swallowed, unsure if she had heard right. 'You are getting married?'

Sabin burst into laughter, his curls bobbing around his face. 'That I am, Norrie, and that's why I am here.'

Elenore forced herself to smile. 'Sabin, that is great but who will marry you? We do not have a Seer here,' was all that she could manage.

'Ah that is why I have come to see Serenity, she is from the ancient line of Seers. She may be able to marry us.'

Elenore shifted her gaze from Sabin to Serenity, dumbfounded.

Serenity smiled. 'I think we all need to sit down and have some tea. I have some fresh scones that I made this morning. Please, come.' She beckoned them to the fire that was almost out. Sabin added some timber and Serenity filled the iron kettle with fresh water, adding some herbs and leaves. Elenore caught the whiff of mint and settled herself on the log opposite Sabin.

Serenity ducked back into her small home coming back with a basket full of scones. 'I haven't had a chance to make some jam, but I dare say if we are here long enough, I might be able to concoct something.'

Elenore was thankful the medicine woman had enough insight to understand her feelings and change the topic. A thousand thoughts raced through her mind and none of them seemed to make sense of what Sabin had just told her. She fully understood what he had told her ... but Edyth! Wasn't she already married? Had Sabin even asked her? This is not supposed to be happening.

'So, Elenore, why did you come to see me dear?'

Elenore looked at the medicine woman as she offered the basket full of scones. Elenore took a scone and forced a smile. 'Oh, it was ...' she took a breath, 'I needed to ask you a favour.' Serenity gave her a questioning look. Elenore looked back at Sabin. 'I need your help too, Sabin.'

'Aye, Norrie, you can always count on me.'

Elenore cursed herself for being selfish. Sabin always had her best interests at heart, yet it seemed she didn't always have his. 'You both have to promise not to tell Merek, he won't agree to it.' Before she gave them a chance to answer she rushed on. 'Huxley holds the key in helping to bring down the Asur. We all know that he is the only person that has ever escaped, he must know something.'

'Aye, Norrie, what you say is true, but I'm not sure if ye have forgotten he doesn't like to talk about it.'

'I know, but I have an idea on how we can get him to talk.' Elenore looked at Serenity. 'This is the reason why I came here today, Serenity, I think you can help.' Elenore took a breath. She was in too deep to pull out now and she hoped that the medicine woman would agree to it. 'Serenity, perhaps you could hypnotise Huxley. We must get him to agree to it and this is where I need you, Sabin. He trusts you. Besides, it might help him heal. I mean, get through the trauma he suffered.' She felt relieved that she had told them regardless of whether they wanted to help or not.

Sabin rubbed the stubble on his chin, 'I think it is a good plan, Norrie' he said quietly.

'I do too, Elenore. But I must tell you, if Merek asks me anything I will be telling the truth. I will keep it secret in the fact I will not be telling anyone, but well like I said if he asks, I will tell him the truth.' Serenity folded her arms, a frown on her face.

Elenore nodded, understanding her predicament. She was a trusted woman of the camp not only to heal but to provide guidance and support to those in need. Keeping secrets from the leader of the same camp would echo a sense of betrayal and weaken the trust people had in her.

'I understand,' she replied.

'Good. Then let us eat and discuss your plan and Sabin's wedding.'

Elenore nodded taking a bite from the scone she held in her hand.

CHAPTER TEN

Zuri

Beneath her mask of stunning beauty, a mystery she possessed,
for her heart held a truth most captivating – a web of deceit.

Elenore

T he tea tasted sweet and minty; Elenore relished the flavour. She was glad that Sabin and Serenity both had agreed to hypnotise Huxley. They decided to go ahead with their plan sooner rather than later. Elenore would have to make sure that Merek did not get a whiff of what they planned and that could prove difficult. Elenore still did not feel comfortable telling Merek of her plan. She knew he would have his reservations and she would not hear the end of it if it failed.

Her husband was not the only challenge they would face; Edyth was not a fan of her and may not agree to having her son hypnotised. Even though Huxley was a grown man and quite capable in making his own decisions, his mother thought otherwise. She often spoke for him and over saw any decisions that concerned him, although this did not happen often as Huxley rarely ventured out. Elenore knew she would need to get past Edyth to talk to Huxley. Sabin would have to work his charm on this one. Serenity had suggested they meet with Huxley in two days' time, giving Sabin a chance to talk to Edyth.

Elenore reached for another corn cake. Aside from a single scone, she had hardly eaten that morning so focused was she on talking with the medicine woman about Huxley. Sabin nudged her gently, bringing her attention back to what they were discussing: his wedding. Elenore groaned inwardly, this was something she was going to have difficulty in getting used to.

'Norrie, remember Nifil village? We stayed there on our way to Dorhall Pass.'

Elenore frowned, trying to remember the village Sabin had mentioned. Slowly the memory came back. In the deserted town, she and Ada had been looking for a place to stay for the night. She shuddered as she remembered the strange home in the middle of the village and the curtain with the exotic patterns and swirls splashed all over it. She had been about to pull the curtain back when Ada had grabbed her, warning her not to. She had never found out why her daughter had been so alarmed or why she felt such a relief that she hadn't pulled the curtain back.

'I remember, it was a deserted village.'

Sabin nodded enthusiastically. 'Well, Serenity is from the people that used to live there. I mean her ancestors.'

Elenore looked at Serenity who nodded, smiling. 'My line of people come from the ancient ones. Some say we are the first humans, our line goes back that far. There were a great many Seers among them. Their gifts were from the Gods themselves. I get my healing powers from them. Although I am not a Seer, I do possess similar...well let's just say similar *traits*.' She smiled broadly taking a sip of her tea. 'That said, I think I have enough qualifications to marry a couple madly in love.' She looked over at Sabin giving him a warm smile. 'It will be good for the people to have some happiness come into their life after everything we have been through.' Serenity took a deep breath before continuing, 'although we are not done with the Asur yet.' Her face took on a sad look as she drained the rest of her tea.

Elenore made her way back to her temporary home in the valley that her husband had found. The sun was beginning to set and a breeze blew, cooling the earth after a hot summer's day. Elenore had so much to consider and think about, her mind was in turmoil. Sabin would announce his wedding plans to Merek in the morning. It was traditional for a man to ask permission from the leader of the village upon which it would be than discussed with the Councillors. There were no Councillors and Eijanbrook did not walk the earth anymore, so it would be up to his son to give consent.

Elenore did not want to take away Sabin's happiness, but she had her reservations. She needed to talk to Merek about them before Sabin spoke to him. Another thought entered her mind and she recoiled from it. She still hadn't told her husband about their unborn child. As she neared their tent she paused to see if Merek had returned from the day's hunting trip. She could not see him and peered into the gloom of the small tent. She noticed his hunting gear thrown carelessly at the bottom of their furs.

He must have been in a hurry, she thought. She turned and looked in the direction he would have come from. The mountains were breathtaking as the sun's rays filtered through their peaks. Her husband was nowhere to be seen. An idea occurred to her: he must be drinking with his friends to celebrate. They had not had a formal celebration to give thanks to the Gods for the valley they had provided them. Even though they had only been there a few days, the ceremony would need to be announced and soon. Failure to do this would bring bad luck for the people that did not show gratitude. Elenore had to find Merek.

Krea offered the water skin to Pancome, giving him a warm smile. 'Pancome, we need to ask the forest to help us like they did you.'

Pancome took a long drink, smacking his lips when he finished. 'I agree with you Krea, but I never asked the forest for help, the Gods did.'

Krea nodded slowly and sighed.

'I will ask Ada to help,' Ulric said.

'How will you do that?' asked Pancome.

Ulric gave a lopsided smile. 'Oh, I think she already has heard the question.'

Pancome chuckled softly. It would make sense that the granddaughter of Anja shared the same gift of mind travel.

Moonlight filtered through the window, casting a soft glow in the small bedroom. Ada lay on the bed. Her eyes closed as she let her thoughts wander her mind. She heard Ulric's question and a faint smile played on her lips. She let her mind wander as it stretched its way to her brother. *'I will ask them, Ulric. You all need to rest, the day has gone and now the moon is shining.'* She giggled as Ulric gave a start at her intrusion in his thoughts. Ulric suggested they find a place to build a fire and share some food and tea before bunking down for the night. He did not mention Ada thinking it best to wait until she had her answer from the Gods, they could be fickle at times. It would be wise not to pressure them. They were fully aware of their situation, and he had to trust them.

Ada returned to her body, feeling light-hearted after connecting with her brother. It was now time to pray and wait for the Gods answer. She had an idea on how to fight the queen of the Asur, but she needed help and more than the advice of the Seer. She respected him greatly, but she was looking for guidance from a higher power.

As she closed her eyes letting her mind open, she felt a presence. Her grandmother had felt it in her dream and Ada had also encountered it. She did not know if it was the Gods themselves, or some other entity, but she knew it meant no harm it was here to help.

'You seek confirmation of what you suggest and if it is the right path to take. Child of the Gods, you know this already. Use the power you have been given. You have used it before in the witch's forest you do not need me to give you permission.' The voice went quiet.

Ada waited, but it did not speak again. *'Please, I need to talk to you.'*

Nothing, the silence remained. She did not know what to say. The questions that she had in her mind had gone. Everything she wanted answered she already knew the answer for. She did not need permission. The Gods had given her powers for a reason, and it was time she used them. As her mind sorted and shifted through the thousands of narratives that ran through her mind, she knew what had to be done. She did not need to ask the Gods for the forest's help. The forest had already become an ally of the humans it provided for. It had been their life force for an eternity and without the forest humanity would struggle to exist.

Elenore made her way to Amzi's people's camp, determined to bring her husband back. The moon had risen, its bright face lighting the way. She looked over at the river that flowed, bubbling quietly as it made its way out of the valley into the land below. The night was beautiful, and she basked in the feeling it gave her: hope. Hope created purpose. It was imperative that they survive and give their children a future, one without the Asur.

As she thought about this, Elenore quickened her pace. She had to get to Merek before he drank too much of the red drink making it impossible for her to reason with him, let alone bring him back to their camp. She picked her way carefully through the throng of people, nodding and saying hello as she did. As she approached the camp, she could see Merek standing next to Amzi's sister. She hesitated as she watched them in deep conversation, suddenly they both burst out laughing.

Elenore felt a wave of jealousy wash over her. She had yet to learn of her name, the woman was both exotic and beautiful, it would be hard for any man not to fall in love with her. Elenore took a deep breath and let it out slowly. She could not walk away, she had to talk to Merek. She thought it strange how they had become distant almost like strangers.

She quickly looked around for Tallot and noticed him on the other side of Merek, talking to Amzi. Taking another deep breath, she made her way to her husband.

As Elenore came closer to Merek, Tallot noticed her. Smiling, he gave her a slight wave. She nodded and returned his smile as she turned her attention to her husband and the woman standing next to him.

'Hello, Merek. I have been looking for you, but I see you have been busy.' Before Merek could reply, she gestured towards the woman standing next to him, 'I don't believe we have met.' Elenore struggled to keep her jealousy at bay. She had always prided herself on keeping her emotions under control, but this had not been the case of late.

'I am Zuri,' the tall woman said with a tight smile.

She doesn't seem to like me either, Elenore thought before returning the smile.

'Zuri means beautiful.' Merek's words cut through Elenore like a knife, and she struggled to keep herself from bursting into an angry spray of words. Not trusting herself to speak, she merely nodded.

Clearing her throat, she managed to say, 'Merek, I need to discuss something with you in private.' She threw Zuri a look of contempt. The tall blonde woman flashed a smile. Her teeth were perfect, her dark blue eyes twinkled, and she seemed to exude health and radiance. Elenore found it hard to stop comparing herself. She is so much younger than me and is in the prime of her life. No wonder she attracts so many men.

'What is so important that we have to discuss it now? It can wait until the morning.' Merek waved his hand as if dismissing her. Elenore had a feeling that he would react this way.

'I need to talk to you, after I finish what I need to say to you, you can return to your party.' She said through clenched teeth.

Merek gave her a hard look. 'Well then, let's get it over with.' He stormed past Elenore, heading back the way she had come.

Elenore trailed her husband feeling hurt and unsure if she still wanted to talk to him, but she knew she couldn't back out now. They made their way to the tent they shared. Merek ducked his head and went inside and Elenore followed.

'Okay, so what do you need to talk to me about? And it better be important,' he growled.

Elenore was surprised by his attitude. 'Why are you in such a hurry to run back to that girl?' She couldn't help herself, she had to say it.

Merek took a step closer to his wife, 'There is nothing wrong with a man spending time with his friends. Why does it bother you? You are always out doing whatever it is you do! A man is entitled to drink with his friends.' He glared. Elenore could smell his breath, the red drink mixed with the meat he had eaten earlier. It almost made her gag. She coughed, forcing the food that threatened to come up back down.

Elenore took a step back unsure whether she should tell him about her reservations regarding Sabin and Edyth's wedding, but she knew this would only infuriate him more.

'If a man is entitled to spend time drinking with other men and women, surely his wife can indulge in the things that make her happy. That's what I do Merek when you are not around.'

'What is it you need to tell me?' Merek said as he turned away from Elenore, running his hands through his long hair.

'Sabin is getting married.'

Merek turned back to her and laughed. 'What? Sabin? Who to? The woman with all those kids? He is mad!'

'Merek, I am worried about him. I mean, I don't think Edyth is the right one and—'

Merek held up his hand. His face was furious. 'You drag me away to tell me this? Seriously, Norrie, what has gotten into you? Sabin is a grown man, if he wants to ruin his life so be it!'

Elenore knew that Merek had not gotten on with Edyth and that she had held him responsible for her husband and sons' disappearance, but he had always expressed that he would try and make amends. This new attitude was a complete surprise.

Sighing, she said, 'I thought you should know. He will want to talk to you tomorrow about it. I also think we need to have a gratitude ceremony for the valley we have found.'

Merek nodded, his face softening. 'Yes, you are right. I will organise one tomorrow. Norrie, do not worry about Sabin, he has the right to make his own life and his own mistakes.' He offered her a smile which she returned. He took a step closer, glancing down at her abdomen, Elenore had started to show. her stomach had swelled to a little bump. 'Norrie, I think you are the only one that is putting on weight since fleeing from the Asur.'

Elenore was speechless, she had not anticipated Merek noticing the small change in her weight.

'Merek …' she began. He moved closer, crushing her mouth with his and silencing the words that she wanted to say. She responded, leaning into him. He pulled away and cupped her face with his hands. 'I know what you are going to say, that you want to stay and build a home here but Norrie you know the answer we simply cannot.' He let out a soft laugh, letting her face go.

Elenore's mouth fell open and she felt the sting of tears. 'You have no right to take my dream away Merek.' Anger begin to build, replacing the hurt.

'Right. And you have to be practical, Elenore, we will not have a home until all, I mean *all*, of the Asur are gone!'

Elenore looked away, tears began to well. She wiped them away, not wanting him to see her weakness.

'Go,' she whispered.

He let out a soft chuckle. 'So I have permission to leave now?' Elenore looked at Merek, completely dumbfounded by his arrogance. He had never treated her like this before. He had had his moments when under stress and pressure, but never this conceited.

'I said leave!' Her tone came out harsher and louder than she had intended.

Merek shook his head. Turning he headed out of the tent. 'Get some sleep, Elenore.'

The new day greeted Ogda with clouds that the sun failed to penetrate. He had not slept well, and his body was tired and stiff. He had asked Ludwig to make his favourite tea to serve with warm oatmeal. Although it was summer, the day was cool and breezy. Rain had begun to fall when Ada and Anja made their way into the kitchen. He greeted them warmly,

'Please help yourselves.' He gestured towards the food that sat on the table. A comfortable silence grew as the three of them ate breakfast.

When Ada had finished her last mouthful and pushed her plate away the Seer smiled at her. 'Do you have some information to tell us, dear child.'

Ada smiled warmly at the Seer. He always knew what people were thinking and when they had something to say. 'I have an idea about how we can get to the Asur.'

'Go on, Ada, I am curious about what it could be.' Anja pleaded.

'The forest knows we need help. If it can probe the earth like the queen of Asur then we can find where they are. I will, with the help of the forest, use the tunnel system and burn the probes of the queen. She will be rendered useless if she cannot use her tentacles.'

'You are a brave and clever girl, dear Ada, but there is one problem,' Ogda told her. Ada gave him a questioning look. He chuckled. 'I know you say the forest knows we need its help, and you are right, but how do you propose to communicate with it?'

Ada frowned and shook her head. 'I am not sure, do you have a suggestion?'

The Seer nodded. 'There are ancient trees like the one Ulric found that helped him find the tunnel system that led to Mohsin. These trees are like the Elders of the forest, the oldest. The Asur would have burned almost all, however, there is one that is the oldest and most ancient of them all. This is the tree we need to seek. It holds the most power and the forest listens to it.'

'So where is this tree?' Ada asked.

'That is our problem. I know where it is, and we have just come from there.'

'Shakurta village?'

Ogda nodded. 'Yes, Shakurta village. It all makes sense now! That is why the Gods took me there; we must go to the ancient tree. Without it's help you will not be able to find the tunnel system.'

Anja cleared her throat. 'I am sorry, but I don't understand how the rest of the forest isn't angry with the people of Shakurta since so much of the Majestic Forest has been burned to the ground.'

The Seer rubbed his chin. 'Yes you have a valid point, Anja. I have asked this myself. The only thing I can think of is that they simply do not know. It has been kept hidden from them. They are far away from other civilisations and trust their people to be their custodians, who have been for thousands of years. There would be no need for them to start worrying now.' The three of them did not speak for a while there was a lot to consider.

Ogda asked Ludwig to make more tea and serve it in the room where guests would usually sit and greet him. It had been the room where they had originally met to discuss the rising threat of the Asur. Once again, there was a need to discuss a plan, time was running out. The Seer had hoped to have already left to make their journey to Merek, it was imperative that they all meet in the valley.

The future would see a great battle. He had foreseen it and it was part of the bigger plan that the Gods had made. Not all would survive, however in war times there was always loss and sacrifice. The most important thing was that humanity survived and continued for generations. This would only happen if the world was finally rid of the Asur.

Elenore had cried herself to sleep. She woke to a grey dreary day that matched her mood. Merek had not come back to share their furs, which only made her feel worse. She rolled over onto her back, looking up at the tent ceiling. Her tears had all been used. She knew she should get up and wash her face and make some tea, but she lacked the will power.

It was hard to grasp how much her and Merek had grown apart, especially given all that they had been through it did not make sense. She missed him and desperately wanted, *needed* him next to her, to wrap her in his strength. Rain began to fall. It reminded her of the tears she shed. An emptiness filled her, and she had never felt so alone.

The tent flap suddenly opened causing her to jump. Looking up she saw Sabin, his dark curls dripping wet, and worry covered his face.

'Aye, Norrie, what's goin on here?' A fresh set of tears began to fall, and she thought she had no more to shed. Sabin bent down next to her. 'Norrie, please don't cry. Shush now.' He patted her awkwardly and Elenore could sense his discomfort at seeing her so upset. 'I will go get Merek, I thought he would be here.'

'No, Sabin, please I will be okay. It's just my condition.' Nodding he stood up. 'Let me get ye some water.'

Before Elenore had time to protest, he grabbed the water pail and went back out the tent flap. Elenore sighed and sat up. She had to pull herself together, she couldn't just fall apart. Pulling her hair back she reached for the tie she used to put it up. Pulling on a fresh tunic she picked up the furs, giving them a shake to freshen up the bedding. The desire to have an actual home and proper bed reminded her of the home Eijanbrook had built for them.

A fresh wave of tears threatened to consume her again and she forced them away. Sabin came in with a pail full of fresh water and she thanked him. She quickly washed her face.

'Did you see Merek?' she asked. He shook his head. She smiled. 'Guess we best go find him and tell him your news.'

'Aye, missus, as long as you are up to it.'

'I am Sabin, please do not worry about me.' She strode past him and out of the tent. The rain had eased to a light drizzle as the pair made their way to where Elenore had seen Merek the previous night.

By the time they had made it to Azmi's camp the rain had stopped and the sun was trying to push through the clouds. Elenore felt a little better and was starting to feel hungry. She had not eaten since early the previous day. Some of the men of the camp were tending to the horses while the women stoked fires and cooked breakfast. The smell of food cooking made Elenore's stomach grumble and mouth water. She forced herself to ignore it and focus looking for her husband.

'Aye, Norrie, I can't see him.'

Elenore combed the camp but could not see her husband. 'I can't see him either. Maybe we should ask someone – wait, there is Amzi.' She pointed to the tall blonde man on the far side, he had just emerged from his tent.

'Good idea, you are clever,' Sabin chuckled.

Amzi greeted them and indicated inside the tent when Sabin asked where Merek was. The two of them peered into the gloom of the tent. Elenore made out the shape of her husband and stepped inside to confirm that it was him. Merek was lying face down among some furs, his long hair tousled, his body sprawled spread eagled. Not far from where he lay, Elenore could see Tallot, naked from the waist up and snoring loudly. A woman lay next to him, and Elenore was unsure who she was. She began to feel uncomfortable, like she was intruding and should not have come.

Sabin lent next to Merek, gently shaking him. Merek rolled over pulling the furs up to his chin. Sabin got up and looked at Elenore.

'Aye, Norrie, I think we should let him sleep. The Gods only know that he will have a sore head when he wakes up,' Sabin laughed. Elenore knew he was right, and she was eager to leave. As they left the camp Sabin suggested they see the medicine woman.

'That's fine, but I need to have some breakfast I am famished.'

'Aye, you should eat. You have a wee one growing inside ye.'

Elenore smiled, 'Why don't you come back to my tent, and I will fix us something. It has been a long time since we shared a meal together.'

'Sounds good,' Sabin replied.

As they walked back a question tugged at Elenore. She had tried her best to ignore it, but it wouldn't leave. 'Sabin, who was that girl next to Tallot?'

Sabin chuckled. 'Best you do not worry about things like that, Norrie.' When Sabin did not say anymore more questions began to worm their way into Elenore's mind. She fervently pushed them away, but they were stubborn and would not leave. She bit her lip to stop herself from asking them, but it was to no avail. 'Sabin, please tell me I am curious.'

Sabin stopped walking, turning to face her. 'Norrie, I told ye not to ask again it is none of yours or my business. Tallot is a single man, a warrior, he has a right to sleep with who he likes.' Elenore noticed Sabin had taken a serious tone which was rare for her curly haired friend.

She gave him a weak smile. 'Okay, you win, I won't ask again.'

'Good. Let's go and eat, I am starvin'!'

Elenore put together some leftovers she had from the previous day adding some extra herbs that Serenity had given her. They ate in silence.

Sabin wiped his mouth with the back of his hand. 'Aye, that was delicious. Thank ye.'

Elenore beamed. 'Why thank you Sabin, it was my pleasure. I think we should go see the medicine woman now.'

Sabin nodded, stood up and stretched. Elenore put out the fire before packing away the utensils she had used, she would take them to the river to wash later. They made their way to the medicine woman's camp and Elenore noticed how long a walk it was. The main camp stretched itself over at least half of the valley. People had begun to fashion temporary homes with the branches of trees like the medicine woman.

Merek had warned them not to cut down the older trees and focus only on the young saplings, taking only what they needed. He had always had respect for the forest and what it provided them. Now his respect had deepened, and he felt that he owed it to the forest to take care of it. Humanity would not survive without it. Family life had resumed a kind of normalcy with children running and laughing.

People were swimming in the river or sitting under the shade of the trees. Some were cooking or building or mending tunics and furs. Elenore smiled. They had not felt this relaxed in such a long time and she wondered how long it would last. Her dream of being in her home with her family was still strong and she could not shake it even if she wanted. The memory of Merek's harsh words the previous evening surfaced. She shook her head as if to dislodge them and she willed herself to think of something else. She rubbed her stomach fondly thinking of the new life growing inside her. She loved the baby even though they had not met.

'Aye, Norrie, have ye told Merek about the wee one?' Sabin startled her out of her daydream.

She blushed and shook her head. 'He was not in the mood to talk last night, Sabin. I will though, when the time is right. It has been, well, a little crazy at the moment.'

'Aye it has, but ye need to tell him soon, Norrie. He won't forgive ye if you don't.'

Elenore looked out over the camp. The rain had revived everything, and she could smell the freshness. Taking a breath, she closed her eyes, savouring the moment. She did not want to think about Merek. He had hurt her, and she knew she would have to confront him again soon, but not now.

She took Sabin's hand. 'Sabin, thank you for being such a dear, sweet friend.' She hesitated. She knew she should tell him about Edyth and her reservations about the marriage. 'As a friend, I need to ask you if you are sure that Edyth is the right woman for you. I mean, you are getting married, and it has not been that long since you have met.' She turned to look at Sabin. He looked back for a moment before throwing his head back and laughing. Elenore frowned. This was not the reaction she had been expecting.

'Norrie, I am totally in love with her. Please be patient. Ye and her will be friends cause, well, ye are both so much alike.'

Elenore could see how happy he was at that moment and decided not to push the issue. She had told him about her feelings towards it and he persisted on marrying the woman. It would not be fair to push it further.

'Okay, have it your way if you are truly in love than I wish you all the best. But you have to promise me one thing.' She wagged her finger in front of him. He gave her a lopsided smile. Elenore could not help but laugh at him. 'You must always come to me if you need to, I am forever your friend.'

Sabin laughed again before embracing the woman before him. 'I promise,' he whispered into her ear. 'Now, let's go. We are wasting time.' He pulled away from her and began to walk to the camp that lay at the back of the valley.

Anja took a swallow of the tea savouring the taste. 'It is delicious! Ludwig you have outdone yourself this tea is absolutely divine!'

'Ah, missus, you are very welcome. It is a personal favourite and I like to serve it on special occasions.'

'You have mixed in,' – Anja took another sip and closed her eyes trying to detect the mix of herbs that Ludwig had used – 'Berry, a dash of mint, and apple?' She frowned. 'I think I can taste a hint of honey too.' She swallowed.

'You are very clever, Anja, that is precisely it! You know your herbs and tea.' Ludwig said, chuffed by her appreciation.

'Ludwig, I think we will need more tea by the sounds of how Anja is enjoying it. We have a lot to get through, so please let us get this started.' The Seer instructed him. Ludwig gave a small bow to Anja and his master before shuffling back to the kitchen to prepare more tea.

Ogda cleared his throat. 'As you know, it is imperative we get to Shakurta village and seek the assistance of the ancient tree. We cannot mind travel there as we have found out the Seer has made a pact with the devil. I have decided to send Ulric, Kacha, Krea and Pancome. Ogda paused for a moment as he collected his thoughts.

'Pancome will be evidence of how a human was able to outsmart and escape from the Asur without being caught. He will be able to convince the ancient tree of his escape. All Pancome's memories will be collected by the tree, and it will learn of the destruction that has been created. It will also learn of the burning of the Majestic Forest, and it will want to seek revenge. What happens next will go two ways: either the Seer of the village will confess and beg for forgiveness, or he will flee and use mind travel to warn the Asur. I have a feeling he will do the latter.' The two women nodded in agreement. 'Once we have the help of the tree, Ada you will find the way to Dardanos. The village will honour the tree and travel to where Merek is hidden. Ulric and the others will go with them. In the meantime, Anja, you will help me guide the people who are fleeing and those that are ready to join Merek.' Ogda paused and took a breath before he continued.

'There are still villages being burned and plundered as we speak, I cannot stress enough that we are all in grave danger. The war may have begun, but the battle has yet to start. Once we have finished, Ada, will have done her part in finding Dardanos. All of us will need to make haste and leave.' The Seer took a sip of his tea and smiled as he said, 'I agree, Anja, Ludwig has done a fine job of the tea.'

Ulric turned onto his side, trying to get comfortable. He felt Ada next to him. He knew he was dreaming, and his sister was trying to connect to him. He let his mind open, and the dream become a lucid reality. *'Dear brother, you need to wake before the sun graces the sky. Make haste to Shakurta village, the Seer and our grandmother will guide you. It is important Pancome goes with you, he will need to speak to the ancient tree. You must hurry, we cannot afford to lose the war against the Asur.'* She touched his cheek, smiling, her green eyes flashed. *'Goodbye Ulric.'*

She was gone and Ulric rolled back to his other side. He opened his eyes, coming fully awake. A deep sense of foreboding began to well, clutching him and it took him all his strength not to pack up and flee. He reached to the side of his furs and grabbed his waterskin. The water was cool and refreshing and helped calm him. He wiped his brow; sweat had started to bead. His heart was still pounding, and he forced himself to take deep long breaths.

Finally, the fear that had grasped him began to settle to a simmer but did not leave. He sighed and closed his eyes. How long would it take before he would fall back to sleep? Would he rest any more before it was time to leave? Another thought took hold: what if I fall asleep and do not wake until the sun has risen.

This made him sit up. He threw back the furs and crawled out of the tent. He stood, looking up at the stars. They twinkled and winked down at him. He sighed. The sun was a long way off from rising. Resigned for the long day ahead, Ulric quickly busied himself in collecting small pieces of wood that they would need to make for the fires along their journey to Shakurta village. He filled all the water skins and rubbed down the horses. By the time he had finished, the soft grey of dawn was beginning to appear. He made tea and a small breakfast for himself and the others. It was time to wake them to eat, drink and make haste.

CHAPTER ELEVEN

Huxley

Breath held, heart a drum. They come with darkness,

stalking, eager for human flesh.

Huxley

The healer was waiting for them as she perched on the log next to the fire she had extinguished earlier. 'Finally, you both have come. I have been waiting.' Elenore's eyes widened with surprise at the older woman, taken aback that Serenity knew they were coming.

'We are here. We had to have some breakfast, I was starving!' Elenore gave a soft chuckle, hoping the medicine woman would be happy that she was eating. Serenity clucked her tongue, giving Elenore a nod before grabbing her bag. She hoisted it over her shoulder and led the way behind where she had made her temporary home. Elenore and Sabin followed.

A dense forest flanked the valley on both sides and thinned out to a large meadow where most of the people had set up makeshift homes. A river coursed through the western side of the forest while the mountains that rose to meet the Gods created a breathtaking backdrop. The clouds had dissipated giving way to a sky of blue. A fiery sun basked the earth in its warmth. The day ahead promised to be a warm one.

Elenore had changed into a light tunic and had run a brush quickly through her long dark hair before she had made Sabin breakfast. She had not had time to put it in a bun and it hung down to the middle of her back. Edyth was hanging clothes on a makeshift line and the children played not far from her. She threw them a questioning look but softened when she saw Sabin.

'Aye, Edyth, I have bought the healer and Norrie to help with

Huxley.' He went to her and wrapped his arms around her, kissing her fully on the mouth. Elenore watched them and slowly realised why the Gods had made him love this small woman. Losing children and a husband whom she had loved would have been heart breaking. Sabin, with his love of life and jovial personality, was the medicine Edyth needed. Elenore sighed. Things had a strange way of working out and it was something she was becoming familiar with.

The healer was watching her intently and Elenore felt suddenly awkward, like she had read her mind. Edyth extracted herself from Sabin and looked directly at Serenity. Sabin had already advised her of Elenore's plan.

'My boy has been through a lot. I don't want him hurt again.'

Serenity nodded, giving her a warm smile. 'You have my word, Edyth.'

Edyth cast Elenore a long look, but did not say anything. 'He is out the back, chopping wood. Follow me. I haven't told him you're coming, or you would of not being able to find him.' They followed her to the back of her camp. The children, seeing their mother leave followed curiously behind. The sound of the axe splitting wood could be heard as the they rounded the corner. Huxley's long hair was pulled back in a ponytail and his beard hung long and unkempt. He did not pause to look at them, preferring to ignore them and continue with the chopping of wood.

Edyth cleared her throat loudly and waited for Huxley to stop his chopping. He continued for several more moments before he turned to the group of people in front of him the axe hung casually by his side.

He lifted his head and directed his question at his mother. 'What do they all want?'

Edyth went to his side and spoke to him in a low whisper. He grunted several times before swinging the axe to the top of his shoulder. He shook his head before looking at Elenore and then the healer.

Elenore walked over to where he stood. 'Hello, Huxley. We need your help. Please, we need to know more about the Asur. I know you want to help, and it may seem daunting, but I wouldn't ask if I didn't think it important and it may help save us all.'

Edyth threw Elenore a hard look but stayed quiet. Huxley stared at Elenore for a moment before looking back at the wood he had been chopping.

He nodded. 'Okay. I will do it.' He placed the axe next to the wood giving a stern warning to the children not to touch it. Elenore reiterated his warning and gestured for them to follow not trusting that they would heed their advice.

'Let us go and make some special tea,' Serenity said as she began walking back to the tent Edyth shared with her children.

Edyth had sectioned off a small area for the kitchen, where there were stashed sacks of vegetables, herbs, and flowers. Edyth was a survivor and had learned to scrounge and seek whatever she could to help feed her brood. Grabbing a couple of pails, she ordered her older daughters to go and fetch some fresh water. Peeling back an old potato sack that was in the corner of the makeshift kitchen she picked up some dried branches. This would help start a small fire for the tea.

Elenore watched her, fascinated. Edyth moved with purpose, sweeping through the kitchen like a small warrior intent on getting on with the task that lay ahead.

Sabin folded his arms letting out a soft chuckle. 'Aye, will ye look at this? Me lady has it altogether. Ah, Edyth, me love, ye are strong one.'

She paused in her bustling and smiled at Sabin but did not make a comment. Instead, she asked them to follow her out to where she had her fire pit. The girls came back moments later with the water which Edyth poured into a pot to boil. Serenity poured the contents from a small pouch into the pot giving it a quick stir. Huxley watched quietly.

They sat on the logs around the fire pit while Huxley sipped the tea. Some of the children had grown restless and Edyth ordered them to go and find her some herbs she would need for dinner later that day. When they had left, Serenity began to softly chant.

Huxley drained the last of the tea and the healer asked him to lay on the ground. She explained that sometimes people passed out after she spoke to them under hypnosis. Huxley hesitated and looked at his mother. Edyth nodded, giving consent that she trusted the medicine woman. Huxley lay on a mat that Sabin had fetched from inside the tent. Serenity sat next to him continuing to chant. A faraway look slowly descended on his face as if his mind had gone into a different time.

'Huxley,' began Serenity. 'Can you hear me?' He nodded. 'Remember you are safe in the valley, but you need to listen to my voice.' He nodded again. 'Good. I need you to be back to when you were taken by the Asur. Can you do that for me?'

A look of fear crossed Huxley's face and a shiver went down Elenore's spine. For a man such as Huxley to have that much fear was astonishing. 'Remember, Huxley, you will be safe I will guide you. We need your help Huxley are you ready?' He gave another nod. 'Okay, let's start.' The medicine woman turned to the others. 'I need you all to remain quiet. I am the only one who will speak. Do you understand?' The healer gave a stern look at Sabin, Edyth, and Elenore. They murmured that they did. She turned her attention back to Huxley. Taking a deep breath, she began. 'Huxley, tell me about the time when the Asur came looking for you.'

Huxley's face turned pallid and his body trembled, but he did not remain quiet instead he began his story.

'I remember the day was a perfect sky of blue. Pa said that we could go with him and Merek. My older brother convinced my Pa that I was old enough to go and that there would be more of us to kill the Asur. He was hesitant at first, but eventually caved into our demands. We left on that perfect day to go hunting for demons. It was rumoured they had ventured to the east coast. It took us a week to get there. We were too late to save the village they had burned to the ground. My father and Merek were hell bent on revenge after they saw the devastation. My brother was excited to make his first kill of the Asur. We trailed them to a path that led directly to the coast. My father and Merek wanted to get there before the Asur. We pushed our horses as fast as we dared and that's when they ambushed us.' Huxley grew quiet.

'What do you mean they ambushed you?' Serenity prompted.

Huxley took a deep breath; it was evident that he was struggling re-living the past. 'They came out of nowhere as if they had some premonition we were there. I mean it was unbelievable they would have never known we were trailing them they were so far ahead of us. They are the devil the ugliest meanest creatures I have ever come across. Even the beasts they rode were full of hate. Jarrod lost his mind; he used his bow and arrow killing one of the giant brutes they rode which angered them more. They came at us with such ferocity. I was terrified, the legends they tell you when you are a child does not do justice for these monsters.'

Again, Huxley went quiet, and Serenity had to prompt him again. He took another deep breath, but his voice was unsteady as he spoke. 'We knew we were outnumbered, and Merek shouted for us to retreat. Our horses could not outrun the beasts that the Asur rode they were faster and stronger. They went for Jarrod as he had killed one of the beasts. I heard him scream and turned back for him. He yelled at me to run and leave him behind, but I could not.' Huxley began to whimper as the memory of his brother came back bringing the buried grief with it. Serenity gave Huxley some time to release the pent-up misery. When his sobs had subsided, he wiped his face with the sleeve of his tunic. The healer offered him water and gave him more tea. Huxley drank the tea greedily. She waited for the effects of the tea to settle before starting her low mesmerising chant.

'I don't remember much detail of what happened, it all went so quick.' Huxley's voice trembled. He ran his tongue over his lips and laid back down on the blanket. He closed his eyes, taking deep, steady breaths. Elenore thought he had fallen asleep when suddenly he began to talk again. 'I could hear shouting. Merek was screaming at us to run, but they had Jarrod and Papa would not leave him behind. They knew they had his most precious thing in the world, his son. They dragged Jarrod kicking and screaming, lifting him onto one of those huge beasts. I went after them, my sword ready, but I was hit from behind. I don't know much else what happened after that. I guess the Asur fled the scene they had prisoners. It would have delighted them to capture not only one son but two! Two sons from a father.' The tea had helped Huxley remember but there was still so much more for him to re-live they needed every detail.

'What happened after that?' The healer asked. Huxley shook his head. Serenity talked in a low soothing tone before Huxley began his story again.

'I woke in a cage in a cave.' He shivered involuntarily. Serenity beckoned Edyth to fetch her son another blanket. She had been quiet as she listened to the events that had changed her world forever.

Elenore felt her heart soften for the woman who had lost so much. *I need to stop being so selfish. This woman deserves love in her life I must try and become her friend,* she chided herself.

'I could not see my brother. My head was bleeding from where they had clubbed me. I called out for him, but there was no answer. I did not see or hear from any of the Asur for days. They left me a skin of water but no food. They have no compassion remember that.' Huxley's voice was barely a whisper. 'When they came back, my brother was with them. I did not recognise him at first. He had been beaten to an inch of his life. They threw him in with me, laughing their horrible laugh.' Again, he shivered involuntarily, no blanket could have warmed him enough from the cold he felt. 'I gave him some water which he drank through swollen lips.' Huxley groaned.

Elenore looked over at Edyth; tears ran down the woman's face. She had always wanted to know what had happened to her first born, finally she was hearing it. Sabin put his arm around her waist, and she buried her head into his chest.

Huxley began to shake uncontrollably and thrust his hands under his arms. Serenity leaned over pulling the blanket more closely around him before she began to whisper soothingly in his ear. He blew out his breath through clenched teeth. After a few minutes he took up his narrative again.

'Jarrod had been a fighter, he was always rebellious and full of courage, but he had picked the wrong entity to start a fight with. His stubbornness and wilful streak cost him his life.' Huxley paused, his hands now gripped the blanket in a tight grasp. He took a deep breath, it seemed that he wanted to shed the pain and retreat to his silent world. Tears streamed down his face, his punishment was to live in the mental torment of not having protected his older brother.

'They came for us not long after, dragging both of us from the filthy cage. They brought us to their queen Dardanos.' Huxley wiped his face with the edge of the blanket.

'Do you remember what it looked like where she lived, Huxley? Try to remember as much detail as you can it may help.' Serenity prompted him.

Huxley frowned, as if trying to sift through the memories to give as much detail as he could. 'She lived far along some passageways; it felt like they were dragging us forever. We did not put up much of a fight we had not eaten for some time. She sat upon a throne made of granite and was the most disgusting, vilest thing I have ever seen. She had tentacles that stretched out like long thick lines of flesh, probing and waving. When she saw us, she laughed it filled and vibrated throughout the mountain that we were hidden in.' Tears once again streamed down Huxley's face.

'You are doing great, Huxley, we are learning so much. Please, we are nearly there, keep going,' Serenity coaxed.

Huxley drew in a deep breath. 'She snatched my brother in one of those tentacles, lifting him up she bit off his head!' Huxley let out a loud scream.

Edyth ran to her son.

'Sabin, take her, she can't wake him he is still in a trance!' Serenity yelled at Sabin. Sabin dragged Edyth who had become hysterical, Elenore moved to help her friend.

'You! It was your filthy husband who did this to my boy. He took him from me!' Edyth spat at Elenore before Sabin was able to drag her into the tent.

Elenore wiped the spit from her face. The healer's voice interrupted her thoughts.

'Elenore this is no time for self-pity, come!' The medicine woman beckoned Elenore to Huxley's side. His face had paled, and his knuckles turned white as he grasped the blanket once more. Huxley's eyes suddenly flicked open in a vacant stare.

'You must watch him, I have to make some more tea. We must keep him in a hypnotic state to stop him from being lost from us forever. I also need to show Sabin how to make Edyth some relaxant tea. Talk to him, tell him anything, just keep talking!' Elenore nodded. Serenity bent down next to Elenore her face close to hers. 'You need to keep talking Elenore or we lose him, do you understand?' The healer spoke in a stern voice.

'Yes, I will keep talking to him. Please, I will be okay, go and tend to Edyth.' Satisfied, the healer left rushing into the tent where Sabin and Edyth had gone moments earlier.

Huxley felt the cold fold itself around him like a giant cobra. He began to shiver and felt vulnerable. He could not hear the healer anymore, it was as if he was in another time and place. A fog had descended, and he could feel the cold, hard rock under his feet. He realised he had gone from laying down to standing. He thought this odd, but his brain was having difficulty making sense of his motions and thoughts. The strong scent of the earth enveloped him as if he had been thrust into the bowels of the world. In the distance he could hear the distant horn of the Asur, and fear clutched him, stifling him. He struggled to breath as he willed himself to flee but his legs were rooted to the rock he stood on. His body defied his commands as he silently screamed at himself to run. He could feel the ground begin to vibrate as the army of the Asur approached.

Ada had retired to the small bedroom she shared with her grandmother. She felt exhausted, she had so much to think about. Anja had stayed with the Seer to discuss which villages they would travel to. As she went to lay down, a sickening feeling gripped her, and she doubled over as if in great pain.

Her head began to swim and moments later she could made out the blurred figures of Ogda and Anja in the room with her.

'Something is wrong!' She could hear Anja, but it was as if she was far away. The Seer sat on the bed and placed his hands on her head.

He stiffened. 'Quick, we must find Huxley, he is in grave danger. Quick!' Ogda commanded. Anja sat next to Ada, placing her hand into hers as her mind searched to make a connection. She could feel Ada and then Ogda. It was not long before they began their desperate search for the young man.

Their minds reached far and wide, but to no avail. The Seer knew they were losing time and slowly the opening to be one step ahead of the Asur was closing. If they did not find Huxley, the Asur would find Merek, and all would be lost. He called for the Gods to help, a desperate plea to save humanity.

The Asur had thrown the world into chaos. Ogda could hear the fervent whisper of the leaves of the trees, as if they were trying to speak. He slowed his mind and opened it to the green warriors as they shouted their rebellious cries. An entity entered his mind and at first, he was not sure where it had come from, he was surprised to hear it. He felt no threat and stayed calm, waiting for it to speak.

'What you seek is hidden, but it seeks you and when it finds you it will destroy you. You are looking in all the wrong places. The very thing you look for is beneath your feet.' The voice vanished as quickly as it had come. Ogda was astonished, however, this was not the time to reflect; they had to get into the underground tunnels.

He called for Ada and Anja, directing them to comb the Asur's labyrinth of tunnels. Desperately they searched, looking near where Merek had hidden his people. Anja felt her sons that were so close, it seemed an eternity since she had seen them. Since losing her husband, she yearned to hold them, be with them. The Asur had taken a large piece of her life and an anger simmered. Fuelled by silent rage, Anja scanned the burrows under Dorhall Pass.

A gentle vibration could be felt as she probed, looking for Huxley. The vibration grew stronger, and it dawned on her that it was the Asur marching towards someone. It had to be Huxley. She called for Ogda and Ada. As she raced towards the sound, she started to feel the energy of a fearful young man.

'Go to him, Anja, take his mind from here. Ada and I will blur and confuse the minds of the Asur.'

Anja made her way to the energy source and gently greeted Huxley. He was gripped in a frozen panic.

'Come, Huxley, it is Anja, do you remember me?' His mind tried to hold onto her words, trying to make sense of them. *'Come, we must leave here. It is not safe, Huxley.'* She felt his mind respond, desperately connecting with hers before being lured away.

'I think he is coming back!' Elenore yelled towards the tent.

The healer raced out and kneeled beside Huxley. 'You are safe, Huxley. Come back now, we are here waiting for you.' Huxley sucked in his breath and blinked. He struggled to sit up. The healer and Elenore helped him. 'Just sit, there is no rush,' the healer told him gently. Fear was still in his eyes as he looked from Serenity to Elenore.

'I will finish making the tea,' offered Elenore.

'No!' Huxley almost shouted. The two women were shocked. Edyth and Sabin came from the tent upon hearing Huxley. Edyth ran to her son's side, embracing him. 'Please, mother, I am fine. I need to tell you the details you were seeking. We need to rid the world of the Asur, they have taken too much.' He sighed and looked at the distant peaks of Dorhall Pass. 'They are near us but do not know where we are. They have a network of tunnels that help them move quickly. If we do a surprise attack, we will have the upper hand. The forest and humans are their enemy. It is important we unite to fight our common adversary. The great Seer has a plan, we need to help Merek too. Anja rescued me, they are coming.' Huxley paused before burrowing his head into his mother's chest like a small child. Elenore stood, telling them she would go and make the tea it had been an exhausting experience.

'So, we have found out a few things—' Ogda was perched on his favourite cushion reflecting on their rescue of Huxley.

'Yes, we know where the Asur are,' Ada interrupted. Anja threw her granddaughter a stern look. 'Sorry,' mumbled Ada.

Ogda smiled. 'Ada, we do not know where they are exactly.' Ada frowned but held her tongue and waited for the Seer to continue. The Seer softly chuckled when he saw Ada's bewildered expression. 'My dear, we know the approximate location, but they know we are seeking them. The place where Dardanos resides, her nest, I cannot describe it any other way is secret and that is what we must find out. Hence your meeting with the ancient tree. The Asur will be on high alert, they will not let their queen become a target and be placed in a vulnerable position. She is their asset, their treasure, the one that commands and leads. Without her, they are lost. So it is important we find her and destroy her, it will be the only way to rid this world of the Asur.' Ada and Anja both nodded there was a lot of work ahead of them. 'We must rest and when the evening falls, we will do our work. Everything we have planned we must finish tonight; the clock is ticking, and the countdown has begun.' Ogda closed his eyes, taking a breath before opening them again. He cleared his throat. 'I must tell you both something and I know you have both experienced the same thing. When we were searching for Huxley, a voice, I do not know whose or where it came from, helped me find where the Asur were.'

'Yes!' Both Ada and Anja cried together.

'Who was that, is it the Gods?' Ada asked.

Again, the Seer chuckled, 'Ah! Dear girl, that as I said, I do not know. But, I think time will tell and it is not important. The important thing is that this voice has come to help us when the situation has become dire or when we seek answers when there appears to be none.'

'I agree,' Anja said as she remembered how the voice had calmed her when she felt the epiphany that she would be the next Seer.

'So!' Ogda clapped his hands together. 'We must get some rest before we head out. After tonight we will be leaving to reunite with Merek. Time is of the essence.' The two women nodded and murmured their agreement, leaving the Seer to take some much-needed rest.

CHAPTER TWELVE

Courage

I was not born a warrior, but I was
born to face the monster that follows.

Ulric

The sun had risen fully, radiating warmth upon the riders below. Anja had instructed Ulric to ride to the east with much haste. He did as she had instructed. The feeling of fear had not quite left him; it had been impossible to shake. His canine companion, with Krea's pet wolf, ran alongside the horses playing and wrestling as they enjoyed being on the move again. As they started to climb up a stony ridge, both the dog and wolf let out a low growl. Ulric looked down at the animals as they crouched beside him.

'What is it, Kanji?' The dog momentarily looked up at his master before flattening his ears and turning back to climb up the steep path. Krea let out a low whistle as she drew her sword.

'This doesn't feel right.' Kacha had ridden up alongside Ulric as he scanned the top of the ridge. The wolf whimpered as he heard Krea's whistle, hesitant in coming back to her. She scolded the wolf for not coming back quickly.

Pancome, who was perched behind Krea, sucked in his breath. 'We are in danger. They are coming, we must turn back.' He looked up towards the top of the ridge, his face pale. Suddenly, the earth began to vibrate. Krea's stallion reared in fear, and it was all she could do to keep the animal under control. Pancome held onto Krea's waist, nearly falling.

'Quick!' Ordered Ulric, 'we must hide, it's the Asur.'

They desperately searched for somewhere to conceal themselves. Ulric called to Kanji, but the dog had climbed higher up on the ridge. He called him again, his voice desperate for the animal to respond.

Krea let out a low whistle, trying to get Kanji's attention. The dog paused, his growl louder as he crouched even lower to the ground as if stalking prey. The vibration grew stronger, and the ground began to tremble. Krea let out another whistle. This time, the dog responded.

Ulric fought to hold his temper as his disobedient dog came to his side. Kanji had never deliberately disobeyed him like that before. They turned from the ridge, hastily making their retreat downhill, struggling to keep their panicked horses under control.

The ground began to shake violently, loosening rocks and stones that started to tumble down the hill. The horses whinnied in fright as they half slid, half ran, down the slope. Kacha pointed to a copse of trees that lay to the left of the ridge. It was not much to hide them, but it was all they had. Ulric and Krea followed the young warrior as they galloped towards their hiding place.

Ulric immediately dismounted, leading his horse in further before grabbing his dog. He did not trust him not to bark or growl. No sooner had they hidden themselves, a roaring could be heard. They looked up at the top of the ridge and gasped as they saw the Asur, an army of demons sitting astride beasts that resembled horses.

A horn sounded and Ulric felt the hair rise on the back of his neck. One of the Asur bent in its saddle, commanding the hound beside him to go search. The dog let out a blood curdling howl before racing down the ridge.

'They know we are here, Ulric,' Krea said in a low whisper.

'And they won't stop until they catch us.' Pancome said as his grip around Krea's waist tightened, a terrified look was on his face.

'Don't run,' ordered Kacha. Ulric briefly looked at the brave young man next to him. Kacha had reached for his sword, waiting for the hound to make its way to them. Krea also readied her weapon, while Ulric placed an arrow in the bow ready to take aim and fire the shaft into the animal.

The hound came closer. It had picked up the scent of the wolf and dog. Letting out an excited bark, it ran to the clump of trees. Ulric let his arrow go and watched it whistle threw the air before meeting its target. The hound gave a yelp before staggering and coming to a halt. It let out a growl before falling to its death.

'Now, we run,' whispered Kacha. Ulric and Krea needed no further urging, they turned their horses kicking them into a gallop.

Ulric didn't know how far or fast the Asur would trail them or how quick they would catch up, but he did not dare look back. Kacha led them towards the forest that had not yet been burned. Once again, humans were seeking the shelter and refuge of the forest that provided so much. Ulric gave a quick prayer to the Gods as they entered the dim light of the thick canopy of trees. He called out to his sister Ada for her help.

He could hear the distant horn of the Asur, they had been alerted to their presence after finding their hound shot dead by one of Ulric's arrows. Deeper and deeper, they went into the thick foliage and still Ada did not answer Ulric.

'Where is she? Pray to the Gods or we will die here!' Ulric's fear had been replaced by anger as he waited for his sister to respond. The horses were beginning to tire as they felt the earth vibrate from the advancing army that pursued them.

Kacha had started to slow, and Ulric dared a quick look over his shoulder. It seemed that the forest had closed in behind them providing a thick backdrop of leaves and branches. Soon, they reined the horses into a trot and then a walk. The three of them took another look from where they had come, all that could be seen was trees and shrubs. Ulric came to a halt, tilting his head to one side as he listened. Silence.

Kacha, Pancome and Krea also listened, nothing but silence. Even the birds had grown quiet. They waited. Nothing just quiet. Suddenly the trees began to rustle, their leaves rubbing together. Ulric looked up at them. Their tall trunks thick and impressive. The branches splayed open as if giving thanks to the Gods above for the life they gave them. Ulric noticed not every tree was the same they were all different in some way. A uniqueness that was breathtaking.

A new appreciation overwhelmed Ulric as he admired their beauty. Once again, they had helped save their lives. Dismounting, he walked over to the tree, remembering how he had once heard one speak when they had gone through the witch's forest. Placing his ear to the tree, he listened. The rustling grew more fervent.

'Follow the path that is made for you. Follow the path that is made for you. Follow the path that is made for you,' the tree chanted.

Ulric looked at the others who both gave him a puzzled look.

'What did the tree tell you?' Pancome asked.

'We have to follow the path.' Ulric answered.

'What path?' Kacha asked in an uncertain tone. Ulric shrugged as he looked around, he could not see any path.

As they scanned their surroundings something caught Kacha's eye. 'Look! Over there!' He pointed to where an almost concealed trail seemed to lead off to one side. They made their way towards it. The trail led to a large opening which appeared very similar to a cave, except that it wasn't. 'Ah, the forest have made us a tunnel that we can take the horses in. This will lead to our destination in no time. Trust the forest they are on our side,' Pancome said as he jumped down from behind Krea and walked to the front of the group venturing into the dark opening.

Elenore ran the comb through her hair. The comb was a luxury she could not live without. She had found a quiet spot where the river had paused to fill a large waterhole. It was a perfect place to bathe, and there had been no one there when she had arrived. Elenore sat semi-clothed she had taken the time to wash her hair and was enjoying the warmth of the summer sun that dried it. She had served the tea and excused herself, leaving Edyth with her son, the healer, and Sabin.

There had been a few revelations during Huxley's hypnosis. One was that they were close to the valley where they now hid, the other was that the Asur had a labyrinth of tunnels. She shuddered at the memory of Huxley screaming.

She also had learned how much Edyth despised her and Merek. A sadness overcame her when she remembered the look of hate in the small woman's eyes. She paused the combing of her long coppery hair, she thought she had heard something.

Turning, she saw Tallot and Flamma coming towards her. She immediately felt shy and awkward and quickly reached for her tunic. Her face blazed as the two men greeted her. She found it difficult to look at them and wondered if they had seen her nakedness.

'The healer said you might be here.' Flamma smirked as he ran his eyes over Elenore. Elenore looked up at the two men and she was taken aback at how much Flamma looked like his older brother. He was not much older than Merek had been when she had first met him and fallen in love.

'Yes, I decided to wash my hair and bathe.' She shifted uncomfortably, looking over at the waterhole.

'Hey Tallot, I think we should take a dip,' Flamma said. Without waiting for Tallot to answer, the young man threw off his tunic and jumped into the water. Tallot chuckled as he watched Flamma swim to the other side.

'He has a lot to learn. The first thing is to get over the jealousy he has for his brother. They are a lot alike, he reminds me of Merek,' Tallot told Elenore as he sat down beside her.

'Is Merek looking for me?' Elenore turned to the man next to her.

Tallot gave her a lopsided smile and shook his head. 'He had a big night, Elenore, sometimes it's good for a man to drink himself to oblivion.'

'That is not how a leader should behave, Tallot. He is not being responsible,' She retorted. Elenore bit her lip, her brow puckered into a tight frown. She suddenly wondered why they had been looking for her. As if Tallot had read her mind, he asked if she had spoken to Merek about the gratitude ceremony that was customary to pay thanks to the Gods.

She shook her head. 'I mentioned it to him but it's obvious he hasn't bothered to organise one.' She gave him a brief smile.

'Okay, well I guess I will have a chat to him when he decides to wake up.' Tallot replied. Elenore did not comment, instead she pulled her legs up under her chin, rounding herself into a ball as she looked over at Flamma in the water.

She could feel her baby, which brought a smile to her face.

'So, when do you think I will get a chance to talk to him? I mean, when do you think he will wake up?' She turned back to Tallot.

He held her gaze for a moment, before looking away. 'Elenore, your husband is a leader and warrior, we do not question his actions.'

Tallot's remark stung. 'I am his wife, Tallot, surely that counts for something.' She felt the hurt ignite her anger.

'You still have a lot to learn,' Tallot snickered. Elenore was surprised. Tallot had always been kind, but this was another side to him. But she knew he was a warrior, a former Protector. The group that would hunt and kill the Asur, they were meant to be hard.

'Hey!' shouted Flamma, 'are you coming in, Tallot?' Tallot stood, grinning. Stripping off his tunic and leaving his undergarment on, he went to join Flamma. Elenore watched them as they frolicked and splashed one another. She stood, leaving them to enjoy the water.

She made her way back to her tent and suddenly felt tired. The bathing had revived her, but now the warm sun and the encounter with Tallot had sapped her energy. She also felt the pangs of hunger. She decided to grab her basket and look for some berries and herbs before taking a nap.

The sun hovered close to its midway point as she made her way to the forest that flanked the outer edge of the valley. She had heard people say that there was an abundance of berries close to the forest edge and she was determined to pick a basket full. She noticed other women out gathering berries, wood, and herbs.

She knew Tallot was right, they really did need to organise a gratitude ceremony, and quickly. Else the Gods would remove their favour to those who were not grateful. The Gods had saved them and now provided not only shelter, but an abundance of food.

A warm breeze blew, ruffling her hair and blowing it gently behind her. It did not take long for her to fill her basket and collect some branches for the fire she would start later that day. The day had grown quite warm when she returned to her temporary home.

As she neared, she saw Merek and Amzi standing to one side they were laughing as they talked. Elenore felt her breath catch in her throat; her husband was becoming a stranger to her. Now she felt nervous even to approach him. The last few encounters had not been positive. Both men paused when she neared them, she nodded a hello before ducking in under the tent flap. She placed her things beside the furs and sighed. She half expected Merek to follow her inside, but he stayed outside with Amzi. She laid down on the furs. Tiredness overrode her curiosity about what the men outside were saying. As she lay there in the comfort of her bed, her eyes grew heavy and she felt herself fall into a deep, dreamless sleep.

The horses were hesitant at first to enter the gloom of the tunnel, but after some gentle persuasion they followed their human masters. Pancome felt confident as he led the others along the earthy passageway that seemed to twist and turn.

'Are you sure about this, Pancome?' Krea asked.

The older man chuckled. 'You will learn that the forest is our greatest ally.'

'We are grateful that they are on our side, Pancome,' replied Ulric. Even though the tunnel was dark, they were able to see through the gloom. Ulric once again tried to connect to Ada, but she remained quiet. He wondered if she was okay but quickly squashed the worry as soon as it came. He had to remain positive they would not survive on negative energy.

They travelled for what seemed an eternity before Pancome, who was leading them, came to an abrupt halt. 'We need to eat and rest.'

Ulric frowned. He could not detect any changes in the tunnel they had been walking in and wondered how the man knew when and why they had to stop. Pancome smiled at Ulric. 'Trust me, I have travelled these tunnels enough to know that we will be at your destination sooner than you think. We must conserve out energy and truth be told I am getting a little hungry.'

Ulric nodded. He would not argue with the things that made sense. They pulled out the dried meat and a water skin, relishing the short reprieve. It had been an eventful morning and the break allowed them to reflect on the past events.

Elenore woke to the shadows of a late afternoon sun. She sat up, wiping the sleep from her eyes. Her tent was gloomy and quiet. She could not hear Amzi or Merek anymore, and guessed they had left. She foggily wondered how long she had been asleep for. Stretching, she threw the furs to one side and picked up the water skin next to her. She drank and wiped her mouth when she had her fill.

Her stomach grumbled and she groaned inwardly; she always seemed hungry. Remembering the berries she had picked earlier, she stood and went to the basket she had placed in the corner of the tent. She ate all that she had picked and chastised herself that she would now have to pick more the following day. She made her way out of the tent and could hear the faint noise of people singing. She cocked her head. It seemed to be coming from the middle of the camp. She quickly made her way to where she could relieve herself before heading towards the direction of the noise.

It appeared that the whole camp had gathered. Elenore wondered if Merek had finally organised the gratitude ceremony, although it would have been at short notice. She saw the healer help set up large timber tables that had been built when they had first arrived. She could smell the roasting of meats and her mouth began to water. The berries had only placated her hunger.

'Ah, Elenore, I was wondering where you had gotten to,' she gave her a warm smile. 'Merek wants to appease the Gods. I think sometimes when a man relieves stress via the red drink it helps seek clarity.' Serenity let out a soft laugh. Elenore watched her as she adorned the table with native flowers. 'I have not stopped since you left. Zuri came to tell me it is time we hold the gratitude ceremony and that Merek had ordered it to be done this evening. I had to send out a whole party of people to pick the herbs and fruits we would need.'

Elenore suddenly realised why there had been so many people picking earlier that day when she had gone to get berries. 'The Gods must be happy that Merek finally organised something. The hunting party was very successful indeed. We shall eat well tonight, dear.'

She turned to face Elenore giving her another warm smile. Elenore forced herself to return her smile she suddenly felt insignificant.

She had become a stranger to the people she shared her life with. They were her community, but she felt like she didn't exist or even matter anymore. No one had consulted her. Even Tallot had not told her. He had been indifferent to her at the watering hole.

She did not know what to say to the medicine woman. Her mind seemed to have gone blank.

'Here you are, Serenity! I have brought more flowers.' It was Zuri, the tall, strikingly attractive, blonde woman. The energy she brought with her was captivating and she walked with confidence and ease. 'Ah, Elenore, we have not had a chance to formerly meet.' Elenore thought this odd as there had been occasions when she had been introduced to her, and when she herself had forced Merek to introduce her.

Elenore was puzzled, but forced herself to smile. 'Hello, Zuri, lovely to see you.' It was all she could manage as she struggled to control her irritation.

Zuri ran her sharp eyes over Elenore lingering over her abdomen … 'Are you with child?' Elenore blushed. 'Yes, you are! Oh, praise to the Gods, Merek has not mentioned a thing.' She paused for a moment. 'Wait, does he know? He doesn't, does he?' A smirk spread across her face.

Elenore felt the colour drain from her face; she swallowed, her mind was in a complete spin. She wanted to run away, disappear, she felt so humiliated. 'Do not worry, Elenore, your secret is safe with me.' She winked.

The healer could feel the tension between the two women and quickly came to Elenore's aid. 'Elenore, would you be so kind to go to my tent and grab me my bag of herbs? I think it would be wise that I season the meat, it will be even more delicious.' Elenore nodded and smiled gratefully at the healer. She turned and made her way to Serenity's camp, not saying another word to the beautiful woman who had made her feel like a fool.

When Elenore returned with the herbs she noticed Zuri had left. Relief washed over her, she had taken an instant dislike to the woman.

'Ah thank you, Elenore, these will come in handy.' Serenity beamed at Elenore.

'I am glad I could be of some help.'

The healer tisked. 'Do not let others make you feel ashamed, Elenore, but…' – she took a breath – 'I think it will be wise that you tell Merek of the child you carry.'

Elenore nodded. 'I have been planning to but, well I just haven't found the right time.'

The healer placed her hands on Elenore's shoulders. 'There will be no right time. It is best you tell Merek, if anyone tells him it will cause a rift, a mistrust.'

Elenore held the medicine woman's gaze. She was right. Elenore knew deep down she had to tell Merek. 'I know,' she whispered.

'Good,' Serenity said, turning back to the table. She started to rearrange some of the flowers that embellished the tables, talking to herself as she did. Elenore watched her for a moment before excusing herself. She went in search of Merek.

People were starting to notice her pregnancy, and he still did not know he was going to have another child. It confirmed the growing distance between them. Since coming to the valley four weeks ago, their relationship had begun to fall apart. She walked towards the huge fire that had been lit in the centre of the camp.

She saw Tallot standing with Flamma and another woman, who stood to one side. Tallot saw Elenore and called to her to join them. She considered ignoring him but knew it would look rude. Reluctantly, she made her way towards him.

'Elenore, I want you to meet someone.' Elenore could tell that Tallot had indulged too much in the red drink. She wondered why he had been acting so different lately. He had not been drunk earlier at the watering hole, so she knew it was not the wine that had changed him. She gave him a slight nod but did not say anything.

Flamma chuckled, he too must be feeling the effects of the red drink.

'This is Ganika, she is Zuri's cousin.' Tallot gestured to the woman standing next to him. Ganika smiled at Elenore and offered her hand, which Elenore took. She was young, around the same age as her own daughter.

'Pleased to meet you, Elenore. I have heard so much about you, and trust me, it is all good.'

Elenore gave a soft chuckle. 'That is nice to hear. Thank you, Ganika.'

Tallot wrapped his arm around the young girl as if claiming her, which surprised Elenore. 'Have you seen Merek?' she asked.

Tallot and Flamma exchanged a look. Tallot replied, 'Yeah, he was over with the hunting party. They are over the back there.' Tallot pointed in the direction at the back of the camp.

Elenore thanked him and left. Her thoughts tumbled over one another, and she was not sure how she should feel. The last few days had been an emotional rollercoaster and once again she longed for a home, a real home, like the one they had fled. When would all this be over? She sent a silent prayer to the Gods that it would end soon. The gloom of dusk descended upon the cabin, causing shadows to dance and pirouette to the soft candles that graced the room. Ada sipped the tea its unique taste stimulating her tastebuds. She glanced at Anja. Her grandmother had not been the same since Eijanbrook had left the living world. A sadness was now permanently etched on her face, it would seem an eternity before she would be reunited with her soul mate.

Ada had come to the realisation that Anja would be the new Seer. It made sense. Anja embodied all the qualities of a great Seer, and she would be the first woman to fill such an important role. Ada knew she should feel honoured by the Gods, but her torment lay with the loss of her husband. The privilege of being the first female Seer was tempered by the knowledge that she would have to wait many years to be reunited with Eijanbrook.

Anja turned towards Ada, a puzzled look on her face. Ada blushed and shifted her position. The Seer asked Ludwig to bring a pot of the tea, it was going to be a long night and there was much work to be done.

'Ulric and his group have entered the tunnel that will lead them to Shakurta village. The forest has come to our aid yet again. But the Asur are getting better at mind travel, they were able to sense Ulric. I feel they are keeping a close guard on the Shakurta village. That is not the only thing that I am concerned with.' He took a sip of the tea and pursed his lips. 'Ada, Ulric was unable to reach you when he called, *begged*, for your help.'

Ada frowned. She had not picked up on any of Ulric's vibrations and an unsettled feeling descended upon her. She met Ogda's gaze and swallowed.

'I assure you, I did not pick up on any vibrations or sense anything.'

'Hmm.' Ogda rubbed his chin. 'The Seer of the Shakurta village must be able to block some vibrations. This too is disturbing.'

'What do you mean?' Ada asked.

'Yes, what does that mean? I have never heard of a Seer being able to not only tap into someone else's vibration but to prevent it from being sent out.' Anja added.

'This is what worries me. I have only known one other Seer who was able to do this.' Ogda sighed. 'He lived many years ago and was said to be one of the original descendants of the first line of Seers. He was from the Shakurta village. It seems logical that the current Seer may possess the same trait, being that he has a genetic link.' Ogda rested his head on his hand.

'We have to tread carefully,' Anja said.

'Yes, we must have our wits about us. No doubt the Seer of Shakurta village will be expecting us, it already seems he is one step ahead of us.' Ogda encouraged the women to drink more of the tea. The fear that he had felt earlier had come back and he realised it really had never left. He acknowledged the feeling, it had been something new and now he had grown used to it like an old friend.

Ogda picked up the teapot and poured another cup of the special drink. Ada and Anja both took a large swallow of their tea.

'I don't know how many of the Asur can mind travel. It is very possible that the Seer has tried to train as many as he can it is a very important tool—'

'Wait,' Ada interrupted. Anja threw her granddaughter a look of reproach. 'How can a Seer train a beast? I mean, they are hideous and ugly, I don't know how they could even learn that.'

Ogda held up his hand for Ada to stop. 'I can understand what you are saying, but the Seer from Shakurta village has found a way. That is what makes them dangerous.'

Ada opened her mouth before closing it again. They did not have the time to argue this, and she knew it would cross the boundary of respect. Ogda watched Ada and nodded when she decided to withdraw from further questioning. 'So, we understand what our roles are? It is important that we do. Once Pancome has spoken to the ancient tree and we see what chain of events that it sets off we must leave.' The Seer cleared his throat. 'There is something I need to tell you, something I seem to have forgotten. We must go to the villages that Merek did not get a chance to go to and tell them to leave. We will do this after Ada has warned Ulric of the Seer of the Shakurta village. It will need all three of us to do this. We need to recruit as many as we can. Ada, you will be on guard for what the ancient tree knows of Dardanos. If their Seer flees, you must try and locate her. This is vital. Once we eliminate her it will be victory!' Ogda looked up at the roof of the cabin when he said this, as if to confirm with the powers above for it to be true. He sat up straighter and a smile spread across his face. 'Are we ready?'

CHAPTER THIRTEEN

Betrayal

Love lost, fire ignited, They'll face the storm I become.

Ulric

The damp smell of earth permeated Ulric's nostrils and he knew he would be able to smell the smell for a long time to come. He decided to dismount and lead his horse, holding a torch in front of him to fight the dark shadows that were hungry to eat the light. Pancome followed him in silence. They had not said much since entering the dark tunnel, allowing them to reflect on the day's events. Even the dog and wolf seemed reserved.

As Ulric walked, he felt his sister it was like welcoming the comfort of an old friend. He felt relieved when he felt her vibration.

'You are getting better, Ulric.'

Ulric smiled. *'Where have you been Ada? I needed you earlier and you did not come.'* His question barely masked his irritation.

'Please forgive me, we have another enemy who is working with the Asur. He is the Seer of Shakurta village. You must be careful he is the one who alerted them to you and stopped your vibration from reaching me.' Ulric frowned when he heard Ada say this. *'The Seer and Anja will try and stop their Seer from knowing about you when you reach the village however, you must make haste to see the ancient tree. Bring Pancome and he will help convince the tree of the betrayal from its own Seer. We must be prepared in what happens next. Ogda, Anja and I will infiltrate the minds of the recruits that Merek was to find. We do not have much time dear brother. After tonight Anja and Ogda will travel physically to Merek.'*

'What about you, sister? What is your role after this?' Ada did not answer for a moment. *'Ada?'*

'*I am to find Dardanos, the queen of the Asur. The ancient tree will be of help.*'

Ulric rubbed the back of his neck, unsure of how to feel about what Ada had just told him. He felt torn between the natural urge to protect her and the knowledge that she had to do this; the future of mankind depended upon it.

'*Can you promise me one thing?*' He could see her smile and nod in his mind.

'*Yes, brother. Tell me, what is it you will make me promise?*'

Ulric chuckled. '*Please take care and do not take unnecessary risks.*'

Ada let out a soft laugh, Ulric shook his head a grin on his face.

'*Of course, Ulric. I mean, I promise by the grace of the Gods.*' Ulric could still hear her laughter in his mind as he and his group made their way through the long dark tunnel.

Elenore made out the form of her husband as she neared the centre of the camp. Her heart began to beat faster as she approached. Amzi and Zuri were talking and drinking the red drink. Elenore paused, she felt herself wanting to turn around and run the other way. What is wrong with me? This is my husband. I am carrying his child, Elenore chastised herself. Taking a deep breath, she came closer, ready to confront her husband. She saw Amzi nudge Merek and point when she came closer.

Zuri gave her a sardonic smile. 'Oh, look who is here.'

Anger welled within Elenore at the greeting and it took all her strength to squash it. 'Merek, I have been looking for you.' She gave him a tight smile.

Merek turned to Elenore, but his face was twisted with an anger he barely contained. 'Oh! Here you are! I guess you have something to tell me!' Merek moved in front of Elenore, his voice like a low growl.

Elenore took a step back. She looked at Zuri, an even deeper hatred started to grow. 'Don't look at her, Elenore, look at me. I am your husband and you have been keeping this a secret! What were you thinking, bringing a life into this forsaken world?!' Merek had started to shout, his anger now unleashed.

Elenore felt her own tide of anger surge and move forward. 'What do you mean? You had a part to play too!'

Merek grabbed his wife by the arm, pulling her away. Elenore resisted, but was no match from her fury driven husband. 'You are hurting me, Merek!' Elenore pleaded.

'What have you done Elenore?! Don't you think you have hurt me?'

'How? How, Merek? How have I hurt you? You ignore me and hang out with them.' Elenore gestured towards Zuri and Amzi, who were watching the couple quarrel. Elenore threw them a dirty look as she tried to calm her anger and slow her racing heart.

Merek pulled his wife in closer to him and Elenore could feel his breath on her face. 'You have lied to me, betrayed me, and you are supposed to be my wife! How could you? I don't want any more children, there is no future for them. Do you understand? You are a foolish woman, Elenore!'

Elenore managed to extract herself from Merek's grasp. Tears ran down her face. Her heart was crushed. Merek had never spoken to her like that before. She felt the ring on her finger and pulled at it. At first it would not budge, stubborn in its resistance to leave her finger it had occupied for so long. She struggled, wriggling and twisting until eventually is slid off. Triumphant, she thew the ring at Merek.

'I am not your wife. And you are not fit to be the father of our children!' Elenore turned and ran, ignoring Merek's shouts that rang out behind her.

She collapsed on the soft furs and cried; her heart broken. She did not know her husband anymore he was not the man she had fallen in love with and married. Tears ran down her face like a river unleashed. As she sobbed, she did not hear the tent flap lift and open.

Elenore was startled when the healer spoke to her, her voice soothing and comforting in the dark. 'Hush now Elenore, he will come round. He has the weight of the world on his shoulders. Please quiet now, child.'

Elenore pushed herself up and squinted in the dark. She could make out the silhouette of the healer sitting at the base of her bed. Serenity moved forward, allowing Elenore to reach out and embrace her releasing another round of fresh tears.

Villages, or what remained of them, had been burned to a pile of charred ashes. The Majestic Forest that graced the land beside Eijanbrook's village had suffered the same fate. It had stretched and snaked itself all the way to the east coast before turning and heading south. As they looked at the new change in the landscape, a sadness settled upon Ogda, Ada and Anja. A once thriving biodiversity of plants, insects, birds, and animals had been reduced to dust and blackened stumps.

The devastation continued for miles; nature had suffered a huge loss. Occasionally, an old tree was sighted, standing forlorn in the new barren land. Ogda tisked. It hurt to see such beauty wiped from the face of the earth. A beauty that had taken nature years to create, a tapestry of contrast between flora and fauna, a delicate balance that had taken a millennium to design. Some of the forest was still smouldering, and the trees that had been spared seemed to look on despondently. No birds graced the sky, no insects, no call of the wild creatures that had called it home. The Asur had been victorious in wiping out a large chunk of the forest.

Ogda knew the trees would seek revenge on the evil that had destroyed their leafy family. This would work in the favour of the humans. Ogda, Anja and Ada travelled far and wide, finding nothing but a barren landscape.

'Are you sure there are any people left?' Ada asked.

'We must have hope, Ada. Without hope all is lost,' Ogda told her gently.

Ada decided not to comment; she was growing tired of the dreary scenery lit by the full moon above. She didn't think that anyone or any of the forest was left.

'There has to be something left. They can't have caused so much destruction in such a short space of time.' Ada grumbled.

Anja knew Ada was growing tired of finding nothing and was running out of patience. Her granddaughter reminded her of youngest son, Flamma. She wanted the night to be over so she could be reunited with the family she still had.

'There!' Ogda interrupted her thoughts. They swept their gaze to a part of the forest that had not been torched. A patch of green that welcomed and gave hope, a sanctuary for all those that had fled. They could hear the fervent whispering of the trees, a gesture of salutations.

A sense of relief washed over Ogda. A niggle of doubt had been creeping in and it had been a challenge to prevent it from morphing into something more. A village nestled within the forest, a human nest among the foliage. It did not take long for the three of them to infiltrate and spawn dreams to flee and seek refuge in the mountains that lay far to the north. The people were fully aware of the predator that hunted them. It would only be a matter of time before it was their turn to be slaughtered and burned.

They continued further along the forest corridor, encountering more people that were either trying to escape and outrun the Asur or had homes within the green corridor. The Asur had made the job of the Ogda, Ada, and Anja easier as many were grateful for the offer of hope, a chance of survival. Ogda urged his assistants to travel faster. Time was catching up and Ada would need to travel back to Shakurta village to listen to the ancient tree.

The Asur had not travelled very south. It appeared they had concentrated on the north, sweeping to the east, making the exception of Shakurta village. Ogda knew their next attack would be to the South. They were striking more quickly, intent on ridding the world of humans as swiftly as possible. The realisation that the people they could not get to would wake to a certain death weighed heavily upon Ogda.

'You cannot save them all. It is time for the girl with the hair the colour of snow to return to Shakurta village.' The voice vibrated inside the Seer's mind, surprising him. He searched for the entity that was a mystery, but to no avail.

'Did he speak with you?' Ada asked.

Ogda frowned and nodded. 'We need to leave. We have done what we can.' The Seer turned, a heavy sense of loss weighed upon him. The voice was right; he could not save them all.

Serenity and Elenore made their way to the tables adorned with food. Elenore took her place at the banquet table. She had washed her face and the healer had tied her hair into a loose braid. She tried not to look at the faces that turned when she had made her appearance. It would be easy for someone to see she had been crying and that she was not sitting next to her husband. It had taken all her strength to agree to the healer's request to come and eat, and be part of the gratitude ceremony.

Whispers and gossip would surely follow the next day and Elenore felt a deep sense of shame. It had been a long day and she was exhausted.

The moon was starting to rise, casting silver streaks across the heavy timber tables. The healer made her way to the front of the people. It was traditional for a Seer to be Speaker, but times were different, and she was the closest they had to a Seer.

Serenity cleared her throat. 'Good evening all that follow Merek, son of Eijanbrook. We are gathered here this evening to give gratitude for the shelter, food, and chance to live that the Gods have given us. We have been through tumultuous times, and I thank you all for having the courage to stand by your leader and have the strength to carry on.' A quiet cheer rang out making the healer pause. 'Merek will offer the prayer for gratitude before we can eat the foods that have been given to us. I guess we are all a little hungry.' The crowd gave a murmur of laughter. 'Merek, please come and speak to your people.'

Merek took his place beside the healer, thanking her. She took a seat not far away; speeches and announcements would resume after the meal. Merek looked over his people, his hair tied back in its traditional bun, matching the long beard that also was tied the same way. He offered them a smile, which earned him an applaud. He waited for the crowd to become silent again.

'Here we are, in the valley provided by the Gods. I know we have been here for a few weeks now but before we send a prayer to them, I want to say a couple of things. First, the forest that provides us with so much must be respected. We take only what we need. No tree is to be cut down without permission. I will be organising groups of people who will oversee different jobs. It is important we work together. Our great Seer will be here soon.'

A gasp rang out among the people. They had no knowledge that he was coming to them, or even if he was still alive. This new information revived their spirits even more. Merek let them talk for a moment before demanding silence. They turned their attention back to their leader.

'We will eat and drink in excess tonight, but come the new day we will have work to do. We must remain united – I cannot stress that enough. You have all gone through so much and we still have a long way to go.' Another murmur ran through the crowd. 'Silence!' Merek demanded as he clapped his hands to get their attention. 'Let's give a prayer to the Gods that provide for us. I am getting hungry!' More laughter followed before being quickly silenced when Merek held up his hand.

Elenore watched her husband. He had avoided her when he had swept his gaze over the people seated. She struggled to hold back a fresh flow of tears and forced herself to look down at the plate as they started to pray.

They ate hungrily. It had been a long time since there had been an abundance of food. Plates of steaming meat were passed along with cups filled with the red drink. Amzi and his people were congratulated in their foresight for bringing so much wine. It had been classed as a necessity as they struggled to carry so much of it on their journey. Now their efforts were rewarded.

Elenore shook her head when the man next to her offered to fill her cup. She ate her meal in silence and noticed that Merek went to sit between Amzi and Zuri. He did not look in her direction and she felt hurt. Her thoughts strayed to her children. She longed to see Ada and Ulric again. Their return was coming closer, giving her something to look forward to.

The healer, as promised, stood to make the announcements and Elenore soon discovered that she was not the only one expecting new life. She held her breath as Serenity went through the list of families that would be adding new additions come the following spring. She was unsure if her name would be mentioned, and she stole a quick glance over at Merek. He seemed more interested in the food he was eating than who was having children. Serenity did not announce Elenore's pregnancy. Elenore was not sure if she was relieved or envious that other women were able to reveal their pregnancies while Elenore had to hide hers.

'Hey, how come you're not sitting next to Merek? You are his wife, are you not?' The man beside her glanced at her with his eyebrow raised, interrupting her thoughts.

She forced herself to smile at him. 'He needed to discuss things with Amzi, and I was ah' – she cleared her throat – 'I was running a little late.'

The man did not reply, simply nodding and going back to his meal. Elenore felt herself blush and it was all she could do from excusing herself from the table and fleeing back to her tent. If she did that, it would confirm the man's suspicions that there was something not right between the leader and his wife.

Serenity was now declaring the marriages to take place in the spring or when they had settled. Elenore heard Sabin and Edyth's names, and once again stole another quick glance at Merek. He had paused eating his meal, and a faint smile crossed his face when he heard Sabin's name. He did not look at Elenore, but she continued to gaze at him, unable to look away. She found it absurd that they were not able to talk as they once had. A rift had formed between them.

Elenore thought back to Serenity's advice- be patient and keep trying to talk to Merek. She assumed he went to the healer after their last altercation and Serenity had refused to reveal what they had discussed. Frustration gnawed at Elenore. Her brows puckered into a tight frown as she realised that Merek had asked her not to reveal Elenore's pregnancy.

The man sitting next to her had followed her gaze and chuckled softly, 'I think our leader might have a liking to Amzi's sister. I don't blame him, she is beautiful.'

Elenore threw the man a hard look. 'I think you need to hold your tongue.' Elenore stood and left the table, it was more than she could take.

Back at their tent, she placed the iron kettle over the fire and sat on the log that faced it. She did not have much tea left and made a mental note to ask the healer if she knew where she could pick the herbs to make some more. She heard footsteps approaching and quickly turned to see who it was.

Tallot stepped from the shadows. 'What are you doing here?' he asked.

Elenore frowned. 'I live here, remember?'

She wanted to be left alone and felt the prick of irritation. 'You should be with Merek, supporting him, not sitting here making tea.'

Elenore stood and faced the warrior. 'It is none of your business what I am doing. And if Merek needs my support, maybe he should come and talk to me!' Her voice rose, and she curled her hands into tight fists.

'Easy, Elenore, I am just being a friend. People are beginning to talk and that is not good.'

Elenore thought about the man that had sat next to her and she groaned inwardly. Tallot was right, people were talking. This was not a good sign, especially when they were in the fight of their lives. Tallot took a step closer. 'How about we start over? I am sorry I came across harsh. I just think you need to work on your marriage or—' He stopped. When it was obvious that he would not finish what he was going to say, Elenore prompted him to continue. 'Look, Norrie, a man can get distracted, and I think you need to be with him.'

Elenore stiffened. 'What are you saying, Tallot?'

He looked away, before returning her gaze. 'Look, forget it. Just try and be with him, or at least seen with him. The people need to see it, it will help them feel confident.' He turned to walk away before Elenore reached out and grabbed his arm. He frowned. 'What is it?'

'Wait for me. I will come with you, and you can take me to him.'

The warrior hesitated for a moment, then nodded. Elenore quickly snuffed out the fire, 'Okay, let's go.' She forced a smile, which he returned.

The moon had risen high in the sky, a silver beacon against a cloak of darkness. Tallot and Elenore walked in silence. Most of the adults were either settling children to sleep so as they could continue the festivities without demands while others had already begun. Elenore heard a woman's voice ring out in a traditional ceremonial song and it gave her a sense of comfort.

'It has been so long since I have heard that song,' she sighed. 'I cannot wait until all this is over and we can finally settle again.'

Tallot did not answer instead he had come to a halt. Elenore noticed he was looking over towards the group standing not far from them. Merek was standing next to Zuri, his arm around her waist. At first Elenore did not comprehend what she was seeing. She shook her head, but the image did not leave. She opened her mouth and closed it again. Jealousy, hurt and envy, all entwined, coursed through her. Tallot looked at her, waiting for a response, but she just shook her head.

'We have come this far, I am tired of running away. Let us get it over with.' Elenore pushed past Tallot and made her way to her husband. Merek turned when he heard Elenore approach. A guilty look crossed his face when his saw his wife.

'So, you have decided to come and talk to me,' he said mockingly.

Elenore ignored his remark. 'I knew I would find you with her.' Elenore kept her tone even and looked at Merek directly.

He forced a smile, grabbing her arm and turning her around. 'We can't talk here.'

She let him guide her back to their tent, not saying a word. Merek followed Elenore into the tent, his anger was barely under control. 'What are you doing, Elenore?!'

'Maybe I should ask you that?' She yelled back at him. He shook his head, clenching and unclenching his fist. He began to pace the small space. 'You won't talk to me, I have to constantly look for you and then I find you with another woman.'

'Quiet!' Merek stopped his pacing, anger on his face. Elenore felt tears well and she grew annoyed at herself for being weak. 'This is ridiculous!' Merek turned and left the tent.

Elenore stood for a moment before following him. He stood just outside looking up at the sky. 'Merek we can't fight anymore.' Elenore took a step closer to him. He remained quiet and did not look at her.

'Where is your ring?' The question took her by surprise, and she frowned. She remembered she had thrown it at him but did not know where it had ended or if he had retrieved it.

'I am not sure.' Merek turned and looked at his wife. He still loved her, but he was not ready to forgive her for concealing her pregnancy. He did not want any more children; the world was full of evil. Taking a deep breath, he closed his eyes. 'We must be apart for a while I need time to think. I have enough on my plate without this—' he opened his eyes and gestured towards her belly.

'Where are you going to go?' Elenore felt a wave of shock wash over her.

'I don't know. Just don't come looking for me. I will ask Tallot to watch out for you.' Without looking at her he left the way they had come.

They followed the tunnel as it wound and coursed underground. 'How will we know when we have reached our destination?' Krea asked her nephew.

'The trees will guide us and show us a way out,' Pancome answered for Ulric.

Ulric smiled at the older man. 'You have your answer, Krea.'

She frowned but did not comment it seemed they had been walking for an eternity and doubt began to cloud her mind. Tiredness weighed her down. They had been searching for days before finding Pancome and she longed for a soft bed. She was surprised that she was feeling the way she was, as she had always prided herself on being a strong warrior. She cast a quick glance at Kacha, but his face remained expressionless. He was disciplined and rarely showed emotion. She thought about his future marriage to Ada, they suited one another in a way: both were indifferent and kept their feelings to themselves. Both were determined, though Ada was somewhat headstrong and both at times appeared withdrawn and silent.

Krea sighed. The world had changed so much, it still felt like an ongoing nightmare. Krea turned her thoughts to her father, his sacrifice had been an effort to give his family and the people he led a chance to survive. She missed him and she knew her mother must be missing him immensely. Nothing would ever be the same again.

Krea felt an enormous sadness, tears threatened. She had been close to her father, and she had not had the time to grieve they had been so focused on hunting the Asur. She stopped walking and felt the wolf lick her hand, picking up on her emotions.

Ulric turned to look back. Noticing Krea had stopped, he frowned. 'Are you okay?'

'I need to rest,' was all that she could manage. She slid down the back of the side of the tunnel and placed her head in her hands. Ulric made his way back to her concern etched on his face.

'Krea?' He bent down next to her.

'Please, Ulric, I just need to rest for a while.'

'We don't have a lot of time.' She did not answer him, and he soon realised she was crying softly.

Pancome came over to where they sat. 'I will sit with her for a bit.

I think I have an idea what the problem is. It's okay, a short reprieve will do us good. We can have a bite to eat it will help lift our spirits.'

Ulric nodded reluctantly and went to the saddle bags to pull out some of the dried meat they had taken with them. They ate in silence, reflecting on their own inner thoughts. When the meat had been finished and they all had a drink from the water skins they started off again.

Pancome held the torch up higher and peered into the shadows. He could make out a faint light in the distance. 'Ulric, I think we are close!' Ulric handed his reins to Kacha and made his way to Pancome. 'There, do you see the light?' He pointed towards the front of the tunnel holding the torch up for Ulric to see. Ulric squinted, hoping that Pancome was right. He sucked in his breath, there in distance was a faint shade of grey.

'I think you are right, Pancome. We are getting closer, we must hurry.' They made their way to the light with new enthusiasm, hoping they had finally made it to Shakurta village.

Elenore had sat by the fire for most of the night, going over and over what Merek had told her. She had found it hard to comprehend at first and she wondered when she would wake up from the nightmare she was having. As the first streaky fingers of day began to grace the sky she decided to go back to her tent. Exhaustion was replacing the hurt and she longed to close her eyes and fall into a dreamless sleep. As she took a sip from the waterskin she heard someone approaching. She quickly pulled her hair back into a ponytail and rubbed her face to rub away the tiredness.

'Elenore?' She paused before opening the tent flap. Taking a breath, she pushed back the fabric. Flamma stood waiting for her, a jeering look on his face.

She frowned and forced herself to smile, she had not recognised his voice.

'Hello, Flamma, can I help you?'

He smiled at her, 'I am not sure if you can.' He paused. 'Is Merek here?'

Elenore bristled. Flamma must surely know that Merek was not at their tent. He was trying to taunt her. The separation between

Merek and Elenore would have pleased him, and she wondered if he would ever overcome his envy. She forced herself to smile, meeting his gaze directly.

'I am sure you already know the answer, Flamma. I am on my own.'

'Oh, that is a shame. I mean' – he held up a ring, it shimmered in the early morning sun – 'I was trying to find out if this was his.'

Elenore took a step closer. 'Can I have a look, please? I lost mine last night. Where did you find it?'

Flamma snatched the ring away. 'Are you sure it is not Merek's? I mean, he isn't wearing one either.'

Elenore struggled to keep her temper in check. 'Flamma, please show me the ring.'

Flamma shook his head and looked out over the valley. 'What if it is Merek's?' He asked as he turned back to look at Elenore.

Elenore took another step towards him. 'Stop playing games, you stupid boy!' She could not take it any longer, her temper had reached boiling point.

'Did you call me stupid? You are the stupid one!'

'Why did you come here, Flamma? To mock me. Go and talk to your brother. You won't get any answers from me!' Elenore had begun to yell. 'Now either give me the ring, or leave!'

Flamma took a long look at Elenore before throwing the ring into the fire pit. 'Go fetch,' he said, laughing.

'Leave!' Elenore repeated.

Flamma took one last look at her before he turned and left. Elenore watched him leave. She felt her pulse throb inside her head and her mouth had gone dry. Flamma could be dangerous, his jealousy was making him bitter.

Pray to the Gods, we have enough enemies, she thought.

She went over to the fire pit where he had thrown the ring. It gleamed and winked among the ashes. She grabbed a stick and prised it from the embers. She blew gently on it for it to cool. She was unsure whether it was hers or Merek's, but she knew that they were both engraved to tell them apart. After the ring was cool enough, she held it up to the light. Squinting she made out her name. Flamma was right, the ring was Merek's.

They had given each other a ring with their name on it: a symbol that they would always be together, united. She sighed. She did not want to cry, she had shed enough tears. She felt an emptiness, a deep sadness she had never felt so alone in all her life.

Questions began to rise and begged to be answered: How did Flamma have Merek's ring? Why wasn't Merek wearing it? And where did Flamma get it?

As Elenore sat down on the log another thought came into her mind: What if Flamma starts spreading rumours? She groaned. The nightmare was far from over.

Daylight filtered in from a huge, gaping hole. Giant tree roots splayed like latticework towards the end of the tunnel.

'The trees have created this opening. Praise the Gods, they are helping us.' Pancome stood, looking up at the mesh of tendrils that hung from the dirt ceiling.

'We must hurry,' Ulric urged them.

The daylight was blinding, and they waited until their eyes had become accustomed to the brightness. A thick canopy of trees surrounded them, and a fervent rustling could be heard.

Pancome smiled. 'They are speaking to us.'

The group looked around; the forest was breathtaking. Ancient trees reached up to the sky, their branches spread in all directions. Birds sang and darted between the leaves, and the buzz of insects filled the air while butterflies hovered. The woods had morphed into a throng of activity. They soaked up the forest and all its grace and glory. A deep connection could be felt between it and the humans. A relationship that was mutual. As they basked in the splendour of nature, they did not hear the approach of warriors.

A group of thirty men dashed out of the undergrowth, swords and arrows drawn. They circled the newcomers.

'Please, we mean you no harm,' Ulric said as he motioned for Kacha and Krea to lower their swords. The dog and wolf growled as they watched the newcomers warily. Ulric tried to keep his thoughts neutral. Thanks to Ada's warning, he knew the Seer of the village would be expecting them, and trying to infiltrate his thoughts.

A large warrior walked his horse over to where they stood. 'The Seer said you would come.'

'We do not want any trouble,' Ulric told the huge man.

He merely nodded before motioning for his men to take their weapons. They followed them deep into the thick forest. An enormous village spread itself through the thick woodland, cleverly entwined with the forest. People came out to look at the foreigners, whispering and snickering as they were led through their city of flora. An enormous hut stood some distance away from a massive tree. It was the largest tree the group had ever seen, breathtaking in its appearance. It rose like a giant beacon from the earth, and Ulric realised that this was the ancient tree Ada had been telling him about. He had not expected it to stand behind the Seer's home, but it made sense that the custodians of the forest would need to protect their most precious and treasured asset.

A morbidly obese man sat on overly stuffed cushion. His hair was shaved apart from a lock that ran down to the base of his skull. Strange tattoos crisscrossed his body and a thick leather choker wrapped itself around his neck. Ulric felt intimidated by the man's appearance. He had never been a warrior, nor ever desired to be one. Once again he wondered why he had been chosen.

'You doubt the task that has been given to you.'

Ulric frowned and turned to see a small man sitting cross legged, not far from the enormous man. He smiled a toothless grin when Ulric turned to look at him. Kanji let out a low growl. This only made the man laugh louder.

'Kanji,' Ulric called the dog to quieten. The dog ignored him instead he continued to stare and let out a low grumbling, the wolf joined in. The small man threw his head back laughing.

'There is something not right here,' whispered Kacha. Ulric did not take his eyes off the Seer. He could feel pure evil ooze from the man.

The Seer stopped his laughter to stare at the people in front of him. 'You have a nerve, waltzing in here. Didn't she warn you we are the most ancient people on earth?'

The merriment had vanished instead a wicked look covered the face of the Seer. Ulric glanced at the men that surrounded the Seer including the leader who remained silent. 'We are custodians of the

Majestic Forest the most ancient people of all. The Gods have chosen us we are caretakers of the world.'

'Well than you must know that an evil force is burning and tearing down the forest and wreaking havoc by slaughtering people and burning down the villages.' Pancome had stepped forward, he could not remain quiet any longer. Ulric did not blame him he had witnessed and seen so much. The Seer narrowed his gaze turning his attention to the older man.

The Seer nodded to the warriors who had brought the group to him. They grabbed Pancome and began to drag him away.

'Where are you taking him?' Ulric took a step forward, Krea and Kacha both reached out and took hold of him holding him back. The wolf and dog let off a chorus of howls and barks.

'You think you can just come here and try and take away what is ours? You are mistaken, son of Merek. I am the Seer adviser to Takeo and to the forest of the Gods!'

The Seer nodded to one of the warriors who stepped forward and grabbed Kanji. The dog growled and snapped, trying to defend itself as it was lifted by the warrior. Ulric rushed towards his beloved companion, but it was too late. The warrior grinned as he ran the knife along the canine's throat, slitting him from ear to ear.

'No!!' Ulric called out. The warrior let the dog fall to the ground.

Kacha grabbed Ulric pulling him away. 'You will pay! I swear you will pay!' Ulric roared at the Seer.

'Take them away, they are getting on my nerves.' The Seer told the warriors. Ulric pushed at the warrior as he seized him by the arm, roughly shoving him towards where they had first entered the village. They were led from the forest, and their horses were seized. The warrior that had slain Kanji tossed the dog's collar at Ulric's feet. They were left with nothing but the clothes on their backs as they were abandoned at the edge of the thick woodland.

Ulric sank to his knees and tears streamed down his face. He held the collar close to his heart as a heavy sense of despair descended upon him. He could not get the image of his beloved dog out of his mind.

Kacha and Krea left him alone to grieve if only for a short while. The day had just begun and already it seemed it would be one full of sadness and loss.

CHAPTER FOURTEEN

The Newcomers

Some call it a curse, we call it power. We dance with the devil to the tune of forbidden desires.

Seer from Shakurta Village

They had settled back in their bodies as the sun rose, their minds troubled. 'Ada, you cannot leave yet. The Seer of Shakurta village knows who Ulric is. I think I have underestimated him. He is much more powerful than I ever imagined.' Dark circles sat under Ogda's eyes and a mix of weariness and concern were etched on his face, his eyes took on a faraway look.

'We have to be smarter than him,' Ada whispered. Anja and the Seer admired the young girl she was brave and had tenacity.

'You are right dear Ada,' Anja reached out and patted her arm.

'So how do we do that?' Ogda offered Ada an encouraging smile.

Ada frowned she did not know and had no answers to give them. 'I am sure the Gods will help. There has to be a way.'

'You are right, but we are nearly out of time this has now cost us another delay. We cannot keep Merek, and his people hidden forever.'

'Do we know if there were any other groups that survived?' Anja asked Ogda.

The Seer thought for a moment. 'To be honest, I have no idea. I have not picked up on any groups and I am not sure if it would be wise to look for others, we simply do not have the time.' The Seer rubbed his chin, contemplating Anja's question.

Ludwig entered the room, interrupting the Seer's thoughts. 'Master, there are people coming.'

Ogda rose, surprised, and the now familiar feeling of fear gripped him. He looked at both Anja and Ada, they both shook their heads, surprise also on their faces. Ogda never had uninvited guests, his cottage was hidden and protected within the forest. A thought crossed his mind: *has the forest been burned so much that we are no longer well concealed?* He had not thought to check the forest that close to home instead he had focused on casting his search far and wide. He cursed himself for being so foolish.

'How far are they, Ludwig?'

Ludwig paled. 'They are almost here, Master.'

The Seer cursed under his breath. 'I guess we shall go and greet them than.'

Merek absently rubbed the finger that once wore the ring Elenore had given him on their wedding day. He still felt a slow burning anger within him for her betrayal. Even though he had calmed down since he had heard of her pregnancy, he still couldn't fathom that she was pregnant. Washing his face at the river, he quickly pulled the tunic over his body and ran his fingers through his hair. He could not be bothered to tie it back. His head hurt from the red drink and the night was a blur of images. He felt hungry and wondered what he could have for breakfast.

As he made his way back to Amzi's camp, he saw Flamma making his way towards him. His younger brother irritated him at the best of times and today he was not in the mood to entertain his silly, jealous fantasies.

'Here you are.' Flamma grinned.

'Make it quick. I don't have the time,' Merek growled.

'Elenore has your ring,' Flamma said.

Merek felt like striking his brother, but knew it would do no good. He was baiting him.

'So? She can have it.' Merek continued his path to the camp, ignoring Flamma.

Flamma narrowed his gaze and clenched his fists. He would always be the son that would was in the shadows of his older brother. Flamma would never have a chance to lead, a dream he had always had until Merek had showed up at his father's village some months ago. His intention had been to antagonise Merek, adding fuel to his anger. Instead, Merek had ignored his taunt, leaving Flamma speechless.

Zuri was making tea when Merek arrived at the camp. She smiled. Once again, Merek was taken aback with her beauty, she was stunning. Her white hair hung loosely down her back, her honey-coloured skin glowed and as she gazed up at him her deep blue eyes twinkled. She oozed a natural confidence and grace.

'I was wondering where you had gotten to. I thought you might want some tea, especially after last night.' She gave a soft chuckle.

Merek smiled and took the cup she offered. He was not sure what had happened, but he had woken up next to her earlier that morning. A pang of guilt crept over him. He was still married to Elenore and had never been with another woman since they had been together. He still loved his wife. She had been, and he realised was, a big part of his world. He felt torn.

'What are you thinking?' Zuri asked.

He gave her a smile. 'Just what I have to do today,' he lied.

'Which is?'

He shook his head. 'Lots of things. Nothing for a beautiful woman to worry about.' He took a sip of his tea as she put her arm around his waist. Merek stiffened a little, but did not resist her.

'Ah! Here you both are!' Amzi called out. He held up a pair of rabbits. 'Breakfast?'

'You read my mind,' Merek chuckled.

Elenore hid the ring in a leather pouch in a corner of her tent. She thought to visit the healer to see if she could give her a leather choker, which she would thread through the ring. Her hurt was turning to acrimony, and she was at the mercy of it. Changing into a fresh tunic she quickly tied her hair into a braid and set off to Serenity's camp.

'I have been expecting you.' The healer gave her a warm smile. 'Did you talk to your husband?'

Elenore shook her head. 'He is no longer my husband.'

Serenity clucked her tongue. 'Elenore, a heart full of bitterness is one that will consume you. It is not a healthy choice.' She gave her a stern look.

Elenore blushed but did not respond. 'I have come to see if you could make me a leather choker.'

The healer evaluated Elenore for a moment. 'Okay, I won't ask why. I guess you have your reasons. Come, let us have something to eat first. I have made some porridge. It is the last of the oats I brought with me. I am not sure how long we will be here for, but if it is a while, we will need to sow some crops.' Elenore took the steaming bowl of oats and ate. Serenity filled a cup with tea and handed it to her when she had finished the food.

The healer watched her for a moment before going into the tent to find some leather. It did not take her long before she had made Elenore the choker. She handed her the leather necklace.

'Thank you,' Elenore said as she took the band. The healer nodded her reply. 'Flamma came to see me today. He had Merek's ring.' Elenore shifted uncomfortably as she spoke to the healer.

'Ah, is that why you wanted the leather choker.'

Elenore blushed with embarrassment, healers were insightful. 'Why are you so ready to give up on your marriage to Merek? You need to fight for him.'

Elenore felt annoyed at the medicine woman. It was not Elenore's fault that her husband did not want her or her unborn child. 'How can I make someone want me and our child, when it is clear he does not.'

'He is a man for one and is under enormous pressure, not to mention the stress of keeping his people alive from an enemy we are still trying to figure out.'

Elenore thought for a moment before she answered. 'I love him, Serenity, but he has hurt me a lot. I think he is in love with another woman.' As she revealed her biggest fear, she felt a fresh set of tears. Angrily she wiped them away. 'I know he is under pressure we all are Ren. Merek has known about the Asur for a long time it's not like this is all new to him. Just because he has to lead now doesn't mean he can go off with someone else!' Her voice rose as she tried to justify her feelings.

The healer stayed quiet. Elenore wiped her face; exhaustion began to creep its way back. As she rose from her sitting position the healer looked up at her. 'Your children will be reunited with you, and I think that will help bring you together again. Strength is in family and staying by one another's side. Your children will be your strength, Elenore.'

Elenore sighed. 'I hope so.'

'Go and sleep, dear. You are carrying the future, you have to take care of yourself.'

Elenore smiled gratefully at the medicine woman before turning to make her way back to her small, lonely camp.

The sun was fully awake when they exited the Seer's cottage to see who it was that was paying them a visit. Ogda was deeply concerned that none of them had been able to pick up on the vibrations of their uninvited guests.

'Do not be alarmed, they mean you no harm.' The voice had come from nowhere and it startled the Seer. He looked up at the blue summer sky, as if he would find who it belonged to up in the air. He shook his head and smiled to himself. They had all heard the mystery voice and none of them knew who it belonged to. One thing was certain, it appeared to have no intention of harming them.

Before them were three riders: a young woman, an older man, and a teenage boy. Their horses were close to exhaustion as they came in at a fast pace. A white lather of sweat glistened under their saddles, their flanks heaving as their riders pulled them to a halt. Ogda watched as the older man turned in his saddle, looking back at the way he had come; it was evident they were running from something.

'You are safe here for the moment.' Ogda did not take his eyes off the man and soon he began to feel the man's energy and vibration. An avalanche of memories, traumas and thoughts came at him, and he took a deep breath. The man turned back to face the Seer satisfied for the moment that they were safe.

'Why don't you give the horses to, Ludwig? He will feed and take care of them, and you can come inside for some tea.' The older man glanced suspiciously at the odd-looking man standing to one side. 'It is okay, he loves horses. He may look different, but he is harmless.'

The man took another long look at Ludwig before nodding to the other two riders to dismount and hand the reins to Ludwig, who was only too happy to take them.

'Please come inside, you can use the kitchen to freshen up. Ada will get you a jug of water to wash.' Ogda gave them a reassuring smile. The man hesitated then followed Ada inside the stone and timber home.

The Seer waited, seated on his cushion, as Anja quickly put together some of the leftovers. She knew their guests would be ravenous. As the newcomers filed into the room where food and tea waited, the older man went over to the window. The Seer watched him as he looked out as if he was expecting someone.

'It's okay, Papa. Please sit down.' The young girl had bitten into one of the cakes and was watching her father. She was quite thin with long honey brown hair. Ogda could feel her energy; she was kind and shy, devoted to her family. He frowned as another vison came to mind. It was not quite clear, but he picked up that it led to another path. He sighed. He would have to meditate later; he knew that they would not be leaving today.

'We can't stay long, it's not safe.' The man had turned away from the window. His face was weathered, and a look of fear was permanently creased upon it.

'You cannot leave just yet, your horses need rest, and besides where would you go?' Ogda said softly.

The man began to pace.

'Papa please sit down.' The teenage boy went over to his father. His hair was a shade of the setting sun, and he was quite tall for his age. The man looked at his son and nodded.

'Have something to eat with your tea.' Anja handed him a cup with a plate of food. Ogda watched them for a short while as they ate and drank. When he was sure they had enough to satiate their hunger, he asked them who and why they were here.

The man washed down a mouthful of food with a gulp of tea. 'I am Matlin, this is my daughter, Kaiah, and my son is Rory. We are from the Shakurta village and have run away from the evil that lives there.' Ogda cocked his head, intrigued. 'Our Seer has made a pact with the devil. He murdered my wife.' The man paused the pain of her loss was still obvious.

'Go on, Matlin,' Anja encouraged him gently.

'She was the healer of the village and from the long line of Seers. She knew the village Seer's heart had turned to evil. She was a threat to him. She had become a threat when she started to warn our leader and the ancient tree, Arius. Before she was taken from us, she warned me to take the children and run. I didn't believe her until she was killed. After that, we couldn't leave straight away. The Seer had placed a guard outside our hut and watched our every move. It was a living hell.' Matlin took another gulp of his tea. 'We started having these strange dreams of how we could run away and that the trees would help us. I am sure it was the Gods sending us the messages. They told us to flee and come here. Well, that is what the dreams told us.' He grew quiet and did not add anything more.

Ogda looked at the family of three and wondered why they had been spared. Once again, the feeling of a different path came to mind. He looked at the girl, she was barely more than sixteen years and her brother no more than thirteen years of life. The girl intrigued him, and he frowned as he observed her energy. She radiated an aura of calmness and inner peace, something a healer or Seer would have. It instantly clicked why they had been spared; the Gods were choosing people for the future, in the hope that mankind had one. There would be a connection somehow, but he just wasn't quite sure what it was.

Ogda looked at Anja, who had been watching him. She smiled and gave a brief nod, she knew all the thoughts he just had.

'The forest is on fire!' The young girl blurted. The Seer pulled his gaze away from Anja and rested it on Kaiah. 'The Asur are burning the trees alive, they want to rid the world of it. They will come for us once they have finished.'

'How much of the forest is gone?' Ogda asked her.

'It took us weeks to get here, the Asur were everywhere. The trees formed tunnels for us to hide when they could. Like I said, they are being burned alive. There is so much of it gone, along with the villages and the people that used to live in them. They are getting close to where we are now.'

Ogda felt the fear clutch at his chest, and he took a slow deliberate breath trying to slow his racing heart. 'How long do you think we have before they get here?' he asked her.

She bit her lower lip, thinking. 'A week, maybe two, but that's it.' She looked directly at the Seer. He sighed, although they had hoped to leave today it would not be possible. The newcomers needed to rest, as did their horses.

Ludwig came into the room not long after they had finished eating. Concern was etched on his face. 'Master?'

Ogda smiled at his faithful servant. It was apparent now that Ludwig would be coming with them. He could not leave him behind, the Asur would see his cabin and burn him alive in it.

'Yes, Ludwig, what seems to be the problem?'

Ludwig held up a horse's shoe. 'One of the horses has pulled up lame. I have put on new shoes, but he has a sprained fetlock from all the hard riding.'

'That is the gelding of mine. I didn't have time to rest him, I had no choice.' Matlin looked at Ludwig apologetically.

'How long do you think before he will be right to ride again?' Ogda asked. He was beginning to feel frustrated. Time would not wait.

'A week at least, Master.'

'Okay we will leave in a week. I suggest we all get some rest. We have a lot to prepare. Ada, can you help Ludwig with the poultices to put on the horse? We cannot leave it behind, it is too valuable. We must make haste to the valley where Merek is hiding.'

'Merek? I have heard of that name in my dreams,' Matlin said.

'Yes, he is the son of Eijanbrook and Anja former leader of the Protectors. We are to meet with him in a hidden valley before the great battle begins.' Matlin merely nodded. It all made sense, his dreams were coming to fruition.

As Ulric rested under one of the tall oak trees, tears spilled down his face. The wolf tried to lick them dry, and he buried his face into his coarse coat. Krea and Kacha looked over at the young man, feeling for his loss.

'You should go and talk to him,' Kacha suggested.

Krea sighed. Kacha was right, she was his aunt. She made her way to Ulric and the wolf looked at her expectantly, his dark eyes expressive. She bent and ruffled his coat, earning her his wet tongue. Ulric watched the interaction and felt an immense sadness. His beloved canine friend was gone forever.

Krea sat down next to Ulric. 'He is with the Gods now, there is nothing you can do. I know you are sad, but we have to make a plan.' She offered him a sympathetic smile.

Ulric wiped his face. He had to be strong. He would grieve more once he had some quiet time to himself. 'I am okay. I can't sit here crying all day, He is with the Gods now. I have to learn to live without him.' Ulric sniffed and cleared his throat.

Krea opened her arms and embraced her nephew. 'You will make a great leader someday, Ulric.'

The words brought a soft chuckle. 'Oh, I never want to be a leader.'

She laughed at his words and released her hold. It was time they planned.

The sun had risen high in the sky, bringing with it a stifling heat. Ulric looked at the trees, hoping they could provide some way of telling them where they could find water. He remembered the time when they had been fighting the witches in a dark forbidden forest and when he had needed help to escape the Asur. He had laid his ear to the trunk and had heard it speak his name. Maybe these trees could talk to him in a similar way. It was worth a try, so he laid his ear to the large oak he had been sitting under.

At first, there was nothing and then faintly he heard his name. '*Water that you seek follow the darkened trunks.*' He pulled his head away before laying it again against the trunk of the tree. '*Follow the darkened trunks,*' came the response again.

He looked at Kacha and Krea, 'follow me.' He gestured as he set off.

It was not long before they saw a tree with a darkened trunk and made their way towards it. One after another, they followed the trees and before long the gurgling sound of a small creek could be heard. They drank their fill and rested on the bank.

'Something is strange about Shakurta village's leader,' Kacha said.

'How do you mean?' Krea asked.

'He didn't say anything. It was like he was hypnotised. I mean, his eyes were glass-like he didn't bat an eyelid. That is strange for a leader.'

'I agree. I was thinking the same thing when we were there,' Ulric answered.

'The Seer must have him under some power, and I bet the same is for the ancient tree,' Krea added. Both Kacha and Ulric agreed.

'We must get to the Seer and break the spell. I need Ada, but I think she cannot infiltrate my thoughts as the Seer is too close,' Ulric mused. 'We have to come up with a plan to get to the leader and the tree without the Seer noticing. I am not sure how we will do that,' Ulric looked at Kacha and Krea, but neither had an answer.

Elenore woke, her tunic stuck to her with sweat her throat parched, she propped herself up and grabbed the waterskin next to her bed of furs. She took a long drink and stretched. She decided to go to the river and have a swim it would refresh her. She grabbed a handful of berries that she kept for a quick snack; it would do for the time being. She grabbed the piece of material she used for a towel and made a mental note to pick some herbs later that day.

It dawned on her she would have to hunt, or ask someone to hunt for her, as she did not have a husband or son that would provide for her at present. She sighed. She had no idea how long Merek planned on not talking to her, or if he had any desire to get back with her. Though the thoughts still hurt her, she was getting better at how she reacted to them.

The shimmering heat sucked the moisture from the earth below. It was oppressive and energy depleting. As Elenore neared the water hole that was used to swim and bathe, it became apparent that others had shared the same idea. Children and adults alike played in the water, relishing the reprieve it gave them from the hot day. Elenore looked around. She could not see Merek, but Tallot was sitting on a rock that sat next to the water's edge. Ganika sat next to him. She gave them a wave and a brief smile before finding a quieter spot for herself.

The water was cold despite the heat, and it came as a shock as she entered it. Forcing herself to go in, she swam to the outer edge preferring to be away from the others. She dove under, feeling the coolness and freedom it offered. She came back up to the top and climbed out to sit on the bank basking in the sun. Her tunic clung to her, highlighting the small bulge that she knew people would start to notice soon.

She lay down, enjoying the moment and pushing the thought away. As she closed her eyes, she heard shouts from across the water hole, but ignored them. The voices grew louder, and she propped herself up onto her elbow. Squinting against the glare of the sun, she looked over to find out what was causing the commotion. Two men had become involved in a heated argument as they began to push each other, tempers flaring.

Tallot rushed over to one of the men, pulling him away. Another man grabbed the other, restraining him as he yelled obscenities against the other. A minute went past as the two men wrestled to be let go. As Elenore watched, she noticed the crowd step aside and Merek come between the two men. Instantly, they lowered their heads the immense respect they had for their leader was evident. Merek gave them both a stern warning and ordered them to leave the water hole.

He was an impressive man, standing tall and powerful. Today, his hair was pulled back in a bun, his beard hung loose, and he wore only trousers, his chest bare. Although Elenore could not hear his words, she could make out that he had told everyone to return to what they were doing. She watched him talk to Tallot before a tall blonde woman came to stand next to Merek: Zuri. Elenore sucked in her breath as she watched her put her arm around the handsome leader. The crowd had noticed too, and a murmur rippled through them.

As Elenore continued to watch, a woman pointed to her and the group of people turned to look at her basking on the rock. Elenore felt herself blush. So the rumours had started. A valley full of people who had been on the run with no entertainment or distraction from their constant fear of the Asur, it was no wonder they craved for something that resembled normalcy, even if it was the drama between their leader and his wife.

Zuri looked over at Elenore too, a satisfied smile on her face. Elenore clenched her fists. She despised the woman, she knew she was antagonising her. Merek gave a quick glance in her direction. Elenore tried to catch his eye, but he averted her gaze. It was not long before he bid Tallot farewell and left the watering hole. Elenore sighed. She would now be the talk of the valley. Life was about to become so much more difficult.

People continued to stare and whisper for a while, until they grew tired of the drama unfolding between their leader and his wife. Once they had either left or continued with their activities, Elenore made her way back to the other side of the water hole. She grabbed her towel and wrapped herself in the rough fabric. Her appearance on the side that was close to the group of people still enjoying the water created another wave of whispers. Elenore ignored them and made her way back to her camp.

At her camp, Tallot was roasting a hare and her mouth instantly began to water. She gave him a grateful smile.

'Tallot, you must have read my mind I am famished! Thank you! Please let me go and change and I will be out in a minute.'

He nodded without saying a word. Elenore quickly changed into a fresh tunic and pulled her hair up into a bun before heading back out to join Tallot at the fire pit. He had carved slices of the meat and placed it on a plate which he handed to Elenore when she sat next to him. 'Thank you. I would make some tea, but I feel that it is way too hot to have a hot beverage.'

'I can't stay. Merek asked me to check on you. I have some things to do.' He turned to leave.

'Wait!' Elenore placed the plate on the log before getting up. 'Have I done something wrong? You are acting different, and besides, I can't eat all of this on my own.' She indicated to the leftover meat that was still sitting on the spit.

'I do not want to get involved between you and Merek. He is a good friend and leader.'

Elenore narrowed her gaze. 'I thought you were my friend too.'

Tallot did not look at her, keeping his eyes down. 'I have to go.'

As Elenore watched him leave, the emptiness began to return.

Ogda asked Ludwig to make up the spare room for the new arrivals. Kaiah offered to help and went with Ludwig to set up the room. Rory excused himself, heading out to the stables to see the horses. The Seer poured himself and Matlin another cup of tea and settled back into the cushion he was perched on. Matlin eyed him reproachfully, taking a sip of the tea.

'I have a dilemma, Matlin, that involves a small group of very brave souls that are trying to infiltrate your village. My vibrations have picked up that they have run into a little trouble, and I cannot go to them due to obvious reasons.' Ogda sighed and took a sip from his cup. 'I was wondering, actually I was hoping, that you could help me. What are your thoughts about your Seer? What are his weaknesses?' Ogda met Matlin's gaze, offering him a tight smile.

Matlin looked out the window he had peered out earlier. He had finally been able to relax, and exhaustion had crept in, sleep was starting to beckon. He rubbed his chin.

'My wife would tell me that the Asur want to reduce the earth to a barren wasteland. They will stop at nothing to achieve this they will wipe the forest clean from the soil they are anchored to. I think our Seer knew she knew this and that is why he feared her; she was dangerous to him.'

Ogda nodded. 'Go on.'

Matlin let his gaze go back to the window and the view it gave. The trees created a breathtaking backdrop, and a faraway look crossed his face. He cleared his throat and turned his attention back to the Seer who patiently waited for his response. 'She said that a queen must have a king, and it was rumoured that he is very hard to find. Anyway, that has nothing to do with what you want me to tell you.' He shifted uncomfortably, looking down at the floor, as he let out a breath. 'You need to seek the help of the forest. They are key. It is not only your fight, but theirs too.' Matlin looked up at the Seer, at last meeting his gaze.

The Seer smiled warmly. 'Thank you. The answer I seek has been there the whole time.' Matlin again shifted uncomfortably. 'What is troubling you, my dear friend?' Ogda raised an eyebrow.

'My wife told me that some humans have joined the Asur. They have the same evil hearts intent on destruction and suffering. I don't know how many, but I guess they could be classed as a threat and an enemy.'

'What you say is correct. It has crossed my mind that there would be some foolish souls to seek some sort of acceptance from the Asur. It comes as no surprise. Please, finish your tea and go and get some rest.' Matlin nodded and drowned the rest of his tea. Ogda watched him leave, a heavy weight on his shoulders.

CHAPTER FIFTEEN

A Surprise

Whispers rustle in the leaves, secrets in the bark.
The forest shares a clue, and humanity's fate lies within.

Ulric

Elenore woke from her afternoon sleep feeling dazed and disorientated. She sat up, expecting to feel Merek next to her. She felt the emptiness and realised that it was not a dream but reality that Merek was not with her anymore. She got up out of her bed, making her way outside to relieve herself. Her abdomen felt heavy, and she wondered if the baby had grown that very day. She smiled to herself as she made her way back to her camp. Serenity was waiting in front of the fire pit, her hair pulled back in a long braid. She smiled at Elenore as she made her way through the thick bush that encircled her camp which offered her a sense of privacy and security.

'Serenity, what do I owe the pleasure of this visit? I will put on some tea.'

Serenity did not answer Elenore straight away. Instead, she watched as Elenore blew life into the fire, placing the heavy iron kettle over it to boil. 'Merek came to see me earlier we are to wait for Ogda, Ada, and Anja to arrive. In the meantime, we are to grow vegetables it will help feed the people. I think you could be of some help. He also said we are to find and keep as many seeds of the forest as we can. This will help us replant the trees that we have lost. Our future needs our forest. This way, it will ensure that they are not lost forever. It is our way of getting vengeance.' The healer looked at Elenore, gauging her reaction.

At last, Elenore nodded. 'I would be honoured to be part of rebuilding the future.' She gave the healer a warm smile. Serenity leaned back, thankful that Elenore was happy to help.

'Did he say anything about me?' Elenore could not help herself.

The healer gave her a long look before answering. 'As you may know, he is distracted by another. She does not have a kind heart.'

Elenore frowned as she waited for more. It was evident the healer was not going to offer anything further. 'To be honest, I do not like her either,' she said and offered the healer a smile.

Serenity nodded in agreement.

As they worked in the garden Elenore wiped the sweat from her brow. She could feel it trickle down her spine and she longed for a cool breeze to whisk away the heat. Some of Merek's people had come to Serenity's call for help to build a community vegetable patch. It soon became apparent that the healer was not the only one that had the insight to bring seeds with her. Others who had thought about the future had managed to pack seeds that would be vital to feed a community. Merek had instructed some of his youngest and strongest warriors to help build the garden. Dressed only in their trousers, chests bare, they laboured under the hot sun.

Elenore was with some of the women sorting the seeds, while Serenity supervised. As the word got out that a vegetable garden was in the process of being built more and more people offered to help.

'Aye here she is!' Elenore turned as she heard a familiar voice, her joy of seeing Sabin evident as she ran to embrace him.

'Oh! Sabin it is so good to see you, I have missed you!' Sabin let her hold him for a moment before extracting himself gently from her clasp. He held her at arms-length, taking in her gentleness and beauty. It had been two weeks since they had seen each other.

'Aye Norrie, I am sorry I have not been to see ye but as ye know I am with me lovely soon-to-be-wife and her children.' He shook his head, chuckling. 'Aye, I think doin' this vegetable garden will be a break.'

Elenore grinned. 'I am glad you came. Please, let me get you some water.' She led the way to the small table stocked with jugs of water for the workers.

Sabin shook his head. 'I am good, thank you.'

Elenore brushed away a wisp of hair that had escaped from her bun. Sabin felt a stab of sorrow for her. He did not understand why Merek had left her.

'Have you seen Merek?'

It was as if she had read his mind. 'I have not, as you know I am now a very busy man.' He threw his head back and laughed. Elenore could not help but smile.

'I thought I recognised that laugh.' Serenity had come to join them, a smile stretched across her face.

'Aye, Rennie, I thought you could use some help. Believe me it's a break from Edyth's little ones. They can be quite demanding at times.' He gave the healer a wink.

'I can understand, Sabin. You are a good man, please, come with me I need your help in digging the last garden.' Serenity made her way back to the field they were preparing, with Sabin following close behind. Elenore watched them leave before turning back to sorting the seeds that she would sow later that afternoon.

Ogda stood up and stretched his legs, he glanced at Anja who had remained quiet when Matlin had been speaking with him. She offered him a smile, trying to encourage a feeling of hope.

'Anja, we must go to Ulric tonight. We need to infiltrate his dreams and pass on the message about the forest. I need Ada rested, she needs to find the queen and I feel it would be best for her to do that when we leave. Now it seems she has a king, and I am unsure if I should be sending Ada alone.'

'I have an idea about how to infiltrate Ulric's dream,' Anja said.

The Seer raised an eyebrow. 'Go on.'

'We can use Ulric's beloved canine, Kanji. If we use him as a messenger in his dream, the Seer will never know it is us. I think I can do it if you will let me.'

Ogda smiled. 'Ah, Anja, no wonder the Gods have chosen you. This is brilliant, yes, we will use the dog.' Ogda made his way to the window looking out at his beloved garden and the forest beyond. He was at a loss on how he could help Ada, and Anja had not given him any suggestions on the matter. 'We will go and rest, maybe something will come to a fresh mind that will help Ada,' he said as he turned away from the window. 'We will reconvene after dinner and make Ulric dream.' Anja nodded and smiled in agreement.

The afternoon stretched into early evening. Elenore wiped her face with a wet cloth, her body ached, and her stomach grumbled angrily. She sighed. 'I might go to the river for a swim.' The thought brought a smile. The water would wash and soothe her after what had been a long, tiring day. Most of the workers had finished earlier, the garden was finished, including seeds being sown. Serenity was watering the last row.

Elenore grabbed a piece of salted meat that had been left for the workers. She quickly ate, but it hardly placated her rumbling belly. 'Are you hungry again, Elenore?'

Elenore smiled sheepishly at the healer. 'I can't help it. I am constantly hungry. This baby must be a boy, Ulric was exactly the same he loves to eat!'

Serenity shook her head. 'It's good to see you out and about, fresh air and sunshine is good for the body. Your baby will grow like the weeds that will grow in this garden.'

Elenore laughed softly. 'I think there will be too many of us to pull them out before they take hold.'

Serenity chuckled. 'Yes, I think you are right.' A couple had walked into the front of the garden and Elenore could make out that one of them was Merek. She noticed Flamma, Tallot and some other men following, not far behind. Serenity followed Elenore's gaze; her brow crinkled into a frown. 'Looks like we have company.'

Elenore nodded, but did not move. The moment of happiness had gone, sadness taking its place.

Serenity went to meet the small throng of people who had gathered to see the day's work. Elenore noticed Merek look over to where she was standing. He held her gaze briefly, she sucked in her breath, before looking back at Serenity. She felt so disconnected not having him with her, Serenity had told her to be patient and to wait for him. She knew this was going to be hard and wondered if she had enough patience and strength. She glanced over at the group again before deciding to head down to the river, the water was beckoning her.

Serenity had brought Elenore some stew she had made the previous day. She had joined Elenore in the river, enjoying the cool water before making her way back with her to her camp. Both women felt refreshed after the evening swim. A fire softly burned as they finished the last of their meal.

'I might feel your tummy, Elenore, just to check if all is going well.' Elenore looked puzzled but nodded in agreement. They made their way into the tent and Elenore laid down on the furs, lifting the tunic for the healer to examine her abdomen. Serenity clucked as she gently moved her hands over Elenore's stomach. She murmured a few words before placing her ear against the skin of Elenore's exposed belly.

They heard someone enter the tent. Startled, both women jumped as Merek ducked under the tent opening making his way inside. He came to an abrupt halt as he saw the two women.

'Merek!' Elenore hastily pulled down her tunic, embarrassed that her husband had seen her. He threw her an angry look.

'Hello Merek, I was just feeling your baby. It seems there is more than one that is growing, I could be wrong though, it is still early pregnancy.'

Elenore turned her attention back to Serenity. 'What are you saying?'

The healer chuckled. 'You are having twins. Well, it appears that way.'

Merek threw Elenore a condescending look. 'It's bad enough with one but now you are bringing two into this world!' His face had taken on a fierce look. He turned to Serenity. 'Can't you do something?' he demanded.

'No. We will welcome new life, it is our hope for humanity.'

Merek took a step closer to the healer. 'Humanity? Who cares about humanity? Who really cares? We have evil all around us, what hope do we have? We can barely stay alive and look after the people who are here, let alone another mouth we will have to feed!' His voice rose his temper barely restrained. 'You are on your own, Elenore, I want nothing to do with you or the unborn children you carry. I will not be responsible, do you hear me?'

Elenore recoiled from his angry outburst, speechless.

'Why did you come here, Merek?' the healer asked.

Merek turned to Serenity, frowning. He looked around the tent before reaching for a bag he had stashed in the corner. Without a word, he left. Elenore burst into tears. Serenity drew her into a warm embrace, stroking her long red hair.

The candles burned softly, creating a dim light as they ate the food Ludwig had prepared. Kaiah had been a huge help to the Seer's only servant. She enjoyed preparing and cooking the meal, it allowed her to feel a sense of nostalgia of times past. She missed her mother and the thought of her brought feelings of sadness and grief. She would never forgive their village Seer or the Asur. They had ruined her life.

She stabbed her fork into the greens. It had been so long since they had had a proper meal. Her father and brother seemed relaxed, they had been constantly on the run since they had fled their village. She chewed her food, relishing the taste and goodness it gave. As she looked up from her plate, she noticed Ada was watching her with interest.

She offered the girl a smile and shifted uncomfortably, she felt like she was reading her mind. Ada looked away frowning and biting her lower lip. Kaiah was curious to know what was going through her mind, but stayed quiet. She turned her attention back to what Ogda was saying.

'We will infiltrate Ulric's dream, disguising ourselves as his dog. I have had some time to think about how we may not only have a queen of the Asur but a king to deal with as well.' He paused and wiped his mouth with the napkin, taking a sip from the cup of water in front of him. He cleared his throat before continuing. 'It all hinges on what we find out from the ancient tree. As you know, the forest has been key all along and their existence depends on how we work together. We will wait until Ulric finds the answers. I will not send Ada until then. If anyone has any other suggestions or comments, please speak freely.' He sat back on his chair waiting for their response.

'Should I accompany, Ada? I mean I can help her I feel she needs to have an extra person to help.' Anja looked at Ogda waiting for his response. He did not answer her straight away. 'I will go, Anja. I cannot jeopardise you. You know what your future brings.' He held up his hand as she opened her mouth to protest. 'My mind is made up. Anja, praise the Gods it is what is prophesied. I know that now. Please, let's finish eating.' They exchanged a glance before returning their attention back to their meal.

Ulric lay on the soft leaves, looking up at the stars. The day unfolded in front of him, and he could not rid the image of his beloved canine being killed in front of him. He had been given Kanji when he was a boy his father bringing home the small bundle of fur. Kanji at first had been hesitant hiding and whimpering behind Merek. Ulric had patiently coaxed him using dried scraps of meat to lure him into his lap. Kanji had cowered at first as Ulric stroked his soft brown fur but after a few moments he began to relax. He had looked up at Ulric with warm brown eyes before licking his face and that was the moment that sealed a friendship. Ulric hastily wiped away a fresh set of tears, he coughed and cleared his throat as the memory evoked a sense of loss.

A smouldering anger began to fester and the more he thought about the day the more it increased his desire to seek vengeance. A cool breeze brought relief from the summer night's heat, and he soon turned his thoughts to Pancome. He had no idea if he was still alive or if the Seer had murdered him as well. Ulric shifted his position; the ground was hard and lumpy and not comfortable at all. He closed his eyes, willing himself to sleep, he needed to be clear minded to think how they could get back into the village. He sighed, opening his eyes again to look over at Krea and Kacha who were both lying on their sides. The sound of rhythmic breathing indicated they had fallen asleep. Ulric tuned on his side closing his eyes again, trying to find the elusive sleep he desperately needed.

Ulric dreamed he was running through a heavily treed forest, his dog keeping pace with him. The forest reminded him of the one he used to go to when he was a young boy. It had offered him a sanctuary, a refuge, when life forced him to retreat from the world. He ran barefoot along the moss-covered forest floor. The smell of earth and the heavy scent of the foliage overwhelmed his senses. He could taste the air, a powerful concoction of freshness and purity it energised him as he ran faster.

Kanji barked, feeling his master's energy of enthusiasm.

Ulric looked down at his furry companion. 'Let's run to the river. It is such a beautiful day!'

The dog barked a reply and they ran harder, making their way to the river that ran through the woods. Ulric felt euphoric as they ran along the tree line, the river's soft gurgling sounding through the air. A strong wind began to blow, whipping Ulric's hair over his face; he brushed it away, but it blew straight back, blinding him. He slowed his pace, pushing the hair away he was beginning to feel annoyed. The wind blew again, the hair flew back covering his face. Ulric stopped, shoving his hair away, he wished he had tied it back.

The wind stopped and he looked around. The sun had gone, replaced by dark clouds that had gathered in the sky. He looked back from where he had come from. Behind him, the forest was gone, only a barren wasteland was left. He frowned and turned back. The forest was now in front of him.

The sound of a horn broke the silence. Dread washed over Ulric, even in his dream he knew the sound of the horn was to announce that the Asur were on the move. Kanji began to bark, running around his master, Ulric felt the ground vibrate beneath him. Kanji ran towards the forest, before stopping and returning to his master's side.

Ulric was gripped with fear. He could not move; his legs seemed anchored to the ground he stood upon. His little dog pulled at his tunic, barking and whining. The vibrations became more intense and he could hear approaching horses. The wind began to blow again sweeping his hair over his face. He angrily pushed it back as he felt his senses return breaking the trance that had kept him rooted to the ground. Kanji ran ahead barking excitedly, Ulric looked at his little dog and followed him.

They ran towards the forest, knowing it would offer shelter and an escape from the evil that was hunting them. As they entered the dark cool interior of the forest, the giant trees began to whisper, rustling their leaves fervently.

Ulric looked over his shoulder. The Asur were in the barren wasteland, they were searching for something or someone. Panic gripped Ulric at the sudden realisation that they were looking for him.

The trees beckoned; their whispering became louder, as if they were trying to shout at him. He ran harder, trying to place as much distance as he could between himself and the Asur. He had always loved running and he was good at it, now it was helping to save his life. The tree branches scratched his face as he delved deeper and deeper into the darkness of the thick mesh of trees.

Ulric could feel someone shaking him. He sat up as the last wisps of the dream faded away.

Concern covered Krea's face. 'Are you okay?' she demanded.

Ulric coughed and nodded. 'I had a really strange dream.' He looked around, half expecting to see his dog next to him. Loss washed over him again as he remembered he was no longer alive.

'What did you dream, Ulric?' Krea continued to stare at him.

Ulric frowned. 'I think it was meant to be a sign or a message. I mean, it was like I was there, and Kanji was there too.' He sighed and wiped his face. The moon had risen high above the trees casting a silvery light. A soft breeze blew, and the hoot of a howl was heard in the near distance. 'It is the forest. The trees, they will be key. I mean, they always have, haven't they?' He looked at both Krea and Kacha, they both nodded. 'The trees will guide us back to the village. I think that was what my dream was telling me.' Ulric stood and went to the closest tree, placing his ear to its trunk. At first there was nothing, but he waited patiently.

Moments went by before he heard a faint whispering. *'Seek the tree with the silver trunk.'* It repeated over and over.

Ulric stared up at the tree he was listening to. Its branches were high as it stretched itself to the sky, as if in prayer to the Gods.

'We must find the tree with the silver trunk, it holds the answers. We must be quick the Asur are coming!'

Krea and Kacha glanced at each other; this was the last thing they wanted to hear.

CHAPTER SIXTEEN

A Place To Call Home

Mourn those we have lost, but do not live in the darkness that follows for there will be courage to rise again.

Ogda

The silver tree stood high on a slope, its green leaves entwined with white blossoms. Ulric raced up the slope, his heart racing. He paused before reaching out to touch the silver-coloured trunk. Krea and Kacha stood beside him and waited as he connected with the tree.

Ulric could feel a pulsing vibration. He leaned towards the trunk, placing his ear to the rough bark. He could hear a low humming as he waited for it to talk. The tree began to sway, even though there was no wind. Other trees soon joined in moving their branches, leaves rustling, a soft chorus filtered throughout the forest.

'Go, go, go,' came a soft chant. 'The forest will put on a show of fury, we will distract them. Go, go, go!' The chanting was becoming louder as did the increasing movement of branches and leaves.

'Let's go, we have to leave and get back to the village!' Ulric shouted. He did not wait for Krea's and Kacha's reaction instead he made his way down the slope, racing towards Shakurta village.

The trees whipped and lashed their branches, simulating a ferocious storm. The people could hear the commotion, and some crawled out of their huts, half-asleep. The sky had grown dark the moon had vanished as they looked up at the forest. A large crash startled them as branches began to splinter and fall, some onto the roofs of the homes that stood under them. People let out startled cries as they raced to grab children and loved ones, fearing they would become a victim of the falling debris.

The Seer watched his community scatter in all directions, concern etched on his face. He had directed the warriors to help families to relocate to the leader's home as it was a much bigger, stronger hut, and would provide a better shelter.

'Where is the old man?' he asked his oldest and most trusted warrior.

'We have him locked up in the cells with the others.'

The Seer nodded, his thoughts racing. He could sense a looming battle and that Dardanos had redirected some of her recon party back to Shakurta village. He had a feeling there were greater forces at work, but he could not pick up on them vibrationally. 'Behead all that are in the cells except for the old man.'

'What do you want done with him?'

'Leave him. I have other plans. We have to get the people out after this' – he waved his hand at the trees – 'and set fire to the forest. I will come for him later.' The Seer had been caught off guard, something he was not familiar with.

Ulric ran as fast and as hard as he could. Krea and Kacha struggled to keep up and soon started to lag. Ulric loved to run, and he was pleased that he could still outrun warriors bigger and stronger than himself. He heard Krea call to him, and he slowed his pace to a jog so that they could catch up.

'Praise the Gods, Ulric. They have given you the speed of a flying horse,' panted Kacha as he drew alongside. Ulric smiled as he came to a halt, a small hut was not far in front of them.

The trees were blowing incessantly, and a loud swooshing noise could be heard. It could easily have been mistaken for a savage storm passing through.

The trio crept quietly through the thick undergrowth and as they made their way. It was evident the impact the forest was having on the village. Branches had fallen on top of the roofs of some of the homes and people were rushing around in a panic. As they watched the scene unfold in front of them, they knew the forest was set on revenge.

'We need to get to Pancome!' Ulric shouted over the roar of the trees.

'How do we do that?' Krea asked.

Ulric had no idea where Pancome was being held captive, or even if he was still alive. He shrugged his shoulders. 'I don't know.' He looked up at the trees wildly moving above him. 'I think first we need to get inside the village and try not to be noticed. Maybe Kacha you could ask one of the villagers if they know where they keep prisoners.'

The tall, lean warrior beside him nodded.

They pretended to be like the people fleeing, hoping to assimilate and escape notice. Most of the villages showed little if no interest as they raced around, trying to make sense of what was going on. Kacha stopped a man who was holding a small child, asking if he knew where the prisoners were kept.

'They are kept underground, near where we harvest the vegetables. Why do you ask?' The man threw Kacha a questioning look. Before Kacha could answer the child the man held in his arms began to squirm and let out a loud wail. The man turned his attention to his son, giving Kacha the opportunity to join Ulric and Krea. They fled, not sure where the vegetable harvesting area was.

Krea pulled Ulric to one side as they slowed to a walk. 'Ulric, I think this place must be in an area where the forest is not so thick. They can't grow vegetables under a canopy of trees, they need sunlight.'

'Yes, you are right. But which way? This village is huge.'

They looked around them trying to find evidence of some clearing. 'It must be near the leader's hut.' Ulric and Krea turned to Kacha. 'It makes sense they would have the largest home in the centre of the village, but not where the house could be burned or like in this situation have trees falling on it. Plus, punishment is usually given out by the leader and his Council so yeah, most villages have the prison close to the leader's home.'

Ulric scratched his head. It made sense, and they had no other ideas. 'Okay, let's go, but we have to be careful. I am sure the Seer must know something is up.'

The torches that lit the paths around and through the village flickered as the trio made their way to the centre of the village. A loud shout was heard as they approached an enormous hut. Concealing themselves behind the trunks of some large trees, they could see crowds of people making their way to the enormous timber home. Warriors were rushing madly, shouting orders at the panic-stricken families.

Ulric noticed some men walking to the far side of the hut before disappearing. He motioned to Krea and Kacha and pointed to where they had gone. Another warrior was making his way to where they had gone, a woman followed him shrieking.

'That has to be it.' Krea smiled at Ulric. He nodded in agreement.

'I will go and get him,' Kacha said. Both Ulric and Krea blinked at Kacha. 'You both need to stay here in case something happens. You must make it to the ancient tree.' He held up his hand before Ulric and Krea had a chance to protest. 'I know we need Pancome to persuade the tree, but we also do not need all of us to die in some hole. All would be lost.'

'You are not going to die Kacha.' Krea frowned at the young man. 'Besides, the Gods have promised you to be with Ada.'

Kacha grinned when he heard Ada's name.

'Be careful, Kacha,' Ulric said as the young warrior made his way to where they thought Pancome had been held captive.

The darkness was beginning to fade when Kacha staggered out with a half-conscious Pancome. Blood ran from Kacha's nose, a knife wound caused blood to trickle down his arm as he approached his friends. Krea ran forward, grabbing Pancome as he slumped over her shoulder. 'What happened?' she demanded as she gently laid Pancome on the ground.

Kacha collapsed, leaning back on the tree they sheltered under. Ulric stepped forward to examine the man's wounds.

'There were so many, it was all I could do to keep them off me. They were beheading so many of the poor souls that were down there.' Kacha gasped and squeezed his eyes shut. Sweat trickled down his face. Ulric ripped part of his own tunic making a torniquet to help stop the blood flow that had begun to pour from Kacha's arm. 'We need to take shelter and rest until Pancome has the energy to help speak to the tree.'

'Ulric, in case you haven't noticed, we are in the middle of the enemy's village. Where are we supposed to hide and how do we even get to the tree?!' Krea shook her head at her nephew.

'It is easy to hide when there is chaos all around you. Don't worry, I am sure we will be safe here. No one has spotted us yet. We will only be here for a short while.'

Krea glanced around them; Ulric was right. There was no one who had even given them a second glance and it seemed that no one had even noticed them! She nodded as she turned her attention back to Pancome.

The ancient tree was perhaps the oldest tree on the planet. It stood some distance behind the leader's home and it was part of the largest and oldest village that had ever been. Its trunk was thick and gnarled, and its branches disappeared into the thick canopy above. It took up room as it spread wide and far, surpassing the large home that stood not far away. The top of the tree was lost in the clouds. Legend spoke that it was the staircase to the Gods. Some had tried to climb, never to return. Ceremonies were held under it: weddings, funerals, and prayers. Sacrifices and daily rituals were part of the everyday existence of the tree. It stood huge and proud, father to the flora that flourished. A deep respect and a sense of awe was felt by all that came to pay their respects. Now, it seemed its days were numbered.

Time was running out. The darkness helped hide them and it was rapidly disappearing as the sun began to rise. Ulric paced as he waited for Pancome to have the energy to make it to the tree.

'I am ready, Ulric, we do not have time for me to sit around while the enemy advances.' Pancome offered a weak smile as Krea helped him to his feet. His face had gone deathly pale and it was evident it was an effort for him just to get to his feet. He leaned on Krea for support, looking towards the old tree that loomed in front of them.

'We will help. Lean on me,' Krea instructed as they took their first steps.

'Ulric and I will cover you until you get to the tree.' Kacha stepped out into the chaos, his hand poised on his sword. People scattered in all directions. Trees lay uprooted, their branches clutching the air like skeletal arms. Debris filled the air, swirling in a chaotic dance. Lost children screamed their cries echoing in the howling wind. Roofs had been torn off joining the swirling debris. The village had become mayhem. Ulric admired Kacha's tenacity and bravery. He knew the young man was struggling as he hobbled into the turmoil. Blood still trickled from his wounds, and he swayed slightly as he walked. Ulric glanced at the people who were trying to make their way to the hut that offered a place to shelter. He could see warriors ushering people, but none paid them any attention. How many had Kacha been able to slay?

So far, no one had given the warning that an enemy was in the village. Time could only favour them for a short time. It was inevitable that someone would come across the dead bodies. He beckoned Krea and Pancome to go behind the large timber house, away from the front where panicked crowds had gathered.

As they made their way to the back of the structure, Ulric noticed Takeo still sitting on the overstuffed cushion. He frowned. *How odd that a leader is not directing his people in a disaster.* Ulric also thought it strange that Takeo's people did not question it. Pushing the thought to one side, he led the way to the foot of the enormous tree.

He turned rushing to Krea's side as he placed his shoulder under one of Pancome's arms sharing the weight of him with his aunt. Together they carried Pancome over to its base. Pancome leaned against the tree, placing his hands on the roughened bark. Ulric followed suit as Krea and Kacha stood guard.

At first, he felt nothing. Seconds passed. Ulric glanced over at Pancome, but then he felt a vibration and a deep-rooted sense of knowledge, as if he had gained a wisdom that surpassed his years on earth. A white light appeared in front of him. He felt confused, panic gripped him, and he tried to shake his head and pull his hands away.

'*Do not resist, one with the mark of a tear drop. I know the old man's thoughts, memories and all his desires and his secrets. I have taken his soul; he will rest now with the Gods. You have come to warn me of the devil that wants to burn me to the ground.*'

Ulric could not answer the voice. It was as if his mind had been plucked from inside his head and it was being scrutinised. *'I have been fooled, Ulric son of Merek, grandson of the legendary leader, Eijanbrook. Those that have betrayed me will pay.* Ulric drew in a breath he felt his heart in his throat and his pulse quickened. *He had no control over his thoughts or his body it was as if the tree was observing him, looking into his very being. Assessing his worthiness. You need to flee from here as fast as you can. Your sister and your Great Seer Ogda will know what to do.*

You must join them and your father. We have lots to do to prepare for battle. Our very existence hinges on it. The Asur have plans for a barren wasteland where they can rule for an eternity. They are an ancient enemy that we must crush.'

Ulric heard Krea and Kacha calling for him to hurry. The village warriors had discovered the dead bodies of their comrades.

'Go Ulric, you will find your horses in a paddock to the west of here. You must make haste!'

Suddenly the light was gone and he fell backwards, crashing into Krea. He scrambled to his feet. 'Hurry, we have to go!'

'That's what I just said!' Kacha replied.

'What about Pancome?' Krea strode over to the man, placing a hand on his shoulder. Pancome sat lifeless at the foot of the tree. Krea gently closed the eyes that were open in a vacant stare.

'Leave him, he is gone. Come on!' Ulric could barely restrain the rising panic as he made his way from behind the hut. He sucked in his breath as he heard the Seer yelling commands at the warriors to find them.

Suddenly, the ground began to tremble. The roots of the ancient tree began to rise to the surface like gigantic snakes coming from the ground. People screamed and came running out of the hut, fleeing. Ulric, Krea, and Kacha took advantage of the added chaos and ran with them, before turning west as the sun began to rise in the early morning sky.

Elenore placed her hands on her abdomen, running them gently over her stomach. A smile touched her lips as she wondered what her unborn children would look like. She had cried herself to sleep once again and she was determined that it would be the last time. She had to be strong for the two babies she was carrying. At least now she knew why she was constantly hungry. The thought caused her to let out a soft chuckle, and she pushed the hurt that Merek had given her to the back of her mind. She knew people were talking and would talk more once they knew her condition. Leaving his pregnant wife would not be favourable for their leader. Many would ask questions. She sighed and started to make her way back to her camp. She hated the Asur more than ever, they had taken so much from all of them. Her brow puckered into a tight frown. Merek had changed. He was certainly not the man she married. She suddenly wondered if she would ever forgive him if and only if he apologised and asked for her forgiveness. Elenore felt her shoulders droop and a hollow feeling sat in the pit of her stomach. He had forgone all responsibilities as a father and husband. He had discarded her like she was a bit of rubbish. Swallowing she closed her eyes wishing for it all to be over so that they could go on with a normal life.

Flamma and Tallot were waiting for her when she returned. She nodded, offering them a shaky smile but she was not impressed to see them.

'There is a morning meeting for the camp. Everyone is waiting for you,' Flamma said, a smirk on his face.

Elenore felt her jaw clench and struggled to keep her temper in check. Flamma rubbed her the wrong way. 'I will be there soon,' she told them, but it soon became obvious they were going to wait for her. She hastily put her things away and followed them to the main fire pit, wondering what the meeting was about.

People were gathered. Some were seated, while others stood as they waited for their leader to speak. Elenore felt a stab of jealousy as she saw Merek standing next to Zuri. Flamma remained beside her while Tallot went to Merek's side to whisper that Elenore was now present. Some people turned as they noticed her appearance. She felt herself blush as attention turned to her.

'I have brought you here today to talk about our future,' Merek announced. Elenore frowned. She had not been expecting Merek would be talking about a future since his whole outlook recently had been negative. 'We will be calling this valley our home for some time, not only while we wait for our great Seer to arrive and my children, but also until we win our battle against the Asur!' A roar came from the crowd. 'We need to have a home to protect us, and the Gods have provided this valley. I say let's build one!' A cheer went up and Elenore could not help but smile. Finally, they could have a home. 'There is much to be done and I need every one of you to help. I will send my men to ask the skills you can bring, and you will be placed into working parties. We will need to work together. We have done this, so far and that is why we have survived.' Another roar from the crowd. 'I must stress again that the forest must be protected. It is our ally, friend, and protector. Those that are found disobeying this rule will be severely punished.' Merek had taken a stern and authoritative tone. Murmurs rippled throughout the people. 'Please wait here while someone comes to take your details. Does anyone have any questions?' Merek asked his people.

'Will everyone have a house?' someone shouted. Another murmur of agreement went through them.

'Everyone is entitled to a home, but they will not be big, in order to preserve the forest. For larger families we will have to try other ways to accommodate so if you have ideas, I am open to them.'

Elenore felt the familiar pull of admiration towards her husband, but she quickly squashed it. The last several weeks had been immersed with hurt and resentment began to simmer. All the reasons why she had fallen for Merek were evident in the speech he had just given, he not only was a good leader, but he radiated reliability and strength which some leaders lacked. But why had he been so cruel to her? Elenore bit her lip as she tried to work through her feelings that were starting to change towards Merek. Her thoughts turned to Zuri, and she wondered what he saw in her. The answer came to her almost immediately: she was beautiful, many men would find it hard to resist her.

'What are ye thinking, Norrie?' Elenore jumped as she heard Sabin's question. She gave him a brief embrace in greeting.

'I was wondering why Merek has fallen for the woman who stands next to him.'

Flamma who was still standing next to Elenore interrupted, 'Have you seen her? Look at her! She is stunning. My brother is a lucky bastard!'

Elenore shifted uncomfortably, she had temporarily forgotten he was still near her.

'Aye Flamma, it maybe she is the most beautiful woman in all the land, but I feel her heart is not quite as ye may think or as beautiful.' Sabin glared at Flamma.

Merek's brother shook his head. 'I don't care what her heart is, if she is beautiful that is all a man wants and desires.'

Sabin chuckled. 'Aye, but not all men think the same.'

Flamma laughed. Elenore had grown uncomfortable though she was grateful for Sabin's interjection. 'Think what you like, Sabin, but I know for sure she is a good one. Wouldn't mind her for myself.'

Elenore felt repulsed as she heard Flamma talk.

'Aye, Norrie, let's go sit down.' Elenore was grateful for Sabin's suggestion and readily agreed. The pair left and sat on a log, watching as a group of men and women came around with a list taking people's details. 'I will try and talk to Merek. The healer told me about him not wanting to accept the babies.'

Sabin put his arm around Elenore, offering her his charismatic smile. She returned his smile. Sabin was kind and attractive, he had a heart of gold and many a woman had tried to catch him, yet he had chosen Edyth. She had been a woman that was hard to get to know and though Elenore forgave her for not wanting to become her friend, she still wondered why Sabin had fallen for her so deeply.

'Thank you, Sabin you are a good friend, he may listen to you. His unborn children will need him.'

'Aye, they will, that is for sure. I do not like the woman he shares his bed with now.' Elenore recoiled as she heard Sabin's last comment. She had hoped that Merek had not slept with Zuri, that he had enough integrity and love for his wife to not cross that boundary.

Sabin realised he had said too much as he saw the look of hurt cross Elenore's face when the words left his mouth. 'I am sorry, Norrie, I thought ye knew.'

She shook her head, not trusting herself to speak. Deep down, she'd thought Merek was just going through some phase of not accepting more responsibility, but now it seemed his relationship with Zuri was becoming more serious. Sabin reached out and took hold of Elenore's hand giving it a squeeze.

'How do you know, Sabin? I mean, have you spoken to him?' Elenore could not help herself, she had to know.

Sabin shifted uncomfortably. 'Men talk, Norrie. Not for women's ears, ye understand?' Elenore remained silent and when Sabin pressed her further, she mumbled that she understood.

Tallot soon appeared to take down Elenore's details.

'Tallot?' He looked up from what he was writing. 'I am having twins, so I may need a little extra room.' A look of surprise crossed Tallot's face. She was over the shame and suddenly wanted everyone to know that Merek had not only abandoned her, but also his unborn children. Her anger was manifesting.

Tallot cast a quick look at Sabin who offered a weak smile. 'Aye, Tallot, it is true. Merek and Elenore are having twins.'

Tallot gave Elenore an approving look before writing down what she had just informed him. 'We will do our best, Elenore.' He looked up at her with a gentleness now in his eyes.

Elenore offered him a smile. She had always been attracted to Tallot and had wondered why he had pulled away from her. Zuri came to mind.

'We are also taking down what skills you have and what you can offer in rebuilding a village for the future?' he said. Elenore frowned at the question. She did not know what skills she had.

'I am not sure. What help do you need?'

Tallot scanned the list he had been taking. There was a moment of silence. 'How about I let you know when we are finished? I am sure you could be of help somewhere,' he finally said.

Elenore offered him a warm smile. Tallot began to ask Sabin his details, turning his attention to the curly haired man.

Elenore made her way to the giant vegetable patch that she had helped build. Serenity was watering the freshly sown seeds and gave Elenore an enthusiastic hello as she came through the gate.

'Hello, Elenore, I was hoping to see you today. I need some help in watering.' She gestured to the garden beds. Elenore took the empty water skins that lay beside the healer and offered to fill them up. As she made her way back from the river she felt a hand touch her on her shoulder. Elenore wheeled around Zuri stood before her, her arms folded her face pinched with anger.

'What are you trying to do, Elenore? Get sympathy? Merek does not want you, or your brats!' Zuri's face was twisted.

Elenore stopped. Sabin's earlier words went through her mind and she instantly understood what he had meant. Zuri's beauty had vanished, replaced by a look of ugly hate.

'I only told the truth. Why, does it bother you so much?' Elenore mocked. 'The only reason my husband is with you is because of them,' she added.

Zuri spat at the ground, narrowly missing Elenore's shoes.

'Remember, he is sharing my bed not yours, regardless of the children you do or don't have,' Zuri sneered.

Elenore felt like a knife had gone through her heart, her feelings crushed. She could think of nothing to say and pushed past the horrible woman. Zuri dug her shoulder into her as she went past, nearly knocking her to the ground. 'Be careful, Elenore, I don't let anyone push me around.'

Elenore turned to face the tall blonde woman, her anger mounting, 'Neither do I!' she retorted.

Sabin promised Edyth he would come back soon and help her with the washing. He had told her about Elenore's current situation, and he had noticed her attitude soften towards her. She had lost twins, and to know another woman was carrying a pair offered a possible connection. Giving birth was risky enough, having two at once was even more precarious.

'A good leader does not abandon his wife when she needs him most,' she said as he turned to leave. Sabin nodded in agreement and set off to find Merek.

Merek was with a group of men surveying the forest trying to work out how many trees to fell without making too much of an impact. He broke into a grin as his curly haired friend approached. Although Sabin knew Merek doubted his decision to marry Edyth, it seemed his friend had still missed him.

'Sabin, what brings you here? I haven't seen you in ages!' Merek ruffled his friend's curly black hair.

'Aye I have been busy, as ye can imagine.' Sabin let out a soft chuckle.

'I can imagine. Edyth does have a few children, they would definitely keep you busy.'

'Aye, they do, Merek. But I love em' they are little gems.' Merek nodded. 'Can we go somewhere and talk in private, Merek?' It was not often that Sabin was serious. Merek looked at the other men who were waiting for him to resume their discussion. 'I promise ye, it won't take long.'

'Sure,' Merek answered, telling the men to take a break and that he would be back soon. Merek and Sabin walked far enough away to be out of earshot.

'I saw Norrie this morning, Merek. She told me ye was expecting twins and I think she needs ye.'

Merek's clenched and unclenched his jaw. 'Sabin, I appreciate your concern for my wife, but she knows how I feel and that won't be changing.'

Sabin frowned. He was shocked by his friend's indifference to the children he had helped create. 'What should she do, then?' Sabin asked in a low voice. Before Merek had time to answer Sabin continued, 'She can't raise em' alone, she needs ye and ye did have a part in making em'.' Sabin deliberately kept his tone calm, as he could see Merek's growing anger.

'I am with someone else now, Sabin. I appreciate your concern. You are a good friend of mine and Elenore, but I don't want to discuss this with you again. Now I have a village to build.' Merek turned, not giving Sabin another look as he made his way back to the waiting group of men.

Sabin watched him go feeling a deep sadness; not only was Merek throwing away his life with Elenore, but he was also pushing his friendship away.

Ulric tried to put as much distance as he could between them and Shakurta village. The ancient tree was destroying the village that had been its custodian since the dawn of time. He was not sure if the tree would survive, and he worried that this would hamper their efforts in locating Dardanos.

'Ulric, we have to rest the horses we still have a long way to go,' Krea interrupted his thoughts.

He nodded and reined in his gelding. They combed the landscape to find a suitable place to rest. Kacha pointed to a rocky overhang not far from them. Ulric nodded and they made their way to rest until the following morning. It had been a long night and morning.

After they had tended to the horses Krea offered to go hunt with Romulus; they were all famished. Ulric tended to Kacha's wounds, tearing another strip from his tunic and rebandaging the large gash.

'How long before we get to Ogda's house?' Kacha asked. Ulric offered him a smile his friend looked pale, and he knew he had lost a lot of blood.

'I think it will be a few days. We will take it easy for you, don't worry, Kacha. You saved us today.' Kacha nodded weakly before falling into a deep sleep.

Anja, Ada, and Ogda strolled near the tree line that faced the modest home. A bird shrieked before breaking out into a melodious tune in the hope of finding a mate. The Seer had a heavy heart; he knew that his beloved forest would soon be reduced to ashes.

'Ulric has succeeded in telling the ancient tree of the betrayal of his people. There has been a lot of destruction, the Seer has fled with his warriors, taking as many as he can to offer to the Asur. Many of his people have died or have been left homeless. The Asur are on their way to seek vengeance and burn down the oldest plant on the planet. I am afraid they will succeed.'

'This can't be! I have to get to the tree, it is our only hope!' Ada cried.

Ogda sighed. 'I know. We will go and take the tea, and mind travel there now. The Seer has gone so we do not have to worry about being seen. We don't have much time and yes, the reason is we had to wait for them to leave. Anja you must prepare to leave. Mind travel to find out where the Asur are located so you can map out the best way to get to Merek. Now let's go back inside we have work to do!'

The village had been reduced to rubble; trees had fallen leaving an enormous gaping hole in the thick canopy of forest. People staggered about the ruins in a state of shock, lost children cried, calling for their parents. A feeling of despondency and loss enveloped Shakurta village.

Ada's heart ached for the people who had now become the Asur's latest victims.

'We don't have time for pity, Ada, they are almost here,' Ogda warned.

Ada forced her mind away from the loss that she felt and focused on locating the ancient tree. It was not long before they could see it, looming high above the canopy: a lighthouse in a sea of green.

The tree sensed them before they had an opportunity to introduce themselves and ask questions. *'You seek the king and queen of the evil that has been a common enemy to us both. They are hidden in an underground labyrinth near where Merek has sought refuge—'*

'Thank you, Arius, this will help us immensely,' Ada interrupted.

'Tread carefully, they are stronger than you think and the Seer who has joined them is more sinister than I realised. He fooled me and the people he was supposed to take care of. He has made a pact with the devil. The trees will help you. It is important you keep working as one for one cannot survive without the other. There is a tree that the Gods have chosen to replace me.

Arius paused, both Ada and Ogda held their breath this information was new to them. *'As you know, we seem to believe the illusion of living for an eternity when we can't. We are only mortal, not the Gods we sometimes think we are. My time on earth is finished. I cannot run from the fire that will be set. Have faith and do not give up hope. Courage will carry you through. Now you need to leave, there is no more time to discuss this further, it is not safe here anymore!'*

Ogda nodded. He did not want to argue with the tree. It had been an honour just to speak to such a legendary piece of flora. The smell of smoke filled the air as Ada trailed the Seer. The forest was on fire. The Asur had arrived.

'Wait!' Ada paused, looking back to where they had left the ancient tree. 'What about the people? They will be burned alive, they can't escape a raging fire.'

'Dear Ada, we do not have time to save them, or we will perish too. Sometimes we must sacrifice a few to save many,' Ogda said gently.

Ada did not reply, she knew he was right. She took one last look at the ruined village, the lush forest, her chest tightened and a lump came to Ada's throat. 'I never want to return; this land has been cursed.' She fled returning to her physical body as quickly as she could bringing with her the hurt, she felt for all that had been lost and all that were going to perish.

Ada and the Seer returned exhausted; mind travelling was draining.

Ludwig was preparing lunch when they emerged from their deep, dreamless sleep. They joined the others seated around the timber table, and Ogda drew comfort from the people gathered.

'Did you find what you were looking for?' Matlin asked after he finished his first mouthful of food. The Seer nodded and grimaced at the thought of the village burning.

'Do not ask questions unless you can handle the answers.'

Matlin was caught off guard, then quickly realised Ogda knew exactly all the questions he had in his mind. 'I just want to know what happened to my people and the forest we protect.'

The Seer gave a long sigh and looked directly at the man seated in front of him. 'They are both gone.'

Matlin held Ogda's gaze for a moment before looking away. Kaiah buried her head in her hands, overcome with emotion.

'Can't we do anything?' Rory asked. The Seer shook his head.

Ada moved the food around on her plate, images of lost children and a devastated people clouding her mind. 'We have to move on and plan the beginning of the end of the Asur.' She looked up from her plate, a determined look on her face.

Kaiah wiped her face with her napkin to remove the tears that streamed down her face. 'What do we need to do then?'

Ogda gave them a faint smile. 'We will wait for your horses to rest and recover, and you will all leave for Merek's hidden valley. Anja will go with you. Ada and I will wait here for Ulric and the others to arrive. We need somewhere safe to hide our physical bodies, and I am afraid the Asur are closer than I would like. They will come and burn the forest and the home you are now in. We will join you in the valley, and there we will plan our battle. Ada and I need to find Dardanos and her king.'

Kaiah smiled weakly at the Seer, thankful that he had been honest with her.

'Why can't we all go together?' Rory asked.

'You cannot afford to wait for the others, and we still have work here to do,' Ada explained.

Rory frowned. 'What work?'

Matlin touched the young teen's arm and shook his head. Rory frowned and pursed his lips before placing a forkful of food in his mouth.

Ulric built a fire while he waited for Krea to return from her hunt. He glanced over at Kacha who was still sound asleep. He had made him as comfortable as possible with what little supplies they had. The sun had risen high in the midday sky, and he moved away from the warmth of the fire. It was already a hot day. He hoped Krea would not be much longer, the fire was only to cook the meat she would bring back.

Ulric was thankful they had their horses. It would have been a massive loss if they had not been able to find them. He sat against the edge of the stony wall that framed the outcrop of rock that offered them shelter. Ulric closed his eyes, thinking of all that had transpired in the last few days. He groaned inwardly as the images of a displaced people came to mind; their home taken from them by the very thing they were meant to protect. Sleep beckoned him and it did not take much for him to give in to its demand.

Elenore licked her fingers. The roasted meat had tasted delicious, and her hunger finally had been satiated. Edyth watched her closely; Sabin had suggested they invite her for lunch which she had agreed to. The curly haired man had offered to take some lunch to Huxley, leaving both Elenore and Edyth alone.

'What are your plans, Elenore?' The small woman's direct question and gaze took Elenore off guard. She took a drink from the cup in front of her and sighed. It was time to try and move on and make a life for herself and her unborn children. But a stubborn persistence of not wanting to throw away her marriage to Merek kept tugging at her.

She looked away for a moment, before returning Edyth's gaze. 'I am not sure.'

The small woman's eyes narrowed. 'You need to take charge of your life. You cannot wait for him, he has caught the whiff of the devil's whore and now shares his bed with her.' Elenore felt like she had been slapped, but Edyth did not wait for her to respond. 'Get your house sorted, the ones that they are promising and have your babies. If it was me, I wouldn't take him back. I mean, what sort of man leaves his wife when she carries his child?' Her tone became harder as she spoke. 'He doesn't deserve you. Don't you take him back, Elenore. He is with that stupid girl who thinks she is all that!' Edyth tisked. Although Elenore had been hurt by her words, the reference Edyth made to Zuri made her chuckle. She, along with others, had realised that her heart was full of ill doing. 'Thank you. I guess you are right, I do deserve better, and I will have my house built.' She grinned as she took another sip from her cup. Edyth grunted and stood to clear the dishes. Edyth was strong and full of courage, she had learned to survive. Elenore admired her, she was a pillar of strength. 'How is Huxley doing?'

Edyth paused in stacking the plates. 'To be honest, he is doing better. The hypnosis made him remember the reason why the Gods spared him. He wants to seek revenge on the bastards that took so much from us.' Her tone was bitter, and her face took on a hard look. Elenore nodded. She understood the hate he felt towards them. 'You fight for those babies you carry Elenore, you fight for them!' Edyth came to stand in front of Elenore.

Elenore smiled weakly. 'I will Edyth.'

Ulric ran after his sister, her long white hair flowing behind her. He could hear her giggles which brought a smile to his face. The large rock pool lay in front of them, and he watched as she did not hesitate to enter the water.

'I won, Ulric!' Ada turned to splash water at him her laughter filling the summer day.

'That's only because I gave you a head start!' He splashed her back. Suddenly the rock pool vanished, and they were standing high on a cliff, looking at the valley below them. 'You can't leave yet. One of you may not make it. You must stay until he heals. A leader will be told where to find you he brings many men. Wait for the other to heal and for him to arrive than make haste to our Seer's hidden home. Remember, the Asur are near.'

Ulric woke with a start. He wiped his face and ran his hand through his hair. Ada's words echoed through his mind and he jumped to his feet, making his way to Kacha. He was still out cold but as Ulric came closer, he noticed a bead of sweat trickling down his face. Ulric put his hand against Kacha's skin and pulled back instantly; he was burning up.

The fire had long gone out and late afternoon shadows darkened the shallow cave. He looked around for Krea, but she still had not returned. He unbuttoned Kacha's shirt and gently pulled it over his head. Kacha murmured, but did not wake. Ulric grabbed the only water skin they had it was almost empty. He poured a little water on the tunic and carefully sponged Kacha's face.

'What's happened?' Ulric jumped, startled to hear Krea's voice.

'I think he has a fever.' Ulric turned to face her.

Her brow pinched with worry as she kneeled next to Kacha. 'It must be from the wounds he sustained, they must be infected.' She touched his face with the back of her hand. 'He's burning up, Ulric.'

'I know and we do not have any water left. Did you come across any close by?'

Krea stood up but kept her eyes on Kacha, as if her gaze would prevent him getting worse. 'Yes, I found a little stream not too far from here and' – she tore her eyes from Kacha to look at Ulric – 'I found a wandering pack horse. I would say the Asur got to its master, and it managed to escape. I also brought down a couple of hares, so we won't starve tonight.'

Ulric nodded. At least Krea had brought good news. He helped her unpack the horse she had found and was delighted to find there were another three waterskins, a small bow and arrow and some dry rations.

'This is excellent, Krea!'

She smiled at him and offered to go and fill the waterskins. When she returned, Ulric proceeded to tell her about the dream he had had earlier.

She pursed her lips. 'Ada can mind travel, which is a good sign, but I do worry about staying here. The Asur are all around. I picked up on their tracks when Romulus and I were out hunting.'

'We don't have a choice. Kacha needs to rest and heal, and we have to wait for the leader that is to arrive.'

Despite his words, Ulric was also worried. He would have to quickly skin and cook the hares they could not risk having a fire. One of them would have to stand guard, they were not well hidden, and the Asur were good at finding their prey. A creeping sensation sent chills and he felt fear clutch at him.

CHAPTER SEVENTEEN

An Injustice

The tapestry of humanity is incomplete without the vibrant
threads woven by women.
Elenore

Takeo reined in his large stallion and wiped away the sweat that had begun to run down his face. The day was hot and windy, and the smell of burning trees hung in the air, stifling his lungs. The Asur were behind them setting fire to the forest that Takeo and his ancestors had protected since the dawn of time. Now, it was coming to an end. His home, family and community were all gone except for the few brave souls that would follow him to the ends of the earth.

He had awoken from his trance and was horrified at the scene that was playing out in front of him. Chaos, turmoil, and confusion surrounded him. The screams of his people still rung in his ears and would haunt him for the rest of his life. He had tried to make sense of what was and what had happened, and his loyal supporters had quickly filled him in advising him of their Seer's betrayal. At first, he was in disbelief but as he came to terms with not only what he was hearing but what he was seeing, an enormous rage began to fester within him.

He turned in his saddle. They were stopped on top of a ridge and could see the tree line in the distance. Smoke billowed high in the sky, a thick black cloud of soot. Takeo was a heavily built man with a long beard that reached down to his abdomen. His dark skin was covered in tattoos of differing shapes and symbols. He glanced over the group that had steadily increased in numbers during the week since they had fled their home. Most were fleeing, trying to find a safe place to hide from the evil casting its sinister net. A few had told him of the reoccurring dream they'd had of making their way to Merek, son of

Eijanbrook. A hidden valley they had said, a place to hide and gather strength to fight the Asur.

Takeo frowned when he thought about Merek. Somehow, he had heard the name before, but could not place where.

'They are only a day's ride away, we must increase our pace,' A younger warrior advised as he reined in his horse beside Takeo.

'I understand, but my horse is not a runner he is more like a cart horse, powerful and strong, meant for pulling carts not fleeing the devil.' Takeo sighed. 'The girl that makes me dream has told me Ulric is not far from here. We should make it by nightfall. Our fate is in the hands of the Gods.' He did not wait for a response instead he urged his horse forward, leaving the young warrior behind.

Ludwig hobbled over to the pack horse, placing the last of the food rations in one of the saddle bags it carried. Even though he loved the extra company it had been draining and it made his body ache. Ludwig had been deformed at birth, a cleft palate and curvature of the spine. His mother had died in childbirth, leading to his father leaving him to the Gods in the Majestic Forest.

Ogda had dreamed of finding the newborn and had rescued the infant. Ludwig had been with him ever since and adored the man who had given him a second chance. He was relieved when his master had relented in letting him stay and travel with him to Merek. '

Thank you, Ludwig. You are truly a gift, I don't know how we could survive without you.' Anja smiled at him warmly. Ludwig beamed and embraced the older woman.

'Take care and we will see you soon, Anja,' he sniffed. Anja carefully extracted herself from his grasp and mounted her mare. Matlin, Kaiah, and Rory were waiting patiently as they watched Anja say her goodbyes.

'You know where to go. The Gods and the forest will guide and protect you. Make haste, we must prepare for the battle ahead.' Ogda advised them. Ludwig brushed away a tear and glanced over at Ogda. He noted his eyes were streaked with bloodshot veins, his shoulders drooped forward, his slight frame sagging with fatigue. A tremor ran through Ogda's hand as he held up his hand to bid the group farewell. Ludwig had never seen him like this before and it frightened him.

'You have my word. Please do not worry unnecessarily, you know where to find me.' Anja offered him an encouraging smile. Ogda merely nodded his eyes gazing over Anja's shoulder at the forest that lay behind her.

Elenore heaved on the shovel to dig up the hard ground beside her half-built cottage. The progress the community had made was astounding. Nearly every man, woman, and child had offered to help in any way they could. It had soon become obvious that the group that had been assigned originally to Eijanbrook were full of valuable skills which now had come in handy in building a new village. Elenore often wondered what had happened to the other groups that had been split to increase the odds of human survival.

She sighed and took a drink from her waterskin. The day was getting hotter, and she was determined to finish the little garden bed at the front of her soon to be home. It had not rained for a while making the ground hard and difficult to dig. Her back ached and a mixture of dirt and sweat covered her tunic. The thought of leaving everything and going to the river to bathe and swim was almost too much to resist. However, a new thought of Merek and his new partner gave her the energy to persist and finally with a grunt she was able to dig the hole deep enough.

Serenity had given her a handful of seeds she had collected on the journey to the valley. She had said they were the seeds of a beautiful flowering shrub and would be perfect for Elenore's garden. Elenore was consistently amazed at what the healer provided, she was always on the lookout for things that would come in handy. She sprinkled the seeds into the freshly dug earth and watered them with the last of the water from the waterskin. She sighed, finally she had finished. Returning to her tent, she retrieved a fresh tunic and some trousers to put on after her swim in the river. She quickly put away the gardening tools and grabbed her towel off the makeshift clothesline before heading down to the pool of water.

She had slowly become used to her loneliness and looked forward to seeing her older children. Tallot had been helping by hunting for her and checking in to see if she needed anything. She still felt a strong attraction to the handsome warrior.

Flamma still tried to manipulate her feelings and she loathed him even more. Her friendship with Edyth was steadily growing, but the woman possessed a deep hatred towards her husband, and Merek's rejection of Elenore and his unborn children had only fuelled her animosity.

Edyth was not the only one who had become aware of the situation between their leader and his wife. Some had offered their sympathy, others had sided with Merek as Zuri was such a beautiful woman. However, Elenore could feel that there had been a shift away from Zuri, her cold heart and mean streak had surfaced numerous times. She had even noticed Merek beginning to change towards her. In time, he would come to realise exactly who she was and the mistake he had made.

The sun was at its midway point as she approached the watering hole, it was quiet and she was pleasantly surprised. *I have the whole pool to myself,* she smiled.

Elenore quickly undressed and dove into the cool water. She swam and enjoyed the delicious feeling of freshness the water gave her. As she reached the far side, she noticed Merek sitting in the sun, drying himself. At first, she wanted to flee, but something stopped her, and she felt helpless, unable to leave, nor tear her gaze away from him.

She had always been attracted to Merek and it had only grown over the years. They had been together for so long and she felt the tug of the familiar heartache pull at her. He was an impressive looking man, tall and powerfully built. His long wavy hair hung loose and wavered in the breeze and his olive skin glistened in the sun. Merek was completely naked, letting the sun dry him and turning him to a deep golden brown.

Elenore dragged her eyes away from him and quietly turned to make her way back to the other side. She threw one last look at her husband and sucked in her breath as she saw he was sitting up and had noticed her. He offered her a smile, making her heart melt and tears began to well.

'Norrie, I think we need to talk.' The fact that he had used her pet name pushed away the last bit of desire she had to leave. She looked to the far side of the pool it seemed far away and quiet, not a soul was in sight.

Merek was pulling on a pair of trousers. She made her way towards him and took the towel he offered her. He waited for her to settle herself next to him and squeeze the water out of her dark coppery hair. Merek offered her a brief smile Elenore averted his gaze. 'I know you will never forgive me and that is not what I want to talk to you about,' he began. Elenore kept her mouth closed. She did not trust herself to speak afraid she would burst into tears. 'People have been talking and I am their leader. In the best interest of the community, I think it would be wise that we are seen to get along.'

Merek paused and pulled at his beard. A thousand thoughts ran through Elenore's mind and soon she began to feel the familiar sense of betrayal. The feeling of bursting into tears was surpassed by her growing anger.

'Is there anything else you wanted to talk to me about?' She kept her voice low and even, struggling with the rage that stormed inside her.

Merek looked over to the far side of the water hole, avoiding making eye contact. 'I want you to share meals with me occasionally and to help with the ceremonies.'

'Is that all?'

His expression turned to irritation at her response. 'You make everything difficult,' he growled.

'My reaction is how any woman would feel after her husband abandons her when she needs him most. No. I won't ever forgive you Merek! Go back to that whore who warms your bed and ask her to help, because I won't!' Elenore had unleashed the raging storm inside her a tide of pent-up emotions had come crashing down. Her body shook as she flung the towel at him and dove into the water, making her way back to the other side.

Elenore pulled the tunic over her head grabbing her towel she hastily left the watering hole. Her body seemed to vibrate with barely restrained energy and she struggled not to break into a run. Taking deep breaths she entered her tent grabbing her comb she plonked herself down on her furs. She pulled the comb through her hair. The motion was soothing and helped calm her. Her encounter with Merek at the rock pool had shaken her and she struggled to grasp how much her husband had changed. He was not the man she had fallen in love with and she wondered how he could have changed so much.

She sighed and put the comb down and laid back on her furs. After their argument she had walked the circuit of the valley, losing track of time as she tried to calm the inner storm within her. Elenore sighed and closed her eyes, but her mind kept drifting back to the scene at the rock pool. She opened her eyes again and glanced around her small, makeshift home.

The late afternoon sun cast dancing shadows that bounced around the tent walls. It was too early for her to sleep and as she sat up, she heard the horn calling the community group to the main fire. She groaned inwardly. The last thing she felt like doing was seeing Merek again, let alone Zuri.

What if I don't go? The question hung, dangling, daring her to explore it further. *What could he do? People are beginning to become unhappy hence the reason why he had asked me to help him when we were in the rock pool.* The more she thought about it, the more she became convinced that she wouldn't go. She went to her tent opening and poked her head out. The sound of people making their way to the main campfire could be heard.

Elenore ducked back inside, not wanting to be noticed if someone walked past and asked her why she was not going. She had no excuse, except for the simple fact she did not want to go. She waited. The horn sounded again to warn the stragglers that the ceremony or speech or whatever the reason for being summoned was, was about to begin. She held her breath, but did not move.

Her body began to tremble. She had never rebelled or completely disobeyed rules before. In normal times, if a person did not have a valid reason, a punishment would be handed down. It was believed that for a community to live in harmony it was important for all to be involved in special gatherings and decisions, though ultimately the end decision rested on the Council and village leader. Elenore stayed rooted to the spot.

The shadows soon grew to darkness, but she dared not light a torch for fear someone would see the light. She had decided her excuse would be that she had fallen asleep and had not heard the horn. Pregnant women needed to rest and slept more than usual. She laid on her furs, her heart still pounding as she waited for the ceremony to finish. She could hear distant talking, shouts and then whistles.

The evening dragged on, and soon laughter was heard above all else. Elenore knew they must have been celebrating something, the red wine had been brought out by the sounds of all the laughter. She wondered when it would ever run out. It seemed they had a never-ending supply of it. Suddenly she heard approaching footsteps and she squeezed her eyes shut, forcing her breath to slow.

'There you are!' The tent flap was flung open and Tallot peered inside the gloom of the tent. Elenore was relieved that he would not be able to see very well inside. She held her breath. 'I know you are not asleep, Elenore.' Tallot's voice was slightly slurred, indicating that he had had some of the red drink. She did not respond and in the faint light that filtered through the tent opening, she could see him trying to locate her in the small space inside.

Tallot squinted, trying to make out where Elenore was. As he took a step closer to her furs the toe of his boot caught hold of the edge of one of them. Frantically trying to balance himself Tallot reached out before falling face first into the soft bed underneath. Elenore rolled out of the way, but the image of Tallot's flailing arms and look of surprise made her squirm with laughter.

Trying hard to contain herself she managed, 'Tallot, are you okay?'

'I knew you were not asleep.' Tallot propped himself up, rubbing his nose.

Elenore reached out, touching his face but soon was overcome with laughter once again. She fell back onto the furs writhing with merriment. Tallot began to chuckle the red drink had relaxed him. He also fell back among the furs.

'Should I leave, Elenore?' Tallot asked his voice barley a whisper.

Elenore had grown quiet, with only the odd giggle. Tallot sat up on one elbow and looked down at her. His eyes had become accustomed to the gloom and as he gazed down at her Elenore noted the look of admiration and desire. She felt her breath catch in her throat as he stared back. She could not tear her gaze away from him. Tallot bent closer, his lips brushing against hers. He waited, as if expecting her to turn away, but she continued to lay there, her eyes closed.

Tallot's mouth crushed against Elenore's, and she felt her desire grow as she leaned into him. She felt his hands move over her, then he was fumbling with the belt that held his trousers. A part of her screamed to make him stop, the other part urged her to make love to him. What did it matter what she did? Merek did not love her anymore.

Her breathing became rapid as she felt her body tingle and her yearning grow. Tallot was struggling to take down her underwear and she lifted her hips, trying to help him. The sudden rustling of the tent opening made them both jump. Tallot instantly rolled off her and pulled up his trousers. Zuri stood at the doorway, a torch held high as she realised what she had just interrupted.

'Well, what is going on here? Tallot, Merek asked you to find Elenore and find out why she could not make the ceremony, but it looks like you got sidetracked.' Her eyes flickered gleefully like a cat that had just caught its prey. 'Best you both get dressed, I am sure Merek will be only too happy to serve out some sort of punishment for adultery.'

Elenore stood from her furs. 'That is calling the kettle black, Zuri considering you are sleeping with my husband!' Elenore raged.

Zuri took a step closer to Elenore, a wicked expression on her face. 'That is where you are wrong. You see, a man can choose to sleep with who he pleases and who can blame him? I mean look at you. Pregnant, not so young anymore, and you couldn't even keep him in your bed,' she hissed.

Elenore slapped Zuri. Hard. 'Get out! You are a witch!'

Zuri held her cheek and took a step back. 'I am going to make your life a misery. You are not going to get away with this.'

'Get out, you evil woman! Go and join the Asur, that is where you belong!' Elenore took a step toward Zuri who backed away and fled from the tent.

Tallot joined Elenore at her fire. 'I think I had better go, Elenore. It won't do us any good if he sees me here with you, it will only infuriate him more.' Tallot gently kissed the top of Elenore's head, before tenderly pushing away a strand of hair.

Elenore nodded but did not say anything. She was disappointed with herself; she had almost slept with another man and now the person she loathed the most had caught her. Life did not seem fair, and darkness descended upon her.

She watched Tallot go and soon could hear someone coming towards her camp. Merek stormed through the undergrowth. His nostrils flared and a furious look covered his face.

'Where is he?'

'He has left, Merek,' Elenore said quietly.

'What were you thinking?'

Elenore turned her face to Merek but stayed seated on the log. 'I was not thinking and—' she stopped herself from continuing and cast her eyes back to the ground at her feet. Zuri was right, men had more rights than women. Regardless of what they did, they were able to get away with far more. She would be the one in the wrong. Not only was Merek still her husband, he was also leader of their community.

Merek clenched his jaw. 'You are going to pay for this, do you hear me?' He reached forward, cupping her chin making her look at him. 'I am so disappointed in you Elenore.' Merek let her go and spat, then stormed back the way he had come.

A week later Elenore woke to a distant thunder. Her tent was rattling with the wind and cloaked in darkness. She peered out of the opening, and a dark menacing sky greeted her. She glanced over at her almost finished hut and wished she was already in there. The weather had been kind since they had come to the valley nearly three months ago, but now it was taking a turn for the worse. She wasn't sure how her little tent would hold up. She had managed to patch the holes that had started to appear, but she doubted if they would hold up to a storm.

She sighed. She would have to see if she could move in with Serenity for a little while until her own home was finished. She went back in and quickly began to pack her things. The sound of her name being called startled her and she quickly went out to see who it was.

'I thought it was you!' Elenore embraced the medicine woman.

'Elenore, there is a big storm coming, you will need to come and stay with me.'

Elenore smiled. 'I was just about to do that. I have already started packing up my things.'

Serenity chuckled and followed Elenore inside to help her pack her things. Elenore was surprised by the number of things she had acquired and as they went back for the last lot of her belongings the wind began to blow even harder.

Serenity urged Elenore to hurry, worried they would be caught in the approaching storm. The women ran to Serenity's home as a heavy deluge erupted from the black sky.

'We made it girl!' Serenity said as she burst through the front door. Elenore followed her into the kitchen, dumping the rest of her things on the small table. Serenity busied herself in lighting the fire to make some tea.

Elenore felt envious of the healer. She was one of the first to be able to move into her home. Merek had made his wife wait until last, knowing how important it was for her to have a home. That had been a cruel blow.

'Merek still hasn't told me what my punishment will be.' She sat on one of the chairs in the small kitchen.

'Hmm that is strange.' Serenity mused.

'He couldn't wait to serve out Tallot's.' Elenore closed her eyes to block out the image of Tallot's public flogging. She had been humiliated and surprised at the ferocity of what Merek had decided. Merek had made Elenore watch and used it as an example for others. Elenore had not seen or spoken to Tallot since that day, and she felt a deep sorrow for the man.

'When will a Council be decided?' Elenore asked.

'Soon, I should imagine. Merek has sent out scouts to search for the other groups. He is focused on looking for survivors.' Serenity handed Elenore a steaming mug of tea. 'Your mother-in-law will be here soon, she brings others that will be part of your future.'

Elenore almost dropped her cup as she heard what Serenity had just said. 'What? I mean *when*? Praise the Gods! This is excellent news, Serenity!' Elenore clapped her hands together. Finally, someone would be able to talk sense into Merek.

'I knew you would be excited. I am sure they will be here by this evening, if my feeling is right.' Serenity chuckled. She enjoyed seeing Elenore happy. She had been through a lot, and the healer was taken aback by how Merek was treating her. Many women had confided in her that they thought he was too harsh on her, and that Zuri was the wrong woman to be with.

'I will have to get ready. There will need to be a ceremony and—' Elenore stood up and began to pace. '

Sit down, dear girl, we will prepare once the storm has passed. Please, I have not told a soul you are the only one.' Elenore nodded and sat back on her chair. She was thrilled and excitement bubbled inside her.

'Wait until I tell Anja she is having twin grandchildren. Merek won't be able to continue to ignore their existence then.' Elenore took a sip of her tea, barely tasting it as her mind raced.

Anja shaded her eyes, looking at the dark clouds that gathered over the peaks of Dorhall Pass.

'Do you know how much further the valley is?' Matlin said as he walked his horse next to Anja's mare.

'We will seek shelter Matlin, and reach the valley this evening.' She paused and swept her gaze over the open landscape. It was breathtaking and she revelled in the scene in front of her. It had been a long time since she had been this close to Dorhall Pass, and yet it was still so far. An unsettling feeling brushed over her and she shivered.

Matlin noticed and frowned. 'What is it?' She did not answer him straight away. Instead, she once again looked at their surroundings, this time it was not to appreciate the beauty of it.

'They are watching.'

Matlin snapped his head around a look of fear on his face. 'Where?' he demanded. Anja again swept her gaze over the landscape that flanked them her lips pressed in a tight line.

'I don't know but they are watching, Matlin. They have become smarter than they once were. Your Seer has been busy educating them.' The chill had not left her, and she felt exposed as they stood on the open plain. There were very few trees, hardly any protection. If the Asur wanted to attack them, this would be the ideal time.

Rory and Kaiah picked up on Anja's concern and their father's fear. Both children glanced around, their eyes wide and their faces drained of colour.

'We must seek shelter now!' Anja commanded. As she scanned

the area, Anja noticed a small patch of trees clumped together in the near distance. Matlin pointed to them. Anja nodded and they made their way towards them. The trees would help conceal them until they felt safe enough to venture out and continue their journey to the hidden valley.

The scout pulled his panting horse to a halt before quickly dismounting and making his way to Merek's hut. Merek had noticed the scout and came out the front door before the man had a chance to knock. 'What is it?' he demanded.

'Master,' the man bowed his head. 'Your mother is almost here. She brings a man and two older children.'

Merek raised an eyebrow. He had dreamed his mother would be coming soon, but he didn't realise how soon. 'Good news, you can go now. There will be a welcoming ceremony later this evening.' Merek dismissed the man. The scout scurried away leaving Merek to think about the preparations he would have to make.

Zuri opened the door, joining him on the small porch. 'What is it, my love?' she breathed in his ear.

Merek merely grunted, not ready to tell her that his mother would be at their home within a couple of hours. She did not push him by asking the question again not wanting to spike his temper. Zuri had full intentions of becoming his new wife and help run the village when he was away. The thought brought a smile to her lips.

Darkness had started to descend, and a community of people were once again looking forward to another ceremony, this time, to welcome their former leader's wife. Excitement hung in the air, creating a festive atmosphere. Merek had built a large fire to cook the deer that had been hunted for the night's feast. Storms had passed through earlier that morning, bringing heavy rain and gusty winds. The men had been happy that all the huts had withstood the storm's damage, giving another reason to celebrate. A sense of normality was being restored among them, increasing the population's reverence towards Merek. He had succeeded in keeping them safe and offered them a new place to lay down their roots. For most, that was all that mattered.

Merek had sent warriors out to meet Anja and guide her to where the trail lay concealed. Merek himself waited with half-a-dozen warriors at the top of the trail, intent on being the one to lead his mother down to their small village. People began to gather as far as they dared along the trail to wait for Merek and Anja.

Elenore felt a mixture of apprehension and excitement. She had missed Anja, she had been like a mother to her. Her mind reached back to when she had left her original village with Merek and their children. It had been sudden and traumatic, and she felt a sadness at all the people they had left behind. They would not of stood a chance, oblivious to the evil that was about to raid and burn their village. Her parents had long been deceased, but she'd had friends that were like family, and she hated herself for not being able to warn them.

Anja and Eijanbrook had become her new family and it had been a long time since she had seen Anja. 'They're coming!' Someone shouted. A roar went up from the gathered crowd.

Elenore peered through the throng of bodies and made out the procession with Merek in the lead. She saw Anja mounted on her mare, a look of relief on her face. She had the same blonde hair as Ada, and it hung down to the middle of her back. Merek led them to the centre of the camp, young teen boys rushed to take the horses as the small group dismounted.

Tears pricked the back of Elenore's eyes and she tried to blink them away.

'Aye, this will be interesting.' Elenore turned to find Sabin grinning next to her. 'This will put that witch in her place.' Sabin chortled.

Elenore embraced her friend. 'Where is Edyth?'

'Aye, she is with the little ones, just over there with Huxley.' Sabin pointed towards the back of the crowd.

'Huxley came to see the ceremony?'

Sabin giggled. 'Of course. He wants to see the look on Zuri's face when Anja asks for ye.' Elenore smiled but shifted uncomfortably. She knew Merek would become angry with his mother when she demanded to know what happened between him and her. Elenore had always been the one to calm him, but it appeared that Zuri took enjoyment from stoking his fiery temper.

Anja handed the reins to the boy who would be looking after her horse. She had already introduced Matlin and his children to Merek, but she could not see Elenore.

'Merek, where is your beautiful wife? I have missed her terribly.'

Merek cleared his throat and looked directly at his mother. 'We are no longer together. I have taken another.' He beckoned a stunning woman who was waiting not far away.

Zuri stepped out and in front of Anja. 'I am pleased to meet you, Anja, wife of the great leader, Eijanbrook.'

Anja took a moment to recover from the shock of finding out that Merek was not with Elenore. She had not even picked up that there were any problems between her son and his wife. She forced a smile and awkwardly embraced the young woman. 'Come mother, we have prepared a feast and welcoming ceremony.' Merek indicated towards the meat roasting over the large fire. Anja wore a puzzled expression as she followed her son to the tables that had been decorated in celebration of her arrival.

Elenore watched as Anja made her way to the tables. People began to take their seats once she had taken hers.

'Aye, Norrie, ye need to go and say hello.' Sabin told her softly.

Elenore shook her head. 'I am not ready for that, Sabin. I don't like causing a scene.'

'Norrie, ye have to be stronger than her haven't ye been listening to Edyth?'

Elenore smiled despite herself. She was grateful for the friends that she had.

They made their way to the tables, and she was surprised to find Tallot seated next to the seat she had been allocated. She hesitated. 'Zuri is up to no good.' She whispered to Sabin.

Sabin nodded in agreement. 'I think ye might be right.'

Elenore sat down, offering Tallot a smile. He looked away, a look of uneasiness on his face. Elenore began to feel uncomfortable; she was right, this was Zuri's idea.

Serenity was seated opposite Elenore with Edyth next to her. Sabin was seated on the other side of Serenity, which also did not make sense.

'That evil witch has seated us. She knows I need help with the children.' Edyth hissed as she sat down. Her brood of children sat down quietly, the youngest nestled next to his mother. Huxley was seated next to Elenore. The table at which they had been assigned was the last in the row. Elenore could barely make out Merek and Anja at the far end. The red drink was offered, and Elenore wished she could have some. It would have settled her nerves. She sipped her water trying to slow her racing heart.

Food was carved and handed out. The night was cool with a gentle breeze, the air fresh from the morning's rain. Merek offered a prayer to the Gods to thank them for bringing home his mother and her friends safely. He also paid respect to the trees that had been felled to build the homes that they needed. He gave a quick tally of the number of homes that had been finished.

Edyth stood as he gave the numbers. 'Merek, you forgot to add that Elenore's is still being completed.' She was a small woman, but had the courage of a lion. Elenore felt herself blush as all eyes turned to their table.

'I am aware of that, Edyth. Elenore will have hers completed this week.'

Edyth stood for a moment longer before returning to her seat at the table. Elenore grinned at her new friend murmuring her thanks. Edyth did not fear anyone, not even the Asur, though Elenore suddenly felt that she had another enemy: Zuri.

Edyth turned to Elenore, her face set in stone. 'Don't let him push you around, Elenore.'

Sabin chuckled at his fiancée's remark. 'Aye she is right, Norrie.' He raised his cup and took a long drink.

The long list of commendations was read out for all those who had gone above and beyond. It was a way to celebrate, acknowledge, and encourage a community to work together. Next, Merek announced that a new Council would be put together and asked for people to come forward if they wanted to be a Councillor. He updated the status of the recon party advising that they had found no survivors so far. Once the announcements, prayers and acknowledgments had been made, he gave permission for his people to eat.

Elenore ate in silence, desperately thinking about how she could start a conversation with Tallot. An awkward silence hung between them. She pushed the food around her plate, stalling for time.

'How have you been, Tallot?'

'Elenore, please do not talk to me. We are in enough trouble as it is. I know it is not your fault, but it will only make it worse.' He offered her a tight smile before returning his attention back to his plate. Elenore sighed and concentrated on finishing her meal.

Tallot left as soon as he had finished his food. Elenore spoke to Serenity for a while before she excused herself too. People were starting to drink the red wine and she was getting bored.

She made her way back to Serenity's hut, her mind consumed with thoughts of how she could get the opportunity to speak with Anja. She let herself into the cosy home and smiled. The healer had created a welcoming space and she felt secure and safe. Serenity had a home that comprised of two bedrooms, the second was to be her patient's room but for now it was Elenore's. The healer was using her front room to see her patients until Elenore's home was finished.

Elenore pulled back the covers of the bed and slipped under the warmth. She blew out the candle and settled, waiting for sleep to take her into its embrace.

A flutter. She opened her eyes and instinctively placed her hands on her abdomen. There! Another flutter, her babies were moving! Tears ran down her face as she felt the movements of her unborn children.

A knock at the door startled her and she instantly sat up. She had not heard a knock on the door for a long time. It instantly brought her back to the time when the Asur had knocked at the door Eijanbrook had built for them. She shuddered and cautiously got out of bed. Grabbing the shawl she had flung over the table near her bed, she padded out to the front door.

'Who is it?' Elenore asked, her heart racing.

'Elenore, it is me, Anja.' Elenore released the breath she had been holding and quickly unlocked the door.

Anja stepped inside the small home and embraced her daughter-in-law. 'Elenore, it is so good to see you! My love, why aren't you with your husband?' Elenore stiffened when Anja said this but continued to hold onto the older woman. Anja gently extracted herself and held Elenore at arms-length. 'You are with child?'

Elenore blushed and nodded fervently. 'Yes. I am, well, we think I am carrying twins!' She had waited for this moment for so long and finally it was here. The women hugged again before Anja once again held Elenore at arms-length. She frowned as she continued to look at Elenore.

'Things are not right with you and Merek. Another has caught his attention.'

Elenore looked away. The hurt of what she had endured came to a head and she began to weep. Anja embraced Elenore and spoke in soothing tones to comfort her. After Elenore had finished crying, she wiped away her tears. It was time for Anja to know everything that had happened.

She explained Merek's reasoning of not wanting to be with her in that he did not want any more responsibilities and to bring children into the present world was shameful. She told Anja about Zuri and how she had found Tallot in bed with her. 'I promise you, Anja, nothing happened but we both have been punished. I am still waiting for my home to be finished and Tallot was publicly flogged.' Elenore and Anja were seated in the kitchen, and the pregnant woman leaned back on the chair, feeling a weight lift off her.

Anja clucked her tongue, shocked. 'Do you still love him, Norrie?' She asked in a low voice.

Elenore bit her lip and nodded. 'Yes, I do. but I don't know whether I can forgive him.'

Anja sighed and shook her head. 'That is to be expected. Norrie, I cannot tell you how to feel but I can offer you advice. Merek needs you. This community needs you, your children who will be here soon need you, and the unborn children you carry need you. Merek is a fool and the woman he beds is a bigger fool with an evil heart. She is Amzi's sister?' Elenore nodded. 'I see. Well, I have a plan that will stop her from getting her hands on my son.' Anja paused concentration on her face.

'Merek will need to share some of the blame for this ridiculous situation as well. I can't believe what he has done.' Once again Anja clucked her tongue and shook her head.

'What is the plan?' Elenore could not help but ask.

'I will tell you in due time, dear. Please, let me worry about that.' She patted Elenore's hand. The front door opened and both women turned to see Serenity enter, carrying bags of herbs and supplies. Anja stood up and embraced the healer.

'I knew you were coming,' Serenity informed her.

'I know you come from the ancient line of Seers.' Anja replied. Serenity nodded, offering to make them more tea. Once she seated herself down, a cup of tea in hand, her face took on a sombre expression. 'I picked up on your fear Anja, when you hid in the cluster of trees. What frightened you so much? Was it the Asur?'

'Yes, Serenity it was the Asur, and you do have a skill for seeing. They are watching us, I am sure of it. I would not be surprised if they know where we are hiding. The people that came with me today are from Shakurta village. The man, Matlin, his wife was a healer, and she also came from the long line of ancient Seers. She had picked up that the Seer of the village had made a deal with the devil. They would leave their part of the forest alone if he taught them how to mind travel.'

Serenity sucked in her breath, and her face paled. 'We are in grave danger, all of us. Ogda, Ada, Ulric, and the people they have rescued including the chief of Shakurta village will arrive here in a week. I just hope the Asur do not attack us before then. Ada and Ogda will mind travel to find their queen Dardanos, and it now seems she has a king who no one ever knew about and this makes things a bit more complicated. We have two that will need to be brought down.' Anja explained.

Serenity shook her head. 'We all thought we were safe here.'

'We will never be safe until the world rids itself of the Asur.' Anja sighed.

'Have you told Merek?' Elenore asked.

'No, I haven't. You, Serenity, and I will see him first thing in the morning. We have a lot to organise.' Anja stood, thanking Serenity for the tea. 'I must go now. I am tired, and I think we all need to rest.'

Elenore walked Anja to the door, finally someone would be able to talk some sense into Merek.

CHAPTER EIGHTEEN

Cursed

May the whispers in the wind turn to accusations, Merek.
Let trust crumble like sand through your fingers, and your
leadership wane until you are no longer worthy, and the light
that guides your people fades to a flickering ember.
Seer from Shakurta Village

The day promised to be hot and steamy after the previous day's rain. Elenore and Serenity made their way to Merek's home. Elenore could feel the trickle of sweat running down her back, and she was beginning to wish for the season to change to autumn. Two warriors guarded the door as the women approached, they demanded the reason for their visit.

'We need to speak to Merek and Anja, it is important,' Serenity said in a determined voice.

One of the warriors went inside and it was not long before he returned. 'He will see you now follow me.' The two women followed the warrior inside.

Merek's new home was the largest in the village, as was traditional for the chief or leader. The inside of the home was sparse, however a large table stood in the middle of an equally large kitchen. It made sense, as most meetings between Merek, future Councillors and warriors would be held over food and wine. Merek was already seated, a cup of steaming tea in front of him as he held his head between his hands.

Anja was dishing food into bowls as she hummed. Zuri was nowhere to be seen.

'Ah, please be seated ladies. I have made us something to eat. It will be very good for you, Norrie, and the babies,' Anja said.

Elenore stiffened and cast a quick glance at Merek. He did not lift his head or acknowledge them. Serenity and Elenore sat and ate their food in silence. Anja placed a bowl in front of Merek. He looked up and pushed the bowl away.

'No thank you, mother. I am not hungry.' Elenore watched as he clenched and unclenched his jaw. She could feel the tension in the room and suddenly felt like leaving.

As if she had read her mind, Anja placed a hand on her shoulder. 'Stay, Elenore. Merek needs to face the things he has been avoiding.' Elenore was taken aback. For a moment, she had forgotten how well Anja could read people's feelings and thoughts.

'Merek, you will start by looking after your wife. She is carrying your children and the future of humanity. We must unite. A great battle is coming you cannot be distracted by another. Zuri has been promised to another man.'

Merek slammed his fist on the table. 'What gives you the right to decide my future and organise my life?!' he roared.

'I am your mother and soon to be the greatest Seer. It is in your destiny to stay with your wife and raise your children. That is, if she will have you back.' Anja paused for a moment for the words to take affect before she continued. 'You have been chosen to put an end to the Asur it is in the prophecy. Zuri was chosen a mate from birth, something that Amzi failed to tell you. But why would he? He didn't think that your relationship with his sister would go this far,' Anja told her son calmly.

Merek stood up from his seat. 'Prophecies can change. I do not want to be with her!' He pointed to Elenore his face twisted in an expression of hate. Merek stormed from the kitchen, grabbing his sword before he opened and slammed the front door.

'This is only the beginning of things to come. We must remain strong. Merek is not thinking straight. Give him time, Elenore.' Anja offered Elenore a smile as she took her seat at the table. Elenore bit her lip. She was not sure if she wanted Merek as a husband again and she voiced her feelings to Anja.

'Norrie, I understand but in time I think we will come to know the source of what has changed him. Please trust me on this.' Anja handed

Elenore another steaming plate of food before patting her arm. Her eyes twinkled and held a wisdom, Elenore slowly nodded. Anja was like a mother to her and even though she knew Anja was asking a lot, she would never do anything to hurt her. There had to be a reason for Merek's behaviour that was out of his control.

Merek made his way to Amzi's home, a growing fury raged within him. An unsettling feeling formed in the pit of his stomach, perhaps his mother was telling the truth about him not facing responsibilities. Merek did his best to shrug it off. He was in love with Zuri, she would make a good wife. He did not want to bring more children into the world and the disgust that he felt for Elenore grew stronger. Zuri had promised him she would not give him children, but her brother had failed to tell him about a promise of marriage to another man.

He rapped on the leader's door. The door opened and Zuri stood there, a surprised look on her face. 'Hello Merek, I didn't expect you.'

Merek pushed past her. 'Where is your brother?' he growled.

She looked confused and slightly hurt.

'What is the problem, Merek? You have woken us all up,' Amzi said, looking annoyed as he came into the main room of the house.

'My mother informs me that Zuri is promised to another. Is this true?'

'You came here to ask me that? Couldn't it wait until later?' Amzi could barely mask his irritation.

'No, it cannot. I have to sort my private affairs first before I can plan a battle. The Seer is on his way here with my children. I cannot afford to be distracted.'

Amzi sighed and looked away. 'Yes, Zuri was, and is, promised to another.'

'Why didn't you tell me, Amzi? I planned to marry your sister. Is the other in this village?'

Amzi bit his lip. 'Yes he is but he does not know.'

'I didn't even know I was promised to another and I don't want to marry anyone but, Merek, don't I get a say?' Zuri interrupted her arms folded.

Amzi pursed his lips. 'Traditionally, no, not really. Our father promised the other man's father before you were even born. It would not be a good example to set, we would be mixing up the future and any prophecies that have been foretold. The Gods would not be happy. I don't think this is the right time to make them unhappy.'

Silence descended upon the trio. 'I have an idea,' Zuri announced. 'What if we convince Elenore to ask Merek for a divorce? He would be free of her then. Merek would then have the choice to ask me to be his wife. He is leader, would that work?'

Amzi frowned. 'Maybe, Zuri. I cannot say for sure, it would be up to a Seer.'

'That's it then, we will persuade her to divorce you.' Zuri clapped her hands, delighted with the idea. Merek did not seem convinced but for the moment he had no other solutions.

'Come Merek let's go and eat I have some leftover stew on the fire we can share,' Amzi said, relieved that he had been able to placate the leader. He placed his hand on Merek's shoulder, steering him toward the kitchen.

Ogda instructed Ludwig to pack as many seeds as he could harvest from the vast vegetable patch. He knew Ulric would be arriving by mid-afternoon. They would need time to rest their horses and themselves. He looked out the window and began to pace the room. Normally he would have meditated but he felt too unsettled, something he was not used to.

He knew the Asur were after them, trailing maybe a day or two behind. Two days would be the most they could rest, and he hoped none of the horses were lame. The Seer would not be able to travel fast, another problem that would delay them. His old cart horse would go the distance but only at a steady pace, Ludwig's gelding was the same. Ada's small grey mare and the pack horse were probably faster than the Clydesdales. He had considered fastening them to the wagon but knew the sharp, winding trails that led to Merek's valley would not allow room for them. He had to take as many supplies as possible, seeds and grains were vital in helping to feed a new nation.

He stopped pacing only when he noticed Ada staring at him from the kitchen entrance.

'I have made some tea. You need to calm your restless energy.'

He gave her a smile, relieved that she was travelling with him. Ogda drank the tea and picked at the food Ada had made him, she had been a big help to Ludwig.

'We have everything prepared, we can leave once their horses have rested.'

Ogda offered her a smile and sighed. 'You are right, dear girl, but I cannot help the feeling that we should have left yesterday. There is never enough time and unfortunately it is not on our side.'

Takeo had been relieved when he had found Ulric, the one with the tear-stained mark on his face that he had dreamed about. Ulric had been expecting him and welcomed the growing group of people. It would be another day before they travelled again, giving time to the rest their horses and allow extra time for Kacha to heal. Takeo told Ulric of his concerns that the Asur was trailing them. They pushed their horses as hard as they dared without risking one of them going lame.

Ulric constantly worried about the devil that pursued them, and it was getting harder to move the growing number of humans fleeing the same enemy. It took them three days to reach the Seer's hidden home. Ogda was waiting and pleasantly surprised at how many had taken refuge by joining Ulric and Takeo.

'It is good to see you Ulric, and nice to meet you Takeo, former custodian of the ancient tree.' The Seer bowed, paying his respects to the large man.

'I am afraid that we all won't fit in your home, Seer. I think we will camp out under the stars.' Takeo returned the greeting with a faint smile on his lips. 'I will organise patrols to keep watch. The Asur are not far behind.'

Ogda nodded, his suspicions confirmed. 'How long do you think you need to rest?'

Takeo and Ulric looked at one another the answer was already decided, they simply did not have a choice. 'We can leave after a day's rest. The Asur are fast approaching.'

The Seer let out his breath, thankful that both men had the foresight to acknowledge the limitations set by the Asur.

'You must come in and have some tea, Ludwig and I have been

preparing for your arrival.' Takeo, Ulric, Krea, and Kacha filed into the Seer's home.

Ulric felt exhaustion descend as he sat on the overstuffed cushion. He could not wait to reach his father and the hidden valley. He felt that he had been running away from the Asur his whole life. Ada and Ludwig served them food and tea before setting out to help the group of people who now were settling in to rest at the front of the Seer's home.

'They have destroyed my home, my forest, and they will do the same to yours,' Takeo said grimly. His desire to seek vengeance on the Asur had only grown stronger they had taken everything from him.

'You have no family left?' Ogda asked.

'I have one son. He is out there, helping the others. My wife, daughters and other son have all perished. I do not know what happened to them. Our Seer took them away and they have not been seen since.'

'Why did he spare one?' Krea asked. She had not had an opportunity to speak to Takeo since she had met him.

Takeo frowned. 'To be honest, I am not completely sure. I think it was that he was too young to be a threat. Our Seer kept me in a trance for many years.'

'It makes sense, Takeo. I am sorry to hear you have lost almost all your family. Hopefully once all this is over, we can re-build our lives again,' Krea said, vocalising what everyone was thinking and hoping.

Elenore was weeding the community garden when she noticed Merek come through its front gate. A sickening feeling clutched her; she had not wanted to see him again since the previous day's outburst. Every time they met it always ended up with her feeling sad and lonely. She did not deserve how Merek was treating her, and she could not understand why he had changed so much. She continued to dig up the weeds as he approached.

'I thought I would find you here.' She did not look up or acknowledge him. 'I was thinking we could make a deal.' Elenore paused and sat back on her haunches and gazed up at the man looking down at her. She hated herself for the fact that he still managed to take her breath away and make her heart pound. Yet only moments earlier she loathed him, she was struggling to make sense of it. 'Are you interested?' Merek's eyes narrowed.

She wiped her mouth with the back of her hand. The day was warm, although it was only early morning. 'It depends on what it is,' she mumbled.

'You need to get up,' he snapped.

Elenore stayed seated on her haunches, ignoring his demand. 'No thank you, I am more comfortable seated.'

Merek looked out over the vast vegetable garden, seeming to try to calm his temper. 'I will finish your home if you ask the Seer when he arrives for a divorce.'

Elenore was shocked by his request. 'No. That would not be fair, everyone else had a home built. It was all part of the settling in program you announced.' She picked up her small shovel and began to dig again. She almost expected him to hit her, but he stood there glaring down at her.

'You will pay for this Elenore!' he said before making his way from the garden. Elenore continued to dig. Her heart and soul had been crushed again and the encounter had shaken her, but she had stood up to him.

Anja invited Elenore and Serenity for dinner, as she had important news to share. Elenore was hesitant about going, with her earlier meeting with Merek still vivid in her mind.

'It is important you continue to go to Merek's home Elenore, it is your home too.' Serenity told her as they walked towards the leader's house.

Elenore casually picked at a thread that had become loose from her dress. 'How do you mean?'

'You are his wife, and you should be living with your husband. Ogda will not be impressed when he finds out what has transpired between the both of you. Merek has defied the laws of marriage. You have not consented to divorce, which thankfully you have to do to make it happen. You are legally allowed to live in that home.'

Elenore blanched. 'That would really set him off. Besides, I am not sure I want to move in with him.'

Serenity came to a stop and placed her hands on Elenore's shoulders. 'He deserves a wakeup call, Norrie.'

Elenore sighed and averted Serenity's gaze, 'I just want things back to the way they were.'

'Give it time, dear girl,' the healer said gently.

Anja had prepared a mini feast for them and the smells that wafted through the kitchen made Elenore's mouth water. 'Oh, Anja you have always been a wonderful cook.' Her stomach began to growl as if in agreement, and Anja giggled.

'Take a seat. The food will be ready in a few minutes.'

'Where is Merek?' Elenore asked.

'Do not worry, I have not seen him all day and Serenity has already told you that this house is yours.'

'He came to see me today, in the garden.'

Anja raised an eyebrow. 'And?'

'He said he would finish my house if I gave him a divorce.'

Anja clucked. 'What was your response?'

Elenore frowned. She sometimes wondered why Anja asked questions when, as a Seer, she already knew the answer to them. 'I told him no. Everyone else has a home and it would not be fair that I didn't get one.'

'Good girl, Norrie,' Serenity said.

Anja served the food and sat down. 'Let us give thanks to the Gods for this wonderful valley and food that has been provided. Now I want you both to eat while I tell you what I found out while meditating this afternoon.'

Elenore stabbed at the food on her plate she was famished. They ate in silence for a while before Anja put down her fork. 'The Gods have provided some answers about Merek's unkind and erratic behaviour of late.'

Elenore froze, her fork poised halfway to her mouth. 'What is it?'

'The Seer from Shakurta village has cast black magic on our leader, my son, your husband. There have been times when Merek has not felt comfortable with being with Zuri and neglecting you. He is fighting an inner battle. It is like he has been possessed by a demon. The Seer is a clever fellow and deceptive. They are watching us. I know they are, but they don't quite know where we are. To have his marriage in disarray has caused a distraction, and a distraction means things can be overlooked, especially when preparing for battle.'

Elenore shook her head. 'I don't disagree with you, Anja, but he does not want our babies. He really doesn't, that is what started all of this.'

'You are right, and that is what sparked the Seer's sense of trouble. He was able to pick up on the turmoil and acted on it. He is more powerful than I thought.' She sighed and took a mouthful of food.

Elenore pushed her plate away, her mind racing. 'So how do we get rid of this curse?' she asked.

'I am not sure, Norrie, but I think Ogda will know. In the meantime, you must not give in to his demands. This house is yours and I want you to move in.'

Elenore stiffened. 'Move in here? I can't. Anja, he hates me.'

'You will and I will be here to protect you. Please do not worry, I will not let any harm come to you and your unborn children. Once we have eaten, Serenity will help with bringing your things.'

Elenore opened and closed her mouth, but she could see Anja was adamant.

'You will be safe with Anja.' Serenity patted Elenore's hand.

Elenore liked her space, and she had grown used to living alone in her small tent.

'It is not safe for you to be on your own, and my duties mean I am not always there to keep you from harm,' the healer continued, more softly. 'Besides, you are the only one who is not living in an actual house. That ends now. You are carrying our future, they must be protected.'

Elenore swallowed. Her life was about to change. She felt afraid of how Merek would take the news of her moving in.

The women finished their meal and Serenity went to help Elenore with her belongings that were still at Serenity's home. Elenore's small tent had survived the storms, but the patches had torn open with the heavy deluge of rain.

Just as they brought the last of her things, Merek entered the front door. Elenore wanted to run and hide, and she quickly went into the spare room that Anja had set up for her. Merek's house boasted three bedrooms. It was easily the largest of all the homes built.

She loved her mother-in-law, but she was unsure whether this was a good idea. It was not long before her suspicions were confirmed. She could hear Merek's rage as Anja told him about her moving in. He left the house, slamming the door behind him.

Once he was gone, Elenore crept from her bedroom. Anja was seated at the table, a concerned look on her face.

'Anja, maybe I should leave. He clearly does not want me here.'

'No. You will stay and fight, Elenore. You have to fight for what is yours, remember he is under the curse of black magic.' Her voice had taken on a hard tone and Elenore merely nodded.

Merek slammed his fist into his hand before running his hand through his hair. He let out a shaky breath and came to a halt. He turned and looked back at his home that he had just left, his mother's words echoing in his mind. For a moment he felt sickened at the way he had just acted.

He loved Elenore.

He wanted to run back and hold her, tell her that he indeed did love her and that he wanted more than ever to take care of her and their unborn children. However, his legs failed to move, stuck to the ground they were planted on. A darkness crossed his mind clouding the feelings of love and compassion. Merek shook his head, turning he continued his way leaving his home behind him.

Dawn broke in the eastern sky as Ogda mounted his draught horse. The forest had started to burn; the Asur had started their attack. He thanked the Gods that at least the Asur hadn't been able to make their tunnels. They did not have the time to be making tunnels in a new territory, instead they focused on burning down the trees that had hidden the Seer's home. The speed in which they had been able to catch up to them was a cause for alarm. Ogda wasted no time in leaving and he looked over his shoulder at the home he had lived in for many years, it would be the last time that he would ever see it. Sighing he turned back in his saddle urging his big gelding into a trot. They were on the run.

Merek did not return to his home for the next few days. Elenore began to relax and enjoy living in an actual home, it had been so long. All she ever dreamed of was to have a home again, a place to raise her children to feel safe and secure.

When Merek returned on the third day she went and hid in the bedroom. He argued with Anja before leaving abruptly again.

Anja called for Elenore. 'Elenore do not hide anymore. You have to be strong, there is so much ahead of us. We must break the curse, I am positive that is what it is. The more he is around you, the more he will think of you. He loves you, you are his soul mate. The prophecy cannot be broken what he is doing is very wrong. He is a leader and must set an example we cannot risk not having a united community.'

'He loved me once, but I am not so sure he loves me now. He is with another, remember?'

Anja held Elenore by her shoulders. 'You are his wife, his love for an eternity. I lost mine, he is with the Gods. I cannot talk to him unless it is in meditation or prayer.' She held Elenore's gaze. 'Believe me when I say you will not survive without him.'

Elenore pulled away, shaking her head. 'Anja, I am sorry, but I think I have been looking after myself pretty well without Merek.'

Anja gently took Elenore's hand and gave it a squeeze. 'Things are going to get hard Elenore, and we will lose a lot of people. The beginning of the end has only just begun and if humanity is to survive, it must unite with each other and the forest that helps sustain it. We need Merek to be the leader that he is destined to be, or everyone will die.' She let go of Elenore's hand and went back into the kitchen.

Elenore followed, watching her mother-in-law as she began to cut the vegetables.

'Edyth hates him.' Anja did not pause in her slicing. 'What if other people hate him?' Elenore leaned against the doorway. Her arms folded.

Anja stopped her cutting and turned to face Elenore. 'That is the very reason why you must forgive him and fight for him. He is leader to these people. Yes, he has done wrong. We all make mistakes some are not easy to forgive I understand that, but we must put our grievances to rest. Eijanbrook and I looked after Edyth and her children for so long and I have been to see her only yesterday. She has been through so much, but she will follow Merek, she has no choice. She will bury the hatchet for the sake of her children, their fate rests on the decisions their leader will make. Now please, start acting like his wife you must be strong and fight for him.'

'That is very unfair. I have tried my best to give him a chance and fight for him as you just said but I—' Tears tracked down her face and Elenore angrily brushed them away. Anja made her way to Elenore, embracing her. 'You weren't here, Anja. I tried my best.'

Elenore pushed herself away and went to the wash basin. Splashing the water over her face she grabbed a towel to dry it. She looked out the small window above the basin that faced out to the thick forest that framed their camp.

Anja was right. She did need Merek, and she could not survive on her own. But she had tried to make things right with him. It all seemed so unfair. Her mind whirled with thoughts. She leaned against the kitchen bench trying to make sense of her feelings. It was only a matter of time before the Asur found them and her husband would need to go into battle.

The thought of Merek dying in battle made her heart ache. Although he had hurt her a lot, deep down, she loved him. They had been promised and they were soul mates. For Merek to be with someone like Zuri, surely it would have taken a curse to be placed on him.

Elenore sighed and turned back to Anja. 'I will keep fighting for him. You are right, my children deserve their father.'

Ogda handed Ludwig the reins of his horse before seating himself on the log of a fallen tree. It had been a long night of riding and he was feeling sore and stiff. He had not ridden so far in many years. Ada sat next to him, a serious look on her face. She had ridden with Ulric for most of the night and was delighted to be with her brother and Kacha again. However, a feeling of doom settled over her.

'We have to distract them, they know where we are and are watching, always watching.' She hugged herself as she watched some of the men start a fire to boil water and roast meat. The camp only dared to have a fire during the daylight hours, as they had resorted to travelling at night. The group had learned to work together, some assigned as scouts, others to hunt for local game, and others to build fires.

Families that were on the run had started to join them as they travelled, traumatised by witnessing their villages being burned and loved ones taken away or murdered. 'We cannot risk the Asur following us to the valley. There are so many of us now.' Ada looked over at the vast group.

'What you say is correct, but I do not know how we can distract them,' Ogda said quietly.

'I may have an idea,' Ada said.

Ogda raised an eyebrow. It should not have come as a surprise that Ada would have a solution. 'My power is fire, so why not use it like the Asur? I mean, I will not burn down our beloved forest, but I can burn the grassland. It will force them back and there are open plains just before we reach the foothills of Dorhall Pass.'

The Seer stroked his wispy beard, he did not know where the tunnels lay that the Asur used to get to Dardanos, but he knew they were near to Merek. 'It is a good idea Ada, but I have concerns about the tunnels that lay nearby. If they find out about our intention of setting a fire, they will use them. I want all the women and children in the middle of the group, we cannot afford stragglers. The ones that are slow will also be in the middle I won't be going back for a rescue mission.' Ogda shifted uncomfortably. He had wanted to surprise Dardanos, but she would already know where they were and where they were headed.

'Don't worry we will still surprise Dardanos, but we must not let the Asur find father's valley.'

The Seer chuckled despite himself, Ada was so perceptive. 'Will you be able to use your power? You cannot control it at will.'

'The Gods will help. They did once before, when we were in the witches' forest, I am sure they will rescue us again.'

Ogda pulled at his beard again and scratched his chin. He was not completely at ease with what she proposed, but it was all they had. 'Okay. I will let Takeo and Ulric know. We will set fire to the grasslands when we reach the foothills of Dorhall Pass.'

Anja had organised Matlin and his children to stay with friends before moving them in with Serenity. People had started to come to Anja to talk, ask for advice and just to be around her. She was a kind, strong woman and many missed her husband Eijanbrook. Anja welcomed her people, but she noticed that some of the things people were asking should have been directed to her son; he was their leader.

She hoped that Ogda and Ada would arrive soon. She was sure once Merek saw his children it would help break the curse. Merek had done a remarkable job of selectively clearing parts of the forest to build homes and make fires. He even had organised a group to help harvest seeds for replanting, in fact Merek had assigned every able-bodied adult a task to do. The people were kept busy and were given a purpose, which helped keep them happy and productive.

Anja began to give Elenore more jobs to do involving their community. She wanted her to still be seen as the leader's wife. Elenore, along with Serenity, would go door knocking to check on the welfare of the people and make a tally of how many women were expecting. Merek could not deny every baby born. Anja also organised Elenore to meet Kaiah, future wife of Ulric. Anja decided that a dinner with Kaiah and her family could be a way to bring Merek and Elenore together.

'Norrie, I have told Merek to be home for dinner. I have some news to share with you both. Also, the people I travelled with are coming as well. It has been more than two weeks since we have arrived, and I feel that a dinner together is long overdue. It should be a nice evening.'

Elenore nodded, setting off to the vegetable garden to pick greens for the night's dinner.

Anja served the casserole into bowls as the group of five waited seated at the table. One spot was empty, and Elenore fidgeted glancing towards the front door. She chatted to Serenity and Matlin while Anja served the food. After a prayer of gratitude, they began to eat. Elenore gave Anja a questioning look, but she shook her head and mouthed, 'don't worry' before returning to her food.

A few moments later, the front door opened, and Merek and Zuri walked in.

Elenore sucked in her breath and cast a quick look at Serenity. She rolled her eyes and shook her head; it was a bold move by them both. Anja got up from the table, excusing herself. Elenore could hear heated words from Merek as Anja spoke to them and she placed a hand over her face.

Anja's anger towards Zuri and Merek had only increased, and she was taken aback at how unabashed Zuri truly was. Anja returned to the table with the couple. Merek took a seat next to Elenore, Zuri next to Rory. Elenore shifted uncomfortably, Zuri threw her a cold stare as she sat down.

'I believe I have some news to share with some of you tonight,' Anja began. 'As you are aware, Merek and Elenore have two beautiful children that are on their way to us as we speak. Their eldest, Ulric, has been assigned a soul mate. Sometimes a good Seer can pick up on who the couple are. When this happens, it is traditional to let the parents know of this future union. I have you all gathered here this evening, I would like to share this news.'

Anja paused and looked around the table at the guests seated. Matlin leaned forward.

'I am pleased to announce that Kaiah and Ulric will be married and that the Gods favour this union.'

Elenore beamed. Kaiah would be an excellent choice for Ulric, and she was sure her son would fall in love with her. The girl was attractive, kind, and shy. Elenore rose to embrace her. Merek sat back on his chair and rubbed his forehead.

'What are your thoughts, son?' Anja asked.

Merek looked up and nodded. 'Yeah I guess it is fine. I mean, it's good. I cannot argue with the Gods. Congratulations Kaiah and Matlin.' Merek rose and shook the other man's hand.

'Do you have anything to say Kaiah?' Elenore asked as she sat down.

The young girl blushed. 'It is an honour to marry the son of a leader, thank you.'

Elenore, Serenity, and Anja laughed. 'Welcome to the family, Kaiah.' Anja held up a cup of water and took a sip. Merek smiled despite himself. He did not realise how much he had missed his family.

'It is good news, Merek. I am happy for our son and future daughter in-law' Elenore said, turning to Merek.

His smile faded and he looked down at the table before returning her gaze. 'I agree. It is a good match for both of them. I am looking forward to seeing our children when they come home.' Elenore felt a flicker of hope; perhaps the curse was losing its grip on Merek.

CHAPTER NINETEEN

Hunted

Beneath our feet they toil, clawing the earth

in the search of souls for reasons as dark and deep

as the tunnels they carve.

Ada

A vast open plain of grasses lay in front of the people Ulric led, before transcending back to forest that made its way up the foothills of Dorhall Pass. The scene was breathtaking. A summer's blue sky stretched above them, and a faint breeze blew ruffling Ada's long white hair. Takeo and Ulric had organised the people how the Seer had instructed, the slow people in the middle of the group. Ogda had addressed the group and told them what had been planned. A sense of anxiety rippled through them as they approached the open plain. There was no forest to protect them, and they felt exposed on the open grasslands.

A herd of deer could be seen in the distance, but they did not have time to hunt. The Asur had started to gain on them, and it was only a matter of time before they caught up. Ada rode up to the Seer, her small mare prancing as she picked up on Ada's nervous energy.

'It is time. Ulric and Krea will come with me. I will meet you at the valley. I think it should only be a two-day ride from here, even with the slower ones.' Ogda looked at the back of the group and turned his big horse around.

Takeo made his way over to the Seer and Ada, his face tight with worry. 'I will lead them. One of the scouts' reports seeing the Asur only an hour away. The other scout has not returned, and I don't think he will.'

The Seer felt fear clutch at him and quickly sent a prayer to the Gods. The Asur were getting even closer. He hoped Ada's plan would work or they all would be gone.

He made his way to the back the group with Ada before she demanded that he go no further. Takeo had urged them to move faster, and it would not be long before Ogda would be left behind if he stayed with Ada for too long.

'You have to trust me, it is our only chance.'

Ogda sighed and nodded. 'May the Gods be with you.' He turned his big horse around, leaving Ada with Ulric and Krea.

The trio waited until the group was just a small speck on the horizon and as they did the faint sound of a horn could be heard.

'They are coming.' Ulric looked at his sister, hoping she was able to produce the fire with her hands. She dismounted her pony, handing the reins to Krea. She walked forward, chanting to the Gods. The horn of the Asur grew louder and the ground beneath them began to tremble.

Krea exchanged a desperate look at Ulric, but he only shook his head. They had no other options. Ada walked further and further, and the horn grew louder and louder. Ulric and Krea walked a little way behind her. The sound of baying hounds came next, and it sent a shiver down Ulric's spine. Again, he sent a prayer to the Gods asking for their help.

Ada continued to walk, but there was no fire that leaped from her hands. Ulric's heart began to race, and he sucked in his breath, the urge to flee was beginning to tug at him. An outline of an approaching army could be seen. Another sound from the horn and the hounds baying increased, they had picked up their scent.

Krea's horse stamped his feet and snorted; a musty smell filled the air. Soon Ulric's gelding began to prance nervously, half rearing as panic filled him.

'Ulric, we may be able to outrun them if we leave now,' Krea hissed. She was barely able to hold her stallion. Ulric did not answer, instead he kept his gaze on Ada. Suddenly, the arid smell of smoke filled the air; fire was coming out of Ada's hands.

She held her palms slightly apart, directing the flames so the field would quickly catch on fire. Soon the plains of open grassland would be blazing. Ulric and Krea scanned the distance. The Asur had come to a halt.

'It's working!' Ulric felt relieved. Finally, the Gods had answered their call.

Ada walked in different directions, ensuring that the whole plain was on fire. When she was satisfied, she turned to look for Ulric and Krea who were waiting some distance away, watching her.

Without warning the ground began to shake violently and the horses whinnied with fear.

'What is it?' Krea asked, trying desperately to hang on to her horse. Ulric observed the ground as it began to part.

'They are making tunnels to get to us! Look!' he yelled. Krea could see the earth opening giving way to movement that ploughed its way underneath. 'Hold my horse!' Ulric jumped off his nervous gelding throwing the reins to Krea.

'Wait! What are you doing?'

Ulric did not answer her, instead he waited for the split in the ground to widen before making his way inside.

'Ulric! No come back!' Krea called. She desperately looked around for Ada, but could not see her. Flames leaped from grass to grass, black smoke filled the air. Krea began to cough as she fervently scanned the plain for the white-haired girl.

'Where is, Ulric?' Krea jumped. Startled, she turned in her saddle to find Ada staring at her. 'Ada, you gave me a fright! He is in there,' she turned back to the direction she had just come from, pointing to where Ulric had jumped in the tunnel. Ada kept her face expressionless, and Krea had a feeling that she already knew he had gone down there, and she was seeking confirmation from her.

'Wait here with the horses, I will go down. I can't use my mind the devil is close.' She did not wait for Krea to respond but jumped down into the open wound of dirt that snaked across the plain.

The tunnel was hot from the fire that raged above. Ada waited for her eyes to become accustomed to the gloom before she made her way forward. She trusted her instinct in the direction she took. She could not mind travel, it was too dangerous. Slowly, she made her way through the deep passageway, and it was not long before she heard the cries of men fighting.

A hound bayed above as it picked up on Ada's scent underground. She hoped she could locate Ulric quickly, the Asur would be intent on capturing him. She could hear swords clashing and as she rounded the corner, she made out her brother locked in battle with three of the Asur. Ulric had never mastered the sword, instead he had become an expert at the bow and arrow and at running away from his enemies.

Ada paused, watching him for a moment, she could see he was struggling. It would only be a matter of minutes before he succumbed to the bigger, more powerful beasts. She moved so that he could catch her in his peripheral vision. He glanced over at her which almost cost him his arm.

The Asur turned to where Ada stood, an evil grin played on their faces. The one closest to her tried to seize her.

Ada dodged. 'Run, Ulric, quick!' she yelled as she danced away again as the second Asur tried to slice her with its sword.

'No! you need to go back to Krea!' he shouted over his shoulder. Ada could see Ulric's arms beginning to tremble and his movements were becoming slower and heavier. Her brother was starting to tire.

'Ulric, it is not your time! We have to leave together and now!'

The third Asur lunged at Ulric, ramming him into the wall of the tunnel. The side of the tunnel began to cave, showering them with dust and dirt. 'Ulric!' Ada called. She had been temporarily blinded with the rain of dirt. Silence. The tunnel wall had completely caved in covering whatever was in its path with dirt. Ada called again, but nothing. She waited for the dust to settle before carefully making her way to where she had last seen her brother.

The tunnel seemed empty. She made her way further along, almost tripping over one of the Asur. It lay unconscious, unmoving. Ada did not look down as she continued along her path. Time was starting to run out. She had to find Ulric and get back to Krea.

Still no Ulric. She could not see or hear him. She squeezed her eyes shut and took a breath, she would have to mind travel and quickly. Ulric's sister cast her mind along the tunnel looking for Ulric. She could feel another trying to tap in, but she shut it out. It was like a thousand fingers probing her mind, trying to clasp at her thoughts.

She shook her head and returned to her physical body. It was no use, the more she travelled the more dangerous it became.

'Rest, Ada, he is making his way to you. When you have been found you need to run for your life!' It was a voice she had not heard before. She frowned and wondered about its source. She took another deep breath and made out the shape of her brother as he limped towards her. He pulled out an arrow, turning he let it fly before grabbing Ada.

'Quick, we have to hurry!' Even though Ulric was seriously wounded, he was still fast. Holding his sister's hand, they raced back up the tunnel to the surface, where Ada had left Krea.

Krea looked relieved when she saw them at the mouth of the tunnel. 'Give me your hand I will help you out.' She leaned down, first pulling Ada and then Ulric. Krea hoisted Ulric up onto his gelding. The wound in his leg poured with blood, and he was unable to hold his weight. 'Ulric, I think I should dress this wound or at least try and stop the blood flow ...'

'No time, Krea, we have to leave. They're after us, so many of them,' he panted.

'Wait!' They both turned to Ada as she turned back to the tunnel. 'There is something I have to do. It will help slow them down.' A twisted grin spread across her face as she leaned towards the hole that went underground. Flames burst from her hands, and she directed them into the tunnel. A roar of pain and shock echoed back to them. Ada let off another flame ball, a look of wicked delight crossed her face as she turned and grabbed her mare's reins from Krea. 'Now we can go.'

They rode long into the night before Ada forced them to stop. Ulric was barely clinging to life he had lost a lot of blood. She had found them a small cave hidden in a thicket of vast undergrowth.

'Krea, tear some strips off your tunic you need to change anyway,' Ada instructed. Ada shook her brother. He was barely conscious. 'Before you sleep, you must drink and eat.' She grabbed the water skin, pouring a trickle into Ulric's mouth. Grabbing the dried meat from her ration pack, she tore off a piece. Chewing it until was a pulp, she spat it into Ulric's mouth, forcing him to swallow it. She offered him another sip of water and noticed that Ulric's eyes were growing heavy. Ada gently shook him.

'Not yet you have to stay awake.' Ada demanded as she carefully placed a thread through a needle. Krea packed Ulric's wound with herbs, a sharp gash on his left thigh while Ada prepared the needle and thread. 'Keep talking to him Krea.' Ada said as she worked in closing the wound. Ulric let out a sharp cry and squeezed Krea's hand.

'How long do you think we will need to stay here?' Krea said as she watched Ada work.

'I have a plan,' she answered simply.

Krea frowned and waited for Ada to explain. Since they had reunited, she'd noticed Ada had started talking like a Seer, almost in riddles, or only short answers that begged for more. When she did not elucidate on what she had just said Krea resigned to wait for her to finish stitching up Ulric's wound.

Krea waited for the water to boil to make herself and Ada tea. She ate the dried meat and reflected about the previous day's events. The Asur had come so close the thought alone made her heart race. Ada had said she would mind travel to Anja to let her know that they needed help. It would take weeks for Ulric to heal, and they needed a rescue mission. She estimated they were at least another day and a half ride away. The fire that she had created would slow the Asur down, but it wouldn't burn forever. They would come after them with even more hatred and fury. She sighed, exhaustion was settling in, and she found it hard to resist. Ada had ensured her they were safe for the moment which gave her a sense of comfort. Her eyes felt heavy, and the lure of sleep became too much to ignore as she let herself give into its beck and call.

The rain fell heavily on the roof, a torrent that turned muddy puddles into small rivers. Elenore woke and waited for her eyes to adjust to the darkness. She could hear someone moving about the house. She felt her stomach clutch and a chill slivered down her spine. She chided herself for being so dramatic as her thoughts conjured up frightening images of the Asur. A soft knock on her door made her get out from her bed.

'Anja?'

'Yes, dear child, we need to talk.'

Elenore quickly opened the door. 'What's wrong?'

Anja's forehead was creased with worry. 'Ulric has been hurt. We must send out a rescue party.'

Elenore sucked in her breath. 'How bad? Is he okay? What about Ada and Ogda?'

Anja pulled Elenore gently to the bed, making her sit down. 'The Seer will arrive tomorrow evening, but Ada, Krea and Ulric are in hiding. Ulric was cut by one of the Asur. Ada travelled to me tonight. They are about a day or so ride away. Merek will need to bring a stretcher, Ulric will not be able to ride.'

Elenore felt panic grip her and the desire to run and save her son became almost too much to bear.

'I will go and tell Merek.' She grabbed her shawl, wrapping it around herself.

'No need, dear. I have told him in a dream. When the rain eases, he will wake and come here. Now I cannot sleep, so I will go and prepare something for us to drink.'

Elenore merely nodded as she left the room.

As the night shadows began to shrink and the sun's fingers painted a light over the horizon, Merek and a search party of six prepared to leave the village. The rain had stopped, and a cool breeze stirred the early morning sky. Tallot watched the men leave. Merek still had not forgiven him and he felt the sting of his banishment.

'Are you okay, Tallot?' Elenore asked, standing next to him as she watched the riders disappear. He did not answer her straight away, instead focusing on a spot in front of him.

'I don't think we should be talking. We came close to doing something we shouldn't have, and it has cost me a lot. Let's just stay away from each other.' He left without waiting for Elenore to reply.

'Hmm looks like someone doesn't like you anymore.' Elenore had not noticed Zuri arrive behind her and she took a step back. Zuri smiled as she saw Elenore's discomfort with her presence.

'Do you really enjoy seeing people not liking each other, Zuri?'

Zuri let out a wicked laugh. 'You have been living under a rock! No wonder your husband left you. I pity you! Someone must put things right. The men from your village needed waking up! You're too nice! They crave a challenge and drama and a woman who can give them all that and more. I warned you to be careful, dear Elenore, it's not just the Asur you should fear.' Zuri had taken a step closer to Elenore her face twisted with anger.

Elenore longed to reach out and shake her, but then a sudden feeling of sorrow overcame her. Zuri lacked kindness and empathy, she possessed a deep seated hatred and jealousy that consumed her. She would never know the real love of having friends or someone who would truly love her. How could she? Zuri's interests were all selfish spawned from a desire to hurt others. This realisation brought an inner calm. Elenore shook her head and instead of responding to her she simply walked away.

Anja and Elenore stayed up most of the night talking and sipping tea. They were both too worried to sleep. Anja was cautious about mind travelling with the Asur so close, and she did not want to take unnecessary risks. Elenore was thankful that her mother-in-law was home, as she enjoyed her company.

She relayed her encounter with Zuri, which made the older woman tisk. 'Good will triumph over evil. I pity the man she is destined to marry.'

'Who is he, Anja? And why wouldn't Amzi want his sister to marry the person that is for her?'

'The horse people are a strange group. I do not know that much about them. Eijanbrook would only go to select horses to help with our own breeding program, his stallion was a foal from one of their best mounts. Amzi is under Zuri's spell as well, I guess. I mean his actions very well show that he is. Amzi hasn't confronted her about how she has been behaving and like you said why doesn't he want her to marry the man who is destined to be her husband.' Anja took a sip from her cup and sighed. 'Do not worry Elenore the Gods have their way of handling things it will all work out just don't stop fighting for Merek.'

Ogda could make out Tallot and Anja standing near the top of the trail, and Ogda smiled for the first time in a long while. Finally, they had made it to the hidden valley.

'Anja, it is so good to see you! Please let me introduce Takeo, leader of the Shakurta village.' Ogda said as he removed himself from Anja's embrace.

Anja took hold of Takeo's hands and bowed her head slightly. 'It is an honour to meet you, Takeo.'

'It is an honour to meet you, Anja,' he replied. Anja looked over at the large crowd standing behind him, she was surprised that there were so many.

'You have saved a lot of people. How many are there?'

Takeo chuckled. 'I think the last count there was nearly one hundred. Not all are from my village, we have picked up a few that were fleeing from the Asur.'

Anja nodded and motioned them to follow her and Tallot as they showed them the way to the valley. People from Merek's community came to see the newcomers, welcoming them into their sanctuary. Anja had organised Serenity to find temporary lodgings for the newcomers, but she did not expect so many and ordered tents to be erected as temporary shelters. This would have to suffice until Merek returned and organised a more permanent solution.

She ushered the Seer, Ludwig, and Takeo into her home where Elenore was waiting. She had been busily preparing a meal for the hungry travellers.

'It is so good to see you, Elenore,' Ogda said as he entered the kitchen. Elenore bowed her head respectfully before embracing Ludwig and introducing herself to Takeo. Aromas of freshly baked food wafted through the house, and it did not take long before they were all seated and enjoying the food Elenore had prepared.

Anja excused herself so that she could ensure that there was enough food for all the people that had arrived, she had a feeling that Serenity would need help. 'I will be back later this evening there is so much for us to discuss!' Anja said as she quickly left.

Ogda leaned back in his chair and closed his eyes. The frown on his face eased and a slight smile played across his mouth as he began to relax. After a moment he let his gaze linger on Elenore as she served the food.

'You are with child, Norrie, perhaps more than one.'

Elenore blushed and glanced down at her stomach; the bump was getting bigger. She looked back at the Seer and could feel his mind reading hers. It was an eerie feeling and she quickly looked away. 'Merek has been cursed.' Ogda did not stop gazing at her. She did not answer him at first, instead she finished what she was doing and sat down.

Takeo and Ludwig remained silent.

'Shall we offer a prayer to the Gods for returning you all safely to us?' Elenore felt awkward and the Seer immediately began to say a prayer, releasing Elenore from his scrutiny.

They ate the meal chatting about the journey and the weather before Ludwig and Takeo said they would wash and change. Elenore let them have her room as she would temporarily have Merek's. Ogda waited for her to finish gathering the spare tunics and trousers for them to change into before he beckoned her to follow him back into the kitchen.

'Dear child, you have suffered much. You have been through a terrible ordeal.' Ogda shook his head, his eyes full of compassion. 'I also have grave concerns about our leader. I am not sure who has placed the curse, but I feel our enemy knows more about us than we do about them.' The Seer took Elenore's hand in his. 'I know it will be hard to forgive him, Elenore, Merek has not been kind but believe me when this dreadful curse is lifted he will feel nothing but remorse.'

Elenore sniffed and swallowed the lump that had come to her throat. 'I don't feel like I can forgive him at this moment Ogda I think it will take time.' Elenore said as she hastily wiped away the tears that began to spill down her face.

'I can understand however it is the only way to move through this. I know you have suffered, but time will help heal our wounds. Merek, like all of us, has much to lose if we are not united. And unity starts with our leaders.' Ogda placed his hand gently over Elenore's.

Elenore wiped her nose on her sleeve, she felt torn, one part of her wanted to forgive her husband the other felt a festering resentment. 'Take some time to consider what we have discussed, dear child. You must be strong, your path has been set. You will be reunited with Merek again, once the curse has lifted, and you must not show weakness this is what the black magic feeds upon.'

She looked up at the Seer and offered him a watery smile. He patted her gently. 'I must change, and rest now, please show me to Anja's room we have a lot to discuss.' He followed Elenore back out to the main room.

Merek strapped the stretcher to his big stallion and ordered some of his warriors to look for any signs of the Asur. They had travelled all through the night before they found his sister, son, and daughter. The horses were exhausted, and Ulric had not woken, forcing Merek to make the decision to rest through the next day. Evening now settled itself as the sun left the sky. Ada poured her father a tea as they waited for the warriors return. It had been a long time since she had seen him, and she had much to discuss.

'Papa, how is mother? I miss her terribly.' Merek clenched his jaw, choosing the words he wanted to say. 'Is something wrong?' Ada's gaze was intent, and he shifted uncomfortably.

'She is well.'

Ada frowned. 'Something is not right I can feel it.'

Merek stood. 'I might go check on my men, they should have returned, and I want to be leaving soon.' Ada watched him go, an uneasy feeling descending upon her.

They travelled through the night, stopping only when they had to spell the horses and have a short reprieve from riding. Merek was determined to put as much distance between him and the Asur as possible, he needed to get his son home.

When the sun graced the sky the next morning, Ulric began to stir. They stopped near a stream, filling their waterskins as Ada checked on her brother. Krea gave him some water as Merek watched over him.

'Ulric?' Merek leaned down and whispered in his son's ear.

It took Ulric a moment to orient himself. 'Papa, is that you?'

'Take it easy, son. We are taking you home.'

Ada checked Ulric's wound and offered some dried meat. After he had finished the food and taken another drink, they began their journey again. Merek did not let his group rest he was determined to be home by early evening. As they made their way up the rocky path that ascended Dorhall Pass, it soon became apparent that the steepness of the slope could cause Ulric to slip from the stretcher. Merek halted his horse, contemplating on how he would get his son up to the top of the trail. Ulric had slipped into unconsciousness again.

Merek dismounted and gestured for two of his men to help fasten a strap around his son. 'Be careful of his wound.' He said as he watched his men tie a leather belt around his son and the stretcher.

Krea had come to help her brother and nephew. Cautiously, they slowly coaxed Merek's stallion up the path. The horse snorted and Merek kept a close watch on the strap holding Ulric in place. He talked soothingly to the animal, calming him as they made their way up the mountain path.

Ada watched, concern etched on her face. Merek nodded to one of his men to go and alert Anja. They had to get Ulric to the valley as quickly as possible. Although it was not ideal having him carried this way, it was all they could do given the situation. Slowly they made their way up the trail.

Elenore ran to the front of the camp when she heard the news that Merek was making his way up the trail. Scouts had come to alert Anja who, together with Tallot, Amzi and Sabin, raced to where the trail tapered off to the hidden entrance. She waited halfway up the path, her heart racing. It had been so long since she had seen her children. The minutes ticked by and she began to fidget. The sun had travelled higher in the sky, blessing the earth below with its heat and rays of sunshine, and Elenore began to sweat. She wiped her face with her hand and took a breath to calm her racing heart.

As she waited, she saw movement up ahead. The shape of a man leading a big horse could be seen, with people walking either side of him. She recognised Merek, Krea, and Ada.

Anja, Sabin, Amzi and Tallot followed Merek with the rest of the warriors bringing up the rear. She ran forward as she saw her son lying motionless on the stretcher.

'Ulric!' Merek brought the stallion to a halt. Elenore touched her son. He felt cold, and fear rose. 'What happened?'

'The Asur got to him. We have to get him to the healer,' Merek replied as he took a step forward continuing the path to Serenity.

'Mother!' Elenore turned as she heard the familiar voice of her daughter.

'Ada!' She embraced her daughter. It had been such a long time and she thanked the Gods that she had been brought back unharmed. Tears began to spill down her face as she continued to hold Ada.

'Aye, Norrie, she is home now ye can let her go.' Sabin chuckled. Elenore and Ada joined his laughter and Elenore released her daughter. Even though she had grave concerns for her son, she was overjoyed that her daughter was home too. Finally, they were all together again.

They made their way to the camp, chatting and discussing anything and everything that came to mind. Elenore watched Merek make his way to Serenity's home, and silently sent a prayer to the Gods for Ulric's recovery.

Zuri was waiting, with many of the camp's people. She strode up to Merek, smiling, then she kissed him. Merek returned her embrace. Ada frowned and many looked away at the bold show of affection.

'What is going on, mother?' Ada turned to look at Elenore.

'He has been cursed, Ada.' Elenore said softly.

Ada shook her head in disbelief. They may have come home, but it seemed not everything was the way it should be in her family.

CHAPTER TWENTY

Revenge

I will come like the darkness that follows. Soon, I will find

you, and you will yearn for the light you extinguished.

Zuri

The healer clucked her tongue as she grounded up some herbs for the wounded man who lay still on the bed. Elenore, Ogda, Ada, and Merek watched in silence, worry carved into their faces.

'He will survive. Please, you must not worry,' the Seer told them in a quiet voice.

'When will he wake?' Elenore felt physically ill. Her son had not stirred since they had arrived the previous evening. Serenity busied herself with preparing many differing herbs and potions. His wound looked infected, and she had added a poultice to help it heal.

'Elenore, my dear, he has an infection. We must give him time to fight it.'

They had all taken turns in watching over him during the night.

'He does not have a fever anymore, thank the Gods.' Serenity poured the drink she had just made into a cup and made her way to the bed Ulric was asleep in. Carefully she placed his head in her lap and spooned the mixture between his lips. Merek helped sit him up so that he would not choke. Slowly they fed him the entire mixture.

'I am hoping this will help wake him.' Serenity told them as she went back into the kitchen. 'I will take first watch,' Merek announced.

'I will too,' Elenore added.

Merek glanced at her, unamused.

'Don't you want mother to stay with you?' Ada was direct. Her anger with her father had only intensified when she had seen him with Zuri.

'I think your mother has enough to do with the garden.'

Ada came to stand next to Merek. 'I think mother is old enough to know what is important, and being with her son takes priority.' She glared at Merek.

Merek was the first to look away. He did not want to argue with her.

'So, it is settled then. Merek and Elenore will do first watch. I will come with Anja later and I think Sabin said he would join you, Ada.' The Seer half smiled at Ada as she turned to look at him.

Elenore sponged Ulric's face and she watched for any sign of him waking. 'Do you remember when we got separated, Merek? And Kacha's healer saved you?'

Merek sighed. He had remained silent the whole time he and Elenore had taken watch over their son. Serenity had made another potion, instructing them to give it to him in three hours' time. The healer was exhausted and had gone to bed once they organised who would be watching over Ulric. The camp was growing and so far, she was the only healer and future midwife.

'I remember.' Merek did not look at his wife, preferring to keep his gaze on their son. 'Have you thought about a divorce, Elenore?'

Elenore sucked in her breath and closed her eyes; she had tried to push this away. 'I will never divorce you, Merek.' Her tone was cold as she willed herself to have the courage to stand up to him.

Merek clenched his fists into balls as his face darkened with anger. 'How will that serve you? I don't want to be your husband any longer. You need to get over this thing that we are going to get back together!' he hissed.

Elenore felt her own anger begin to grow. 'I don't think we should be arguing in front of our son.'

Merek started to pace the room. The sound of the front door opening startled them, and Merek went to check who had come in. Elenore could hear Zuri's voice, and her heart sank. She despised the woman. *Didn't she have any decency?* Despite herself, Elenore peered out the doorway into the main room. Zuri had jumped into Merek's arms, and her legs wrapped around his waist as they kissed.

Elenore felt both humiliation and disgust. She wanted to shout out to Merek that she did want a divorce and it was all she could do to stop herself from doing that very thing. Wiping the tears that began to flow, she went and sat beside her son's bed. The image of her husband and Zuri lingered in her mind, and she could not shake it. *How can I ever be with Merek again? It will never be the same. If the Asur had never come, none of this would have happened.* Bitter thoughts tumbled through her mind, stoking her fury.

Elenore looked out the window. Night had come, dark and daunting. A fluttering in her stomach brought her attention back to where she was. She placed a hand on her stomach; her babies were moving. So absorbed in trying to connect to her unborn children, she did not hear Zuri and Merek come into the room.

'What are you doing?' Zuri asked, making Elenore jump. She snickered as she saw Elenore's reaction.

'I am feeling Merek and I's babies move. They are healthy, which is what every mother and father want.' She glared at Zuri.

'I think you need to go home and rest, Elenore. Better make sure they continue like that you know how things can change.' Zuri folded her arms over her ample chest. Elenore wanted to gouge out her eyes.

She stood and took a step towards Zuri, then pushed her. 'Get out. You are not welcome here!'

Zuri pushed her back, forcing Elenore on to the bed. Elenore's patience snapped. 'I told you to get out!' She said as she once again shoved the younger woman towards the door.

Merek came to stand between them as Zuri reached forward to grab Elenore's hair. Elenore let out a startled cry as Zuri pulled with all her might. Elenore toppled back, landing on her side on the floor.

Merek pushed Zuri aside. 'Leave her!' he growled.

Elenore lay on the wooden floor. A sharp pain tore down her side as she panted to catch her breath.

Merek hunkered down beside her. 'Are you okay?' She did not answer him.

Serenity had woken after hearing Elenore fall and raced into the room. 'What is going on here?' she exclaimed.

Elenore sat up. Her head swam, and she reached a shaking hand up to her forehead. She could feel a small gash and blood was on her fingers as she pulled her hand away. Merek offered his hand to help her up.

Elenore pushed it aside. 'Leave!' she told him. Merek continued to look down at her. 'I said, get out!' Elenore shouted.

'Leave her, Merek, she is not worth it.' Zuri grabbed Merek's arm, leading him from the room.

Serenity kneeled beside Elenore. 'Don't get up just yet. Let me look at the cut on your head,' she said gently. The healer clucked her tongue, examining the wound. 'Not too bad, Norrie. It won't need stitching. Take it slowly when you get up,' she offered.

Elenore nodded she felt exhausted. She took the healer's hand as she hoisted herself up. The healer looked her over once more. 'Does everything feel okay?'

Elenore nodded. The healer helped her to the chair beside Ulric's bed. Elenore sat down and glanced down at her son.

'Serenity, he is moving! I think he may wake up!'

Serenity smiled and came closer to the bed. Ulric was indeed stirring, and as he moved on to his side his eyes fluttered open. Elenore got up from the chair and kissed his cheek. 'Welcome back, son.'

People busied themselves in gathering food, water, and timber for the night's welcome ceremony. It had been three weeks since they had arrived at the valley. Ulric had recovered enough to be able to participate, and there was excitement in the air as the burgeoning village prepared to welcome their new guests and soon to be community members.

Anja sipped her tea. Ada, herself, and the Seer had discussed in great length preparations for the coming battle and the situation between Elenore and Merek.

'I think we need to announce Zuri's future husband tonight at the ceremony. We won't have time to have another one, it will be too risky,' Anja said thoughtfully. Ogda reflected on her proposal, it was a good suggestion. He had his concerns with the Asur finding them and it was crucial that Merek be restored to full capacity before the Asur arrived. Ogda scratched and pulled at the wisps of beard that sprouted from his chin.

'There is another thing I think you need to be made aware of.' Anja sighed.

'Go on,' Ogda said as he raised an eyebrow.

Anja glanced away for a moment before meeting Ogda's gaze.

'In the last few days Merek has failed to send scouts out to look for any sign of the Asur. Tallot came to tell me.' She let out a slow breath. 'Merek is now starting to neglect some of his leadership duties, and I am sure that it has to do with Zuri being the distraction and the curse that has been placed on Merek.

Ogda shook his head. 'We have to get this situation under control.' Concern covered Ogda's face.

'We have to convince Amzi to be on board. He has a right to decline, as he is her only living male relative.'

'I will send Ada to discuss it with him, but this cannot go on any longer. Someone has cursed my son, we need him focused on the battle ahead.' Anja pursed her lips.

'Do we know the man who is intended for marriage with Zuri?' Ada asked.

'We do. He is from a different family, one that joined Merek when they were on their way here.' Anja smiled. She had not met the man, but the Seer had pointed him out. 'He is a carpenter, his skills are highly regarded. I have heard good stories about him.'

Ada chuckled. 'A bit different to a leader. Zuri won't be impressed.'

'It will humble her. I think she needs a lesson in that.' Anja smiled.

People were seated at the long timber table that was adorned with decorations and tableware. A woman sang a song that told a story about a couple in love, her voice reverberated through the night sky. She had a beautiful voice and Elenore listened to it intently. When the singer had finished Ogda stood in front of the gathering of people. He welcomed the newcomers and did a speech of how grateful he was to be back with them. The crowd applauded and whistled when he had finished. Excitement rippled through the people seated.

The Seer proceeded to read out the list of the upcoming weddings. He asked each couple to stand and be congratulated and announced that weddings would take place in four weeks' time. A murmur went through the crowd. It was so soon. Ogda ignored them, merely giving the explanation that time was of the essence, their world was not a permanent one.

'The last wedding that will take place will be between Zuri and Arcus. Please wish the couple good health and fortune.' The crowd gasped at Ogda's words, and a wave of whispers went through them. Elenore sucked in her breath, and she felt her son squeeze her hand. He had been briefed by Ada of all that had transpired between his parents.

Elenore quickly scanned the crowd for Zuri; she wanted to see how she was taking this news. Zuri was sitting next to Merek, an angry scowl on her face. Merek was trying to placate her and was losing the battle badly. Elenore watched as Zuri begrudgingly stood up, honouring the traditional practice of good wishes. She quickly looked over to the far side of the table, where a handsome dark-haired man stood. He was young, with shoulder length hair and a broad smile. Zuri did not meet the man's gaze, preferring to look away.

The village wished them well and raised a toast for the soon to be couple. Elenore noticed Merek direct his gaze at her. The look of hate sent a shiver down her spine. She averted his gaze and instead stared down at the plate of delicious food. Suddenly her appetite vanished and an uneasy feeling settled upon her.

Elenore made her way back to Merek's home. Ulric walked beside her, adamant on escorting her home. He was bitterly disappointed with his father and had barely spoken to him once he had found out what had happened between his mother and father. Elenore felt exhausted, her stomach felt heavy, and she wondered how she would be in four months' time when the babies were due. As they neared the large hut, Zuri came walking towards them an angry look on her face.

'Can you give us some privacy, Ulric? I need to talk to your mother,' she growled as she neared them. Ulric frowned, irritated that she had the audacity to dismiss him.

'No. Whatever you need to say to my mother, you can say to me.'

Her eyes flickered over Ulric and a look of repulsion settled upon her. 'Very well, have it your own way. Elenore, I know that you are behind this and I am going make you pay! Merek is mine, do you hear? He loathes you and you sicken him!' As she spoke, she took a step closer to Elenore, waving her finger in front of her.

Ulric stepped forward and pushed her roughly away. 'Get away from here. My father is not thinking right, he has been cursed. You are the one he should be hating. How dare you speak to the leader's wife like that!' Ulric continued to steer Zuri away from his mother.

She pulled away from him and turned to look back at Elenore. 'I am going to make you pay for this, Elenore!' she spat.

Ulric took a firmer hold on her. He had not yet regained his full strength, but his patience had run out. Pulling her arms, behind her he began to lead her back to the main camp.

'I will wait back at the house, Ulric!' Elenore shouted after him. Ulric raised his hand, indicating he had heard her.

Ulric was determined that he would face his father and put an end to this ridiculous love triangle. He also wanted Zuri punished, something he would have to discuss with the Seer. Zuri twisted and squirmed, trying to escape Ulric's firm hold.

'Stop trying to get away, it won't help you. I have had enough of this rubbish!' Ulric scanned the crowd, desperately trying to locate his father.

'Are you looking for your father?' The small voice startled him, and he looked sideways to see Kaiah standing off to one side. He felt himself blush. It was not a good time to be talking with her. She did not wait for him to answer. 'He is with Anja and the Seer, over near the healer's home.' Ulric mumbled a thank you and made his way to Serenity's home.

His father was seated in front of a small fire, the Seer, Anja, and the healer seated opposite him. They were in a deep conversation as Ulric approached. Reaching them, he shoved Zuri forward, his fury evident.

'This woman is to be punished! She threatened my mother, your wife!' Ulric directed his gaze at Merek. Merek stood as Zuri ran to him. He placed his arms around her, giving her a quick embrace.

'I decide who gets punished. I am the leader of this village.'

Ulric strode towards his father. 'You are not fit to lead this camp. You have abandoned your wife who carries your children! What sort of leader does that!' Ulric demanded.

Merek clenched his jaw.

'He is right, Merek,' Ogda whispered. 'Zuri is promised to Arcus. Amzi has given his consent. We have tried to warn you. This union between yourself and Zuri is doomed and will forfeit everything we have worked for. Your wife needs you. I will be the one overseeing the punishment for this woman.' The Seer straightened his shoulders and faced the woman who had caused so much trouble. 'Zuri, you will go and work with the people who collect the seeds, and you will be banished from seeing Merek. I do not want to say this, but if you break your punishment, you will be banned from the village.'

Zuri let out a cry.

'Banning someone from the village will ensure certain death,' Merek argued.

The Seer sighed. 'I cannot risk the fate of all for the needs of one.'

Merek sat back on the log, holding his head between his hands.

Zuri sat beside him, stroking his arm.

'You should leave now. Please do what you have been told.' Merek did not look up at her. Zuri paused her hand halfway in the air. 'Leave,' Merek growled.

She stood, as if she had been slapped, her face full of shock. 'As you wish. You will regret it.' She turned and fled while Merek continued to look down at the ground.

Elenore busied herself by helping both her daughter Ada and son Ulric's wedding arrangements. She gathered native flowers that grew in the valley and had begun to sew Ada and Kaiah's wedding dresses. Anja also helped, making the decorations that would grace the wedding table. Each wedding table would have its own unique array of decorations made by the families of the bride and groom. Usually, they would have months to prepare, but with the Asur almost at their door they had only four weeks to organise the grand event.

'Hold still, Ada.' Elenore carefully placed a pin where she wanted to put in a decorative thread.

'Kacha will love all your home cooking. Ludwig tells me you have been such an immense help and that he has shown you how to make many things.' Anja chuckled as she watched mother and daughter.

'Ludwig is a talented cook and I am looking forward to trying out new recipes.' Ada added. Elenore sighed. If only they did not have an enemy at their backs and Zuri had not been in their life. She wiped away the loose strand of hair that had fallen across her face and pushed aside the negative thoughts that were starting to surface. Concentrating she inserted the needle near to where she had placed the pin previously. She began to sew the decoration that she had chosen for Ada's dress. Elenore wanted to see how it would look with the dress on unsure of the location of the decoration. After a few minutes she was satisfied with her decision. Ada breathed a sigh of relief and gestured to Kaiah that it was her turn to have her dress decorated.

Elenore lay on her side for her afternoon nap not only was she weary from all the wedding arrangements; she could not lay on her stomach any longer. Serenity had given her different herbs to take every day to help with the growth of her unborn children. Merek had returned to his home a few days after he had told Zuri to leave him. He was quiet, withdrawn, said little, and refused to sleep in the same bed as Elenore.

At first, she had been hurt with his rejection but after some time she grew to accept it. Elenore had also noticed Anja's frustration and annoyance with her son. From the dirty looks Anja constantly threw at Merek to her impatience when he refused to discuss their next step in finding and getting rid of the Asur. An uneasiness had formed between both Merek and Anja and Elenore wondered how long it would go on for. She knew it was important they have a plan in place it was only a matter of time when the Asur would come for them. Merek's priorities both as a father and a leader were beginning to become less important.

A shiver went down her spine when she thought about the Asur. They created a fear that never left any of them. Although the village had started to relax and resume normal life, she knew it was imperative that they formulate strategies and designate people tasks if they were to survive the inevitable attack.

The room had grown warm, and Elenore hoisted herself up. She got up from the bed and felt a pain go down her side. She paused and waited for it to go before making her way to the kitchen. Ada and Ludwig were cooking, they had become very close. Kaiah was sitting at the table, peeling vegetables. She smiled at them before making her way out the door and towards the river. She wanted to bathe and hoped the coolness of the water would lift her spirits.

The river was full of people, but she managed to find a quiet spot away from the crowd. She could see Zuri talking to some younger men, and she shook her head. *I hope Merek comes to his senses and sees what she is really like.*

She wondered where Merek went during the day now he had fallen into a deep depression. She washed her face and dunked her hair in the cool water. Zuri had caught sight of her and whispered to the young men she was flirting with. They smirked and laughed as they looked over towards her.

Elenore felt herself blush and decided to leave, uncomfortable being the butt of their jokes. She hated Zuri and wondered if she would ever forgive her. As she stepped out of the water, she felt another pain, causing her to cry out. She reached out to support herself with a small tree that stood in front of her. The pain lasted longer this time, and a growing sense of alarm began to develop.

'I will go and see Serenity, there must be something wrong.' She could hear someone behind her as she slowly walked away from the river.

'Hey!' Elenore squeezed her eyes shut and took a breath. She did not have the patience to have a conversation. She felt a hand on her shoulder, and she turned to see who it was.

'We were hoping you would stay a little longer.' One of the youths who had been flirting with Zuri was grinning at her.

'I have to get home.' Elenore did not like the look he was giving her. His mouth twisted into a wicked grin. He reached down and grabbed her wrist, pulling her towards him. Elenore felt her heart beat faster and she swallowed trying to calm her growing panic. 'Please leave me alone I just want to go home.'

The young man had pulled her close enough that she could smell his breath and she looked away. 'You can go home after we have had some fun. Zuri tells me you love playing in the water.' He snickered and pulled Elenore towards the water's edge.

Elenore looked over to where Zuri and the other men were sitting. They began to jeer and shout as they saw their friend dragging Elenore into the water. Elenore pleaded for the man to stop, but he only laughed at her as he pulled her further in. She desperately looked around for other people, but it seemed most of them had already left. She spotted a family on the far side and began to call out for help.

The man roughly placed his hand to cover her mouth. 'Shut up!' he growled. 'Now you can either do it my way, nice and easy, or we do it the hard way. I don't think you will like that.' Elenore felt tears run down her face. 'Are you going to keep quiet?' he demanded.

She nodded. He gave her one more look before releasing his hand. Elenore took a breath. The water was up to her waist, and she looked over to Zuri who was watching intently. Elenore let the man drag her to the rock ledge that Zuri and three other men were sitting on. The pain had started to return, and she willed it to go away. She sent a prayer to the Gods and screamed silently for Ada or Anja to pick up on her dilemma.

As they approached the others she pleaded once again for the man to let her go.

'What's wrong with her?' Zuri called out.

'Arh! she doesn't want to play with us,' he snickered.

'Stop your whingeing Elenore and get up here.' Zuri came over and helped the youth pull her out of the water.

Elenore carefully sat down, not looking at them. 'So, what game do you want to play?'

The other men had come over and surrounded her. Elenore's thoughts tumbled over one another. She had to get away from them. She looked over to where she had seen the family across the other bank, they were leaving. She felt her breath catch in her throat and her stomach clenched.

'I told you to be careful, didn't I?' Zuri kneeled beside Elenore, pushing a strand of her hair away from her face. 'Look at me!' She grabbed Elenore's chin, pulling her to face her.

Elenore stared into the other woman's blue eyes. A cold, hateful look filled them. It sent a shiver down her spine.

'I want you to pay for what you have done. You have ruined my life and now it is my turn to ruin yours!' Zuri spat. She pulled Elenore up by her hair, forcing her to cry out. 'Shut up you stupid bitch' she snarled in Elenore's ear. Elenore knew her life depended on her getting away and thought desperately on how she could escape.

The pain in her abdomen had increased, giving her the strength to fight. An anger washed over her as her desire to flee became too much to bear. Elenore pushed Zuri with all her strength, forcing her back onto one of the young men behind her. Zuri leaped up as Elenore ran towards the edge of the rock ledge.

'Grab her!'

Elenore felt the hands of one of the men grab her hair, reeling her back towards them. She turned and began to claw at his face. He released his grip, giving Elenore an opportunity to make another dash to the water. She surged forward before she felt herself being pushed from the side. Elenore became unbalanced and toppled sideways. She held out her right arm to brace her fall and an immediate pain shot up from her forearm as she fell heavily on her side. Her stomach cramped and she cried out from pain and shock. She squeezed her eyes shut. The pain was unbearable, and she dared not move.

'Get up!' Zuri leaned over and placed her foot into Elenore's side. Elenore lay still.

'Have you killed her?' One of the youths came to stand next to her.

'No, she is pretending.' Zuri gave a swift kick, causing Elenore to moan. 'I told you she was still alive. Now get her up!'

They sat Elenore up and she watched dazed as they peered down at her. She could feel a dampness between her legs, and she glanced down at herself. A bright red patch was beginning to form at the front of her trousers. 'You're making her lose her baby!' One of the men shouted. Elenore heard Zuri laugh in satisfaction. She could not move the pain was too great and she suddenly felt exhausted. The numb feeling of sleep enveloped her, and she gave into its embrace.

When Elenore woke, her arm was throbbing and the pain in her stomach had slowed to a dull ache. Blood had dried on her trousers, and she was relieved that the bleeding had at least stopped. She looked around her. The sun was descending, casting shadows on the water. Zuri was locked in an embrace with the man who had dragged her into the water. The other three were engaged in conversation.

'She's awake!' The youngest man leaped from where he had been sitting.

Zuri rushed over to Elenore, a wicked look on her face. 'Good you are awake, now we can have some fun.' She forced Elenore to sit up. 'I want you to mess her up. That way Merek knows what he really missed out on.' She sneered as she instructed the two youths closest to Elenore. They laughed and jostled before Elenore felt a hard blow to her face. A dark curtain descended upon her as she fell into a dreamless sleep.

CHAPTER TWENTY-ONE

A Second Chance

Sharpen your swords, for the devil stirs. We will stand
together and bring the devil to heel.

Merek

The hard rocky ledge was pushing into Elenore's spine, and she groaned as she moved to make herself comfortable. Her eyes could barely open and her lips felt swollen. She struggled to remember where she was. Attempting to sit up, a sharp pain shot up her arm. She lay back down, and waited for her eyes to become accustomed to the dark.

Crickets and frogs sang a chorus to the evening sky. Her jaw ached and she rubbed it as the memory of what had happened earlier came back, like a dim light slowly becoming brighter. Panic seized her and she swept her gaze around the rocky ledge. They had gone; she was alone. She sighed in relief. The enormity of what had happened began to grow and she quickly moved her hands along her abdomen. Her babies were quiet, there was no movement. Tears welled and rolled down her face as she began to sob. *She has won, she has killed them.*

Elenore's sense of loss was overwhelming, and she felt broken, her soul shattered. Suddenly, all she wanted to do was sleep and she gave in to its pull and welcomed it as it took her to the depths of unconsciousness.

The rain smelled sweet as it hit her face, waking her once more as it cooled the summer night. Opening her eyes Elenore reflected on the reason she was lying on a rocky ledge near the river's edge. *I have to get off from here, nobody knows where I am.*

Taking a breath, she slowly sat up. Her right arm still throbbed, and her face felt swollen. She looked at the dark river lapping softly at the bottom of the rocky ledge. During the day, it had beckoned her, offering relief from the heat and a way to wash away the dirt, but now it didn't seem so friendly. The rain continued to fall, soaking her tunic and trousers. She had to get into the water and swim to the bank if she wanted to survive.

Zuri and her male companions had left her for dead. She wanted to prove them wrong and seek vengeance for what they had done to her unborn children. They had dragged her to the top of the ledge, making it harder for her to get down to the water's edge. Slowly, she tried to stand up. Her head swam and she nearly fainted as she stood, she took a moment to steady herself before taking a step.

Cautiously, Elenore made her way to the edge. Every step brought pain and she clenched her jaw to shut off her cries. The water lay below, dark and surly, the rain pounded against her. Taking a breath, Elenore shoved herself into the water. It was cold. The icy water seemed to freeze the very air in her lungs causing her to gasp. She kicked her legs, making her way to the opposite bank. She was thankful it was not that far away, and she clambered up, gulping for breath. Every movement brought pain, but she still had a long way to go.

The lights of the village could be seen in the near distance. Elenore stumbled, making her way towards them. She had never realised how far the village really was from the river. Her fear in coming across Zuri dogged her steps. She willed herself to keep going, the lure of sleep was getting harder to resist.

As she neared the edge of her community, she fell to her knees, the pain and exhaustion almost too much to ignore. Taking a breath, Elenore began to crawl so determined in reaching the main camp that she dared not to stop. Soon she could make out the bright light of the torches and main campfire. People were engaged in conversation while adults rounded up children to put them to bed. She began to call out, but all she could manage was a whisper.

'Help!' She tried harder to make her voice louder. She had to get closer so someone would see her. An overwhelming tiredness pulled at her, demanding to take her to the dark world of unconsciousness. Elenore tried to shrug it off. She had to get nearer, and she willed herself to keep going. Suddenly she heard someone call out, finally somebody had seen her! She stopped and saw them run towards her, now she could give in to the sleep that refused to let go.

Elenore blinked her eyes open; several men were carrying her on a stretcher one of them was her dearest friend!

'Sabin,' she croaked.

'Aye Norrie, ye awake. Please stay still, we are taking ye to Serenity. I have told Tallot to fetch Merek.' Elenore smiled. Sabin had always been there for her. His face was creased with concern as she continued to blink up at him.

Serenity was waiting for them as they pulled up at the front of her hut.

'Quick, get her inside!' She peered down at Elenore. 'For the love of the Gods, what happened, Norrie?!' Elenore began to weep as the memory of what happened surfaced. 'Hush now, child. Do not cry, all will be well.' Elenore thought about her babies, and she cried out. Serenity reached down and patted her shoulder before making the men lift her gently to the bed. Ada, Anja, and the Seer burst into the room as Serenity began to cut away Elenore's-soaked clothing.

'Mother, what happened?' Ada rushed to her side.

'Zuri,' was all that Elenore could manage.

'I knew it!' Ada snarled. Anja started to help Serenity, bathing Elenore and talking to her in soothing tones. 'She is going to pay, I am going to make sure of it!' Ada said as she looked worriedly at her mother.

'My babies, Serenity, I think I have lost them.' Elenore glanced at the healer as she examined her belly.

Serenity clucked. 'You have a lot of injuries, Norrie, but I will start with your babies.' She prodded and gently poked, clucking and tisking. She looked at Anja and shook her head.

'What is it?' Elenore attempted to sit up, but the healer gently pushed her down. 'Norrie, you have a baby in there, it's the other I cannot feel. I am sorry.'

Elenore screamed. Ada ran to her mother, holding her as she wailed. When Elenore had succumbed to quiet sobs, Anja and Serenity tended to her wounds. Her arm was fractured, and it was evident she had been beaten badly.

Ada made a broth and attempted to feed her mother. Elenore refused.

She did not want to eat, she just wanted to sleep and pretend that nothing had ever happened.

'You must eat, mother. You still have a baby that needs nourishment' Ada coaxed. Elenore sighed. Her daughter was right. She took a sip of the broth; it was delicious. She took another and soon the bowl was finished. Ada smiled at Elenore. 'She will pay. Don't worry mother.' Elenore nodded.

Ulric burst into the room, startling them. 'Anja just told me what happened! What the hell!' He ran to Elenore's side, a look of revulsion crossing his face as he saw her battered body. 'Where is father? He is the cause of all this!' Ulric ran his hands through his hair.

'Sabin has been trying to find him,' Ada replied.

Ulric leaned down to Elenore, brushing his lips over her cheek. 'I will make whoever did this pay, starting with your husband.' Ulric cast a glance at Ada before striding from the room.

Ogda came to see Elenore too. His face reflected his shock at seeing her battered body. He shook his head and muttered a prayer to the Gods. He sat with her for a while before Sabin came to pay his friend a visit.

'Aye, here she is!' His easy tone brought a smile to Elenore's swollen lips.

'Has anyone found Merek yet?' the Seer asked Sabin, barely able to keep the irritation from his voice.

'Aye, Ulric found him. I had to prise the youngster off him. He can have a temper when he wants.' Sabin chuckled.

Ogda sighed the camp was in disarray and a persistent feeling of doom lingered. This would be the perfect time for the Asur to attack. He had hoped that he could mind travel with Ada and seek out Dardanos, they had been delayed for too long. Heavy footsteps brought him back to the present and he glanced up to see Merek leaning on the doorframe.

Shock and concern lined the leader's face. He had been drinking heavily for several days until his son had sought him out. Merek gingerly touched a dark bruise on his cheek, bestowed by his son it would seem, as he stared at his wife.

At first, he could not register what he was seeing. Her body was covered in bruises and scratches, her lips swollen, and one eye was closed. She lay lifeless on the bed, barely moving when he called her name. His drunken stupor began to lift taking the brain fog with it. He blinked and came to sit beside her.

'Aye Merek, she is in bad shape.'

Merek ignored Sabin's remark as he gazed down at Elenore. He saw her slow look of registration when her eyes met his. She tried to smile with cracked lips, but it was obvious that her face hurt. Merek felt the enormity of what happened come down on him like a crushing blow.

'Norrie, I am so sorry my love,' he stroked her hair as his heart ached. 'Who did this?' He whispered.

Elenore swallowed. 'Zuri and her male companions.' Her voice crackled and rasped. Her whole body ached, and she longed for a warm soaking bath. 'Our babies … Merek, I think we have lost one of them.' She began to sob.

Merek stood. His beard hung long and unkept, along with his hair as he pushed it back and paced the room. He swallowed. The realisation that his affair may have cost him his own child clutched at him. A wave of nausea swept over him. He stopped his fervent pacing and wiped away a tear. He sniffed and cleared his throat, inner rage now festering.

'She is going to pay. She will no longer be allowed in this village,' he growled.

'We will deal with her and her adversaries correctly.' Ogda interjected.

'And Merek, please, no rash decisions,' Ogda added.

Merek met the Seer's gaze and cast another look at Elenore. 'Look at my wife and what Zuri has done!' Merek shouted.

The Seer merely nodded.

Zuri and her three companions that had attacked Elenore stood on the wooden platform. Merek was seated at the table in front of them, Ogda and the newly elected Councillors on either side of him. The Seer had pushed Merek into creating a Council and to put the accused on trial. He was determined that the community they lived in believe in justice and it would be provided fairly.

The people had come to Elenore's aid, leaving her donations of food, clothing and well wishes. Edyth stayed with her most days, until the demands of her own children got too much for Sabin or Huxley. When the village had heard that one of Elenore's babies may not have survived an angry sentiment rippled through it. This forced the Seer to place Zuri and her companions in a secret location for their protection, until justice could be served. Arcus had relinquished his consent on the marriage between himself and Zuri after finding out what had happened.

Merek looked at the woman he thought he had fallen in love with, revulsion hitting him. Her evil heart had diminished her beauty and he could barely stand to look at her. A crowd had gathered to watch the proceedings and Merek had strategically placed his warriors to help contain them.

'Does anyone object to the sentence of banishment for the four people that are on trial for the assault on Merek's wife Elenore?' called out one of the newly elected Councillors in a shrill voice.

A murmur went through the crowd before a voice could be heard. 'I beg for forgiveness for my sister, please!' Amzi pleaded.

'Why should she receive forgiveness? This is the second time she has done the same thing!' A member of the crowd replied.

'Explain why she should be granted forgiveness?' The Councillor asked.

'She is sorry for what she has done, ask her!' Amzi argued.

The Councillor turned to the four shackled on the platform. 'What is your response?'

Zuri spat on the ground in front of her before casting an angry look at the gathered crowd. 'I would do it again and I am not sorry. She deserved it!' She began to laugh as the crowd erupted into barely restrained anger. Merek stood, his own temper rising.

'Sit down, Merek,' Ogda demanded. Merek thumped his fist on the table, glaring at Zuri.

'You enjoyed me, Merek!' She goaded. The Seer motioned for Tallot and a few other warriors to grab Merek as he took a step away from the table.

'Get your hands off me! I won't touch her, let the Asur do that!' he snarled.

Amzi shook his head it seemed his sister had gone mad and there was nothing he could do. He prayed to the Gods for them to spare her soul and he turned and left the scene.

Zuri and the young men were given horses and supplies before being led, blindfolded, to a location far from the village. They were advised that if they were to return it would mean certain death. The people were satisfied with the punishment and followed the warriors to the edges of the valley's forest, cheering as Zuri and the youths were banished.

Elenore finally was well enough to be in her own bed. Her bruises and cuts were starting to heal, and she was able to move around with minimal discomfort. Her arm still throbbed at night and Serenity had strapped and placed it in a sling. Elenore was astounded and surprised by the amount of support that her community had given her. It was an example of people being united and working together to help one of their own when it was needed. Something that would be vital when they battled with the Asur. Merek stayed with Amzi, offering his support for the man who had lost his sister. Though their friendship had remained, it was not as it once was, an undercurrent of animosity ran through it.

Elenore lit the candle beside her bed. Rain hammered against the window as the summer storm passed over the village. She laid on the bed, running her hands over her stomach. Although she was grateful that the curse on Merek had been lifted, she prayed every night to the Gods to feel some movement to confirm that at least one of her babies was alive. She tried to relax, taking deep breaths and placed her hands lower, waiting for the familiar fluttering.

She waited.

Nothing.

Disappointment washed over her, and she bit her lip to stop the tears that threatened to spill. She heard the front door open, and she wondered who would be coming in so late in the evening and in the rain. She sat herself up further on the pillows before there was a knock at the door. She swallowed as fear took her in its grasp. She was still unsure on who it could be.

'Come in.' She said hesitantly.

Merek opened the door, his hair and beard dripping from the rain, he looked at her sheepishly.

'I um, can I stay here tonight?'

Elenore still was unsure about her feelings towards Merek. 'Okay,' she said slowly. Merek nodded and reached for the towel that was draped over the chair next to the bed.

'Do you mind?' He asked as he held up the towel. Elenore shook her head and watched him as he dried himself off. 'What were you doing?' He asked casually.

Elenore could not take her eyes off him. It had been so long, and despite everything that had passed between them, she felt herself longing to be held by him.

'I was just trying to feel the baby.' She looked away, unsure what his reply would be. Merek had not mentioned their unborn children, even when Zuri had been cast out and she worried if this would become an issue again.

He sat on the bed beside her and placed his hands on her stomach. Elenore sucked in her breath. Suddenly, there was a flutter and then another. Elenore gasped before breaking out into a smile.

'Merek, did you feel that?'

He grinned. 'Yes I did.' Elenore felt her heart melt and moved her hand to touch Merek's face. He kissed her fingers before leaning forward to brush his mouth against hers. She moved in towards him as he gently began to nibble her neck. Merek pushed Elenore back on her pillows, carefully positioning himself so that he would not lay on her arm or put his weight on her stomach. Elenore could feel his desire grow as he began to make his way to her breasts.

Suddenly an image of Zuri with her legs wrapped around Merek's waist replayed in her mind.

'Please Merek, I am not ready.'

He paused and groaned before carefully extracting himself from her. 'I understand. We will take it slow. Is it still okay for me to stay here?'

Elenore looked away. Her heart hammered, and she began to feel uneasy. It would take some time before she would feel comfortable around her husband again. She slowly nodded her consent.

Merek ran his fingers through Elenore's long dark red hair. 'I am sorry for what I have done to you and my family. I owe you so much, and I hope one day you will forgive me.' Elenore opened her mouth before Merek placed his finger to her lips. 'Please, do not say anything. I can't explain my actions and I hate myself for them. I must make it up to you and I will do everything I can. I can't live without you, Norrie. I am such a fool for nearly letting you go.' He rubbed his face as if trying to erase the past.

'It will take me some time and I ask you to be patient. I also want you to know that nothing happened between myself and Tallot.'

Merek clenched his jaw and looked away. 'Okay,' he mumbled. Elenore was unsure if he believed her but decided not to push the issue. She missed Merek, but she would have to work hard to put the last few months behind her and forgive him.

'I can sleep in the other room if that makes you feel more comfortable,' Merek offered. Elenore sighed. She desperately wanted things to be back to the way they had been before Zuri came on the scene. She shook her head and patted the bed beside her. Merek went around to the other side of the bed and slipped under the covers, beside her. 'Hold me,' Elenore said after a moment. She scooted over and placed her head on his shoulder.

Merek wrapped his arms around her, gently pulling her closer. She could feel his breath on her cheek and a feeling of comfort and security came over her.

'Goodnight, Merek. I am so happy that you came here tonight. Please, this is our home, do not leave me or it again.'

Merek kissed the top of her head. 'I won't, my love,' he replied.

The Seer had gathered the warriors to discuss their formations and the training that would be required. Merek sat to one side as he did a quick head count. He had begun training men who had shown an interest in fighting the Asur and he was pleasantly surprised by the number that had put up their hands. There were close to two hundred men gathered to run training drills in front of his hut and still a few more stragglers were making their way towards them.

Merek looked over at his sister, she had a few of her own female recruits. Merek smiled and shook his head, she was always ready to take on a challenge. He had noticed her training some other women on how to fight and use the sword in the last couple of weeks and he admired her.

As the crowd began practicing their formations a nervous energy coursed through them. Merek had advised them that training would intensify, and patrols would be increased.

'You will need to train them hard Merek. We will need every one of them.' Ogda ran his eyes over the large group. They had started to practice their sword skills and the air rang with clashing metal.

'Have the scouts returned?' Ogda leaned in and whispered. The scouts had been on a week-long mission to try and find evidence on where the Asur were.

'I am expecting them any day.'

The Seer nodded. He planned to mind travel that afternoon with Ada, but had hoped that the scouts would have returned by now. Ogda had felt the now familiar feeling of fear return. He sensed chaos and destruction on a level that they had never seen before. The people in the village had already experienced being misplaced and losing loved ones, this would be an even greater calamity. He pushed aside the thoughts that ran through his mind; it was imperative that he stayed focused.

Ogda asked Ludwig to make the special tea for himself and Ada to assist with their mind travel, as he arranged large cushions for them to sit on. The day had become cloudy and dark; a storm was starting to build over the mountainous Pass. Ada stood at the window, watching the clouds gather to an ominous purple.

'There are riders on their way, I can feel their energy they have something important to tell Papa.' She frowned and glanced at the Seer.

'They are the scouts. I have been waiting for them to arrive, we must speak to them before we start our meditation. Come let us go and meet with them. I think Merek is at the main camp.' They made their way to the main camp as six riders came in. They were talking excitedly to Merek and by the way their horses' flanks were heaving, it appeared they had ridden hard to get to the valley.

A strong wind began to blow, whipping Ada's hair around her face.

She pushed it back, annoyed; the storm was getting closer. Merek turned as he noticed his daughter and the Seer approach.

'Wait, I want you to tell everything you just told me to Ogda and my daughter Ada, they need to hear what you have to say.'

The scouts were filthy and looked as if they hadn't rested in many days, but they nodded their heads to Ada and the Seer respectively. 'We came as quick as we could. The rest of the forest is on fire and there are many people fleeing. The Asur are killing everything and setting it on fire. They are travelling quickly.' The lead scout shook his head and ran his tongue over his parched lips. 'We were lucky not to have been caught and praise the Gods we all made it back here alive.'

'Did anyone see or follow you?' Merek asked, concern etched on his face.

The scout looked down at the ground. 'I cannot say for sure, master. We had to leave as fast as we could. We rode all through the night but there appeared to be nobody following us.'

Merek sighed. 'That does not mean that somebody was not.'

'Sorry, we just didn't have time for extra precautions.' The scout continued to look down.

'Did you see anything else?' Ada asked gently. The scout looked up at her as she studied him. He shifted uncomfortably, Ada was reading his thoughts and it was unsettling.

'You saw humans with them.' It was more of a statement than a question. The scout was taken aback and shot Merek a quick look. '

Tell us. I won't let you leave here until you tell us everything.'

'Sorry, master. Yes, what your daughter says is true, we saw humans with them.'

'What were they doing? Were they prisoners?' Merek demanded.

The scout shook his head. 'No, they were – I mean, it was like they were helping them.'

'Go on,' Merek prompted.

'I can't be certain, but one of them looked like Ranco. He was riding with one of their generals. I could not get a close look as we had to run, but I am sure it was him.'

'That evil, filthy rat. How many more?' Merek growled.

'A few. Actually, there was a woman too. She was quite beautiful.'

Merek looked at the Seer who shook his head, but did not say a word. Merek knew his decision to be with Zuri, regardless how brief it was, would haunt him for the rest of his life.

'Thank you for your information,' Ada told the scout quietly. Merek waved his hand giving the scouts permission to leave.

Ogda came closer to Merek. 'We have a serious problem, Merek. If Zuri has taken up with the Asur they can very well make their way to the valley.'

Ada held Merek's gaze. 'I will cloud her mind when she is away from the others, erase her memories if I can.'

'Can you do that?' Her father looked at her dubiously.

The Seer clucked his tongue and shook his head. 'It is a risk. You know that they can mind travel now,' he clasped his hands behind his back.

Ada ignored his warning. 'How long has it been since Zuri and her friends were taken away from here?' Ada asked her brows puckered into a tight frown.

Merek sighed. 'Around three weeks ago. Enough time for her to meet up with the Asur. Obviously, she was able to charm them. I would say they had people with them, and that is who she convinced.' Merek pulled at his beard.

'I think you are right, Papa. She was beautiful, but her heart was ugly.'

Merek blushed slightly, he had been taken by Zuri's beauty and it had nearly cost him his family.

'We must hurry and find the queen, Merek. Ada and I cannot have anyone disrupting our sessions. Serenity can take care of the village's needs and Anja will help. Your wife is an angel, she will also assist.' Merek smiled 'you have my word.'

CHAPTER TWENTY-TWO

An Entity

Her mind now mirrored an abyss, dark and consuming. The entity slithered whispering ungodly secrets that no mortal was meant to know.

Ogda

Anja insisted on Ada and the Seer having a meal before they went into their world of mind travel. She had her concerns about Ada trying to erase Zuri's memories, but could understand the importance of it. Ogda pushed his food around his plate, worry was beginning to build and he was barely able to hold in the panic that threatened to overtake him. He looked up at Anja as she congratulated Ludwig on how well he had done with cooking yet another meal. He sighed. There was so much to lose; the very fabric of humanity hung on the decisions they would be making.

'We must go and meditate now, Anja. Enough of the chit chat.' The Seer had taken on a serious tone as he stood. 'Ludwig has made another batch of the tea' – Ogda gave her a brief smile – 'bring it to the room please, Anja.' Without another word he left the table, making his way to the room where they would be meditating.

As Ada's mind travelled through the forest, she could smell the burning timber. She shuddered, hearing their cries of agonising pain as they were burned alive. Nobody gave a second thought to a tree burning, but their agony was real. She gave a silent prayer to the Gods, acknowledging that the forest was as much their creation as the humans that walked the earth.

Ada saw Zuri sitting cross legged near some other people. They were eating and talking quietly to one another. Quickly scanning the group, she searched for Ranco, but could not locate him. She paused before she entered Zuri's mind, Ada wanted to be sure that no other entity had picked up on her presence.

One of the Asur nearby struggled to stay awake as he stood watch over the humans. Ada inhaled and moved into the mind of the woman who had stolen her father's heart. Images and memories bombarded her, and she pushed them away until she came across one that had reference to where the village was located. The secret valley came to view, a strong memory with Merek at the forefront. Ada quickly blurred it, giving her an image of Eijanbrook's village. She knew it was possible Zuri would question and be confused as to why she had this memory as she was not from this village. Her people were horse people, her brother's village. But Ada had no memory of this village. She had never been to it and could not replace it with her own memories.

Fear gripped Ada. Suddenly she felt another as if something had picked up on her presence; it was a strong presence and one she had never felt before. Quickly she backed away, fleeing and praying that whatever it was did not have the time to work out who she was.

'Ada,' the Seer shook the young woman gently. Ada blinked and opened her eyes, gasping as she sat up. 'What is it? Did you erase her memory?' Ogda's weathered face came into view as she grew accustomed to her surroundings.

She nodded. 'There was another.'

The Seer raised an eyebrow. 'Who?'

She shook her head. 'I don't know, but it was strong, and I have never felt it before.' Ada slumped back onto the cushions, exhausted. Something had tried to find out who she was, and it was powerful so powerful it made her tremble. She let out a slow breath.

Ogda noticed her shiver. 'We are in grave danger, Ada. Whatever it was, was quick enough to not only pick up on you, but to try and find out who you were. You were only gone ten minutes!'

Ada frowned. She thought that it had been longer. 'You are right, we must be careful. They know we are watching them, so I was subtle. We need to find the queen as soon as possible.'

Ogda sat back on the overstuffed cushions, thinking about the next mind travel they would take. 'Ada, do you remember what the ancient tree told you?'

She nodded. 'Yes, she is close to us, and we have to be careful they know we are after them and she is their leader.' Ada ran her tongue over lips. 'I just need a drink of water and we can try and find her.' The Seer poured her a drink from the water jug Ludwig had provided. He then moved the large teapot side to side to mix the leaves that helped them find clarity as their minds explored the world around them without their physical bodies.

'Take a break and have some tea.' Putting his concerns aside, Ogda tried to alleviate Ada's fears. She offered him a tight smile and took the cup he offered.

Elenore laid on the bed as Serenity felt her stomach. The healer tisked and clucked as she usually did, moving her hands over Elenore's exposed belly. Elenore raised her head, trying to catch the healer's eye, but she continued her examination, ignoring Elenore's questioning gaze. Elenore laid her head back down, letting out a loud sigh.

'The baby has grown, but is still small and I still can't feel the other one.' She continued to feel Elenore's belly, frowning.

'What is it?' Elenore said. She knew the healer was not telling her everything.

Serenity removed her hands from Elenore's abdomen and faced her patient. 'I don't want to get your hopes up—' she began. Elenore pushed herself into a sitting position, waiting for the healer to tell her more. 'I think I felt something, but I am not sure if it was the other baby or if it is the bigger one laying in an awkward position.'

'So, I could still be having two babies?' Serenity had gone to the bowl of water she kept for washing her hands after examining patients. She did not answer Elenore straight away, instead she finished washing her hands before sitting in the chair beside the bed.

'I am going to be honest with you, Norrie,' she started gently. Elenore felt her heart skip a beat and fear clutch at her. 'I think you probably do have two babies, but odds are either one is very small and may not make it, or it may have already died.'

Elenore felt her heart sink and tears began to well and spill down her cheeks. Serenity embraced her. 'I have to tell you the truth, Norrie. Please don't cry, child, shush now.'

Elenore pulled herself away and wiped her face on the cloth Serenity handed her. She thanked the healer and left, making her way to where Kacha and Krea were staying. Merek had finally finished the small home that was originally promised to her, but since she had moved back with Merek it was now Kacha's and Krea's.

Krea had finished the garden Elenore had started at the front of the small timber home giving it a welcoming feeling. The female warrior was sitting on the small porch sharpening her sword and broke out into a huge grin when she saw Elenore.

'Norrie, what a lovely surprise.' She stood, giving her sister-in-law a warm embrace. 'Ada was here just yesterday to see how Kacha was getting along. His wound has healed nicely, and he jokes with Ulric about them having matching scars.'

'I am glad Ada is spending time with him the weddings are in a few days' time.'

'Yes, I am excited Ada will live here and I will have another female in the house.'

'And I will have two children soon to be married.'

The two women made their way inside and Krea made some tea. 'I am not much of a cook, Norrie. I prefer to be out practicing the sword, another reason Ada will make a wonderful house companion, I know how much she loves to cook with Ludwig.' she softly chuckled.

Elenore smiled and sipped the tea Krea had made. She continued to chat to her sister-in-law about the wedding preparations it helped them keep their minds off the looming war with the Asur. Elenore left the small cosy home feeling more relaxed than when she had first arrived. The afternoon was warm and part of her wanted to go to the river. She had not been there since the incident with Zuri. She sighed and wondered if she should have asked Krea to go with her. She didn't feel like turning back and decided to head for home, maybe Anja would feel like a swim.

The tunnels were wide and dark, a long, never-ending void. The Seer and Ada were flying blind, trusting only their sense of smell and hearing.

As the tunnel wound and twisted itself a strong pungent smell began to fill their senses. Ada coughed and spluttered, the smell overpowering her senses and bringing a deep feeling of death.

Ogda was beside her, trying to calm her as she fought the urge to turn back and flee. 'Don't let it consume you, rise above it. You have to be stronger.' Ada could not answer him, instead focusing on bringing her mind under control as panic began to take hold. The smell grew stronger, and she struggled to breath. Her mind began to wane as the Seer's voice faded. *'LEAVE!'* The booming voice blasted in her mind. The panic that was barely under control rose and crashed over her like a giant wave. She screamed and fled back through the blinding tunnel, her only wish to be reunited with her physical body.

Anja felt her granddaughter's panic before she heard her screams. She threw the piece of clothing she had been folding back into the basket and rushed into the room where Ada and Ogda were mind travelling. Ada's screams filled the house as Elenore entered through the front door. She jumped as she heard her daughter's distressed shrieks.

She too raced into their room. Anja was cradling the young woman like a baby as she continued to screech. The Seer still had not returned to his body as Elenore kneeled beside her daughter.

'What's happening?'

'I don't know,' Anja said. She spoke to Ada in soothing tones.

'Should I go and get Merek?' Elenore asked a helpless expression on her face as she continued to watch her daughter in her distraught state. Anja nodded. She knew it would help Elenore to feel like she was doing something, and Merek would offer support when both the Seer and Ada returned.

Elenore left the house, her mind racing to where her husband could be. She made her way to the main camp and desperately searched for him. The memory of Huxley going through a similar fate made her catch her breath, he too had seen things she could never dream of. A man with dark curly hair stood with his back to her, Sabin! He would know where Merek was. They had been spending more time together reconnecting their friendship.

'Sabin!' she called breathlessly. Running was difficult with her heavy belly. Sabin turned around at the sound of his name and frowned at

Elenore's anxious look. 'Where is Merek? Ada and Ogda have been mind travelling and Ada is in trouble,' she gasped.

Sabin could see the fear on Elenore's face and he quickly looked for Merek. 'Aye, he was here just a minute ago, said he needed a toilet break.' Sabin swept his gaze towards the tall grass that framed the camp site. Suddenly he saw Merek emerge and quickly waved him over.

Merek frowned as saw his wife and Sabin standing together both with a look of worry on their faces. It was not like Sabin to be troubled.

'Merek, thank the Gods. Quick, ye must come, Ada is in trouble.'

Merek did not wait to ask questions, instead he grabbed his sword and raced to his home with Sabin and Elenore trailing behind.

Ada was sobbing when they entered the room. Her face was pale and sweat beaded on her forehead. She was speaking incoherently as Anja continued to rock her. Elenore stole a quick glance at Ogda who still had not returned. She swallowed as she kneeled beside Merek, again feeling helpless as she watched her child struggle. Sabin stood awkwardly and for the first time in his life he could not think of anything to say.

'How long has this been going on for?' Merek demanded.

'About half an hour. Something has scared her. We just need to wait until she calms down and get her thoughts under control.'

Ada began to shake and gasp, fighting for breath. Elenore began to weep.

'Sabin, take Elenore out to the kitchen and get her to make some of the sleeping tea, quick!' Sabin gently grabbed Elenore's arm and helped her to her feet. She let herself be led out to the kitchen and numbly made the tea.

'Sabin, can you please carry it to Anja I can't go back in there, I can't see her like that.'

'Aye, Norrie, ye sit down and have some of that tea ye made Ada,' he patted her arm as she sat down at the kitchen table.

Ogda felt Ada turn and flee before his mind became clouded overcome with a darkness that was spawned from evil and he could not escape it. The control he possessed was slowly disintegrating, squashing all rational thoughts as he descended into a gloomy abyss. He did not know how long he was in the void, but as his senses returned, he heard voices and the awareness of touch. Ogda opened his eyes and familiar faces swam in front of him. He gasped and drew in a long breath as he attempted to sit up.

'Easy now, ye have been out cold for a bit.' Sabin's accent was strong as the Seer made sense of what he was saying. As he looked around the room, he noticed Merek and Anja with Ada. The young woman was weeping, her face drained of colour. The memory of the tunnel along with the sickening smell they had encountered came back to him. It had been right before Ada had panicked. His mind tumbled and turned as he tried to make sense of it all.

'Is she coherent?' His voice came out slurred, as if he had been drugged.

Merek and Anja looked over at him and Anja offered him a warm smile.

'She will be soon. I have made her drink some tea that will help relax her. She just needs time.'

Merek stood and ran his fingers through his hair. They were vulnerable all of them including the whole village. It seemed that the Asur knew where they were and were waiting to attack them.

'I am going to see Norrie,' he said, leaving before they had time to reply.

Elenore was sitting hunched at the kitchen table, an empty mug in her hand. 'How is she?' she asked as Merek sat down beside her.

'She is getting better,' Merek replied. Once again, he ran his hands through his hair. Elenore had become to know this as one of his nervous habits.

'What is on your mind, other than Ada?'

Merek clenched his jaw. 'I think the Asur know where we are, and they are just waiting to pounce,' he said in a low tone.

Elenore sat up. Something inside her agreed with him. 'What are we going to do?' She whispered.

He rubbed his chin. 'I am not sure. I have to talk to Ogda when he is up for it, and our daughter.'

'The Seer is awake then? I mean, he has come back?' Elenore felt relief flood over her as Merek nodded. 'Maybe I should make him a tea or bring him food.'

Sabin came into the kitchen as she finished her sentence. 'Aye Norrie, I think I need some tea Ogda will be out in a minute, and I reckon he will want tea and food.'

Elenore gave him a brief smile. 'How is Ada?'

'Ye have a fighter there, that's for sure. She has stopped crying and is starting to converse. Maybe put some food on for her too.'

Elenore rose and began to prepare a casserole. She frowned. 'Where is Ludwig?' She had temporarily forgotten the faithful servant and was surprised that he was not bustling around the kitchen.

Sabin was unable to help himself as he let out a soft chuckle. 'He is with Amzi. As ye know, he loves horses, and he couldn't help but go and get acquainted with em'.'

Elenore smiled. She could understand Ludwigs's desire to check out the best horses in the land. She busied herself making food as Merek and Sabin chatted about how they could outsmart the Asur. Merek had revealed to Sabin that he thought the Asur already knew where they were. Sabin agreed. He too had a similar feeling.

After she finished making the food, Ogda, Anja, and Ada made their way to the table. Elenore took a long look at her daughter. Her face was deathly white, and tear-stained. She looked as if she had been to hell and back.

Elenore served them food and poured water from the jug, along with placing the heavy black kettle filled with tea in the middle of the table. She sat and the Seer offered a prayer to the Gods before they ate the food.

When they had finished their meal they cleared the table. Anja helped Elenore with the dishes and poured the tea.

'What happened to you both?'

It was a question that was on everybody's mind and begged to be answered. Ogda took a deep breath and cast a quick look over at Ada. Colour had begun to return to her face, and she gave him a brief nod, indicating she was okay.

'I am not sure, to be honest. We are up against something much bigger than we anticipated and...' his voice trailed off.

'Something got into my head' Ada finished for him.

'Something got into mine too,' Ogda added.

'They demanded that I leave.' Ada shuddered at the memory.

'If it was the Asur, why didn't they just attack and kill you?' Elenore asked.

'Because, dear child, that would be too easy for them. They *want* a battle. We are a prize to them, something they can tease and torment before striking us when we least expect it,' Ogda told them thoughtfully.

'What do we do now?' Merek began to fidget, it seemed the knowledge that he was not in control did not sit well.

'We will be on the lookout, and we gather as many forces as we can.'

Merek frowned, 'I thought we had as many as we could and isn't that what we have been doing these past few months?'

'We need more. We don't have enough. Anja will mind travel and find more if there is any, after Ada and I have recovered we will try and find their queen again. I don't know how to reach her, but she is still the key to this whole monstrous mess.' Ogda's brow furrowed and his face had become flushed, his calm demeanour had vanished. Elenore was concerned for the ancient man and had a feeling he was growing impatient.

'Maybe they are waiting for us to make a foolish move. I mean, it's like they are taunting us.'

The Seer reflected on Elenore's words. It made sense. 'Well, I guess we will beat them at their own game, we too will wait and unbeknown to them we will gather and prepare an army. We will locate their queen and their king, and we will bring them down.'

Ogda's words brought a smile to Merek, and he chuckled. 'A man after my own heart.'

Laughter rang out across the valley as children played and adults celebrated. The mood was festive and joyful. Ten couples had been married including Kaiah and Ulric, Ada and Kacha, Edyth and Sabin. Kacha tapped his cup and gestured for Sabin to fill it again. Ogda had completed the formalities, and it was now time to rejoice. Elenore watched the couples and her heart swelled. The women looked radiant in their dresses, and she felt an immense satisfaction with how well the decorations had turned out on both Ada and Kaiah's dresses. Suddenly she heard the traditional wedding song and the couples squealed with delight. It was time for them to dance and play the customary wedding games before taking leave to their wedding accommodations. Before the Asur, a special hut would have been decorated for the special couple. It would have been built some distance from the village giving the newly married couple privacy before they returned to settle into married life. However, things had changed, and the couples would be returning to their own homes. Elenore sighed and rubbed her swollen belly affectionally. She forced herself not to think of the approaching doom, she was determined not to ruin the special day.

CHAPTER TWENTY-THREE

New Life

A star whispers, a soul descends, and
with a breath, a new life begins.

Serenity

Summer drew to a close ushering in a new season of autumn that led to shorter days and cooler nights. Merek organised homes to be built for the new couples, and a feeling of contentment settled on the village. It would be easy for one to believe that life had returned to normal and there was no threat of an evil entity that was lying in wait. Elenore had not seen Ada or Ulric so happy.

'Merek, it's good for them to have a normal life, and Ada needs a break.' She kissed him on the cheek as she and Merek had come to help move their things into their homes. Merek nodded and offered her a smile. She frowned. 'You are keeping something from me.'

'Norrie, I am happy for our children I truly am but...' he trailed off and shook his head.

'But what, Merek?'

He sighed. 'We both know that this is not going to last forever. The Asur will come again, and we still haven't got enough people to build an army big enough to take them down.'

Elenore grimaced. She knew they were living under false pretences. She patted her belly instinctively. Her baby had grown, stretching her stomach and bringing a daily backache. The healer had advised that Elenore would deliver her baby late winter not the best time to birth. Elenore pushed away the thought before it could take control of her mood and sour it.

Merek put his arm around her, pulling her in close. 'I will kill every last one of them to protect my family,' he whispered in her ear.

Elenore smiled and turned to face him. 'I know you would, Merek.' He kissed her, fully leaning his body into hers. Elenore felt the familiar desire grow but as usual, the image of Zuri spoiled her mood, dashing away any feelings of intimacy she had for her husband. She gently pushed Merek away. He groaned and ran his fingers through his hair.

'Norrie, will you ever forgive me?' Elenore swallowed. It was a question she constantly asked herself and if she was honest with herself, she did not have any idea or if she had it in her to forgive him. 'Elenore?' Merek's tone was stern, and she could feel he was running out of patience. It had been many weeks since Zuri had been banished. She had to give him something, it would not do their relationship any favours if she kept resisting him.

'I will try tonight, I promise,'

Merek broke out into a grin and hugged her before he kissed her again. 'I love you, Norrie.'

She giggled and pushed him away. 'I said I would try, that is not a promise.'

'Okay, I heard you. Now come on, let's go and check on Ada she needed help with the pots Ludwig gave her.' They spent the rest of the morning setting up home for Ada before checking on Kaiah and Ulric.

Ulric poured his father a large cup of wine. Amzi had started growing grapes to refill the large stash they had brought with them; it was starting to run out. Merek took a large gulp of the fruity drink, savouring the flavour and the feeling it gave him. He smacked his lips, thankful that Amzi had been able to grow the vines of fruit responsible for giving them such a delicious beverage.

'Papa, I think we need to start a battle plan.' The statement threw Merek for a moment. It was the last thing he expected Ulric to say. Even though his son had matured and come to terms with using the sword and seeing combat, he never thought that Ulric would be thinking of preparing for battle. Merek coughed and took another swallow of his drink before answering his son.

'You are correct, Ulric, we do. I will organise a meeting with Tallot, Amzi, and the Seer first thing tomorrow.'

'Have the scouts seen any activity from the Asur? I mean, I can't understand it: they burn down the forest and kill everything that is not of any use to them, only to go underground. It just doesn't make any sense.'

'You are right, my son, and I agree. Ada and Ogda have made preparations for the end of the week to try and find their queen. Last time didn't go very well.'

'Yes, I know, and Zuri and Ranco have taken up residence with them.'

Merek stiffened when he heard Zuri's name and took another swallow of his wine. 'They both deserve to die,' he growled.

'Maybe we should send spies and see what they are up to. I mean, get Ada to find out about them, see what they are planning.'

Merek nodded slowly. 'I think you may have a point, son. I will bring it up with the Seer this evening.'

Ogda leaned back on his chair after he heard what Merek suggested. The plan made sense, they needed to know what their enemy was up to, even if they had grown quiet. As he thought about it, he chided himself for not thinking of this idea earlier. To know what your enemy is planning was nearly as important as organising a battle plan.

'I will go and see what they are up to,' Anja said, meeting Ogda's gaze. She had read his thoughts. He looked at her and then at Ada who also was watching the Seer intently. They had come together for a family dinner, so Merek could discuss Ulric's suggestion. 'I will go tonight we have wasted enough time.' Anja said firmly.

The Seer nodded.

'Why don't you go now? I will do the dishes, Kaiah will help,' Elenore offered. Grateful, Anja smiled at her daughter-in-law and got up from the table. Ogda and Ada followed her into her room so they could help her prepare for her mental journey. Ludwig went to make the special tea and prepare snacks for them; it would be a long night.

Anja felt herself float above the room before disappearing out into the dark night. The coolness refreshed her as she let her instincts guide her to where she thought she could feel the presence of the Asur. Deep into the night she searched until she had left their valley far behind and came to the last remanent of the forest.

Loss and sadness enveloped her as she gazed upon the dark stumps, a landscape that had turned to a grey wasteland. Her senses led her to a tunnel that burrowed deep underground. At first, she was hesitant, but she pushed away the doubt and continued bravely looking for the Asur.

She heard voices well before she could see the beings they belonged to. Not far ahead, a large fire flickered. A group of humans and Asur gathered around it. She instantly recognised Zuri and Ranco, both engaged in conversation. Anja paused, listening intently. A large Asur stood next to the pair, drinking something as it too listened to them. It was odd that something so foreign could converse with the beings that it loathed.

Zuri laughed as she flirted with Ranco. *She hasn't changed at all*, Anja thought angrily. Other humans were drinking and engaging in conversation with the Asur, and Anja wondered how they could betray their own kind so easily. She pulled her attention away from them to listen once again to what was being said.

A group of Asur sitting not far from Zuri and Ranco were discussing when they would take the valley of humans. Anja's mind leaned in, absorbed with what they were saying. Suddenly a voice came into her mind as she noticed one of the Asur sniff and look around, as if he had been alerted to her presence.

'Anja, they know you are here. You need to leave now; you have the information you seek.' She felt confused, both by the voice and whether she had the information she was looking for. One of the Asur pulled out its sword, taking a step forward making Zuri and Ranco pause in their conversation. Anja did not need any more urging, she turned and fled.

Ogda and Ada's faces swam into view as she settled in her body. She gasped as she reconnected with her physical form. Ada offered her some water which she took gratefully taking a long drink.

'Thank you, child,' she said as she wiped her mouth. She gave them a brief smile. 'I found them, and they are planning to take us by surprise.'

'When?' the Seer and Ada asked at the same time.

'They are planning to attack us in the middle of winter, when we would least expect it.'

'They know we are here?' Ada asked.

'Yes, they have known for a long time.'

'Did that evil woman, Zuri, tell them?' Ada asked again.

Anja nodded. 'She just confirmed what they suspected without giving specific details. I guess the blurred memories you gave her only sufficed for a short time. Ranco is with them too, and others. There is no forest left. They have killed all that did not serve them, we will not be getting reinforcements. We need to find their queen. They are closer to us than we think.'

'You have done well, Anja,' Ogda praised the older woman who sat in front of him.

'I think Eijanbrook helped me tonight.' Ada looked at her grandmother, bewildered. 'He warned me to leave and advised that I had heard everything I needed to hear, even though I felt that I hadn't heard it all.' Anja frowned before a smile crossed her face. The thought of her husband helping her after his death was a comfort.

Ogda made a steeple with his fingers under his chin. 'We have a lot to do, and this is good information. We will tell Merek in the morning. I know we don't have enough warriors, but we have gained the upper hand by learning this. The Asur won't know what we are planning so it will be a surprise for them. Good work Anja and I agree, I think Eijanbrook, or some other force, is helping us. Let us pray and meditate before we get some rest for the night, tomorrow will be a long day.'

Merek closed the door softly behind him as Elenore lit a candle on the nightstand next to the bed. She felt a tingling as Merek came close to her his breath heavy with anticipation. She let out a soft giggle, suddenly feeling like she was a young girl again. He reached his arms around her, placing his hands on her stomach before caressing her. She sighed and willed herself to give into the feeling of intimacy. Merek began to nibble her neck as he gently lifted her and placed her on the bed. Elenore was surprised at how strong her husband was and let out another soft chuckle. He carefully laid over her, mindful of her pregnant belly. He kissed her mouth, his passion growing. Elenore could feel his hardness and pressed into him as she pushed away the images of Zuri and her husband.

Merek struggled to pull down his trousers and not hit her exposed stomach at the same time. They both broke out in peals of laughter as his frustration overcame him and he rolled on to his side to pull down the cumbersome pants. Merek turned and kissed his wife again and gently stroked her hair. Elenore gave in to the feeling of warmth that spread through her body. Merek gazed down at Elenore, his face softened with love and admiration. She closed her eyes as Merek kissed her softly and stroked her face.

'Norrie, I love you so much,' he said, his voice full of emotion. Elenore opened her eyes and reached up to touch his cheek. Merek kissed her again more passionately and a moan escaped her. Merek paused as tears streaked down his face, and he quickly wiped them away. He cleared his throat. It was obvious that he was struggling with the tide of emotions that were sweeping over him.

'I want you to want this too, Norrie. Please, I never want to hurt you again.' His voice wavered as he continued to gaze down at her.

'I am ready, Merek,' she whispered. Merek did not need any further encouragement as he drew closer to her groaning with desire.

The sun shone through the open window, caressing Elenore with its warmth. She opened her eyes and stretched. Memories of the night before came flooding back and she smiled and turned to a sleeping Merek beside her. She watched him and gave a quick prayer of thanks to the Gods that the curse that he had been under had been lifted.

Merek stirred and shifted onto his back. She gazed at his muscular physique that had turned to a deep bronze over the summer. His hair fell in disarray and his mouth was open as he continued to sleep. His beard was getting long and hung loose. She noted flecks of grey peppered it. A familiar fluttering drew her attention away from her husband and she smiled as she placed her hands on her stomach. The baby would bring joy to their lives.

Merek stirred again as he turned back on his side closest to Elenore. He opened his eyes and smiled. She kissed him, overcome with the love she felt for him.

'Hmm I think I have made my wife happy,' he grinned at her. Elenore giggled as she pushed him playfully. He placed his arm over her. 'I love you, Norrie,' he told her. Elenore felt tears prick her eyes and she quickly wiped them away. 'I know I have hurt you and I am so sorry,' he told her, not taking his eyes off her.

Elenore leaned in and kissed him, 'I forgive you Merek,' she said.

Later that afternoon Ogda discussed with Merek, Elenore, Ulric, and Serenity what Anja had found out in her mind travel. He had started to involve the healer more as he had discovered she often added wisdom to their conversations about the Asur. 'I think we should give some time before we allow Ada to find their queen. Once again, they have been alerted to our intrusion,' Serenity said after the Seer had finished telling them.

Ogda nodded. 'You are right, dear. We need to have a surprise for them.'

'When do you propose we find their queen?' Ogda smiled at Ulric. The boy had grown into a man and had changed so much since he was a young teen. Ulric casually pushed his copper brown hair to the side as he waited for the Seer's response.

'We will find her at the start of the winter season. If they plan to attack us halfway through, we need to be able to take down their leader. Merek, every person that can fight must be trained and ready. I say we have only a few weeks left before the cold, dark season is upon us.'

Ogda looked towards Merek who sat casually on a timber log, his sword propped up beside him. The weather had been unusually warm, and the days were full of sunshine and blue sky prompting them to hold their meeting around the small fire at the rear of the home.

Elenore breathed in the fresh air, it was so nice to be out, and she savoured the days that were too good not to enjoy. As she listened to the Seer, her concern grew for her unborn child. A few other women were due in the spring, but she was the only one due in the coming winter.

'How can we be safe here anymore, if the Asur know where we live?' She tried to keep the panic from her voice.

'Elenore, nowhere is completely safe from the Asur, but you have many people around you that will protect you,' Anja told her gently. Elenore offered her a weak smile, but it did little to placate her apprehension.

Merek set about readying the village for the approaching battle that would be coming in only a few short months. His people started to feel on edge again and soon the tension began to show. There were more arguments between friends and families, people were more reserved, and many stayed indoors more than they had in a long time.

Elenore, Edyth, Anja, and the healer made daily trips to each house offering support and advice to those who needed it. It helped keep Elenore's mind busy as she struggled not to focus on how her life could change so very quickly. She also knew she was more of a target not only being a leader's wife, but because she had made enemies with her husband's former lover. It did not surprise her that Zuri had taken up with the Asur, she had an evil heart and was only focused on her own ego. She mentioned her concerns to Serenity as the healer conducted her routine check on Elenore's baby. She did not answer her at first, her concentration more on feeling the unborn child. She clucked and tisked, a frown puckered her face.

Ignoring Elenore's concerns about the upcoming battle she asked, 'Have you been getting movement every day?'

'I have, but it is not as much. Why? Is there something wrong?' Elenore replied with a sinking feeling.

Serenity sighed. 'I don't want to alarm you, but your baby has dropped, and I can't feel the other one. We still don't know if it is even alive.' Elenore propped herself up on her elbows, a look of disbelief on her face. 'Please, Elenore, lay back down I need to feel some more. As for your other concerns, it is out of our hands. We must trust the Gods, that is all we can do. You must stop worrying, it is doing you no good, nor that of your unborn children. I want you to rest more. I think your time to birth will be sooner than we want it to be.'

Elenore let Serenity finish her examination. She was alarmed that her babies may come early, and she sent a quick prayer to the Gods that her other child was still alive.

Over the next few weeks Elenore stopped going with the other women for their daily checks on their community. Instead, she laid in bed sipping tea. As the days came and went, she could feel her babies sitting lower in her abdomen, pushing down on her pelvic floor.

Merek and Anja did not let her leave the house or disclose any news that would upset or concern her. Elenore knew they were only protecting her, but she felt shut out and it brought back memories of the time when Merek had pushed her aside.

Elenore threw back the covers of her bed stood and stretched. she noticed a dark red stain on her nightie. Elenore gasped, looking back at the bed. A red patch darkened the furs.

Panic gripped her as she struggled to take a breath.

'Ada!' she called for her daughter, unable to process what was happening. 'Ada!' she called to her again. She was sure Ada was still home it was not that late in the morning. Merek had left early as his usual routine and the Seer and Anja were out in the village.

A sharp pain stabbed across her stomach as she reached for the door. Elenore turned and sat back on the edge of the bed waiting for it to pass. She squeezed her eyes shut as she felt another contraction. Instinctively, she knew she was close to giving birth. She sent a quick prayer to the Gods and hoped her daughter would pick up on her dilemma.

Elenore waited, taking in long slow deep breaths. Suddenly the door burst open, and Ludwig stood with a dishcloth in his hands. He had been busy baking, preparing for the day's meals. He stood, perplexed, unable to speak as he saw Elenore doubled over in pain.

'I-I will get Ada,' he stammered.

'Hurry, Ludwig! The babies are coming!' Elenore shrieked.

Elenore dared not move and again tried to slow her breathing, the contractions slowed as she arranged herself to a more comfortable position. She could not lose her other baby. The thought was almost too much to bear.

Mercifully, she did not have to wait long before she heard approaching footsteps and the door was flung open again. Serenity, Edyth, Anja, and Ada burst into the room. The healer ordered Edyth to fetch towels and water. Anja and Ada removed the stained furs and helped Elenore get more comfortable.

'They are too early!' Elenore said as Serenity felt her abdomen.

'Hush, child, you must relax. They are early, yes; winter is hardly upon us, but their fate rests in the hands of the Gods.'

'When was she due?' Edyth came in with a bowl of water and several towels.

Serenity sighed. 'They are six weeks early.' She pointed to the nightstand for Edyth to place the bowl and towels.

Edyth gave Elenore a look of sympathy. 'Mine were born early, around the same time,' she said quietly.

Ada sat on the bed beside her mother. 'It will work out, mother. Please do not worry, their fate has been decided.'

Elenore smiled weakly at her daughter, unsure if what she said was a good omen or not. Another contraction took hold and Elenore cried out. 'I feel like I need to push,' she gasped.

Serenity examined her. 'Wait until the next one, and then you can push,' she ordered.

Another contraction, stronger than before, washed over Elenore and she gave in to her body's instinctive urge to push.

'I have to get off the bed,' she said as she pushed herself up.

Edyth and Anja helped her to her feet before the urge to push again crashed over her. Elenore screamed; the contractions were like none she had ever felt before. Her body shook as she squeezed Edyth's and Anja's hands. Ada wiped her mother's brow while Serenity placed towels under her.

'They will be here soon. I will get Papa,' Ada did not wait for a reply instead she left the room to find her father. Elenore felt another contraction and pushed and felt the first baby come from within her. Serenity took the baby and quickly dried it, rubbing the child vigorously.

'It's a girl!' Serenity shouted. The baby let out a loud wail, causing the women to smile. Anja gave Elenore a sip of water as they waited for the next child to be born. Minutes ticked by as the women waited.

'This will give you time to recover until the next one is born,' Edyth told Elenore.

Elenore nodded, she was still in a standing position and still had not seen her first baby. Her focus was now on the second one and she prayed that it was alive. Serenity had wrapped the first baby and placed her gently on the bed. A knock on the door startled the women,

'Come in,' Serenity said. Ada and Merek stood in the doorway. 'You have a beautiful baby girl, Merek,' the healer told him. Merek beamed.

Ada went to her mother and pushed a tendril of hair away from her face. 'Have faith mother,' she whispered. Just then, another contraction caused Elenore to call out. She began to push before Serenity looked up at her.

'Elenore, you have to be strong, this one is breech I will have to pull it out.'

Merek stood transfixed, unable to leave. He was unsure if he was supposed to stay, but none of them had told him to leave.

Elenore strained with all her might. 'Nearly there, Elenore! Don't stop!' Serenity instructed. Elenore was beginning to tire, sweat ran down her face and her body continued to shake. She glanced over at the bed, at her newborn baby. The baby girl's face was puckered in a frown as she gazed around the room. Clenching her jaw, Elenore gave one long last push causing the second twin to be born. Serenity pulled the baby by its feet before wrapping it in a towel. There was silence. Elenore cast a look over at the healer. She was rubbing the baby telling it to breathe. Edyth went to the healer's side as Serenity pushed open the baby's mouth to blow air into its lungs.

'What's wrong?' Merek demanded.

Anja looked at her son. 'The baby isn't breathing.' Merek strode over to the healer and Edyth, regardless of whether he was supposed to be there or not, he was not leaving his children.

'Can't you do something?' he said anxiously.

'We are, Merek,' Edyth retorted. Elenore felt her heart pounding and tears roll down her face, she prayed hoping her child would live. Serenity continued to blow air into the baby while rubbing it briskly. 'Don't stop Serenity, please,' Edyth pleaded. Elenore's birth had brought back memories of her twins who had died shortly after birth. Serenity's lips formed a tight line as she once again blew into the baby's mouth. The small infant was turning blue as her life began to ebb. Anja moved over to the bed as Elenore began to weep.

'Merek, go and comfort your wife,' Anja instructed as she took Merek's place. He gave one last look at his baby before he went to comfort Elenore.

'Let me try, Serenity,' the older woman said. Serenity stepped aside, her face showing her despair. Anja blew into the baby's mouth. 'Come on, little one, you must live.'

The baby lay motionless.

Anja blew again, then turned the baby over and patted it on the back. She gently put the baby back on its back and blew once more into its tiny mouth.

The baby spluttered and gasped, letting out a weak cry.

Edyth jumped and clapped her hands. Merek rushed back to the bed, leaving Elenore holding her breath. Serenity took the baby and rubbed it again trying to stimulate circulation. The baby let out another weak cry, bringing laughter from all that were in the room.

CHAPTER TWENTY-FOUR

Dardanos

A nightmare given flesh, it stalks through
dark tunnels, a monstrous shadow with an
insatiable appetite for human souls.

Ada

Elenore nursed one of her twin daughters while Merek gently burped the other. They were both small, however the second baby was even smaller. She struggled to cling to life and Elenore fed her every hour, willing her to fight.

'Have you thought of names for our girls?' Merek asked.

Elenore smiled. 'Yes I have.' He raised an eyebrow, surprised Elenore had not consulted him. 'I had their names picked as soon as I knew I was having twins.'

He nodded. 'Are you going to keep me in suspense all day?'

She grinned. 'No, of course not. I have called her Anwen' – she pointed to the baby Merek nursed. 'Have you noticed she has light coloured hair like her sister, Ada? And Anwen means beautiful and fair.'

Merek kissed Anwen's head softly. 'And the other?' he asked, looking at the small baby attached to Elenore's breast. Elenore looked down at the baby overcome with love and joy.

'She is strong-willed, so I have called her Anhi.'

Merek chuckled. 'How did you know they would be fair and strong-willed?'

This time it was Elenore's turn to laugh. 'I knew one would be a fighter and the other was just a guess, but I did know they would be beautiful.'

'Norrie, how did you know they were going to be girls?'

Elenore looked up at her husband and shrugged. 'Just a hunch, I guess.'

Merek bent down and kissed her. 'Well, maybe I have married a Seer,' he told her as his laughter filled the room.

Ogda held a welcome ceremony for the new babies a month after they had been born. It would be the last for some time. Ada had planned to mind travel the following evening. Welcoming new life always brought a renewed energy and a positivity to a community. This time it also gave hope. Hope that they had a future and for the all the pregnant women who still had not given birth. The twin's survival was a good omen for the future, and all came to celebrate.

Elenore had bled heavily after her birth and the healer warned she may never carry again. It did not bother the leader's wife. She had her family, and she was content. She sat next to Merek at the head of the table. Sabin and Edyth offered to take care of the babies while they said their speeches. Elenore was grateful for all the help she had been given.

'Aye Norrie, I am thinkin' I might convince Edyth to try for another. I think I could get used to being a father.' He chuckled as he nursed Anhi.

Elenore smiled. 'You would make a fine father, Sabin, and Edyth is already a wonderful mother.'

Sabin wiped away a tear, embarrassed at the show of emotion. 'Aye Norrie, ye making a grown man cry.'

Elenore leaned and hugged him before planting a kiss on his cheek. 'You are the best friend I have ever had Sabin, thank the Gods for sending you to us.'

Sabin nodded. For once he was at a loss for words, so overcome with emotion that he did not trust himself to speak.

Elenore ran the comb through her long copper hair as she gazed at the tiny babies that were asleep in the crib next to her and Merek's bed. She felt Merek kiss her on her shoulder, and she smiled, delighted at the feel of his touch.

'My beautiful wife, you have produced some fine-looking daughters,' Merek whispered in her ear.

Elenore chuckled. 'I think you may have had a hand in helping to create them.'

She turned to face him, sitting cross legged in front of him. Merek cupped her face and kissed her fully on the mouth. Elenore closed her eyes, relishing the moment. She opened them again before Merek burst into laughter. 'What is it?' Elenore asked.

He shook his head continuing to laugh. Elenore pushed him back gently and sat astride him, pinning him beneath her.

'Hey, you better not get any ideas. I have to go and hunt and besides, you need to heal from having the twins,' Merek managed to say between bursts of laughter. She grabbed his wrists, placing them above his head.

'I appreciate your concern, but what if I don't let you?' she teased. Merek sat up and quickly pushed Elenore back and began to tickle her. 'Merek!' She squealed. 'You will wake the babies.' She writhed under him trying to escape his hold. Merek was strong and she was unable to break free from his grasp. 'Please Merek, let me go,' she begged.

Merek stopped tickling her and gazed into her green eyes. 'I will never leave you, Norrie. Nothing or no one will come between us again. I promise.' His tone had become serious.

Elenore felt her heart swell with love that she had for the man who now leaned over her. 'Okay I believe you. Now, please, you must get off me. Don't you have a hunt on soon?' She wiggled and felt his grasp loosen. Taking advantage of the opportunity she sat up, kissing him.

Merek closed his eyes before falling back on his pillows. One of the babies stirred and Elenore made her way over to the crib to peer in at the small infant. The baby opened her eyes and looked around the room before noticing her mother.

'Hey, little one,' Elenore cooed. The baby stretched and opened and closed her small mouth.

'Elenore, I have to leave soon, would you like to join me for breakfast before she is fully awake and demanding your time?' Merek smiled at Elenore as she turned her attention from her newborn baby.

'I would love that more than anything. Who is going?' She left the side of the crib to focus back on Merek.

'Tallot and Flamma, and I have invited Sabin and Ulric too.'

Elenore raised an eyebrow. 'Tallot and Flamma? Will you be, okay?' She still felt uneasy when she spoke about Tallot, and she still did not trust Flamma. Flamma had kept his distance since Zuri, and the other men were exiled. She had, however, noticed him looking at her from a distance, a strange expression on his face.

'I want to reconnect with Tallot again, it's important that we can bond and fight alongside each other once more.' Merek paused and pulled at his beard. 'As for Flamma, mother wants me to take him. He has always been difficult and been at odds with his jealous streak.' Merek shrugged and let his gaze linger on his wife who sat in front of him. 'You have nothing to worry about,' he said half smiling.

'I am not worried, Merek. I know you can handle him. Please' – she stopped before rushing on – 'Tallot and I have shared nothing together, except a kiss and friendship.'

Merek looked away and nodded. She felt he did not believe her and there was nothing she could do to change his mind. She leaned into him, breathing in his masculine scent. Merek turned, swinging his legs over the edge of the bed. His back now faced Elenore so that she could not read his expression. He ran his hands through his hair and stood. 'I might skip breakfast, Elenore, I am running late anyway.' He gave her a brief look before pulling on some trousers.

'Are you sure?' Elenore felt hurt with Merek's sudden withdrawal.

'Yeah, I'm sure,' he gave her a quick kiss on the top of her forehead before striding from the room. Elenore's heart sunk, and her feelings were mixed. *How come Merek had a girlfriend, and it was obvious the relationship he had with her, and yet I haven't done anything, and he still doesn't believe me,* the thought raced through her mind. She pushed her irritation away as one of the twins let out a shrill cry demanding to be fed.

Ada felt herself inside a dark tunnel complete blackness engulfed her. She held the candle high so that she could walk without tripping over. She did not know how she had gotten inside the tunnel or how long. Fear wormed itself within her, making her heart race. A strong odour permeated the tunnel, causing her to gag as she reached out to hold the side of the earth wall to steady herself. She waited for the nausea to pass before cautiously taking a step forward. She placed her shirt over her face to help filter out the strong pungent odour. Willing herself to keep moving she once again set off.

She had no idea where, why, or which direction she was going in; the only thing she knew was she had to keep moving forward. Slowly, she inched her way further in the deep dark tunnel. A long throaty cry resonated through the passageway, causing Ada's stomach to clench. She paused waiting to see what would happen next. Another cry could be heard, and she was unsure whether it was a cry of pain or pleasure.

It was like nothing she had ever heard before. Taking a breath, she continued her march forward. The cries now became a chorus, almost deafening, and she struggled to squash the rising panic that threatened to overwhelm her.

'You must get closer, Ada, what you seek is in front of you.' The voice told her soothingly. She shuddered involuntarily. The voice had been a guide in times when she had been unsure, and she wondered the source that it came from. As she ventured further, she could make out a light, it was glowing a bright orange and she made her way towards it.

'Don't go any further,' the voice warned her. She stopped, happy to oblige whoever was guiding her. As she peered ahead, she could see the roots of a tree that had wormed and stretched itself into the tunnel. As she continued to stare, she could see the roots were dark and appeared ancient as they made their woody ascent up out of the passageway. She could not see much of the trunk as the roof of the tunnel closed in around it.

Edging forward, Ada sucked in her breath as she saw Dardanos, the queen of the Asur.

The queen sat within the lattice work of tree roots. Her hair spilled all around her, tendrils that spread out like a heavy coat.

Ada crouched down, fearful that she would be seen. The queen was watching her warriors as they pushed forward a group of humans. The cries were both from the queen and the warriors as they delighted in the fear the humans felt. Ada wanted to look away, not wanting to see the fate that would be bestowed on the terrified people, but she was unable to tear away her gaze.

As she watched, one of the queen's tendrils flicked out, reaching for the closest person to her. The woman screamed as it enfolded her, before dragging her to the queen's mouth. The queen of Asur devoured the woman, cutting off her screams as blood dripped from her mouth.

Ada watched in horror and disbelief as the queen consumed the woman, a bitter, cruel look on her face. The rest of the group who had watched in terror attempted to flee. The queen threw her head back and laughed before waving them away. The warriors pushed and shoved the small group, moving them from their queen, who let out a cruel, wicked laugh. Ada closed her eyes, unable to comprehend the scene she had just witnessed.

'Time for you to leave Ada,' the voice instructed.

Ada woke, gasping. She sat up and placed her hands to her face as tears rolled down. She pulled her legs up, crouching into a small ball. The resolve and courage she had felt had abandoned her. She began to rock, feeling like she had lost her mind. She did not hear the door open, and Anja and Ogda come to her side.

Anja tenderly brushed away a strand of hair. 'We are here, dear child, hush now.' Ada turned and buried herself into her grandmother's chest, her sobs heaving.

Anja embraced the young woman and hummed soothingly, waiting for her to finish crying. After a little while, Ada pushed herself away from Anja's embrace looking for something to blow her nose and wipe her tears. The Seer offered her a cloth which earned him a grateful smile. Ada blew her nose and took in a deep cleansing breath.

'I saw her.'

'In your dream?' Ogda frowned, waiting for Ada to explain. She nodded as a fresh set of tears began to spill and roll down her face. She quickly wiped them away.

'She is hideous. I mean, she is nothing that I have seen or come across before,' she dabbed the cloth at her eyes wiping away the tears.

'Ada, what else would she be? I mean she is queen of a force that is evil and our enemy.' Ogda said gently.

Ada nodded. 'I know,' she sniffed. 'It's just that...' she paused and looked down at the bed. 'She ate a woman!' A fresh set of tears began to flow, and she wiped her nose with the back of her hand.

Anja once again embraced her. 'Dear Ada, she is Dardanos. Her name means to devour.'

Ada cradled one of her twin sisters, seeking comfort from the small baby as she related to her mother and Kacha the dream she had had. Elenore shook her head, taken aback by what her daughter had described. Kacha reached out and touched her arm, his face full of worry for his new wife. Elenore gave both Ada and Kacha their tea with one of the freshly baked scones Ludwig had baked Ada as a special treat. He had grown fond of the young woman and fussed over her when she came to stay.

Elenore gently took the baby from Ada and placed her in the wooden cradle that had been dragged into the kitchen.

'Where's Papa?' Ada asked as she swallowed a mouthful of the scone.

'He is out hunting with Sabin, Flamma, Tallot and Ulric,' Elenore answered as she sat down next to her daughter. She frowned as she wondered how they were all getting on.

'I think I know where she is.' Ada's statement interrupted her mother's thoughts.

'Who, Ada?'

'Dardanos. I know where she is.'

'What?!' Both Elenore and Kacha exclaimed.

Elenore cast a glance around the kitchen, Ludwig was busy preparing vegetables for the evening meal and appeared he had not heard Ada. The Seer and Anja were both out with Serenity, people had been coming more frequently to seek guidance and counsel from the wisest members of the community. Kacha shuffled his chair closer to Ada.

'Please do not worry, I will tell you all when they return.' Ada met Elenore's and Kacha's bewildered looks and gave them a tight smile. Elenore shuddered involuntarily; the memory of Ada's dream still vivid.

Merek had taken the men as far from the valley as he dared. He was rewarded with a new scenery, a mix of patches of forest and open grasslands. The Asur had not yet ventured so far north and destroyed the pristine environment. Large groups of deer and moose grazed, offering a potential supply of fresh meat. Excitement coursed through the men as they worked out a plan on how to hunt down the animals that foraged in the meadow that lay in front of them.

Tallot chuckled. 'Looks like we get a choice of what to bring down.' He ran his eye over one of the bucks that had poked its head up sniffing the air and twitching its ears.

'Hunt and kill as many as you can take back with you, we are low on supplies,' Merek instructed. They did not need any further encouragement as they proceeded to discuss the best method in capturing their intended prey.

The sun was making its slow descent ushering in the cold winter night. Merek finished tying the deer he had brought down before hitching it behind the pack horse. He had not intended to stay out the entire day, but the hunt had been more successful than he had expected. He swept his gaze over to where the others who were also hitching their kill to the back of the pack horses that had been brought with them.

'Aye, I think I see a light,' Sabin announced as he mounted his horse. Merek frowned and looked to where Sabin was watching the horizon.

'I see it too,' Tallot said. A faint yellow light was moving in the distance.

'Who could that be?' Ulric turned to his father, a look of worry on his face.

Merek looked at the sun, it would not be much longer before it disappeared from the sky. 'Ulric, you, and Sabin take the pack horses and head for home. Organise some of the warriors to come back here. We don't know who this is, and I am not taking any chances.' He threw the reins of his pack horse to Ulric before setting off at a gallop towards the distant light. Flamma and Tallot followed suit.

As Merek came closer to the mystery light he signalled for his brother and Tallot to spread out. He wanted to surprise the approaching horseman. The three men walked their horses behind the tree line before coming to a stop to see who was coming. Dark shadows settled over the forest and a hoot of an owl could be heard breaking the evening's silence. Merek shivered the night was growing colder. Soon he could make out three horsemen and was relieved they were not the Asur.

One of the men held a torch to help him see the way he was going and as he came closer Merek recognised him as one of his own scouts. He frowned as his mind raced to which of the scouts were due back from their reconnaissance trip. Merek let out a low whistle, a signal that would not startle the approaching scouts and to alert Flamma and Tallot. He urged his big white stallion out of the tree line and waited for the scouts. Flamma and Tallot joined him as the three men reined in their horses in front of Merek. The first of the scouts jumped from his horse and held the torch up high. He bowed in respect for his leader. Merek could see he had been riding hard for days he was filthy, and his horse was close to exhaustion.

'Master, we came back early. The Asur are on the move, and they have an army!' The scout's words tumbled over one another.

Merek held up his hand. 'Take a breath before you continue, I need to hear what you have to say not a jumble of words.'

The scout nodded and took the waterskin Tallot offered. He took a large swallow, gulping down the liquid before handing it to the scouts behind him. He wiped his mouth and took in another breath. 'Thank you.' He gave a brief bow and looked back up at Merek. 'You sent us three weeks ago to gather information about the Asur. We went way south but close to the sea and all we saw were bodies and burnt forests they left nothing alive. After about a week we crossed the last remanent forest and that's when we saw them. Master, it's the biggest army I have ever seen, they are like hornets coming out of a hive!'

The man's voice rose as he relayed what they had seen. As Merek listened, the night seem to grow colder, his fear of how big the Asur's army had gripped him, and it sickened him to the core.

'How far away are they?' he demanded.

'At least a week, maybe two. We rode back here as quick as we could. We didn't expect to see you so far south.'

Merek nodded. 'Good work.' He clenched his jaw, they needed to get back to the valley and have an emergency meeting with his mother and Ogda. He signalled them to follow him as he made his way back to his people.

Elenore had finished feeding her babies and as she gently tucked them in their cradles, she heard horses approaching. She had felt on edge all evening and could not get what Ada had told her out of her mind. She had pushed the Asur to the corners of her mind not wanting to think about the impending battle that would take place. Fear clutched at her as she heard Ulric make his way in the front door. She went out to the kitchen her heart pounding, the feeling of bad news wormed itself into her mind.

'What is going on, Ulric? Has your father been hurt?'

Ulric shook his head. 'No there was a horseman approaching and he wanted me and Sabin to come back and organise some warriors to go back and meet him. I am here to let you know I have a feeling it is some of the scouts sent out weeks ago.' Ulric did not wait for his mother's response instead he turned to walk back out the door. 'You might want to find the Seer I have a feeling it will be important,' Ulric said over his shoulder. Elenore followed Ulric out the door and watched him mount his gelding before leaving.

Sometime after Ulric's return, Merek was seated with his mother, Ogda, Ulric, and Ada. The scouts had briefly relayed their news to the Seer before Merek dismissed them to get some much-needed rest and decent food. Elenore was in the kitchen, helping Ludwig prepare tea and cake there was much to discuss. She still could not shake the fear that had her within its grasp and the feeling of a coming change was imminent. The concern she had for her newborn twins was enormous and she wondered how they would ever outrun an enemy so intent in wiping them from the planet. She helped Ludwig carry in the heavily laden trays and debated whether she should stay or return to the comfort of the kitchen.

'Stay, Elenore, you need to hear what is being prepared.' Anja threw her a comforting smile, seemingly understanding her daughter-in-law's fears. Elenore returned her smile and settled herself on a cushion next to the older woman.

'How do we fight such an army? How many do we have, Papa? I bet it is not even half the number what they have.' Ulric looked at his father a frown etched on his forehead.

'There is no way we can win a battle against such a big an army as theirs.' Merek let out a deep breath.

'We have a few things they don't have. We can make fire at will, we can surprise them, and they don't know we know they are coming.' The Seer informed them.

'They also don't know that I know where their queen is,' Ada added. The small group looked over to where she was seated. 'I wanted to tell you that I know where she is from the dream I had. I wasn't sure at first, I had to reflect on the details of the dream. I needed to make sure that I had the correct details about the location.' Ada shrugged with a nonchalant expression. 'It will give us an advantage and I have an idea on how we can flush her out.' Ogda raised an eyebrow, visibly impressed by his young protégé.

'I can mind travel to where she is and distract her before setting fire to the tunnels that she resides in. She will call for reinforcements as she does not have a huge army guarding her.'

'That is a good idea, Ada, but what about some of the Asur that can mind travel? They may not be as good as us, but I am sure they are honing their new craft.' Ulric looked at his sister, remembering the village that had been controlled by the Asur.

'Are we sure they know where we are?' Elenore could not help but interrupt.

Anja nodded, confirming Elenore's fears. 'Zuri will lead them straight here, she too has signed a pact with the devil. We have enemies of the humankind as well.'

'How long did the scout say we have until they reach here?' Ogda asked Merek.

'He thinks around a month, they have a huge army, and it takes time for them to move.'

'We need to make plans then. Every person in this village will have a job to do. We have Amzi and his horses they will come in handy in getting to places fast, we have strong battle-hardened warriors that you have trained, and we have magic.'

They all turned to look at the Seer with puzzled expressions. He smiled at their questioning looks. 'Ada can make fire Anja and I can get inside people's minds, and I am thinking of training Serenity to help with the mind travel. She is from a long line of Seers. We will discuss with Takeo about his Seer and any weakness's that can be to our advantage. We must strategize our battle plan, and this will take time. I suggest we start at first light. Our people will need to be aware of the army of the Asur we also need to be able to hide our most vulnerable.' He paused and looked at Elenore. 'Norrie, you will be in charge of this,' he said gently. Elenore swallowed and nodded; things were about to change.

CHAPTER TWENTY-FIVE

An Early Arrival

In the distance a horn blew, and the earth trembled, a
thousand marching feet, a precursor of the inevitable.

Ada

An uneasy feeling had settled over the community of people who were hiding in the secret valley. Merek had advised of the coming of the Asur and had given instructions on how they planned to go into battle with an enemy that would not stop coming. He prayed to the Gods that this would be the final curtain that would descend on an ancient adversary. Elenore, with the help of Edyth, began to make a tally of the most vulnerable; she still had no idea where they all would be hiding. The village had become a hive of anxious activity.

Ada, the Seer, and Anja had talked long into the night when Merek had shared the news of the approaching Asur. Ogda had long known they would arrive, however he had not prepared for it to be so soon. He had advised Ada and Anja that he would need to mind travel as close as he dared to the impending army. He needed to see for himself how big the army was. Serenity was happy to oblige his request of finding out if she was able to learn the gift of mind travel and began to spend many hours with Anja.

'I am planning on dreaming this evening, Anja. Tomorrow we will start actioning our battle plan.' Anja sighed she could not argue with him they had no choice and the existence of humanity hinged on everything they now did.

She met his gaze and nodded. 'May the Gods protect you while you travel in your dreams,' she told him. He merely nodded.

Ogda felt his mind make its way south, leaving his physical body behind. Fear sat with him; it was now a constant companion. He travelled over the vast forests that stood in the path of the Asur and felt a stab of sadness. They would burn everything in their path, leaving nowhere to hide or any tree that could help fight a common enemy. The enormity of the situation weighed upon him, and he struggled to carry it.

In his whole time on earth, he had never been in such a challenging position. It was not long before he could see billows of smoke as they wafted up into the air. Acres upon acres of forest had been reduced to blackened ash.

The Seer slowed his mind, he could feel the Asur, they were close. Carefully, he surveyed the drab landscape. From afar he heard a horn, long forlorn and bone chilling. He drew in a sharp breath. As he gazed out at the rolling hills in front of him, he caught a glimpse of a dark line. He opened and closed his mouth. The scout had not exaggerated when he had said that the army was huge. A procession of beasts, monsters, and a few humans stretched itself long and far. It seemed there was no end to the army before him.

A shadowy string, not unlike an army of ants poured from their nest. Hundreds upon hundreds of Asur marched steadily, making their way to Merek's village, the remnant of humanity. Ogda watched, transfixed by the enormity of such a massive army of evil. Moments went by before he began to feel the probe of another, it startled him. Turning, he fled, he had seen enough. They would need the grace of the Gods if they were to stand any chance of survival.

Ada, Anja and Merek were gathered in Elenore's kitchen waiting for the Seer. The morning was becoming late, rain drizzled conjuring a feeling of melancholy for the group seated at the big oak table.

'He has been asleep for a while, mother. Maybe you should wake him.' Merek had remained standing, too unsettled to sit.

Anja looked up at her son but shook her head. 'He will be here soon. Ludwig could you please be a gem and serve that delicious pie you made earlier.' Anja instructed, hoping that food would take their minds off what lay ahead.

Ogda came into the kitchen as the last of the pie was being served. Ludwig beamed when he saw his master and quickly poured him some tea with a piece of the pie he had saved him. The Seer sat at the table murmuring his appreciation to Ludwig. He was visibly exhausted, and a look of terror was on his face.

Merek folded his arms, seemingly knowing that the news would not be great. Ogda took a sip of the tea and closed his eyes. They waited for him to collect his thoughts and a heavy sense of dread filled the room. The Seer flicked opened his eyes, his face bore the unmistakable marks of exhaustion and dark circles sat under his eyes.

'The scouts were correct. The Asur have gathered an army the likes I have never seen or will see for that matter. Today, we need to put our plan in place. They will leave no man, woman, child, or tree alive. The goal of the Asur is to destroy and eradicate our existence. Now listen carefully, I have some ideas on how we can outsmart them.' Ogda gave a smile and a faint twinkle flickered in his eyes. 'We will once again call upon our friends of the forest: the trees. They will provide us with tunnels that Ada will firebomb to destroy their queen. Ada, you still have powers that will be unlocked. You need to learn what they are. The trees will also help alert us on how close they are. I will send Ulric with Amzi and some of his men to the edges of the forest. Amzi's horses are the fastest so they will be able to get back here quickly.'

'Ulric?' Merek interrupted his eyebrow raised quizzically.

Ogda nodded. 'I know you worry about your son, as do other fathers in the village. But Ulric has spoken to the trees before, in the witches' forest and to seek help in finding Shakurta village. I have a feeling that this maybe his special power.'

Merek could not argue with the Seer, but his face paled when he learned his son would be the first in line.

'Merek, you must organise the warriors into groups. The bravest and best horsemen must ride to intercept the army. They are to remain hidden as much as possible and act as a type of elusive lure. Amzi must provide them with horses they will need to escape quickly and need a mount that is not only fast but swift. You need to organise hidden traps this will help disorientate them and divide them. Anja how is Serenity going with unlocking her ability to mind travel?' He turned to Anja who was sitting next to him. 'She is progressing well and will be able to help blind the generals' minds.' Ogda nodded and smiled. He wanted the army of the Asur to be as unorganised as possible. An unorganised army would be ineffective and would allow them a chance to strike.

'Elenore...' the Seer paused, unsure of how Elenore would react to what he was going to tell her. She looked at him with tears in her eyes. 'Elenore,' he began again, more gently. 'Dear, you must make preparations to leave.' Elenore took a sharp intake of breath and covered her face. 'I gather you have a list of all who have to leave.' Elenore nodded, not trusting herself to speak. 'Good. The trees will guide you. They will create a tunnel that will lead to the heart of Dorhall Pass. You must take as many provisions as you can as you may be there for a long time. Krea and her wolf will help guide you and protect you.'

Elenore turned to Merek as tears trickled down her face.

'We will join you, dear, in time.' Ogda attempted to reassure her.

'When will she need to leave?' Merek asked the Seer. Ogda was not quite sure on the answer to Merek's question, and he was silent for a moment. 'It is best not to leave too early, lest the provisions run out. I suggest once Ulric has returned from the edges of the forest you will need to leave. It will take them a week, maybe two, to get here with that big of an army.' He looked at Merek and then at Elenore both nodded. Their fate was in the hands of the Gods.

Ogda and Anja sat on the overstuffed cushions waiting for Ada to say goodbye to her husband, Kacha. Ada's small home was cosy and comfortable, in the two months since she had moved in, she had decorated it with many throws that she had sewed with bits of unwanted fabric. Kacha had carved her creative sculptures that she placed throughout the home. A feeling of warmth oozed from within manifesting a sense of security that enveloped all who had the chance of visiting her. Ada came into the main room where Ogda and Anja were seated. She smiled as she made herself comfortable on her own cushion.

'Ada, do you feel ready to find the queen?' The Seer asked her.

'I am ready.'

'Good. I plan to start the attack on her this evening as I will be accompanying you.' Ada nodded. 'Has Papa finished all the preparations?'

Ogda sighed. The last two weeks had been exceptionally busy. Ulric had only just returned from his post of sighting the arrival of the army of the Asur. The trees had spoken to him just as the Seer predicted and were intent on ridding their common enemy before all the forest disappeared forever. They had begun their task of creating tunnels for Elenore and her group to leave and for Ada and Ogda to travel to the queen. Merek with the help of his best warriors had created hidden traps within the tree line that was closest to the trail that led into the valley. Every adult that had put their hand up to fight had been training every day, success in victory could only be achieved if they were united.

'Mother leaves today.' Ada looked up at the Seer, concern covered her face.

'Yes. She will be here later to say her goodbyes. She will be safe. Ada, you must focus your attention on the queen.'

It was Ada's turn to sigh. 'Yes, I know I am ready.'

She frowned as suddenly a feeling of déjà vu came over her. Her mind reached back plucking the memory of when she was in the field waiting for her father's arrival with Kacha. It had been the spring, after they had been separated in the blizzard and the village, they were staying in had rescued them. She had not yet met Kacha but knew he was part of her future. Her dream had felt like a premonition, and it seemed it was coming to fruition. The dream had foretold her father gathering his weapons while hiding his family from the Asur. She shuddered at the memory.

'Ada?' Anja said her name, gently picking up on the memory her granddaughter was having. Ada closed her eyes before they flew open again.

'They are almost here!' Panic rose like a wave about to crash upon her. She stood quickly and strode over to the window. Ogda and Anja exchanged worried looks before they too joined her at the window.

'What is it, Ada?' The Seer was becoming concerned he had no feeling of impending doom and wondered how Ada was able to pick up on their trail way before he did.

Ada turned back to Ogda and Anja, 'we have to start preparing now they will be here within an hour!' Her voice was almost a shout.

'I will tell Merek and get Elenore,' Anja said as she turned to leave.

'We must go to the tunnels Ada and find the queen.' Ogda had caught Ada's panic, an infectious grasp of terror.

CHAPTER TWENTY-SIX

Chaos

The curtain of death hangs heavy, a doorway behind to an
unknown realm, a journey we all must make.

Ogda

Merek blew the horn, calling for all to go to their stations as they had practiced so many times. Amzi and his group had raced to the tree line once they had been alerted to the Asur's early arrival. Elenore could not stop shaking as she placed the twins in the carry bag that she would strap to her back. She'd thought she would have more time, but things had taken an abrupt turn.

'Norrie?' Merek strode into the room, sweat beaded his forehead and his face had gone a ghastly white.

'Merek!' Elenore ran and embraced her husband. Merek held her for a moment before cupping her face with his hands. He pressed his mouth against hers. Elenore melted, her heart racing wildly. Merek pulled himself away. 'You must leave, Norrie, they will be here soon. Follow the tunnel the trees have made for you there will be a cave at the end like Ulric described to you. You must wait there, and I will meet you with our children.'

'Promise me, Merek. Please, promise me.' Elenore began to cry. She felt sick with dread and of the unknown. The thought of losing all that was dear to her was almost too much.

'Norrie, you have to be strong. Please don't cry. I promise I will be there.' Before Elenore could reply he crushed his mouth against hers. One of the twins began to fuss and Merek turned his attention to his baby daughters. 'Be good for your Mumma,' he said gently as he bent and kissed each one of them.

A strong pungent smell drifted in the air, making the people of the hidden village gag. Krea led Elenore and the group of more than three hundred people to the entrance of the tunnel that lay on the furthest side of the village. The trees had begun a fervent whispering; their enemy had arrived.

Elenore cast a brief look back at the village that had been her home for the last several months. She had not had a chance to say her farewells to Ulric or Ada. Ada and Ogda had fled down a different tunnel, making haste to find the queen of Asur. She covered her mouth; the smell was overwhelming. As her gaze swept over the small houses that were dotted in the distance, she saw an Asur break through the undergrowth. It held a flaming torch and as she watched, it threw it at one of the wooden homes. The small timber house caught alight, sending flames up into the bright blue sky.

She watched, transfixed as she made out Tallot racing towards the creature, his sword drawn. More of the Asur came crashing through the undergrowth a stampede of murderous beasts.

How will we ever win a battle against so many? Her mind raced as terror gripped her. Krea and the others also had turned their attention to the battle that was breaking out not far from where they stood. Tallot plunged his sword into the beast as it wheeled its mount to turn and face him. Another of the Asur raced towards the warrior intent on bringing him down. Merek and some of his warriors had come to the forefront swords drawn as they met them head on.

'Elenore, we have to go.' Krea touched Elenore's arm, but Elenore ignored her. She was so engrossed in watching the battle raging behind them. Krea directed the group to start their way into the tunnel they had to move before they were seen. More of the Asur spilled from the trees. Elenore stood transfixed, unable to drag her eyes away from the murderous scene. An Asur had come behind Merek an evil grin stretched upon its hideous face. It raised its sword intent on bringing down the leader.

'Merek!' Elenore could not help but call out to her husband. He could not hear her she was too far away. Krea turned as she heard Elenore scream out her brother's name. Tallot had seen the Asur and rushed to defend his leader. Their friendship had recently rekindled and now his friend was in grave danger.

The heavy clang of metal could be heard as it rang out in the afternoon breeze. Elenore covered her ears and continued to watch. Merek wheeled his stallion to face the Asur that had almost killed him. Another of the Asur raced towards Tallot, its weapon held low. Merek saw the evil being as it sprinted towards Tallot. He did not have the time to intercept instead he called out trying to get his friend's attention to the enemy that was coming towards him. Tallot did not hear Merek's shout, locked in combat with another.

Elenore watched in horror as the blade of the sword that the Asur carried sliced through the air, decapitating the warrior.

'No!' Elenore screamed.

'Elenore, we have to leave now!' Krea shouted to her sister-in-law. Edyth had been helping the rest of the group into the tunnel ushering them forward and reassuring her children that they would be safe. She stopped as she heard Elenore's scream and raced back out of the tunnel. She saw Krea make her way to Elenore calling her to leave. The wolf had followed her only to drop to its haunches letting out a soft growl, its ears flattened against the back of its skull. Edyth looked in the direction to where the wolf was pointed.

One of the Asur had heard Elenore's scream.

Edyth ran towards Krea and Elenore, 'Krea! Elenore! Quick, they're coming, we have been spotted!' Her voice rang out loud and panicked.

Krea looked at her wolf whose growl was becoming louder. She pulled at Elenore, 'Move!' she shouted. Elenore pulled her gaze away noticing the Asur that was galloping towards them. One of the twins let out a wail, awakening her mother's instinct to protect her babies. She felt Krea's pull on her arm and raced towards the entrance of the tunnel.

'Take them to safety!' Krea shrieked at Edyth and Elenore. She waited for them to disappear into the tunnel before racing back to the entrance her sword ready.

Ada and Ogda entered the tunnel, holding the torch high to push back the darkness that filled the passageway. They carefully made their way along pausing to listen if there were any approaching Asur. An eerie quiet greeted them as they moved forward, and it was not long before a strong smell filled the tunnel. The Seer was surprised at how close Dardanos had been to where they had lived over the past several months. He wondered if she had known that they were there but as quickly as the thought had presented itself, he was even quicker to dismiss it. Now was not the time for reflecting on such things.

'She is close,' Ada said. A dim light danced in front of them. They pushed forward slowly, stealthily, not wanting to attract attention from a guard. The tunnel twisted and turned exactly like Ada had dreamed it would. She waited for the voice that had always been there to return but it remained silent. They edged closer to the light, the smell overwhelming now. It was all they could do to not to cough and gag. Soon voices were heard, and they stopped to listen. It became evident that the queen was in a heated discussion with one of her generals.

'Ada,' Ogda whispered, 'you need to do it now.'

Ada cocked her head, but could not decipher what the queen was saying. A smile played across her lips as she brought her hands up. It had been a long time since she had used her powers and she was not even sure if they would work. She waited. Nothing. She closed her eyes trying to relax and listen to her inner voice.

'*Be patient, Ada,*' it whispered. She smiled even more. It had not forsaken her.

A flame, and then another, burst from her lifted hands. The flames whipped up and then shot forward lighting the tunnel. It was not long before she could hear screams and a long, drawn-out cry of anger and pain. Ada continued to shoot forward fire and it engulfed the tunnel in a capsule of heat spiked fury. She was not sure on how long she should shoot flames, but she continued until the voice once again filled her mind.

'*You have done your job here, Ada, you must return to the battle that rages outside.*' Ada let her hands rest at her side, they were aching from being held up for so long. 'It is time to go,' Ogda had waited patiently and was eager to return to the village they had left behind.

Merek had witnessed the death of one of his longest friends, but he did not have time to acknowledge his grief, there was just too many of them. Amzi had not returned to advise how the traps they had hidden had worked or if they had been successful in slaying some of the Asur. He struggled with combating and slaughtering as many as he could. Some rode on the huge beasts' others walked as they crawled from the undergrowth that flanked the village. He sent a quick prayer to the Gods that his wife had managed to flee. The Asur had caught them off guard with how quickly they had made their way to the village. He had seen Zuri briefly as she grinned at his surprise when she had accompanied one of the Asur as they pushed their way through the tree line.

The trees swayed and whooshed, their anger evident in the way their branches moved with no apparent wind. Anja and Serenity had hidden in the healer's cabin both attempting to get into the minds of the generals. As Anja concentrated, her frown deepened, another was trying to push her back. She indicated for Serenity to use her mind to find another general, the Asur would not be familiar with the novice mind traveller. Serenity forced down the fear that bubbled within her and called upon the courage that was needed to fight the enemy that was consuming them.

She strained and forced her mind to find the one that was coordinating the attack and it was not long before she found it. As soon as she entered, she began to hum consuming the mind of the general that it belonged to. It disorientated him almost sending him into a mad rage. Serenity felt the mind of the general unravel and struggle to stay in control. The humming would bring on a madness that would leave the brain in a complete state of emptiness, a vacant wasteland of brain matter. Her first victim gave her the confidence to find another as Anja wrestled with the entity that stubbornly tried to block her.

Elenore heard the tunnel fill in behind her and she wondered about Krea. *How will she get back to us?* She shivered not letting herself dwell on the what ifs. Edyth led the way, holding the torch as they made their way along the dark passageway. Elenore sent a quick prayer for the trees who had played such a vital role in saving their lives. She dared not think of Tallot; it would be her undoing. She had to stay strong.

The tunnel wound itself under Dorhall Pass like a giant serpent. One of the twins began to fuss before letting out a loud cry, demanding to be fed. Some of the children began to beg for a rest upon hearing the baby's cry. Edyth halted their march, allowing time for a break. Not only were there children and older people, but a few of the women were heavily pregnant. Spring was not that far away, and many were due with the changing season.

Elenore took off her carry bag, relieved to have a break from the weight of her babies. Anwen was the loudest and always fed first, Anhi sucked on her fingers waiting her turn.

'Elenore are you okay?' Edyth peered at Elenore in the gloom. She held the torch to one side and Elenore was able to see her face puckered in a crease of worry.

'Yes, I am fine how is everyone else?' Edyth looked at the long line of people.

'I think they are tired and scared, but that is understandable.' Edyth was always forthright and never minced her words. Elenore was thankful she was with her; her strength was unwavering. Her son Huxley had wanted to stay and fight the Asur, and she was amazed at how his mother had kept herself together.

She missed Krea, they had no warrior now to defend them. Merek had given each adult a dagger to have some form of protection. The thought of her husband pulled at her heart, and she sent yet another prayer to help protect him and all that were fighting the Asur.

Merek clashed his sword with the vile creature that attempted to unseat him from his horse. He was beginning to tire as the afternoon began to descend into early evening. They had been fighting all day. Amzi and his group of horsemen had stumbled from the forest, but he had not had a chance to ask him anything, the Asur were strong not only in numbers but in combat. He had noticed some of the generals jump from their mount's hands covering their ears and the sides of their heads. Merek smiled when he saw this, his mother and the healer were working their magic.

The homes they had built were on fire, lighting the shadows that the late winter evening brought with it. His warriors were also beginning to tire, and many had been slain. It felt there was no end in sight.

The trees who had not stopped their disconcerted effort at the Asur began to make the earth tremble. Merek was surprised at first, to feel the earth begin to move and quickly looked up at the tall trees that graced the sky above him. It was not long before he realised why they had taken to shaking the ground: the Asur had set fire to them. The trees were being burned alive and the screeches from the flames were deafening. Merek cringed as he listened, and a heavy sense of pain and loss reverberated through the air. It was the beginning of the end.

Ada and Ogda stumbled out of the tunnel and were greeted by a grim scene. The forest was ablaze, and the smell of death hung in the air. Warriors staggered, disorientated and exhausted. The trees were futilely trying to make the ground vibrate, opening gaping holes in the earth, hoping that the Asur would fall into them. It was a losing battle, nearly all the large trees were engulfed in flames.

The Asur were making sport of the men that were barely clinging to life, it was apparent that Merek was losing the fight. Anger simmered and overflowed inside Ada as she desperately searched for her father.

'Ada, it is time to use your other power!' The Seer instructed her. At first, she was unsure on what he meant before realising that part of her prophecy would be the magical powers that she had been blessed with from the Gods.

She walked over to where she could see one of the Asur were about to strike a young woman who was desperately trying to defend herself. Ada held up her hands, her rage evident. Her breath came out ragged as she struggled to keep herself under control. Fire did not erupt this time, instead it was a lightning strike that turned the Asur into a blackened corpse. She smiled. She liked this new power. It was time to put it to work.

Sabin had met with Merek fighting alongside him as he noticed his friend beginning to tire. Huxley joined them, his rage and the desire for revenge consuming him. Merek was thankful for his two friends he had started to lose hope. There were just too many of them.

As Sabin hacked and cursed at one of the Asur he noticed one of their leaders fall to the ground, his hands holding the sides of his head.

'Aye, looks like Anja and Serenity are doing their jobs,' he shouted at Merek and nodded in the direction of where the general had fallen.

Merek cast a quick glance at the general who was now banging his head on the ground. He was grateful that Takeo had advised that his Seer who had betrayed him and his people was only aware of three that could mind travel. Serenity would have been a complete surprise. Watching the general succumb to madness raised his spirits and he plunged on, driving his sword into yet another of the Asur. He was covered in blood, sweat and filth. His arms ached from the sword; he had left his stallion, finding it easier to fight on his feet. The fire had almost consumed the village and the forest had transcended into a bright orange ball. He suddenly thought about his mother and the healer they were hiding in one of the houses he wondered if the house had caught on fire. He quickly looked around to see if he could find someone to go and warn them. He did not want to go himself he was already a target he needed someone they would not expect. Desperately he searched. The battle was starting to slow, and it was easy to see that the Asur had the upper hand. He noticed Huxley sparing with one of the humans who were helping the Asur. Huxley would be able to find and warn them he just needed to get to his side.

Merek plunged his sword deep into the Asur's throat, urgently wanting to finish the beast. He raced to the other side it was closest to the burning forest searching for Huxley. He was sure it was him he had seen just a moment ago locked in a fight with a traitor who had sided with the enemy.

A knife slashed across his leg, and Merek cried out in agony. He spun round to find who had injured him. Zuri stood in front of him, a murderous look on her face as she lifted the knife high in the air.

Merek had never killed a woman before, but he had no choice.

He plunged his sword into her heart, sidestepping and letting her fall to the ground. Bile rose and he swallowed it down, he was locked in a war for survival one in which his enemies would be brought down. He staggered and half limped his way to Huxley who managed to kill the man who was fighting him.

'Huxley!' He shouted. The young man turned to him and made his way to Merek. 'You need to find Serenity and my mother, they are in danger of being burned alive. Tell them to hide, they can't be seen or the Asur will know who is making their generals go mad. Hurry!' Merek did not wait for Huxley to respond, instead he turned back to the fight determined to kill every one of the Asur.

Ada and Ogda continued their wraith on the Asur, burning them to a blackened crisp. The Seer noticed Sabin leaning up against a tree blood poured from a wound on his arm. As they approached, they could see how deep the gash was his muscles and tendons were exposed and he had already lost a lot of blood.

'Sabin!' The Seer ran to the curly haired man and crouched down beside him. Sabin was losing consciousness and struggled to remain awake. 'Sabin, hold on, it is not your time to go,' Ogda told him gently.

'Aye, ye would miss me too much.' He attempted a chuckle which resulted in a cough. Even when death was circling Sabin, he tried to make light of it.

Ada bent down and stroked the man's face. 'Sabin, we still have work to do. I will be back, try and stay calm.'

Sabin managed his lopsided grin and nodded, too weak to talk.

Krea and the wolf rushed at the Asur as it threw its head back, letting out a strange guttural sound. Krea sliced and thrusted at the beast, but it merely sidestepped, dancing away from her advances. Her wolf, Romulus, lunged grabbing the beast's wrist biting down on it and crushing the bones. The Asur let out a loud howl, swiping at the wolf and sending him flying.

Krea saw her opportunity and drove her sword into the back of the beast, her screams of fury echoing through the air. The Asur turned, its pain driving it into a madness as it wheeled its own weapon at Krea. It was her turn to dance as she skittered away.

'You're going to die, you bastard!' Krea roared. She pivoted and whirled before slicing her sword through the monster's torso. She watched it crash to the ground, a sardonic smile on her lips. She glanced over at her wolf who was gingerly walking over to her. 'Romulus,' she bent down and petted him. He licked her face, grateful his mistress had not succumbed to their enemy.

After checking her wolf was okay, she straightened and cast her eyes back to the tunnel where she had left Elenore. One of the Asur was pushing its way in as dirt began to rain down closing the entrance. She watched horrified as it disappeared. The group of vulnerable people stood no chance they would all be slaughtered. A feeling of panic enveloped her as she sprinted back to the tunnel. It had been her responsibility to protect them, but their enemy had distracted her. The tunnel was fully closed by the time she got to it.

'No!' she screamed. She tried to dig her way back in, but it was futile. Her mind raced, unsure what to do. Taking a deep breath, she forced her mind to become calm. The forest on the other side of the village was a burning inferno she looked back to the forest that was on the side of the tunnel. It was untouched, fire had yet to reach there. The trees had created the tunnel to save their fellow humans. The Seer had consistently told them that it was vital they work together if they were ever to rid the world of the Asur.

She looked up from the tunnel entrance. It was hard to tell how far back it went or even the direction. 'Romulus' – she kneeled next to the animal – 'find!' she ordered. The wolf cocked his head. 'Find!' she said again.

The wolf gave a whimper and began to sniff the ground. Krea urged Romulus forward, showing him that she wanted him to locate where the tunnel went. Romulus headed up an embankment, following the scent of the people. He let out a low howl before looking over his shoulder to confirm that Krea was following him.

'Keep going, boy. Good job,' she praised. The wolf wagged his tail and continued to trace the tunnel. She had to try and get ahead of the Asur and drop back down into the tunnel and surprise it. She gave a quick glance up at the trees hoping they were understanding of what she was trying to do.

A strong wind began to pick up, blowing the arid smell of smoke across the evening sky. Krea coughed, the smell was strong and almost overwhelming. She leaned up against one of the tall oak trees trying to get her breathing under control and stop her incessant coughing. Romulus whined when he saw his mistress and waited for her to follow him. Krea placed her hand on the rough bark of the tree steadying herself. A vibration pulsed through the trunk forcing her to pull her hand away in surprise. She looked up at the tree, its heavy limbs reached upwards as if sending a prayer to the Gods above. She coughed again; her lungs had consumed a large dose of the toxic smoke.

'Tell me where to go,' she asked in a hoarse whisper. She placed both hands on the tree, the pulsing was becoming stronger. She leaned closer, had she heard a whisper? A buzzing could be heard like a hive of bees. Krea placed her ear to the rough bark.

'*Krea, follow the wolf until you reach the stream.*' Krea pulled away, her heart pounding. She placed her ear back to the trunk making sure she had heard right and was not dreaming. The tree said the same thing over and over. The wind blew stronger whipping the smoke through the air making Krea cough again.

'Romulus, let's go!' She managed after she regained control of her breathing.

Huxley ran from burning house to burning house, frantically trying to find one that was not on fire. The Asur were burning everything, intent on removing every fabric of mankind that they could. He ducked and weaved, careful not to be noticed but time was running out. There was less than half of the warriors that had started when the Asur had first made their appearance through the forest. The ones remaining were starting to tire and lose hope of winning the battle to survive. If the Asur got to Serenity and Anja, it would be over.

He raced to the edge of the village and looked for the house that sat apart from the others. Huxley had not visited Serenity's new home preferring to live a reclusive life. He rarely ventured out. He knew Serenity liked to have some quiet when she was not seeing people and having her home located some distance away would ensure this. Not far from the edge of the tree line where the fire had not yet started, a small cabin sat nestled under a giant tree. The tree was like a massive beacon, set apart from the rest of the forest. It appeared to have taken it upon itself to stand guard over the little house that sat beneath it. He knew instantly that this would be Serenity's home, she always looked for significance in things and this tree certainly offered something. He sprinted towards it, hoping he would not be spotted he wanted more than ever to rid the world of the Asur they had taken so much from him. He made it to the front porch and instantly hunkered down peering from over the rail to ascertain he had not been seen.

Some of the Asur were making their way to the untouched part of the forest, torches ablaze, ready to set fire to the last remaining trees. Huxley gritted his teeth. His hatred for the monsters was overwhelming. He forced his gaze from them and carefully made his way to the door. Turning the knob, he gently edged it open. He half crawled, half shuffled inside, closing the door behind him. He let out a slow breath and waited a moment for his eyes to get accustomed to the gloom.

Huxley made his way to one of the rooms. He could hear a soft chanting from within. Serenity and Anja sat cross legged on colourful cushions, their eyes closed. He was usure of what to do, he did not know if he should interrupt them and rouse them from their dreaming state. He sat contemplating what the next step should be.

Serenity's eyes flew open. 'Huxley, what is it?'

'You must leave, they are coming to burn down your house. Now!' Huxley hissed. He felt panicked, the Asur would not waste time when they saw the only home that had not been set alight. Serenity tapped Anja, she had no choice but to distract her from her mind travel. Anja simply nodded and stood waiting for Huxley to lead the way. 'Is there a back door?' he asked.

Serenity nodded and led him to the back of the house. Huxley motioned for the women to wait as he opened the door slightly scanning the forest that lay behind it.

The smell of smoke filled the air, and he struggled not to cough. There were two Asur holding torches as they put fire to the ancient trees. Where could he lead Anja and Serenity? There were no safe hiding places anymore.

He closed the door and looked at the two women, his face an ashen white.

'What is it?' Serenity demanded.

Huxley swallowed. He would have to tell them. 'I don't know where to hide. They are setting fire to the other side of the forest.'

'Take us to the tree that stands above the home, it will provide a safe haven.' Serenity told the young man.

Huxley frowned, unsure if this was a good idea. The tree stood high above the village and was not at all subtle in its appearance.

'Trust me,' Serenity said, as if she could sense Huxley's dilemma. Huxley merely nodded and once again opened the door enough for him to peer out. The Asur had noticed the house and were making their way towards it. Huxley would have to distract them, and he knew that this would be his ending. He closed the door again and took a deep breath, his heart was beginning to pound. He fingered the hilt of his sword for reassurance.

'You and Anja run, I will distract them,' he said.

Serenity began to say something, but Huxley did not wait, he pushed the door open running head long towards the Asur.

The Asur were surprised to see a young man burst from the last house standing making his way towards them. Huxley roared letting the built-up anger come to fruition. He had held it in for so long and now he used it to fuel his attack. The Asur were caught off guard and were slow to reach for their swords. One of them threw the torch to set Huxley on fire. Huxley dodged and drove his sword into the monster's heart. The other Asur was upon Huxley slicing the man and tearing open his back. Huxley felt the hot pain from the wound that the Asur had made. He staggered and teetered as he turned to face his opponent. He let out a growl his fury coming to a head. The Asur stepped back its face holding a taunting look waiting for his opponent to strike back. Huxley sent a quick prayer to the Gods before he lunged towards the Asur.

Serenity watched as Huxley raced towards the Asur, she knew he was giving his life to save them. She forced her gaze away from the unfolding scene and grabbed Anja's hand, making her follow her to the ancient tree. The tree had been expecting them. Its long wide roots snaked around the home like giant fingers. The finger like roots burrowed deeper, splitting the ground open and creating a space for Serenity and Anja to step into.

Serenity did not waste any time, it was important that she took up her humming again. She trusted the tree, knowing it would protect them. She also knew the Asur would burn it to the ground, but it would be too late. They would be safely hidden under the giant root system that stretched itself into the depths of the earth.

Elenore did not allow the babies to have a full feed, they did not have time. She felt a sense to run and could not shake the feeling. She carefully hoisted the carry bag back onto her back.

'Edyth, I think something is following us,' she said.

Edyth nodded. 'I do too, best we make haste.' The small woman did not waste any time in calling out to the group to hurry. They could not run, there were too many of them who were in no condition to do so, but they could walk fast. They had to make it to the underground cave the Seer had told them about, there they were to wait for the rest of the village. Elenore's heart raced, and her breaths came out heavy and ragged. She urged her group to move faster, they had to get to the cave.

As Elenore half walked, half jogged, she looked behind her. She was the last of the group, encouraging the stragglers and as she cast her eyes back down the long dark tunnel behind her, she could make out a light. The feeling that it was not Krea sat with her, and she felt her heart flutter. She instinctively touched her small dagger strapped to her waist.

'Hurry!' she shouted. The Asur were gaining on them, and she knew they would never be able to outrun them. She grabbed the old man in front of her by his tunic. 'Wait, you have to take my babies, please give them to Edyth when you get to the cave.'

She quickly took off the carry bag, thrusting it towards the man. She did not wait for his response instead she grabbed her dagger from her waist belt and made her way to the light that was quickly approaching.

Krea saw the stream; the trees were fervently whispering, as if trying to encourage her and confirm that she was in the right place. She quickly scanned for a way to get to the tunnel still not sure if she should try and dig her way in. Romulus began to whimper and whine scratching at the ground. Krea looked at the wolf, there under the leaf litter was a cavity! She rushed to the wolf's side joining him in digging making the cavity wide enough for her and the wolf to squeeze through. The trees fervent whispering had become a crescendo of nature's notes, an attempt to shout a battle cry, a defiance of demise.

Krea lowered herself in, she turned to look up at the big wolf. He looked at her hesitantly, before jumping into her arms. Krea staggered back under his weight. She carefully placed him on the ground, giving him the signal to find again. She was unsure if she was in front of the group or behind. Romulus sniffed the air before lowering his nose to the ground. He gave a low growl and began to edge his way forward.

Krea readied her sword. She had a feeling the Asur was not far away.

They cautiously moved forward. The darkness of the tunnel blinded Krea and she strained to listen to the wolf, using her ears to follow him. It was not long before she saw a light ahead. Instinctively, she knew it was the Asur. She felt herself smile; they would not be expecting her. Romulus gave a low growl as he warily made his way towards the Asur.

Krea waited until the last moment, until they were almost upon the beast, before she raised her sword and plunged it deep into its back. The animal let out a blood curdling scream as it spun round to face Krea. Romulus leaped, teeth barred, going for the monster's throat.

Elenore had caught up with the Asur just in time to see Krea's attack. She wasted no time in sinking her small dagger into its back as it turned to face Krea. The animal roared in pain, the dagger stuck in its thick hide alongside the gaping hole Krea had made with her sword.

The wolf clamped its jaws around its neck as it reeled from Elenore's attack. It stood no chance. It let out another soul piercing cry as it stumbled, trying to fight off the wolf that was fastened to its neck.

Krea dove forward, slicing the beast at its knees, crippling it as it crashed to the tunnel's floor. Romulus had let go of his hold as the beast began to topple. Krea was upon the beast, hacking and striking, her despise for their enemy coursing through the blows she made against it.

Elenore let her go, understanding the hate and loathing she was venting. Krea's arms trembled, and her breath was heavy when she finally took a step back. She wiped her mouth before hawking and spitting at the dead monster that lay in front of her. Krea leaned back against the tunnel wall trying to get her breath back. She closed her eyes and took a deep breath before letting it out slowly. She was thankful it was only one that managed to get into the tunnel, they were strong and like no other enemy she had ever encountered before.

'Krea?' Elenore offered her a smile as Krea opened her eyes to look at her sister-in-law.

'Thank you.'

Krea chuckled. 'No problem, Norrie.' Elenore sighed and both women began to giggle before laughter took them in its hysteria.

Ada and Ogda searched for Merek, destroying every Asur that stood in their way. The stench of burning flesh, trees and blood filled the night air. As Ada looked around her, she noticed the Asur retreating.

'Your attack on the queen has worked, they are going to her aid. The generals have been crippled, succumbing to an eternity of madness. The queen will need to gather her army around her.' The Seer watched in fascination as the Asur turned to flee.

'How do you know we have not killed her?' Ada knew the battle had not finished.

'There will be another time for that.' Ogda paused in his stride. Ada stopped and followed the Seer's gaze. Many of Merek's warriors had perished, others had fallen exhausted it would have been an easy war for the Asur to win. Humans had only a finite source of energy one of their weaknesses in fighting with demons. Merek was locked in a battle with one of the Asur, however the Asur seemed different to the others. It was taller and broader, and a different helmet sat upon its ugly head. Various combat tools were strapped across the heavy belt that adorned its waist.

Merek was losing, no match for the enormous beast. He yielded his sword, swinging and hacking at the animal. He was growing tired, his legs trembling under him, his arms ached and shook, it had been a long day and a longer night. Determination was set on his face, it was evident he was struggling not to give into his exhaustion. The beast roared, barring its teeth as it sensed Merek's exhaustion.

Ada held up her arms, aiming to strike the monster that was determined to kill and bring down her father.

Ogda gently pushed down Ada's arms. 'It will not work with this one.' Ada turned to look at the Seer a frown puckered on her face.

'You wanted to know who the king of Asur was? He stands in front of you.' Ada turned her attention back to her father. Merek's sword clashed with the giant Asur metal against metal rang out in the air.

'What are we going to do?' Ada asked in a panicked voice.

'I will distract the demon and you will run and find Serenity. You will know what to do after that.' Ada was confused she shook her head trying to make sense of what Ogda was telling her to do. 'Now Ada!' The Seer yelled.

Ada took a step back as she watched in horror as Ogda made his way towards the beast. The Asur paused in its attack on Merek, its sword poised in the air. A smile broke out on its face as it noticed the Seer come towards it.

Ada's heart was in her throat, a sickening feeling descending upon her.

The Asur threw down its sword and letting out a loud, guttural sound it made its way towards the Seer. Merek watched in morbid fascination as the Asur reached for Ogda, picking him up like he was nothing at all. It threw its head back, letting out a loud roar that reverberated throughout the dark night.

'Papa!' Ada had found her voice as she raced towards her father. Merek tore his eyes away from the Asur and ran towards his daughter. 'Quick, you must follow me!' Ada told her father. Merek did not argue or ask questions they needed to flee before the king of the Asur came looking for them.

Merek threw one last look back at the Asur. It had lifted Ogda high in the air as if examining the man. Its tongue darted out, as if tasting him. A look of revulsion descended upon Merek. The Asur once again let out a loud roar before reaching inside the Seer's chest to rip out his heart.

Merek and Ada came to a stop, hiding behind a smouldering house. They peered out and watched in horror as the Asur consumed the Seer's heart, licking and smacking its lips as if it had just eaten a tasty treat.

Nausea swept over Ada. She fell to her knees, covering her face before sobs began to engulf her.

'Ada, come, we must leave.' Merek lifted Ada back to her feet. She nodded and suddenly knew why Ogda had never been able to see his own death: it would have been too traumatic. The Gods had spared him, and he had not let them down, giving his own life to save humanity.

Father and daughter picked their way through the carnage to where Sabin still sat, propped up against a tree. Relief swept over Ada as Sabin gave them a weak smile his face was pale and drawn. It took all of Merek's remaining strength to hoist him to a standing position. Merek gently placed his shoulder under Sabin's arm. 'The battle is over, Sabin. We have to get to the cave,' Merek said as they took a step forward.

'Aye, Merek, guess we kicked their arse.' Sabin attempted to chuckle before breaking out into a fit of coughing. Merek grunted in agreement.

Ada turned, the Asur had fled leaving a grisly scene of dead bodies and blackened trees. She knew this was just a prelude to what was to come. The Asur would stalk them relentlessly, seeking vengeance until they were all wiped from the planet. A cold dread settled inside her stomach and she forced down the nausea that rose in her throat. She would need to work on her magic if they had any hope of prevailing against a formidable enemy.

Pushing away the fear that coiled around her heart like a serpent, she turned back towards her father and Sabin. Dawn was fast approaching, it was time to regroup, find their injured and make their way to safety.

New Found Books Australia Pty Ltd

www.newfoundbooks.au

NEW FOUND
BOOKS